The Good
Girlfriend's
Guide to
Getting Even

Anna Bell currently writes the weekly column 'The Secret Dreamworld of An Aspiring Author' on the website Novelicious (www.novelicious.com).

Anna is a full-time writer and loves nothing more than going for walks with her husband, two young children and Labrador.

You can find out more about Anna at her website:
www.annabellwrites.com

Also by Anna Bell

The Bucket List to Mend a Broken Heart
Don't Tell the Groom
Don't Tell the Boss
Don't Tell the Brides-To-Be

The Good Girlfriend's Guide to Getting Even

ANNA BELL

ZAFFRE

First published in Great Britain in 2017 by

ZAFFRE PUBLISHING
80-81 Wimpole St, London W1G 9RE
www.zaffrebooks.co.uk

This is a work of fiction. Names, places, events and
incidents are either the products of the author's
imagination or used fictitiously. Any resemblance to
actual persons, living or dead, or actual
events is purely coincidental.

A CIP catalogue record for this book is
available from the British Library.

ISBN: 978-1-785-76039-6

Also available as an ebook

1 3 5 7 9 10 8 6 4 2

Typeset by IDSUK (Data Connection) Ltd
Printed and bound by Clays Ltd, St Ives Plc

Zaffre Publishing is an imprint of Bonnier Zaffre,
a Bonnier Publishing company
www.bonnierzaffre.co.uk
www.bonnierpublishing.co.uk

To Carlene Wright, fellow sporting widow and very good friend, for the Blackpool darts weekend that left memories I'll never forget (no matter how hard I try). Here's to the next sporting trip our husbands drag us on.

1

'*Ouch!*' I shout as my elbow whacks into the cubicle wall for the zillionth time, and I start muttering swear words like I'm Gordon Ramsay. Hiding in a cubicle in my work toilets and squeezing myself into a tight dress requires the acrobatic skills of a ninja. There seems to be an obstacle at every turn. One wrong hop when I'm putting my tights on and I'll be plunging my foot into somewhere only a bath in Dettol would fix, but hop too far the other way and I risk poking an eye out on the door hook.

It's a tricky minefield, and something I wouldn't be doing if this wasn't a true emergency, but my boyfriend Will and I are meeting my parents for dinner and I'm running late. I'd intended to nip to the gym en route to dinner to have a proper shower and change, but I've been swamped at work and left it too late.

I tried to tell my parents that a six o'clock dinner reservation midweek was a bad idea, but it's my dad's birthday and it was at his insistence. Knowing him, and his frugal ways, there will be some special offer for eating early.

I finally wrestle the zip up my back and make a break for free-dom out of the cubicle to pop some make-up on, only to find a woman standing at the sink washing her hands. No need for the extra blusher I'm about to apply; my cheeks automatically pink up in embarrassment at my swearing.

'Going somewhere nice, Lexi?' she asks, clearly trying not to laugh. She's one of the serious women who works in finance and I can never remember her name. She's probably my mum's age, all twin-set and pearls, and I'm guessing she's never had to do a quick change in the toilet. It's practically an impossible task worthy of *The Cube*.

'I'm off to dinner at Le Bistro.'

'Nice. Special occasion?'

'My dad's birthday.'

'Well, have a nice time,' she says, looking at me again and hiding what looks like a smirk.

I quickly glance down at myself, and can't see what she's smirking at. I think I've scrubbed up pretty well. I breathe a sigh of relief that I'm alone once more, and I focus on my face, slapping on my foundation defiantly.

I've discovered on many occasions that the fluorescent lighting in the toilets is not conducive to make-up application. When they designed the 1960s-style council building, with its minimal windows and abundance of strip lighting, they hadn't thought what that would mean for any girl trying to get ready in the windowless toilets. The lights are so bright it's like being on the telly, and it's very easy to overcompensate, which means that when you go back out into the real world, your office colleagues either mistake you for some type of hooker, or you look like your five-year-old niece applied your blusher.

Make-up done, I give myself a quick look in the mirror. I'm wearing a tight-fitting dress with a floaty lace overlay. I bought it in the sale last year and have been dying to find a reason to wear it ever since. I've perhaps put on a couple of pounds since I bought it, and while it might be a little snug, I think it still looks pretty good – no matter what the finance lady thinks.

At least my mum will be impressed that I'm wearing an actual dress and tights. If I'd turned up in what I wore to work this morning (frumpy black palazzo pants and a baggy, misshapen grey cardie), she probably would have sent me back home to change. The last time she met me from work she looked at my outfit and told me that it was no wonder I was thirty-one and unmarried if that's how I dressed.

I put a final coat of lippy on and rush out of the toilets. The only thing worse than having a dressing-down from my mum about my clothes, is her telling me off for being late.

'Oops, sorry,' I say as I turn a corner and bash straight into someone.

'Woah, there,' says Mike, a colleague who I sit next to. 'Where's the fire?'

I'm tempted to stop and talk to him as he's with the fit guy from the top, better known as the guy that works in the executives' department at the top our building. He's all pin-striped suit and perfect hair, and every time I see him he has a strange effect on me.

I've never actually been this close to him, and I try to force myself to keep moving before I fall under the spell of his hypnotic eyes.

'Sorry, Mike. I'm off to dinner at Le Bistro,' I say, fluttering my eyelids at the fit guy from the top while trying to show him how sophisticated I am – like I'm the type of girl who goes to posh restaurants all the time.

'Uh, before you go . . .' he calls.

'Can't stop, I'm running really late.'

I give Mike a quick wave over my shoulder and hot step it out of the council offices. I feel a bit rude not stopping to hear what he's got to say, but I'm sure it was just a question about the audit we're about to have. We're all desperately trying to get all our ducks in a row before an inspector comes in to see what we do as a department, but it's already five past six and if I don't make it to the restaurant soon, not only will my mum tell me off, but she'll be left unchaperoned with Will. Any time she's alone with him she brings up the topic of him proposing.

I dump my work clothes in my car as I pass, before doing a quick jog, or rather totter in these heels, to the restaurant, which is just off the main high street.

I spot my family straight away as I walk past the window – it's hard not to when they're the only people in the restaurant. Will looks relieved as I race through the door and over to the table.

'I'm so sorry I'm late. Work is nuts at the moment,' I say, leaning over to give my dad a quick peck on the cheek and passing him his present. 'Happy Birthday.'

'Thanks, Lexi,' he says, smiling up at me.

I bend down to kiss my mother, too, and as she brushes my cheek with her lips she stops.

'What on earth do you look like?'

'It's a dress,' I say, standing up straight and brushing it down. 'I thought you'd be pleased that I made an effort to wear something that shows off my figure.'

'It might have been nice if perhaps not quite so much of you was on display.'

I'm about to open my mouth to reply that this is the fashion, and lace is in, when Will gets up and stands behind me. Maybe now, after years of nodding along whenever my mother snipes at me, he's decided to stand up for me and defend my wardrobe choice.

'Lex, your skirt's tucked into your tights at the back,' he whispers.

I close my eyes and wish that I could disappear. When I open them a second later and see my mother still staring at me with pursed lips and a raised eyebrow, I realise that it hasn't worked, so instead I try as best I can to pull the dress out from my tights as discreetly as possible. God love my boyfriend for trying to protect what little modesty I had left.

Needless to say my dress must have been in my tights since I came out of the cubicle. Thinking about it, I bet that was what Mike was going to tell me. He's a good egg and I'm sure he wouldn't have let me walk out like that. And while I'm not too embarrassed that he noticed – I'm guessing he saw worse at last year's Christmas party when I drunkenly fell over and flashed our entire department – I am mortified that the fit guy from the top saw. Not to mention everyone on the high street as I walked here. I wonder if the finance lady saw my mistake as well and didn't say anything – that's almost against the code of sisterhood.

She's off my Christmas card list – well, she would be if I could ever remember her name. Thinking about it, maybe that's why she doesn't like me.

I clear my throat and move away from Will to sit down at the table. I place my napkin over my knees and try to act like I've got some dignity.

My parents go back to looking at their menus. 'You look lovely in the dress,' says Will, using his menu as a shield.

'Thanks. It's always a bit awkward doing the quick change in the loo.'

'Ah, well. At least it was empty in here.'

'Too bad the high street wasn't when I was on my way. Do you know, I even had a wolf whistle! I haven't been whistled at for years – I was well chuffed.'

'I'd whistle at you,' he says, winking.

I smile and I'm about to say something cheeky back when my mum coughs. I'd almost forgotten my parents were here.

Will and I lower our menus like naughty schoolchildren that have just been caught passing notes at the back of class.

'So, I bumped into Vanessa's mum yesterday in Sainsbury's. She's all excited about the big day.'

I feel my muscles starting to tense in preparation. It's as if I'm putting up a force field around myself.

'I'm sure she is,' I say, as if it's no big deal.

One of my childhood best friends, Vanessa, is getting married a week on Saturday. While I'm very excited that she's tying the knot, my mother seems to have taken it as a personal insult that she's dared to get married before me.

'I hadn't realised that they'd only been together for *four* years,' she says in a tone as if they'd only met last month.

'That set menu looks good,' I say, pointing at the handwritten chalk board mounted on the walls. 'I adore monkfish.'

My mother chooses to ignore me, and ploughs on like a steam roller.

'Her mum was saying that Vanessa's dress is from that little bridal boutique off Kimberly Lane.'

'Um, yes, I think it is,' I say, trying not fuel the conversation.

'I see it when I'm on the way to Zumba. It looks magical. I always walk past it and hope that one day I'll be going in there,' she says longingly.

I sense Will getting fidgety next to me. If I'm uncomfortable with this topic of conversation, Mr Commitmentphobe is bound to be. You see, Will and I have been together for seven years and, despite us living together, he's yet to produce a small, sparkly ring. Not that I really care *that* much. In my mind, our joint mortgage is probably more binding and difficult to break than a marriage certificate, but it's a different story for my mum. It's not that she objects to us living in sin or anything. As far as I can tell, she needs me to get married so that she has something to write about in her Christmas letter. Last year, she apparently emailed everyone to tell them she was doing a charity donation in lieu of cards, which I think was because she was too embarrassed to write for yet another year that I was neither engaged nor married.

Sure enough, Will's now looking at his watch as if he wants to get home as quickly as possible and away from my interfering mother.

Luckily for both Will and me, the waitress comes over and takes our order. We've all decided to go for a set menu that includes main course and dessert, so at least we've shaved off twenty minutes by not having starters.

'So have you had a nice birthday, Dad?' I ask, well and truly shutting down the Vanessa conversation.

'I have thanks, love. I got an excellent book called *Match of My Life.*'

'Oh, great. From Mum?'

'No, he bought it for himself. I bought him a jumper from M&S.'

Dad gives me a weak smile. Thirty-five years of marriage and every year he gets an M&S jumper for his birthday.

'I've read that one,' says Will. 'It's really good. Have you seen the *Got Not Got* Southampton book? I was reading it thinking you'd like it.'

'Yes, I got that for Christmas. Great book. So many memories.'

I roll my eyes as Will and my dad get lost talking about different football books. The fact that they're both Southampton fans is the only thing they have in common, and therefore the only thing they ever talk to each other about. I always thought it would be nice to have a boyfriend that got on well with my dad, but when they spend hours discussing the percentages of possession in the last game, I realise that I should have been careful what I wished for.

My father thinks Will's the bee's knees, unlike my mother, who disapproves of him, largely for not yet allowing her to become mother of the bride. Of course, my father's impression is based solely on the fact that Will has a Southampton Football Club season ticket. He could be the world's worst boyfriend, but as long as he went dutifully to every home game, then he'd still be OK. Luckily for me, he's actually a pretty good boyfriend, but still . . .

I try and tune out their conversation about the league table, and that of my mother, who's started telling me about her next-door-but-one neighbour whose daughter just had a baby. I'm sure you can imagine how she feels about grand-children. Instead I use my time to daydream about the novel I'm writing.

We make it through to dessert without me tipping wine over my mum's head, much to my amazement. She was actually quite restrained, having got distracted by telling me all about the scandal of the stolen fridge magnets at her work (it was as riveting as it sounds). My dad and Will are sitting in silence since exhausting their talk about football somewhere between the main course and dessert. All in all, we're on the homeward straight, and bar a cup of coffee we'll be off back home – and it's only 7.30. Gotta love an early dinner.

As another waitress sets down our coffee I notice that Will's hands are shaking as he drops two sugar-lumps into his cup before stirring vigorously. He clatters the spoon so noisily against the china cup that even my dad looks over at him to see if everything's OK.

I know that dinner with my mother would put anyone on edge, but I'm sure he's jumpier than usual.

'Have you got your outfit sorted for the wedding next week, then?' asks my mother.

What was I saying about being on the homeward straight?

I burn my tongue as I try to finish my coffee in a bid to get away more quickly.

'Yes, all sorted. I'll take lots of photos and show you next time I see you.'

Can't wait for that meet-up. I must remember to leave Will at home.

'Ah, perfect. It'll be nice to have some copies of photos of you at a wedding, even if it isn't your own.'

I can feel Will's leg jiggling under the table and I'm just hoping that his coffee is decaf as he's clearly already got way too much nervous energy to add caffeine into the mix.

'Well, thanks for a lovely dinner,' I say, placing my cup down and looking expectantly at my dad for him to summon the bill.

'Yes, thank you,' says Will.

He glances at his wrist and looks in shock at the time, as if he hasn't been checking it every few minutes since we got here.

'The football's just kicked off,' he says, turning to my dad. 'Do you fancy going to the Swan round the corner to watch it?'

'Football? On a Tuesday?' I say, exasperated.

'Champions League,' says Will without missing a beat. 'Real Madrid vs Man City.'

So that's why he's been checking his watch all night. Not because he wanted to get away from my mother, but because he didn't want to miss the game. Honestly, him being that anxious and jumpy about two teams that he doesn't even support is just typical. My boyfriend is so sports-obsessed that he'd watch tiddlywinks if Sky Sports broadcast it.

'Oh, I'd forgotten that was on,' says my dad.

Although he's a big Southampton fan, he's not as addicted to watching sport as Will is.

'We could go to the pub to watch it, and Lexi can take Jean back to ours for a cup of tea until we're finished.'

My mouth drops open.

'Um . . .' I stutter, as the house is definitely not tidy enough to have my mum over. I can't remember the last time I hoovered and I don't even know if I loaded last night's dinner plates into the dishwasher. 'Why can't we come to the pub too?'

I'm not a football fan, and I couldn't think of anything worse than going to the Swan to watch the game, but I feel a bit affronted that we're being farmed off like good little women to drink tea at home while the men go to the pub.

'Because you hate the Swan and you hate football. You'll be much more comfortable at home.'

Really? With my mum turning her nose up at the state of my house? But I can't say that out loud – I wouldn't want her to know how we really live in a pigsty.

'But . . .'

Will is glowering at me with a look so severe that I stop myself from saying anything else.

'Actually, Will, as kind as your offer is,' says my mother, 'I've booked tickets to the cinema for eight o'clock. That's why we're eating so early – it's not just because your dad is tight, Lexi.'

She laughs a little, and my dad even raises a smile.

'Thanks, Will. Some other time, yeah?' he says almost hopefully.

'OK,' says Will, looking crestfallen.

He obviously really wanted company to watch the game. He would usually go with his best mates Aaron and Tom, but they must be busy.

'I'll go with you,' I say, trying to plant an enthusiastic smile on my face.

He narrows his eyes as he looks at me.

'You don't have to.'

'No, I want to. You clearly really want to go and see it.'

'That settles it, then,' says my mother. 'Alan, get the bill, will you?'

My boyfriend smiles, and I see the anxiety fade away. All he wanted was someone to watch football with him. This way at least we can go and have a nice glass of wine together and shake off the dinner with my mother. It's not like I have to watch the football anyway as I've got my trusty Kindle in my bag – one of the many tools I have in my arsenal as a sporting widow. I'm always prepared for being on the sidelines of some sort of sporting activity.

2

'Just think, this time next week you'll be married,' says wide-eyed Cara.

'I know. It's mad, isn't it? I can't believe it,' says Vanessa.

Neither can I. It seems that nearly all my friends are getting married, and most of them met their significant others way after I met Will.

'Maybe one of you two will catch the bouquet,' she continues.

I smile politely. I don't even bother trying to these days. What's the point when I know I'm not going to be next. Will told me a few years ago that he'd ask me at the right time. I've since learnt that his definition of the right time is when Southampton win the Premiership. And I think they've got about as much chance of that happening as I have getting my novel published and it hitting the bestseller charts.

'Not me,' says Cara, 'I stay away from those things. I've got too much exploring to do to be the next one down the aisle.'

'Blimey, Cara, if you're the next one down the aisle then my mum really will have kittens,' I say laughing. 'No offence.'

'None taken,' she says, giving me a little arm rub. 'But I hear that Southampton are doing well this season. Maybe this year's the year.'

'Now you sound like Will.' Ever since Leicester City won the league, he's been convinced that Southampton are going to do the same. 'No, but really, I'm fine not getting married. We practically are anyway – we live together, we bicker, we barely have sex. That's like marriage, right?'

Note to self, best not to make dismissive jokes about marriage to person tying the knot in five days' time. Vanessa is not pulling a happy face. She better hope the wind doesn't change or her super-expensive wedding photographer will be a complete waste of money.

'Of course, I'm sure not every marriage is like that,' I add hastily. 'Why don't I get us some more drinks in? I think we've got just about enough time before writing group.'

'Hey, I caught you,' says Will a little breathlessly. I look up and instantly feel bad that we were just joking about him. I hope he didn't hear.

'What are you doing here? Is everything OK?'

I'm suddenly fearful that he's the bearer of awful news. Maybe someone's died. Why else would he come all the way down here?

'Yes, it's fine. I just came to deliver this.'

He holds up my printed assignment for tonight's class. I'm sure I put it in my bag after dinner.

'Oh God, I can't believe I forgot that.'

'I know. I went to the kitchen to grab a beer and saw it on the table. I know how hard you worked on it, so I thought you'd be disappointed to have left it at home.'

'Thanks, honey,' I say, standing up to take it from him and giving him a kiss. It was really sweet of him to come all the way here to drop it off. 'I'm surprised you came. Weren't you watching the football?'

'I was, but it's half-time. I should only miss five minutes or so.'

I smile – that's my boyfriend. Although missing five minutes is quite a serious sacrifice for Will.

'Well, thank you,' I say, still genuinely touched.

'Right, I best be off,' he says.

'Don't forget to wish Vanessa good luck. The next time you'll see her is on Saturday at the wedding.'

'Oh, um, yes. Of course. Good luck, Vanessa,' he says.

'Thanks, Will.'

He gives us a little wave and then dashes out of the pub back to his precious football.

'That was really sweet of him,' says Vanessa.

'I know, it was. I would have been gutted when I realised I'd left that at home. For once I'm actually happy with my work.'

'I can't wait to hear you read it out,' says Cara. 'Now, are we getting that other drink?'

Vanessa glances at her watch.

'I'm probably going to have to get going. I've still got orders of service to print off.'

'OK, thanks for coming down to see us. I can't wait to see you on Saturday. The next time we speak you'll be Mrs Vanessa Hancock,' I say, excited.

'I know,' she says, the smile reappearing on her face. I've clearly redeemed myself. 'I wish I could have had you girls as my bridesmaids, though. You know that, don't you?'

'We know,' I say, as I give her a kiss goodbye and wish her luck.

'I wish we were bloody bridesmaids, too,' says Cara as Vanessa heads out of the pub.

'Do you? All that standing around, and can you imagine how intense she's going to be the morning of the wedding? We'd have been sprinkling Prozac into her cornflakes.'

'Yeah, but do you know how much being a bridesmaid increases your chances of hooking up with someone? It's like the law that a bridesmaid has to get together with an usher.'

I roll my eyes at her. And there was me thinking she was being sentimental for the fact that we'd been friends with Vanessa for almost fifteen years.

I have to admit I was a little gutted when I found out that I wasn't going to be bridesmaid, as it might have been the closest I'd get to an altar for a long time, but with Vanessa having three sisters and the groom having two, the places had already been filled at birth.

'Despite not being a bridesmaid, I'm actually looking forward to the wedding.'

'I know, me too. It sounds like it's going to be amazing and she seems to have worked so hard on all the little details.'

'Hmm,' says Cara. 'I'm more interested in the seating plan and how far away we're going to be from her cousin Max. I hear he's an usher. Do you remember him from her mum's fiftieth when we were in sixth form? I've been looking for someone to help me test the headrest I've just bought for my swing since Bob the Baker is out of the picture as he did this weird bum thing.'

'Cara, what have we said about over sharing? You know the rules. I don't want to hear about what goes on in your bedroom,' I say, thinking that conversations with her should come with their own form of brain bleach.

'Well, you know what my golden rule is,' she says in a husky way before giggling.

'Isn't it simply that anything goes?'

'I do draw the line somewhere, you know.'

'Uh-huh,' I say, not believing her in the slightest.

'So, seriously, are you OK about this wedding on Saturday?' she says, changing the subject.

'Yes, I'll be fine. I know I was a bit jealous when she got engaged, but I've had plenty of time to get over it. Besides, Will's going to be with me, and we usually have a bit of a mushy time at weddings. Plus, you won't be the only one getting some. Weddings are like the one time we're guaranteed to have sex when we get home.'

'What is it about weddings that they're like the ultimate aphrodisiac?' asks Cara.

'I don't know,' I say, my cheeks colouring at thoughts of the last time Will and I went to a wedding. We ended up getting pretty hot and heavy behind the marquee as we were leaving. If only I could channel the wedding horn and bring it out all year.

Both Cara and I are sitting in silence for a moment, and for once I'm guessing our thoughts are along the same lines. But while mine are like something out of a Jilly Cooper novel, I'm sure hers could be taken from the pages of a Sylvia Day.

'Evening, ladies,' says Janet, our writing group leader as she walks past us.

'Hello, Janet,' I say, looking up, startled to see her. My fantasy had been so vivid that I had expected Will to be standing in front of me.

I fan myself with my writing folder to attempt to reduce the colour in my cheeks.

'I always feel like the naughty girl at the back of the class whenever she catches us having a drink beforehand,' says Cara, draining the rest of her wine glass.

'I know. It's like if you don't want us to have a drink first, don't hold the meetings in a pub.'

'Thank God she does, though, as I'd never be able to read out half of my work without a glass of wine.'

'You're telling me. I think most of the group are grateful that they can down something while listening to you as well. And to think, you don't even go into the really raunchy stuff in class. I nearly had kittens when I read that first sample you gave me.'

'Yeah, hardcore S&M novels can be a bit of a shock to the senses the first time.'

I'd think they would be a shock all the time. I can only just look Cara in the eye again since reading her work.

Who'd have thought she had been the quiet one in our group in sixth form. She barely even said boo to a boy. Yet, something had happened to her at uni and she discovered who she really was, and ever since then she's been a rampant man-eater.

'I'm not too sure that my homework is any good this week. I'm not looking forward to reading it out at all,' says Cara.

'Me neither.'

'But I thought you said earlier you were pleased with it.'

'I am, but I'm just dreading what Dr Doom and Mr Gloom will say.'

'Ah well, you can ignore them. I'm sure it rocks.'

I sigh. If it wasn't for the fact I get to have a gossip with Cara, then the negative comments of those two members of our group would have made me give up coming to this writing group.

I wrote my first complete novel four years ago. So far the only people that have read it in its entirety are Cara and Will. After sending samples and realising it was virtually impossible to secure an agent and get published, I joined the group for help. It's great for making me write and try new things, and it would be perfect without Dr Doom and Mr Gloom who write 'serious literary fiction' and therefore always attack and pull apart the seat-of-your-pants thrillers that I write. Speak of the devils, here they are now.

The middle-aged man (aka Mr Gloom) and the younger failed hipster wannabe (Dr Doom) walk into the pub and mutter hellos as they go into the back room.

The rest of our group are an eclectic mix of writers of sci-fi and fantasy, steampunk, chick lit, historical fiction, poetry and plays.

'Shall we go in?' asks Cara, wrinkling up her nose.

If my commercial thrillers take a beating, you can imagine the reaction she gets for her erotic fiction. The only difference is Dr Doom and Mr Gloom are usually blushing too much to critique her in the same way as they do me.

'I guess so.'

We slowly stand up and make our way into the room, finding ourselves our normal seats.

Once everyone has taken their seats Janet kicks the class off.

'Right then, have we all had a good week?'

We nod enthusiastically.

'Anyone got any news they want to share?'

She pulls her glasses down on to the bridge of her nose as if to inspect us a little closer, her face hopeful.

Every week she asks the same question, and every week you can see the disappointment on her face that one of us has not become the next J. K. Rowling.

She's met with silence.

'Right then. The only bit of news I've got is that my latest novel, for any of you following the series, is published on Thursday.'

Janet is a romance author and seems to have a book published every other week. They're historical bodice rippers of the Mills & Boon series variety – not really my type of thing, but it's nice that the group is at least led by someone who knows about the industry, even if Dr Doom and Mr Gloom like to pretend they know more.

'Now, before we get stuck in, I want to warn you that we're going to spend the next few sessions looking at marketing yourself. I know you might think it's irrelevant, but these days as an author you'll be asked more and more to do self-promotion, and it doesn't just start when you get published. You'll find that it could help you to secure a deal if you're active in promoting yourself and have an existing following.'

I groan. How am I going to get a following? I'm lucky if I can get my mum to like a post on my personal Facebook page.

'We'll spend next week looking at what other authors are doing as best practice, and then the week after I want us all to have a go at setting up a blog. So, have a think about possible topics between now and then. It doesn't have to be about books and writing – it could be about your life or a hobby.

'You'll write the first one for homework, and then I want you to keep on publishing for a few weeks. We can then look at social networking and promotion to see if we can push up your statistics.'

I know that's a couple of weeks away, but I'm already panicking.

'Back to this week and those introductions you wrote as homework. Let's dive straight into the sharing part, shall we? I'm looking forward to hearing them.'

As hateful as this bit of the group is, I think my writing is slowly getting better as a result.

'Lexi, why don't we start with you?' says Janet, smiling her ever-encouraging smile.

'Um, OK,' I say, rising slowly to my feet and digging out my piece of paper.

'*Klaus clutched at his sides as he approached the wooden cabin,*' I start, trying to keep my voice from going all high-pitched and squeaky. I read through the short introduction to a new thriller as best I can. It's pretty hard when my hands are shaking as much as if I were on a rollercoaster.

I finally finish and scrunch up my sheet of paper.

'Lovely, Lexi,' says Janet, beaming the coathanger smile once more. 'Very nicely read.'

Not quite the same as very nicely *written*, but still a compliment.

I sit back down and Cara gives me a thumbs up.

'I thought it was ace,' she whispers.

I smile at her as best I can and tense my muscles in preparation for the onslaught about to come my way.

'So the guy dies of a heart attack?' ask Mr Gloom.

'Uh-huh,' I say through gritted teeth. Here we go.

And as I listen to him and Dr Doom continue to slag off my work, it makes me feel like I'm never going to get anywhere. I try to let the comments bounce off me, developing that thick skin everyone says you need to cope as a writer, but I can't deny that they get to me and I feel like giving up.

Perhaps I just need to accept my situation. I am not destined to be a published writer, any more than I'm destined to get married this side of thirty-five.

3

I press my lips together and make a smacking noise before stepping back and giving myself a final once-over in the mirror.

Looking good, Lexi.

Of course, I'm deliberately not looking too closely or my eyes will be drawn to the white hair that I know is lurking amongst my up-do. And let's not get started on the bags under my eyes that not even industrial amounts of *touche éclat* have managed to hide. But aside from that, I look pretty good.

I probably should put my dress on, but while I'm a little bit ahead of schedule I take the time to practise my smile – trying to gauge the perfect amount of teeth. For some reason, whenever I see myself in someone else's wedding pictures, I seem to be smiling so hard that I look like I'm having my teeth X-rayed at the dentist.

I think I simply get carried away – there is nothing I love more than a good wedding. I mean, how often do you get to dress up in a fabulous frock and get plied with free booze and food all day? Then, it's not only socially acceptable but expected for you to dance around like a sweaty baboon until the early hours of the morning. And even better, today's wedding is not just that of a casual acquaintance or a cousin I haven't seen since way back when, it's one of my best friend's. And the only thing that I think I could possibly love more than going to one of my best friends' weddings would be to go to my own. But, as we all know, with my boyfriend, that isn't going to happen anytime soon.

'You better get ready soon,' I say, as Will walks into the bedroom. He's still dressed in his baggy weekend sweatpants and one of his many old Southampton football shirts.

I curse the fact that men have it so easy that it takes them mere minutes to get out of the door, and yet my beauty regime for the wedding started yesterday lunchtime with a trip to get a mani/pedi. Which was followed after work by a long bath with extra exfoliation and shaving in all the necessary places. I even brushed my lips with my electric toothbrush last night to make them all super smooth for seamless lipstick application. And yet all Will needs to do is have a quick shower and shave before he throws a suit on.

Unlike me, Will hates weddings with a passion. It's not that he hates the social awkwardness of being forced to sit on a table with strangers, or the fact that he has to get dressed up in a suit on his day off. Oh no, in his opinion weddings are the devil's work if they happen to fall on a Saturday. You see, Saturdays are known in our household for being for one thing, and one thing only: the religious worship of sport. It's probably a good thing that we've never got engaged. I mean, when would we ever get married? With a boyfriend like mine, there's always something he wants to watch. Cricket, snooker, rugby league, televised pool, and then there's the American sports that have started to trickle in: NHL, NFL, MLB – FFS – it's never-ending. Most days of the week have some sort of sporting activity that would create a conflict. There's rugby or football on Sunday, Speedway on Monday, football of some description usually on a Tuesday and Wednesday, darts on a Thursday, rugby on a Friday night and so on.

I know what you're thinking: why on earth would I put up with all of this? But as I watch Will in the mirror, I know why. Because it's *him*. I know that's a rubbish answer, but how do you describe the love you have for the person that you've been dating for what seems like forever?

So maybe he's got a spare tyre or two round the belly (who hasn't), and his hair is almost always in a perpetual state of bed hair, but he's still cute. And it's not about the way he looks, anyway. In the wise words of Michael Jackson: it's the way he makes me feel. We're content and comfortable, and that's how I like it.

I know I get ignored on a regular basis in favour of a team of men, but when he's not in super-fan sports mode, he's sweet and loving, and, well, he's my Will. And I'm usually happy, as while he's watching sports, I can write. It's as if he's given me the gift of time: win-win.

I'm just about to apply some more eye shadow, when I see him in the mirror doubling over and steadying himself on the chest of drawers.

'Are you OK?'

I stand up and instinctively go over to rub his back.

'I think I've got a bad belly,' he says, a hint of a groan in his voice. 'I've spent the last half-hour on the toilet and I've got these cramps.'

I look down at him rubbing his stomach.

'You poor thing. Do you think it's something you ate?'

I quickly think back to what I cooked for tea last night, panicking that I've given him food poisoning, but I soon remember we went out for a Thai meal. Phew, at least I'm not to blame. 'Yeah, maybe. I did have prawns last night. Right, I'll slip on my suit.'

He winces as he hobbles over to the wardrobe, pausing for a second before bolting to the door. I hear him thunder across the landing to our bathroom.

I wrinkle my nose up at the thought. It may be a pain that we don't have an en-suite and the bathroom is about as far away from the bedroom as it could be, but at this moment in time it's a blessing. I can't think of anything worse than hearing what's going on in there.

Poor Will.

Of all the times he could get struck down by food poisoning, it would have to be right before Vanessa and Ian's wedding. It's the one wedding he'd been marginally excited about as it's being held on one of the docked ships in Portsmouth Historic Dockyard and it's not every day you get to go on a warship.

I'm pretty excited about the boat as well after hearing all about it for the last few months, or at least I am since I managed to find amazing wedges to wear with my vintage-style prom dress. I'd been in a mild panic when Vanessa first mentioned the no stiletto/narrow-heeled shoes rule.

I slip on my dress and finish getting ready while I wonder what we're going to do. The taxi is picking us up in half an hour, and I know Will only has to throw on a suit and stroll out of the door, but I can't see this belly problem disappearing in time.

Damn it being such an early wedding. If it was later on in the day perhaps he'd have time to get it out of his system.

I try and think of solutions. Perhaps I could pump him full of Imodium and rehydration sachets, or he could just cross his legs all day.

Will appears back in the doorway. His face looks pale and he's clearly agitated, a bit like he was at the restaurant on Monday. Maybe it's not food poisoning after all and he's been coming down with something all week.

'I better get ready,' he says with a slight moan as he rests his head on the doorframe. He seems to be wincing in pain, and I know I'm no doctor, but I think he'll need more than Imodium to get him to the wedding.

He can't go in this state. Even if he could stand up straight, it's not the ideal venue to have a tummy problem in, not when you have to shimmy up and down little ladders between decks to get to the loo.

I can't remember the last time I went to a wedding on my own and I feel my heart racing slightly at the thought. Whose hand will I squeeze during the service? Who will I talk to when I've got an empty space next to me on the table? And what am I going to do when I get all frisky at the end of the night?

No, no, no. I can't go by myself.

I look up at Will, and all my selfish thoughts fade away. He's screwing his eyes up and I think he might even be shedding a tear of pain. Not even I'm cruel enough to force him, no matter how much I don't want to be left on the sidelines when everyone joins in after the first dance.

'You can't come, not if you're feeling this bad.'

'I can't let you go on your own,' he says, pulling his head back upright and walking across the bedroom. 'Ah.'

He doubles over and I go over to support him, leading him to the bed.

'I'll be fine,' I say, lying. 'You stay here in bed. I'll dig you out a rehydration sachet.'

I'm no longer thinking about getting him to the wedding. I just want him to get better.

'Thanks,' he says, using a lame man-flu voice.

I'll forgive him this once for feeling sorry for himself. No one likes a dodgy belly. It's not even like you can lie on the sofa binge-watching TV when you have to keep running back and forth to the bathroom.

'You look nice, by the way,' he says. 'I'm gutted I can't come with you.'

'I'm sure you are,' I say, walking over and rubbing his hair affectionately.

'I'll go and sort out your medicine.'

'OK,' he says.

I pad down the stairs to the kitchen and see that I haven't got long before the taxi arrives. I better pack a bag quickly and get the man sorted.

I hope Vanessa doesn't notice that he's missing, or if she does, I hope she understands. She's laboured over the guest list and the seating plan for months and I know that she's agonised over who could and couldn't come, and who they'd be sitting next to. I hate to think we've messed all that up. She's one of those people who gets stressed out really easily, and I don't want to do anything that might upset her on her special day.

I search the messy kitchen drawer until I find the required medical supplies and fill up a large glass of water.

When I go back upstairs Will is under the covers, his eyes scrunched up – presumably in pain.

Blimey, he must be in a bad way if he hasn't even switched on the TV. I know we don't have the sports channels upstairs, but still.

'Are you going to be all right if I leave you here by yourself? Do you want me to stay around and look after you?'

I'm sure I could do a good line in playing Florence Nightingale. I even have a nurse's outfit kicking about somewhere from the time when we used to make an effort with our sex life. OK, so it's white PVC and probably not something Florence would approve of, but I'm sure the sight of me in it might cheer up Will a little.

I run my hand over his forehead; he doesn't feel hot or clammy.

'I'll be fine. You go. Enjoy yourself. There's no point in two of us having our day ruined,' he says, batting away my hand. 'Plus, Vanessa would kill you if you weren't there.'

That's true.

'If you're sure? Are you going to be OK on your own?'

'I'm sure. Have a great time.'

I lean over and give him a kiss on the cheek, careful not to touch him too much, just on the off-chance it's infectious. I hesitate for a second and wonder if I might have already caught it. What if I give it to everyone at the wedding? I try and weigh up what would be worse, passing on some infectious gastro-illness or facing the wrath of Vanessa? I shudder. Definitely the wrath of Vanessa.

'I will do. I'll try not to wake you when I come back.'

Will winces again and I leave him to it. When you're feeling that rotten all you want is your own space.

'See you later, honey,' I whisper, but he doesn't reply. Presumably too lost in his pain.

I head downstairs and just about have time to shove my lippy, phone and camera into my clutch bag, shove my feet in my shoes and pick up a pashmina before the horn of the taxi goes outside.

'Here goes,' I say, taking a deep breath and trying to imagine what it'll be like to go to the wedding alone. I know that when I was single I used to hate weddings, but it's different now that I'm with Will, isn't it?

And it's not like I'm not going to know anyone. I went to school with Vanessa, and when I was a teenager I think her family saw more of me than my own did. Plus, Cara will be there. Or at least she will be if she doesn't go off with one of those ushers.

Suddenly, I'm feeling a bit more upbeat about the wedding. Even though it's always nice having your other half with you at one, Will does hate them and he spends an awful lot of his time moaning about whatever sports he's missing. Perhaps this is even for the best. I can enjoy the wedding without feeling like I have to babysit a man who's sulking in the corner checking the footie scores on his iPhone.

I slam the door behind me and walk over to the taxi. Yes, this wedding isn't going to be too bad. I mean, as long as I don't get so drunk that I accidentally battle Cara for the usher, then what's the worst that could happen?

4

It turns out that the key to having a good time at a wedding by yourself is drinking copious amounts of elderflower champagne cocktail. The moment the first of those beauties touched my lips, I became relaxed and sociable Lexi.

I've spoken to great-aunts of Vanessa's, practically charmed the pants of her new husband's boss, and I've done my best at matchmaking two awkward teenagers from either side of the families.

Right now, I'm talking to Vanessa's mother. Or more accurately, I'm listening to her. She's done nothing but talk about the wedding and how wonderful it is for the last five minutes. I've merely been required to nod and 'um and ah' in the right places. Not that I'm complaining, she's the proud mother of the bride today and she is entitled to brag about her gorgeous daughter's big day.

'And the florist she used is the same as the one that they use at Chewton Glen. She came highly recommended.'

'They're beautiful,' I say, although, to be honest, I'd only noticed them when her mother mentioned them. Unless you can eat it or drink it, then it doesn't fare well on my radar at weddings.

'Yes, well, I'm sure all this will come in handy for your wedding,' says Vanessa's mother, turning her focus to me as if she's just realised who she was speaking to. 'Vanessa kept this beautiful book, I'm sure she showed you, with all her ideas and research. I'm sure she would lend it to you.'

'Oh,' I say, unsure what to say. It's always handy to be offered materials for the wedding you're not planning. 'Thanks.'

She picks up my hand and shakes her head.

'If only William would propose,' she says, running her hands over my ring finger. 'I bumped into your mum in the supermarket the other day, and she was saying that she's lost all hope that you two will ever get married.'

I try and force my cheeks into a smile, but instead channel my inner Catherine Tate to create an 'am I bothered' face. The truth is, this isn't the first time I've had this conversation today. So far, Vanessa's dad, sister, aunt and one random friend from her hen do have all had variations on this talk with me. I didn't mind it the first couple of times, but it's started to get old now. So instead of replying, I've settled on a winning formula – keep downing my drink until they stop.

'We'll get there one day,' I say, chugging down the elderflower champagne and shaking my head slightly at the aftertaste.

'I'm sure you will,' her mother says. 'Oh, there's Sandra. I must go and say hello.'

She waves at a woman at another table and I breathe a sigh of relief. It sure is exhausting being alone at a wedding. I think people keep making a beeline for me as they feel sorry for the girl by herself.

Cara comes and sits down in the seat Vanessa's mum has just vacated.

'You'd think with Ian being so tall they might have picked another venue,' she says, pointing at him as he walks back into the reception room.

'But it's so lovely and quirky, maybe they didn't realise how much of an issue it would be.'

We both audibly wince as the groom bumps his head yet again. We pick up our glasses and drink a sip; at least it's given us a new drinking game. I stare at my glass in shock, realising it's empty, and quickly refill it with the wine on the table.

'It is nice here,' she says. 'Although dictating what shoes you can wear is a little much. I had to go and buy these things especially. When am I ever going to wear these things again?'

I look down at the gorgeous, wide-heeled sandals that are worlds away from the towering skyscrapers that she usually wears. I'm surprised she was able to walk with her feet flat; she must be so used to being on a permanent incline.

'It's bad enough that I'm single at a wedding, but coming without heels. When you're five foot four you need all the height you can get to bag an usher.'

She looks wistfully over to the top table and I can see the usher she's after – Vanessa's cousin, Max. He's that good-looking that I'm almost tempted to have a go myself. Perhaps I need to cut back on how much I'm drinking.

When Cara mentioned him at the pub the other night I couldn't remember him from the party when we were in sixth form. But that could be because I'd drunk too much Archers and lemonade, my drink of choice back then, or I'd been too far into my indie stage that unless he was sporting a shaggy ape look like a Gallagher brother, then I probably wouldn't have given him a second look.

'I mean, just think, I'll have to take them off when I get lucky. They're not really wear-in-bed heels, are they?'

'Blimey, I can't remember the last time I had sex in heels. These days it's more about what socks I have on and if I can be bothered to take them off.'

Cara rolls her eyes at me and my slovenly sexual ways. I can almost see one of her spice up your life pep talks coming and I need to change the conversation quickly before it does.

'At least you won't bang your head,' I say.

We look up and see the groom bang his head on a beam after coming upright from bending down to kiss and greet a guest.

We drink again. Thank God for the free booze.

'Ooh, he's alone,' says Cara, leaping to her feet. She's lucky she is short, as from the spritely way she bounced up she could have done herself a massive head injury. 'Wish me luck.'

She crosses her fingers and looks like she's going to wet herself with excitement. She's been waiting for Max the usher to be alone all day, but he's had a steady stream of guests to talk to. Pretty much every female from the wedding has had their eye on him, except for me, of course. While I might joke about it, I don't want anyone other than my poorly man.

As I watch her go, I do feel a tiny bit jealous of the giddy rush she's probably feeling. I've been dating Will for so long, I sometimes can't remember what it's like in the beginning. Occasionally, in moments like this, I'm reminded of that heady feeling of lust and tingling loins that I used to get. But those days faded when, not long after we got together, Will felt relaxed enough to fart in front of me.

Perhaps the elderflower champagne cocktails and the wine aren't my friends, after all. I have to admit that when I first saw Vanessa this morning I got really jealous of her bridal glow, but now I'm jealous of Cara for being single – talk about messed up.

I feel my phone vibrate in my bag and I instantly pull it out, thinking that it'll be the patient. I've been trying to leave him alone up until now, allowing him to sleep it off. Plus, I didn't want to rub it in that I was having a great time with lovely food and drink when he's on his death bed.

I still feel the teeniest bit bad about leaving him at home. What if he's too weak to make it down the hall to the toilet? I shudder at the thought of what that could mean, and swipe at my phone. But as I unlock the screen, I see that it's not a text from Will, but one from my work colleague, Mike.

I have a flash of panic that there's been some emergency and I'm being called into work, but really, what could happen in the leisure department of the council at the weekend that an arts officer could fix?

I click on the message and see that it's a photo. As it loads I have a slight panic that I'm going to see something I don't want to, like a naked selfie destined for his wife Louise. What if he's hit my name by mistake?

I squint at the photo through half-shut eyes before opening them fully in shock. While I was right not to want to see its contents, it was definitely a message aimed at me.

There in all his glory is my Will. Not at home tucked up in our bed, but instead dressed in his red-and-white Southampton football shirt, staring at the TV camera. The logo for Sky Sports is clearly visible in the corner, and I can see the edge of Mike's telly.

Mike Williams
Just spotted Will on telly! Cracking game. Bet he's having a brilliant time.

My mind starts to run away with itself, trying to think of logical explanations for the photograph. Maybe it's a practical joke. There's no date stamp on the photo; who's to say it wasn't taken some other time and Mike's only sending it now? Or it could be an old message and it's only just been delivered. The faster my mind works, the more ridiculous the scenarios I think up.

I know in my heart of hearts that the photo is from today. I'm not a fool, despite Will having played me for one.

I give him the last bit of benefit of the doubt by googling the club fixtures to see who Southampton are playing. The search engine results show me that they're playing Everton and as I go back to the photo I can see the scores for the game: Sou 2–1 Eve.

I start to feel sick as I realise he's lied to me. I didn't even know there was a game on today. That's how long he's been planning this. I just assumed that as there hadn't been a week of sulking and moaning in the lead-up to the wedding, that it was an away game which he wouldn't have gone to anyway. But it's blatantly a home game, and he must have been planning to go and watch all along.

Cheeky bastard.

I can't believe he's done this to me. He's lied and let me come to the wedding alone. He's let down Ian and Vanessa, who have paid for the food and drink he won't be consuming – not to mention taken a valuable seat away from someone who might have wanted to come. It's incomprehensible.

The disbelief starts to fade as I try and piece together exactly how devious he has been, and the shock gives way to anger.

I type out a text message to him.

You absolute wanker. I cannot believe you did that!

I hesitate before hitting Send, but I can't do it. As much as I'm fuming, I want him to have the chance to redeem himself. I want him to confess to what he's been up to.

I delete the message and quickly tap and send:

How's the patient feeling? Any better?

I hold my breath. Surely he's going to send a response back that tells me that he's made a miraculous recovery and he's profusely sorry but he went to the football instead of the wedding. That would be the logical explanation.

My phone beeps:

No, if anything I feel worse. Been on the loo most of the day. How's the wedding?

I feel as though steam is coming out of my ears. I can't believe he came back with that. Well, two can play at that game. I type out a frantic reply:

It's good. Missing you though. Should I come home and look after you?

It doesn't take long for him to tap back. Clearly it's half-time, or he knows that he has to be on high alert so as not to make me suspicious. I wouldn't usually get such a quick response when he's at a football game.

I miss you too. Would love to have you here, but really all I'm doing is sitting on the loo and groaning. Believe me, you're best staying away from me at the moment. I'm gross and I stink, and not to mention I'm grumpy. Go have a good time x x

My nostrils are flaring. 'Have a good time. Have a good fucking time!' I scream at my phone. A couple of guests within hearing range look at me and instantly look away in embarrassment. Well, I guess there's always one weird, crazy guest at a wedding. This time it might as well be me.

I hastily type back:

I'll try.

Looks like he's going to keep up the ridiculous lies. I've never known him do anything like this in the past. I try and think if there are any other situations where he could have done this before, but he's usually pretty open with his sporting plans. I'm used to him looking at wedding or christening invitations along with his sports calendar and us negotiating his terms of attendance, e.g. whether or not he can monitor or stream a match on his phone.

I feel stupid that alarm bells didn't ring in my head when the invitation came through from Vanessa and Ian and that didn't happen. Silly me. I had thought that with it being the wedding of one of my best friends, he'd decided it was more important to support Vanessa, and me, on her special day.

I stand up, looking to see where I dumped my little clutch bag. If I leave now, I might just make it home before Will gets back from the game. I have a quick look at my watch. It'll be tight as Portsmouth traffic is always bad, but I should just make it.

'Lexi,' shrills Vanessa as she comes up and practically throws herself at me.

'Ness.'

I hug her warmly and try and hide my rage as best I can.

'Are you having a good time? Did you get enough to eat? Do you like the wine we chose? It wasn't too heavy?'

She's literally holding her breath for my replies to her rapid questions.

'Of course I'm having a fabulous time,' I say, ignoring the last five minutes. 'I ate plenty and the wine is delightful.'

'Phew,' she says, letting out the breath. 'Just you wait until the dessert comes out; it will blow your mind. And mine for that matter as it'll be the first chocolate I'll have eaten in months in preparation for getting into this bad boy.'

She strokes down her dress and I marvel at it up close. The tiny translucent beads that keep catching the light are woven in such an intricate pattern that it is truly exquisite.

'The more important question you should be asking yourself is, are you having a good time? It's your wedding, after all,' I say.

She beams and her whole face lights up.

'I am. I truly am. I mean, it's so true what people say that you don't get to talk to anyone at your own wedding and you never see your husband. But it's so lovely knowing that everyone I love is under one roof. I'm so pleased everyone made such an effort to come.'

Everyone except my boyfriend.

'I'm so sorry again about Will not being able to make it.'

I try and keep the anger out of my voice as I don't want Vanessa to know – the truth would devastate her.

'Oh, these things can't be helped. You're here and that's the main thing. Right, I must go and talk to Ian's aunt and uncle, but please promise me you'll come and join me on the dance floor after the first dance. I want you and Cara boogieing beside me.'

She squeezes my hand before shimmying off to Ian's relatives and I'm left a little stunned. For someone that had lost sleep over the guest list she seems mightily relaxed that Will didn't come. Which can only mean one thing: she must have had a few of those champagne and elderflower cocktails too.

I throw my clutch bag on to the table and sit back down. I can't go anywhere now. I couldn't let her down on the dance floor. I'll just have to get Will to confess when I get home.

Cara comes back over and takes a seat.

'Turns out he's got a bloody girlfriend. She's not here as she's some fucking saint doing a volunteer project in deepest, darkest Peru. Men!' she says, huffing.

Men indeed.

'Did I miss anything over here? Have you spotted any other men that might have potential?'

'Oh, no and no,' I say, too mad to even tell Cara about the text. I'll tell her in the week, as if I do it now I'll probably explode and storm out. 'Nothing exciting going on over here.'

Just the potential bubbling away for my boyfriend and I to have the mother of all rows when I get home.

'Another drink?' she asks, standing up.

I down the one in front of me. 'Abso-fucking-lutely,' I reply. The only thing that's going to stop me from going to defcon 4 is getting so hammered that I forget the train wreck that lies in wait for me at home.

5

It's never nice to be woken up with the bed shaking and the covers being ripped off you, but it's a million times worse to be woken like that when you've got a hangover.

'Sorry,' says Will as he practically sprints out of the bedroom.

I'm in too much pain to try and recover the duvet but the slight chill is almost comforting.

I feel so rough.

It takes a few minutes to allow the pounding to subside enough to replay the events of yesterday in my mind. The wedding – Vanessa and Ian's beautiful wedding. It was the stuff of fairy tales. Perfection around every corner: the venue, the food, the absolute blast we had at the evening reception.

The only dampener being that text message. The hangover momentarily subsides as the anger starts to ripple through my body at the memory of Will's lies.

The image of him in the photo – happy and smiling – is so vivid in my mind, it's as if I was there with him. No matter how many of those champagne cocktails I drank, or the tequila shots that followed, nothing seemed to make me forget. The pain of being lied to is almost as bad as the hangover.

Maybe that's why he's bolted. Maybe he sensed that I know and he's getting as far away from me as possible.

I wonder if I said something to him when I got in last night. I can barely remember leaving the wedding. I have a hazy memory of coming home in a taxi, but aside from that, nada. I must have come straight upstairs, slipped out of my dress and bra and crawled into bed, as I'm still wearing my big hold-everything-in knickers, my tongue is fuzzy, the smell of tequila lingering on my breath, and my eyes are matted together with the mascara I didn't remove.

What I need is a shower and the greasiest fry-up, but I feel like I need to get things sorted with Will first.

My temporary reprieve from the hangover doesn't last long, and the raging around my head commences once more.

'Sorry about that,' he says as he comes back in the room and gets into bed. 'I'm still at the mercy of this belly.'

He pulls the covers back over me, and groans as he wriggles back down under the duvet. Despite the pain it causes me, I roll over to look at him. I stare at him for a moment in disbelief. Is he really going to pretend that he's still ill?

It's a pretty shrewd move, though: who argues with a stomach bug? It's not like anyone would position themselves in the toilet demanding proof.

'You must be really poorly for it still to be going on,' I say arching my eyebrow as I play along.

'I know, it's rough and I couldn't eat a thing yesterday.'

'Poor you. In the house all day long. Weren't you bored?'

'It was so boring,' he says, rolling a bit closer into me. 'But I survived.'

He's using his pathetic man-flu voice, and while yesterday that could have been considered endearing, today it's just adding salt to the wound.

I smooth my hand over his head. 'Poor baby.'

He pouts and I can't believe he hasn't picked up on the sarcastic lilt to my voice.

'But at least I've got my nurse back today to look after me.'

If I hadn't discovered the truth I'd probably be lapping this up by now, cooing over him, feeling guilty for having left him alone. I'm sure that despite the hangover, I'd have been running around after him. Instead, I'm having to lie on my hands to stop them from throttling him.

I should be screaming and shouting and throwing things round the room, but despite being so mad, I can't. I'm too intrigued to see how far he'll go. I need to try and trip him up – he's my boyfriend, after all, not some double agent.

'I heard that Southampton did pretty well yesterday.'

'Yeah, apparently it was a really good game,' he says. 'Tom was there and he was texting me with updates.'

'Ah, that's nice of him. What a good friend.'

'Yeah, he's pretty good like that.'

'It's a shame that it wasn't on TV or you could have watched it.'

I have photographic proof that the match was televised. With our big sports package – that practically requires its own mortgage – he couldn't possibly say we don't have the right channels to cover it.

'It was,' he says with barely a pause, 'but my belly was so rough that I was camped out on the loo and barely saw any of it, which is why I needed the text updates.'

'Ah,' I say, nodding.

'Hopefully this morning I can make it through the Malaysian Grand Prix that I recorded.'

He's rolling out lie after lie, and so quickly. Has he always been this good at lying and I've never noticed? Should I be worried? He could be having affairs left, right and centre and I'd be none the wiser.

I almost laugh out loud. Really, what mistress would put up with his sporting obsession like I do?

Though it does make me wonder what he's done in the past in the name of sport. I mean, how important could this football game have been for him to have gone to such lengths to go and see it? It's still early in the season and as far as I know, it wasn't a special match, which just makes it worse. I might have been able to forgive him if it had been the FA Cup final – maybe – but an average game? He has a season ticket and he goes to nearly all the matches, so you would have thought he'd be able to miss one.

I'm angry that he didn't come to my friend's wedding, but I'm more hurt that he wasn't honest with me. I know I wouldn't have given him my blessing if he'd asked, but I wouldn't have been able to stop him. I'm sure I'd still have been mad as hell, but I wouldn't be feeling as betrayed as I am now.

At least I know where I stand in the pecking order. I always thought that when push came to shove he'd put me first, but now I'm not so sure.

'How was the wedding, anyway? You hung-over?' he says, snapping me out of my thoughts.

'A bit. But the wedding was lovely. It was such a shame you missed it. I felt a bit bad talking to Vanessa about you not being able to make it. She'd really struggled to keep the numbers on the guest list down and what with the empty seat . . . But she was very understanding. You can't argue with a serious bout of food poisoning, can you?'

I start to change tack, hoping I can guilt him into confessing.

'You certainly can't,' he says, nodding in agreement.

Where is this acting coming from? This is the guy that can barely think creatively enough to play charades, and yet this performance is almost worthy of a BAFTA.

He's making me really mad. It's almost like the more angry I become, the more determined I am to get him to confess.

'You know what I really fancy? A KFC,' I say.

I'm being mean now. I know he can't resist a Bargain Bucket.

'I reckon my hangover will just stretch for me to go get one. All that deep-fried chicken, corn on the cob and barbecue beans,' I say, my stomach rumbling as it buys into my lies.

I'm not really going. I'd be over the legal driving limit, but I want to test if he's got the power to resist the food. I can't imagine that he'd want a KFC if he really did have stomach problems.

'Do you want me to get us one?' I ask.

I can see that for the first time he's torn. He's hesitating as if he's contemplating it.

'You get one for yourself, if you want. I don't think my belly's up to it.'

Damn it.

Who trained this guy? I almost feel like I should drag him down to the bathroom and do some water torture. Although who am I kidding, the only water torture I know is when I attempt to dye my own hair in the bathroom without staining all the tiles.

I'm going to have to pull out the big guns.

I roll over to him and snuggle up a little. If all else fails there are always my feminine charms. Now I know I didn't get round to taking my make-up off last night, and my hair is probably reminiscent of that scene from *There's Something About Mary* thanks to the ridiculous amounts of hairspray I used for the wedding, and let's not talk about my breath, which tastes horribly like stale tequila, but aside from that I've got shaved legs, so that has to be a bonus, and I've still got my boobs. My boobs don't usually let me down.

Playing to my strengths, I keep my head and booze breath away from him and rub my bare leg up against his.

'What's got into you?' he says, a look of surprise creeping over his face.

'I've got smooth legs.'

Although I do regularly shave my legs, I went the whole hog for the wedding, new blade, proper Gillette foam rather than my usual conditioner, and I exfoliated and moisturised.

'I can feel that.'

'And there's my boobs,' I say, thrusting them towards his bare chest, but still making sure that I keep my head away from him as much as possible. 'You know, the best bit of us going to a wedding is usually what happens when we get home.'

I try and put a sexy purr into my voice, but thanks to some very heartfelt singing of 'Summer Nights' it sounds more gravelly, like I've got a fifty-a-day habit and am in need of a good hack to clear it.

Will runs a hand up my leg and as it creeps further and further up my thigh I feel like I've got him.

'As smooth as they are,' he says, removing his hand just before it gets to the good stuff, 'I feel far too rough for anything like that. Rain check?'

Humph.

I shift my weight back over to my side of the bed. I can't believe that not even the lure of sexy time worked. The last time my boyfriend turned down sex on a platter was when . . . in fact, he's never turned it down before.

I guess it wasn't a foolproof plan. What was I expecting him to do, confess in the middle of his climax?

'I think I'm going to have to go to the toilet again,' he says, getting out of bed.

I watch him go out of the room and shake my head. I roll on to my back and sigh loudly.

He's never going to tell me, and it looks like he's going to keep up the pretence.

As much as I want to see how long it will be until he confesses, I'm going to have to have it out with him. He can't get away with this. If my head wasn't pounding I'd be tempted to go and call his bluff and burst in on him in the bathroom right now. Catching him – or more accurately not catching him – in the act.

I only wish he wasn't so bloody annoying in an argument. If I get cross and shout at him, do you know what he does? He listens to the rant, he nods his head, he apologises, and he comes over and gives me a cuddle. I used to think it was because he realised I was right, but I've since realised he's managing me. It hit me as

I was watching a friend placate her toddler by indulging his tantrum and repeating to him over and over that she knew he wanted to go on the big slide before his brother, while she smoothed his hair and hugged him until he calmed down. That is exactly what Will does to me. He knows that if he shouts back or gets cross then we'll have a huge row that will see me in a strop for days. Whereas his softly-softly approach means that I've got the rant out, and after he's made a strategic cup of tea and provided me with an emergency bourbon, we're back to normal.

It might seem like a dream, but it's so frustrating. Not to mention, in this situation, it would totally let him off the hook. But what choice do I have?

He gets back into bed and I take a deep breath, wondering how I'm going to tell him that I know. I stare at him for a moment. Am I just imagining it, or does he have beads of sweat on his brow? I wonder how he's made it look as though he's still sweating from his illness.

'So, I was thinking yesterday. You know that week that we've got booked off in November for the DIY.'

'Uh-huh,' I say, dreading the thought of it. It will be the only week of annual leave where I'd rather be at work. We booked it off months ago, at Will's insistence, as we keep putting off doing our decorating. We've had paint swatches on our kitchen wall since the week after we moved in, and we still have space-themed wallpaper hanging proudly on one wall of our bedroom.

I've only agreed to decorating those two rooms, though. If he's been watching *George Clarke's Amazing Spaces* again and wants to pimp out the shed as well, he's very much mistaken.

'I think we should say bugger the DIY and go on holiday. Somewhere a bit exotic.'

'I'm listening,' I say, suddenly thinking I'll bring up the text later instead. To be honest, he could have said go on a holiday to Skegness and I would have been happy if it got me away from the decorating.

'How about we go to Barbados?'

'Barbados?'

'Uh-huh. Next month. I've been looking at package holidays, and there are some good deals around.'

'Um.'

I'm lost for words. This was not the conversation I thought we'd be having this morning.

'It would be all romantic,' he says quickly.

I'm not firing on all cylinders, thanks to the hangover, and it takes me a while for it to sink in. Boyfriend does monumental shitty thing to me one day, doesn't think I know, then proposes mother of all romantic holidays the next. Hmm. I might be slower than usual this morning, but I'm thinking there might be a link. Is this his guilt manifesting? Is it morphing him into a romantic boyfriend?

Usually, it falls to me to submit lots of different dates and options for holidays, and Will checks his sports schedule and lets me know the best one. So for him to take the lead and suggest somewhere so different to our usual holidays is very out of character.

'I've found us a deal in a resort that has little bungalows. The complex itself has a big pool and several restaurants. It's not on the beach, but it's across the road from one . . .'

I'm only vaguely aware of what he's saying. He had me at Barbados – any other information is incidental. In my head I'm already there, sipping cocktails under a giant palm tree, watching the waves crash on the crystal-clear shoreline while in pursuit of the perfect sun-kissed tan.

I've always dreamt we'd have one of those holidays. I thought he'd never be persuaded unless it was our honeymoon. I'm so excited that it seems to have momentarily cured my hangover.

'OK, then, let's do it,' I say, interrupting him waffling on about the transfer time from the airport.

'Really?'

Why does he sound surprised? He's talking about us going to the Caribbean, not Outer Mongolia. I'm sure there are very few girlfriends that would need their arms twisted to go on such a holiday.

I can't help smiling, until I remember the text message. The anger in me had somewhat disappeared, but now it slowly rises to the surface again. I'm suddenly torn between wanting to confront him and wanting to go on my dream holiday. Perhaps today is not the day to tell him I know. Who knows what else he might do to ease his guilt?

Before I can ponder it any more, the radio from my alarm clock breaks the silence and scares the bejesus out of me. Why I set my alarm for a Sunday I don't know.

'*And here's Rowan with the sport,*' crackles out of the radio.

'Oh, turn it off, Lex, in case they talk about the Forumla 1.'

I lean my hand over to find the Off switch when I'm hit with a sudden idea.

Barbados, or no Barbados, if I'm not going to confront him, then perhaps I'll teach him a lesson.

'. . . *There was a shock result in the Malaysian Grand Prix.*'

'Argh, get it off!' wails Will, nudging me in the direction of the bedside table.

I lean over and instead of turning the dial off, I turn up the volume to the max.

'. . . *Romain Grosjean won after Hamilton had to retire, closing the gap at the top of the table of the championship.*'

'Eep, sorry,' I say, as I pretend to jab at the different buttons, none of which will make it stop.

After the results have well and truly been spelt out, I miraculously find the Off switch. I take a moment to compose myself and hide the smile on my face before I turn back to face Will.

'I can't fucking believe that,' he says, groaning.

I'm trying to pull a sympathetic girlfriend face, but inside I'm smiling. I know it wasn't big or clever, and it doesn't go anyway to making up for his lying, but it made me a teeny tiny bit happy.

'I'm sorry. I guess I'm not very co-ordinated this morning. But I'm sure it doesn't matter that you know who won, it's about how it happens, right?'

I know this isn't true. It's like when you find out who's been eliminated from *Bake Off* before you've had a chance to watch it on iPlayer. It's never the same when you're expecting a particular person's cakes to collapse or burn.

'Of course it matters. I mean, what's the point of watching now. Might as well not bother.'

'Oh well, I'm sure there'll be something else to watch.'

Will sighs loudly and I can tell he's going to spend the whole day sulking. Which suits me down to the ground.

'First I have my Saturday ruined by food poisoning, and now my Sunday's ruined too. It's like I'm cursed.'

I feel the hackles on the back of my neck stand on end. He's really never going to let go of this lie. Any pleasure I got out of ruining the Grand Prix result fades away.

Will is going to have to crack eventually about what he did, and in the meantime, I'm going to have to think of a way to control this anger.

6

Since when have two-day hangovers been a thing? I might not have woken up this morning with toilet-bowl tequila breath, but I did wake up with a sickness and lethargy that made me feel like I'd run a marathon before I'd even got out of bed. I did question whether it was flu, but instead of craving Nurofen, I was craving McDonald's. There's usually only one thing wrong with me if I think an Egg McMuffin is going to act as the miracle cure.

Luckily for me, there's a McDonald's en route to work, and I show up at eight clutching my little brown paper bag full of naughtiness that I hope will fix me. I'd usually have the willpower to resist, but after the weekend I've had, I'm feeling pretty low.

'Like that, is it?' says Mike, looking at the bag as I place it on my desk.

Mike may be in his fifties, but he can still spot the classic tell-tale signs of a hangover a mile off.

'Uh-huh. Mondays, hey.'

'Yeah, but I'd eat that quickly if I was you. Don't forget, we've got the audit starting today and I'm sure Robin whatever his name is will be down soon.'

'Oh, crap.'

I'd completely forgotten about that. We're having an audit to prove to the councillors that we, as a department, are value for money. I'm pretty sure it's a paper-pushing exercise, and I can't personally understand how it's cost effective to have someone sitting with us for weeks while they work out what we do, but hey, what do I know? I don't work at the top of the building where this kind of genius hails from.

Despite my reservations, I want to make the best impression I can as, at the end of the day, I want to keep my job. When you work in the arts, you know you're an easy target for cuts. Not that I think I'm going anywhere as (a) I'm good at my job, and (b) they've already got rid of everyone else so that it's only me left.

I look at my brown paper bag, knowing that it's the key to me being well this morning. If I don't have it I'll feel like crap all day, but if I'm scoffing it down at my desk it might not make the best first impression.

Deciding that I should play it safe, I get up and head towards the staff kitchen.

'Ah, here we are – leisure,' says the fit guy from the top.

I stare at him in disbelief, wondering if he's lost, before I clock the big wad of files under his arm and realise what's going on.

He's our auditor? Him that sits up on the top floor with his perfect hair, perfect suit and perfect pearly whites.

I feel sick and it's nothing to do with the hangover. I'm going to be sitting opposite him for the next few weeks. The man that makes me giggle and blush like a schoolgirl. And that's without taking into consideration the fact that he probably saw me last week with my dress tucked into my knickers.

Oh dear lord.

'What's that smell?' he says, sniffing like a bloodhound.

I look down at the brown paper bag in my hands and go to put it behind my back but as I do, he looks straight at it. I'm caught red-handed.

Why couldn't I be one of those clean eaters and have an impressive super-healthy snack in my hands? My head throbs and I remember why I'm eating the Egg McMuffin. I don't think anything raw or without sugar would cut it right now. I wonder what clean eaters eat when they've got a hangover?

'Oh,' he says. 'A McDonald's at eight o'clock on a Monday morning? A woman after my own heart.'

He looks at me as if I'm the only person in the room, and I'm about to blindly give him my Egg McMuffin – hell, I'd give him anything he wants right now – when Mike jumps out of his seat and interrupts us.

'Robin, good to see you again,' he says, reaching out and shaking his hand. I've not seen him this spritely since the time we had a free buffet in the lobby.

'Nice to see you, Mike. How was your weekend? Did your boy's rugby team win on Sunday?'

I watch as they shake hands like they're long-lost friends.

'It was good, thanks, and yes, they won 21–7,' he says beaming.

I hop from foot to foot, not knowing whether I should pipe up and join the conversation or slink off and eat my naughty breakfast.

'I see you've met Lexi. Have you been properly introduced?' says Mike, as if he senses my awkwardness.

'No, I haven't,' he replies, looking between the two of us.

'She's the arts officer. Sorry, arts development coordinator,' says Mike, using my new title, my third in the seven years I've been here in what is essentially the same job. 'You're going to be sitting opposite her.'

'Perfect,' he says, looking down at the empty desk. 'That will do me just fine.'

'Lexi was just on her way to eat her breakfast in the kitchen,' he says, nodding his head at me.

'Yes,' I say, mimicking his head movement. 'I was.'

Of course I was. I regain my composure and force my legs to move.

'Nice to meet you,' I say, still intimidated, and I scurry off to the kitchen.

Once inside, I breathe out and open the bag. I quickly scoff down the Egg McMuffin, before wishing I'd had the foresight to buy a vanilla milkshake at the same time. I make do instead with a vanilla-flavoured coffee from the vending machine, and hurry back to my desk.

'Vanilla coffee?' says Robin, sniffing the air. 'Wow, someone obviously had quite the weekend. Need a sugar rush, do we?'

'Something like that,' I mutter, trying to act cool.

'And what with that McDonald's you just ate. I thought that the leisure department would be all NutriBullet shakes and goji berries.'

I hate the fact that our department is named *leisure*. I constantly have to tell people that a title like *arts and recreation* would be much more fitting, as *leisure* makes us sound like we spend all day lounging around in tracksuits.

The only time that misconception worked out well was when I met first met Will in a dodgy nightclub in Southampton. He'd asked me what I did and I'd told him I worked in the leisure department of a council. He'd assumed that meant I worked for Southampton City Council, and that it might mean I'd get to go to networking events with the Southampton football players. The disappointment was written all over his face on our first proper date when he found out that I worked at a smaller local council and that I had nothing to do with sports. By then we were half way through dinner and he was stuck with me until the end of the night. But somewhere during the main course and dessert, he realised that despite me thinking that the offside rule was him alluding to tax avoidance, I was pretty cool.

'I work in the arts, therefore I'm exempt,' I say, flamboyantly and quite accidentally playing up to the profession's stereotypes. I'm surprised I didn't add a lovey 'darling' to the end of the sentence. I'm so embarrassing. Thank God I'm with Will, as I really suck at flirting.

'Yes, so I've heard. But I'm relieved,' he says. 'I thought you'd all be force-feeding me kale and judging my biceps.'

My eyes fall over his arms as he removes his jacket. They look all right from where I'm sitting.

'The only force-feeding here is cake when it's someone's birthday.'

'Now that I can handle,' he says smiling.

He places his pile of papers down on the desk and looks around.

'Is Jacqui in yet?'

She's my boss, and the head of the department.

'She'll be here in about five minutes or so. She goes to a diary meeting on a Monday with the exec.'

'Of course,' he says.

I'm guessing he can't start whatever he needs to do until she gets back. It's making me uneasy as I feel as though I should engage him in conversation, but I can't for the life of me think of anything witty or interesting to say.

I sip my coffee, burning my tongue as I do so and wincing at the sweetness. I'd get up and get something else to drink, but I don't want to look like I spend all my time eating and drinking.

I try and turn my attention to my work, but I'm so distracted by Robin sitting opposite me that I can't remember what I'm supposed to be doing. Damn Moira for leaving and creating a free desk.

I quickly turn on my PC and busy myself looking in my diary to make it look like I'm terribly important and good at my job, as my brain tries to remember what I should be doing.

I scan my emails, deleting all the forwards from my grand-mother that warn me about the men wanting to climb into my boot with rope at petrol stations, followed by the round-robin emails about things that don't concern me, and then I see Cara's sent me a message:

To: Lexi Hunter <L.Hunter2@SolentTown.gov.uk>
From: Cara Thomas <Cara.Thomas@sci-soton.ac.uk>

Subject: Post Wedding Blues
How are you feeling today? Wish we could do that wedding all over again. And I could do that usher all over again. Why did I have to come to work . . .?
Looking forward to a gossip on Wednesday. Are you OK to pick me up?

I laugh at Cara's email before quickly hitting Reply:

Yes, will see you at seven x

It's our standard Wednesday date – writing group. I'm look-ing forward to seeing her as I haven't told her what Will did yet, as it's the type of story that deserves to be heard in person.

'So how was the big wedding? That was this weekend, wasn't it?' I look over at Mike.

'Yes, it was. It was great, thanks.'

'I was a bit surprised to see Will at the footie, though. You're a lot more relaxed than my wife. She'd never have let me go to the football instead of a wedding.'

I bite my lip. I'm too embarrassed to tell him the truth. So I just smile and pretend that I'm actually some super-cool, laid-back girlfriend.

'Don't you think that's pretty impressive, Robin?' asks Mike.

Oh God. I sink even lower in my chair. Why does he have to bring him into the conversation?

'What's that?' says Robin.

'Nothing,' I say, scowling at Mike.

I know Robin seems really nice, but Mike was the one saying we had to put our best foot forward, and then he starts gossiping and making it obvious that we're talking about our personal lives when we should be working. Of course, I know that I'm multitasking as, while we're dissecting my weekend, I'm browsing my various arts websites like I always do on a Monday morning, keeping up to date with the my industry – but Robin's not to know that.

'Lexi's best friend was getting married at the weekend, and she let her boyfriend go to the Southampton match instead.'

Clearly, Mike is not fluent in the language of scowls.

'That's really nice of you,' says Robin, looking a little shocked.

'Nice? Flipping heck, it's more than nice.' Mike grins at me. 'My wife would never let me do that. Would your girlfriend?'

'I'm between girlfriends at the moment,' says Robin.

For a second I sit up a little straighter until I remember that I'm not between boyfriends. What is it with this man, and why is he making me act like a hormonal teenager?

'But if I did have one, I wouldn't have asked. If it was her best friend, then I'd have probably wanted to go with her to the wedding.'

I stare at him and my eyes widen. I didn't think men actually thought like that. I'm tempted to ask him if I can borrow him and use him as Exhibit A when I have it out with Will, but then I remember that I can't tell him and Mike my shameful secret – that I didn't give my boyfriend permission and he went after feigning illness.

Robin looks up at me as I'm blatantly staring in surprise, so I quickly turn my attention back to my screen.

Not only does this Robin guy look perfect, he is also seemingly the perfect boyfriend.

Talking to these two guys only reinforces my opinion of Will's deceit. Sometimes, I've been known to fly off the deep end and make a big deal out of nothing (who hasn't?), so it's nice to be reassured by these two that Will going to the football when he should have been by my side at the wedding was a really big thing.

Thinking makes my brain ache and my hangover pound even more. I sip at my vanilla coffee, slowly trying to ignore the taste as it's all I've got left in my arsenal to get rid of it.

Jacqui walks into our office, fresh from her meeting. I smile at her as she strides purposefully over to our island of desks. She's only been our boss for about a year, but she's bloody good at it. One of those rare beasts that is not only good at her job but good at recognising her staff's talent too.

'Morning,' she says in her chirpy yet authoritative manor. 'I see you've been pointed in the way of your desk, Robin. Now, do you want to come into my office and we'll get this process started?'

'Happy to,' he says, standing up and taking a big pile of papers with him.

Mike and I breathe out as he leaves.

'He's not what I expected. Do you know him well, then?' I say.

'Not that well. I've met him before, during some planning meetings. He's a really nice guy, though. Seems to take the time to find out who you are and he remembers conversations he's had with you. I only mentioned James playing rugby in passing.'

I wish I was like that. I'm rubbish with names, which is why I give people random nicknames.

'I was pleased when I found out it was him that was doing the audit. The only thing that scares me is that he worked on the environmental health department audit last year.'

That's not what I wanted to hear. I try and swallow a lump in my throat. They've recently suffered a reshuffle and redundancies, probably on the basis of that report.

I look over my diary and see I've got a fairly clear week in terms of appointments, mainly as I thought I'd stay in the office and work on next summer's arts festival. I almost wish I'd booked lots of external visits to get as far away as possible.

I try and distract myself from Robin's report by getting stuck in to listing all the venues and collaborative partners for the festival. I then start brainstorming the possible events based around local writers, artists and performers. I'm just looking up a local band on YouTube when I feel a tap on my shoulder.

I take my headphones off, and see Robin standing over me.

'Jacqui said you'd take me through some of the departmental procedures, if now is a good time? I could come back when you're –'

He pauses and I get the feeling he doesn't really know whether I'm working or playing.

'Um, this is work-related,' I say, pointing to the screen. 'I'm looking at performers for our arts festival.'

'Oh, really? Can we swap jobs? You can work for my fire-breathing boss Beth and compile reports and I'll scout for local bands. I've always fancied myself as a Simon Cowell.'

'As tempting as that offer sounds, I think I'll stick to what I'm good at. Plus, I don't think that you'd be able to pull off the high-waisted trousers.'

I almost slap my hand to my mouth. I can't believe I said that to our auditor – I've only just met the guy. Talk about being overfamiliar.

I'm worried about how he's going to take it when luckily for me, he laughs.

'You're probably right. I don't much like his choice in T-shirts either. I better get on with the audit in that case. So now is a good time, then?'

'As good as any, I suppose.'

He nods his head a little before smiling. 'Don't be nervous. I'm not here to get anyone sacked. If anything I'm here to highlight what a good job people do around here. So just relax and give me the information I need. Jacqui mentioned that your work was really interesting, so we thought I'd start with you.'

I look over to her office and she gives me a thumbs up from her desk. I can't help but feel a little flattered that he's started with me out of the twelve people in our department. I do think I've got the most interesting job out of us, but I'm probably a little biased.

'OK. Take a seat and tell me what you need to know,' I say, trying to calm the confusion of my inner voice that (a) a handsome man is sitting so close to me, and (b) that said handsome man might be bad news for my job.

I take a deep breath and tell myself to get over it. He said it himself: he's not here to get anyone sacked. All I need to do is show him how good a job I do – and not get lost staring into those deep blue eyes of his. And if I can do that, then the month will fly by and before I know it he'll go back to the top of the building and I can go back to acting like a normal human being at work.

7

I've barely pulled up outside Cara's house before she's running down the driveway and jumping into the car.

I know she always looks forward to our Wednesday evening catch-up and writer's group meeting, but this is keen even for her.

'Hiya,' she says, getting in with the same velocity.

I almost expect her to shout *drive, drive, drive*, like they do in heist movies, as she's got that type of nervous energy.

'Hi. Everything OK?' I ask, as I pull away, glancing at her house in the mirror as we drive down the road.

'Yeah, fine. The usher came over,' she says, sighing. 'I couldn't wait to get out of there.'

'The usher that you took home on Saturday?'

'That's the one.'

I had to check. I wouldn't have put it past her to have been working her way through the rest of the bridal party.

'So what's changed?' I say, wondering if I'm going to live to regret that question.

'I invited him over last night and he came over with a *bag*.'

'Oh no, a bag,' I say, laughing.

She gives me a stare. Apparently this is no laughing matter.

'What was in the bag, then? I'm guessing it wasn't the kind that Christian Grey would carry around with him.'

'Oh no, that I could have handled. It was much worse. It had slippers inside.'

'Slippers?'

'Yeah, slippers,' she whispers, as if it's a dirty word. 'Ones like my dad would wear. You know the type, made of slightly flexible sturdy fabric, in dark blue velvet.'

She shudders.

'Maybe he just likes to have warm feet.'

'We had a one-night stand, and when I invited him for a follow-up he brings grandad slippers. Come on, that's like me showing up at his house with my hot-water bottle.'

Now is not the time for me to tell her that I once showed up at Will's house with a hot-water bottle, but in my defence his house was bloody freezing. I swear that was the reason that we had so much sex in our early relationship. If we didn't have a little bit of under-the-cover action, we'd be shivering like ice cubes for an hour after getting into bed. Hmm, maybe we should have a central-heating failure in our house.

'That's hardly a reason not to date someone.'

'Isn't it?'

I shake my head.

'So wait, he came over last night, with his slippers, and what, he didn't leave?'

'He did – he went to work this morning. Then he came back after work to collect his bag.'

'And you've just left him there?'

'Well, yeah. When he showed up we had a quickie, obviously, and then he got dressed and put his slippers on. He made us both a cup of tea and then settled himself into my armchair. I didn't know what to do, and then I saw your car, so I mumbled that I was off, and ran out.'

I can't help but laugh.

'I can't believe you just left him there. Do you trust him?'

'Well, as much as you can trust any man.'

'True dat,' I say, thinking back to my weekend.

'And don't forget, he's one of Ian's best friends. So he's like Vanessa-approved. Which means that of all the people that come through my house, he's already been properly vetted.'

'Ah, I'd forgotten that. Shouldn't that have given you a clue – with the slippers?'

Vanessa's new husband is the kind of guy that would have been a pipe-and-slippers man back in the day. A pint of real ale. A knitted cardigan. He's practically a hipster by accident.

'Oh, yes, I see my mistake. Anyway, he'll let himself out, I'm sure.'

'Uh-huh. If he's brought his slippers, he's probably there for the long haul.'

Cara sighs.

'At least he gives good head.'

'Oh God. Overshare,' I say, as I screech on the brakes and try to put a halt on the conversation. Luckily, we've made it to the pub and I can escape. I climb out of my little car and we head inside.

'So how was your hangover after the wedding?' Cara asks as we make our way to the bar. 'I haven't seen you that drunk in a really long time. Was everything OK?'

'Let's get a drink first, you're going to need it.'

'Sounds interesting,' she says, raising an eyebrow.

She dispatches me to find our usual table while she heads over to the bar. I go and sit near the little back room where our group meets. We've got just enough time to have a gossip beforehand.

'Right, then, fill me in,' she says, sitting down and sipping her wine like's she's settling in to watch the latest instalment of a favourite soap.

I'm just as eager to start the story. I've been holding it in for over seventy-two hours now, and if I don't tell someone soon, I'll burst.

'Well, you know when you went and chatted up that usher – not the usher in your house, the other one with the chiselled jaw?'

'Of course,' says Cara, her eyes lighting up. 'Damn shame about him and his nun of a girlfriend.'

'Indeed it was. Well, while you were trying to get him to sow some wild oats,' I say, getting into storyteller mode, 'I got a text message.'

'Intriguing,' says Cara, leaning in closer. 'Tell me more.'

'It was from this guy Mike that I sit next to at work. He sent me a picture message.'

'Oh my God. With his bits out? Was it like some sort of I've got the horn for you message?'

I roll my eyes at Cara. She totally wants to be the next E. L. James, and her mind is almost permanently in the gutter.

'No,' I say, not telling her that that had been my first thought too. 'It was of Will.'

'This is getting weirder by the minute. Do I want to know the rest?'

'Let me save you some time. The photo was of fully dressed people, and there was nothing remotely sexual.'

'Oh,' she says, leaning away from me, her interest waning.

'It was of Will watching the Southampton footie match on Saturday. He was on Sky Sports and Mike took a photo.'

'Is that all? I'm sure with all the home games he goes to that he gets snapped all the time. I'm surprised he doesn't have a showreel.'

Actually, so am I now that she's mentioned it.

'But it was *this* Saturday,' I say waiting for the penny to drop.

'So . . . oh, wait. When he was supposed to be at the wedding?'

'Uh-huh,' I say, the ripple of anger washing over me again as I say it out loud.

'But he was supposed to have food poisoning.'

'I know,' I say, in a high-pitched squeal. 'He spent the whole day pretending that he was tucked up in bed when all along he was at St Mary's drinking beer and watching his beloved football.'

'Oh dear. So what happened when you confronted him?'

'Well, that's just it. I didn't tell him.'

'What do you mean, you didn't tell him? Didn't you go nuts when you got in? Granted, you might not have been able to do anything in your drunken stupor on Saturday, but surely you went mental on Sunday?'

'Believe me, I wanted to, but I was hoping he'd come clean by himself.'

'And did he?'

'No. I really thought that he might be a bit sheepish and confess, but he kept up the lie. Do you know, he even had the gall to get up the next morning and run to the loo? In fact, he spent until about five o'clock that evening pretending he had stomach pains and walking around feeling sorry for himself.'

'And you didn't let on that you knew?'

'No, I kept trying different things to make him crack. Making him feel guilty for wasting a place at Vanessa and Ian's wedding, asking him about the footie game, and I even offered him sex.'

'And?' says Cara, hooked on every word.

'He turned it down. He was like a flipping clam – he didn't give anything away. He just kept churning out lie after lie. If he hadn't been lying to me, I might have been impressed with the speed at which he could come up with them. I mean, who knew that Will had it in him?'

'This doesn't sound like him at all,' says Cara, shaking her head in disbelief.

'I know. He's not usually devious, but I think he felt guilty, as he suggested we go to Barbados.'

'You what? Really?'

'Uh-huh, he wants us to go in November. You know, when we'd planned to do our DIY. How amazing is that going to be? A tan before Christmas.'

'I'm so jealous, but let me get this straight; you haven't had it out with him because you're going on holiday? Surely you must be fuming?'

'Absolutely, and Barbados isn't the only reason I'm not confronting him. I'm not that easily bought,' I say, trying to convince myself. 'It's just, you know what he's like when we argue. He'll do his usual cuddly apologetic thing, and that will be the end of it.

'I did try and get my own back on him. He shouted for me to turn off the radio so that he wouldn't hear the Grand Prix results, but instead of turning it off I turned it up. He'd recorded the race to watch later on and he was so cross. I know it is nowhere near in the same league as what he did to me and Vanessa, but it did make me feel a tiny bit better.'

'So that's it? You're just going to let it go?'

'No, I just haven't decided what I'm going to do about it yet.'

'Are you going to go all woman scorned? Get your revenge?'

I think back to Sunday. Revenge did make me feel better for a tiny bit.

'I don't know if I'm cut out for that. It worked on Sunday because it was spontaneous. It just sort of happened.'

'Well, why don't you make it sort of happen again? You could accidentally phone up Sky and get your sports package removed. Just think of the money you'd save.'

She's right. We'd save a flipping bundle if we didn't have BT and Sky Sports. Our mortgage advisor told us we'd be able to have a three-bedroom house rather than a two-bedroom if we added that money into our mortgage each month instead. Of course, Will told him we'd worry about that when we had a need for a third bedroom.

'Hmm, I don't think I could do that – as much as I'd love to. I know from when we looked to change providers that you have to give them a month's notice.'

'So just talk to him and tell him you know. I mean, what if he does it to you again?'

'I know, I've thought about that,' I say, pausing to consider. 'I will talk to him, but if I go in all guns blazing, all he'll do is apologise and I feel like I need something more. Besides, he doesn't have to know when I found out about the game, does he?'

Cara sighs.

'If I was you I'd be ripping up his bloody season ticket and then telling him exactly why I did it.'

'Blimey, I do still want to be in a relationship with him. I'd pretty much be given my marching orders if I did that.'

'You know that I once ripped up Wes's cricket tickets? Did I ever tell you that story?'

'No,' I say, almost spitting out my mouthful of drink.

Wes, or Wanker Wes to give him his full title, was one of Cara's rare boyfriends. She broke up with him as it turned out he was cheating on her with the local barmaid.

'We had this huge fight the night before he was due to go to the cricket with his mates, and I lost it completely and ripped up his ticket. His friends had to go without him.'

'God, that seems a bit extreme.'

'Yeah, it was a little, and I did feel guilty, until I found out that he was sleeping with that bitch. Then I wished I'd done something a little meaner.'

'I think I need to do something more subtle. I want him to be the one in the wrong at the end of this, not me. I want to make sure he doesn't know what I've done so that I have the moral upper hand when I confront him.'

The leader of our writing group walks past and says her hellos before going into the back room.

'I take it that's our cue to go in, then,' says Cara.

'I guess so.'

'Marketing today.'

'Hmm. Can't wait,' I say, groaning.

We pick up our stuff and head towards the room. I don't know why I'm bothering tonight. I'm supposed to have been thinking about my own blog, but I've been far too distracted by my lying boyfriend to do any writing.

For once my normal life seems as depressing as my aspiring-writer life, and I've lost all motivation.

8

Despite me trying to channel my inner creative genius since late last night, I am still no further forward on a blog topic or a revenge plot.

Luckily for me, last night's writing group was all about benchmarking and looking at blogs, so I've got a whole week to write my own before we look them up in class.

So although my personal life is in a state of flux while I work out what to do about Will, I'm focusing my attention on writing my blog and taking advantage of my previously underused lunch breaks.

It's actually quite refreshing to step away from my desk and into the fresh air. I'm so used to grabbing a quick sandwich or, if I'm feeling adventurous, heading down to the subsidised staff canteen. And it really is adventurous since you can never be too sure if there are vegetables in the veggie lasagne, or just what meat is in the meat loaf. But today, I'm heading outside and away from my computer to a coffee shop to sit behind . . . my laptop. Yep, OK, still a screen, but at least it's a *change* of screen.

With the noise of the coffee machine, the chatter of fellow customers and the windows steamed up with condensation,

I can indulge in my fantasy that I'm a full-time writer working in some big exciting city, rather than a wannabe writer in a small coastal town on my lunch break.

All I need to do is think of a topic to write about. Janet, our group leader, said it didn't have to be book-related and that it could be about our real lives. I've only got to come up with half a dozen different posts for class, it's not like I've got to keep it going. Yet I'm still stumped.

I'm just about to start typing – really I am – when a shadow falls across my desk.

'Hey there,' says Robin, as I look up at him. 'Moonlighting, are we?'

'Oh,' I say, looking up in surprise. I thought I'd gone far enough away from the council offices not to bump into colleagues. I'm a bit flustered and I don't want him to think I'm here applying for other jobs or running some sort of secret company. I need to think of a good excuse for what I could be doing. 'I'm just doing a bit of writing.'

I groan internally. I hate new people knowing about my hobby. By telling them, it's like I've invited them into a secret room, and once they know about it, people start poking around and offering advice.

I close the lid of my laptop, as I don't want him to see the empty page in front of me. I'm too embarrassed to admit I've got writer's block.

Robin sees this as an invitation, pulls out the chair opposite me, and sits down.

'Don't worry, I'm just waiting for my panini to cook and then I'll leave you to it. So what do you write?'

I sigh. This is where it starts.

'Thrillers, mostly. Although, today I'm working on a blog post. You know, establishing my social networking platform,' I say, pretending that I know what I'm talking about.

'Good for you,' he says in a tone that sounds a bit patronising, but from the look on his face I don't think it was meant in that way.

We sit for a moment in silence and my eyes drift over to the counter in the hope that his panini is forthcoming. But the waiting staff seem busy with other customers.

'So . . . do you come here often?' I say, trying to change the subject, before I realise what I've said and cringe. I really hope he doesn't think I'm flirting with him.

'Well, I would if I knew . . .' He laughs at his own joke and it only makes me cringe more. 'Yes, I do. I have a real weakness for their tuna paninis. I know it's a long way to come, but they use red onion and really good mozzarella. You should try one, you know, if your taste buds aren't too damaged from all that fast food.'

'Hey, that was a one-off. It had been a big weekend.'

'Right, the wedding. They can be rough. Especially the older you get. My hangovers seem to go on for days now,' he says.

'Me too.' I knew that must be a thing. 'I'm not looking forward to getting any older if this is what's to come.'

'I think you're OK yet. You're what, twenty-five, twenty-six?'

He's looking at me like he's trying to count my wrinkles, as if they're the circles on a tree stump.

'Actually, I'm thirty-one.'

'Oh,' he says with a look of almost shock. 'You're looking really good for your age, then.'

'Um, thanks,' I say, not knowing if it was really a compliment. One of those awkward silences falls over the table and I wonder what to say. 'How's your work going?'

'OK. I mean, it's still early days, but I had a quick meeting with my boss Beth this morning and she seems happy with my outlined proposal for what I'm going to look at. Or as happy as an ogre can be.'

I feel goosebumps prickle my skin at the thought of Robin's report. I know he told me that he's not out to get us fired, but I do still feel uneasy about it.

'I tell you, you're so lucky to have a boss like Jacqui. She seems to really focus on the talents of her staff. You should have heard the things she said about you.'

'Were they good?' I squeak in hope.

'Yes, let's just say if you ever needed another job, your references would glow more than Regent Street at Christmas.'

I know that should make me feel a little better, but I also know that whatever happens after the report, it won't be Jacqui's decision to make.

There's another pause, and I'm wondering if they've gone to catch the tuna for Robin's lunch.

'How long have you worked at the council, then?' he asks.

'Um, about seven years.'

'In the same job?'

I know what he's thinking, that I should have moved on by now. I'd only ever meant to work there for a year or two, as a stepping stone for something bigger, but the lure of staying in my home town was too appealing. Having moved from a bedsit in Tooting, I had found that I could afford to rent a flat that I could swing a cat in and have money left over at the end of the month. My two best friends (Vanessa and Cara) had moved back after university too, and it was handy that my parents were round the corner. What really put the nail in the coffin, though, was when, a couple of months into the job, I met Will. With all those reasons to stay – and a genuine love of my job – I haven't wanted to climb the career ladder.

'Yeah, but I love it,' I say, giving him the simple explanation. 'I couldn't imagine doing anything else. And you?'

I know from my own private observations that he's been there for a few years.

'It'll be four years in January. It's crazy how quickly time flies.'

'Do you think you'll stay?'

'For now. There are quite a lot of opportunities for me still. I've bought a flat on the Hamble, and I really like it. So unless I take a job at one of the other local councils, I think I'll be here for a bit.'

'Where are you originally from, then?' I ask, trying to guess, but pinning him down to the Home Counties with his plain, slightly posh accent.

'Leatherhead, in Surrey,' he says.

I almost do an air punch. I would so have said Surrey. He's got that look about him.

'Avocado on toast with a baked egg,' says a waitress, hovering over us.

Robin and I both look up and I raise my hand.

For once I'm pleased that I didn't go for the pulled pork sourdough that I'd so craved. It would have looked like all I ate was stodgy, fatty food.

'I'm sorry to be a pain,' he says, flashing a winning smile at the waitress. 'I was just wondering if my panini will be ready any time soon? No hurry, just when it suits.'

The waitress looks like she's going to swoon, and I think if he'd asked her to murder puppies for his panini, she'd have obliged. He's got that old-fashioned, proper gent charm down to a tee.

'I'll get it right away,' she says.

There's a colour to her cheeks that I would have had in a similar situation up until a couple of days ago, but I'm slowly building up immunity to his charms. I've realised that he makes everyone feel special and I keep reminding myself of that so that I don't get sucked in.

'So, social networking,' he says. 'What does that entail, then? Posting to Facebook?'

'I'm playing around with a blog. Mainly just about my life.'

I hope he doesn't ask any more questions as I don't really want him to know the details.

'I'm sure you must have lots to write about. Your job seems interesting with the different artists and organisations you get to work with.'

'Yes, it is,' I say, nodding. 'But I don't blog about work. I like to keep my private life separate.'

'Of course. Plus, most of the interesting blogs are about people's personal lives, aren't they? Look at all those YouTube people that have become famous.'

'I guess, but I can't imagine people would be dying to see my daily life here, my commute to the council building, my house that's covered in paint samples and dodgy wallpaper from the last owners.'

Robin smiles. 'I'm sure people are just as fascinated with actual real life as they are with what they see on Instagram.'

'Are they? Are they really? Don't we all just wish we lived liked Tom and Giovanna Fletcher?'

'Who?'

My mouth drops open.

'Um, Tom – from McFly.'

'Are you sure you're not twenty-five?'

'Whatever,' I say, picking up my fork and starting to eat my food before it gets cold.

'Couldn't you write about your relationship? Aren't you the ultimate laid-back girlfriend? Not minding that your other half goes off to the footie instead of going to your best mate's wedding. It could be called the Good Girlfriend's Guide.'

I almost choke on my avocado. If only he knew the truth about what was going on at the moment. With all the anger and the thoughts of revenge, if I wrote down what was actually going on in it would be more like the Good Girlfriend's Guide to Getting Even.

The waitress finally comes over and gives him his paper bag, along with a big smile. I'm guessing he gets that a lot.

'Right, well, I should leave you to it. Good luck. You never know, you might become the next Princess on a Shoestring.'

I look at him confused, as I have no idea what he's talking about.

'She was a blogger turned bestseller. My sister's getting married, and she carries her book around like it's the Bible.'

I almost splutter a laugh at the thought that someone would want to publish a book about my whining.

Robin gets up and leaves the coffee shop and I slowly pull the laptop screen up. I try to turn my attention back to the task in hand.

I stare at my blank screen. But what's interesting about my life? I work all day in a job that I enjoy, but it's really not of that much interest to the wider world. I am content in my long-term relationship with my boyfriend. I'm so far a failing aspiring author. We don't even have a pet that does interesting things that I could talk about.

It's hardly bookmark material.

I laugh for a moment at the thought of writing about my relationship with Will, like Robin suggested. I'm not sure that it would go down so well. I cheekily type out the bio that Janet said we should write for our page.

I'm Lexi, thirty-one-year-old woman, in perpetual long-term relationship with sports-mad boyfriend. Follow my blog to hear of our perfect domesticity, where I have my life organised around the fate of eleven men in red-and-white stripy shirts and the Sky Sports schedule. Expect much swearing and exasperation, from both him, at whichever umpire/referee of the game he is watching, and me, from being ignored – AGAIN!

I read what I've written. It's actually funny. I'm not sure if it's just because I'm laughing at how pathetic my life seems, or if I'm actually harbouring a comedy genius inside. Perhaps Robin was on to something.

My boyfriend and I have been together seven years. SEVEN. And in that time, I've learnt an awful lot, mainly how no matter how many times he is told, the toilet seat will always be left up and the answer to the question 'What should we do today?' will always feature a time window as there will be some sporting event to be watched before/after. Yes, my friends, I am a sporting widow.

You might be one, or you might know one. You can usually spot them a mile off – they're the ones that are sat in restaurants not talking to the men they're with as they'll be looking up scores on their iPhones. The ones who get dragged along in the freezing cold to the arse end of nowhere to watch games against teams they've never heard of, as that's the only way they get to spend time with their partners. The ones that have to hunt for their men in social gatherings, only to find them holed up in a corner having found a TV to watch the sports on.

I'm sure, like me, they're the ones that can probably tell you the name of every football ground in England, what an LBW is in cricket, and the new rules in Rugby Union scrums. The only saving grace of such useless knowledge is that it will hopefully come up in future pub quizzes.

I stop typing and glance over what I've written. I like the warm tone to it, and it sounds quite witty, but I can't help thinking it's lacking something. Would I really want to read a blog that is just someone moaning about being ignored and having acquired enough knowledge to go on *A Question of Sport*?

I highlight the text, hit Delete, and then pause for a minute. I think back over the best-practice blogs that we looked at in our writing group last week. All of them had an interesting angle or a hook.

My fingers hover over the keyboard. I know what the hook for my blog should be, I just don't know if I want to write about it. I take a deep breath and tell myself that I can just see what it looks like on the page – it's not like I'm going to be posting it live right now.

Sporting Widow Seeks Revenge

Up until a week ago, I was a happy sporting widow. OK, maybe happy is a bit too strong a word, but let's just say I didn't mind playing second fiddle to my boyfriend's sporting obsession. I was content writing my novel and fitting our social life round his seemingly never-ending sports watching. When it came down to it, I always thought if he had to choose between the sport and me, he'd pick me. Oh, how wrong I was.

It all started when I got a wedding invitation from my best friend. I should have had my suspicions then, when he was quiet about it. Usually when an invitation arrives there's a frenzy to check the date so he can work out if his beloved football team are playing, or if there are any other sports he might miss. It's often worse than a Middle East peace summit, trying to arrange his terms for attendance as we negotiate how and when I'll allow him to monitor the game/match – phone, mobile app, TV (e.g. he's banned from checking during the service/speeches/first dance). So when we RSVPd without his usual strop, I thought that was either because (a) his football team were playing away, or (b) he knew her wedding was too important for him to kick up a fuss.

The wedding day arrived and we were getting ready to go (so far so good) when my boyfriend was struck down with food poisoning. He was hobbling round, wincing in pain, groaning as he ran to the toilet. Believing he was almost at death's door, I tucked him up in bed after administering Imodium, like the good girlfriend I am, and then I trotted off to the wedding alone. I was having a grand old time until I got a picture message from one of my work colleagues showing his TV screen – with my boyfriend at the football on display. That's right, my lovely boyfriend had faked an illness to miss the wedding and go to a football game. I don't need to tell you how livid I was.

I'm sure you're already imagining the mother of all rows we had. But in truth, he doesn't know I've found out about what he's done. Instead, I want to make him pay for it – I'm going to get my own back. One piece of revenge at a time.

By the time I'm finished with him, he'll be missing that much sport he'll be the sporting widower.

Blimey. My fingers stop typing and I stare at how much I've written. I read it back through and I think it works. It fulfils the brief. It's a blog. It's interesting (or at least I think it is), and I should have enough material to fill the next few weeks of class. It does make me sound like a little bit of a *Fatal Attraction* 'bunny boiler' – but I'm allowed to embellish the story a bit, aren't I?

What am I thinking? I highlight the text and hover over the Delete key. These blogs might be a pet project in our writing class, but they're still going live on the Internet. There is the potential that someone other than my writing class might stumble across it and read it. Do I really want them to?

I know that not many people will read it, but I feel a bit guilty talking about Will like this. I mean, he is my boyfriend, and I love him dearly – sports obsession and all – and having what he did down on paper in black and white when I haven't told him that I know feels a little bit like I'm betraying him.

But then what would the alternative be? I take a deep breath and instead of deleting the post I save it. I can decide later if I'm brave enough to post it.

I close my laptop down and triumphantly eat the rest of my avocado on toast. Now, if only I could solve the problem of what I'm going to do about Will's lying as easily.

9

It's one thing to talk to Cara about getting my own back, it's another thing entirely to go through with it.

It's been almost a week since the wedding and I still haven't formulated a proper plan for what I'm going to do. I like the idea of an eye for an eye. If he missed the wedding for a Southampton game, then I should stop him going to see one. But I'm stumped as to how to do that. Every time I think of something, I imagine a way that it could backfire.

My first idea was to give him a good dose of laxatives as I thought that a real case of upset belly would be poetic justice. But there were too many variables. Trying to get his body to react at the exact right time would have been almost impossible.

The only other thing I've come up with is handcuffing him to the bed and 'losing the key' – I've clearly been hanging out with Cara too much. But there are far too many things that could go wrong with this plan. Him demanding I put the radio on to listen to Radio 5 Live before I left. Him being like Houdini and escaping. Him refusing to get in the handcuffs in the first place. Bondage isn't really our kind of thing, and with him turning me and the boobs down last week, I worry that the lure of me in bed wouldn't be enough on a game day.

I've got to do something soon, though, as I'm still really angry whenever I'm reminded of what Will did, especially as he keeps referring back to his illness. Today at breakfast, he started talking about how he'd been drinking Lucozade all day at work yesterday to get his electrolyte levels back up so that he had enough energy to play five-a-side football last night – five days after his ordeal. Miraculously, even though he still felt a bit ropey (his words, not mine) he managed to make it to the pub afterwards for a few pints with his mates.

So, while I was eating my berry-infused porridge I came up with a plan. I'm going to continue doing low-level acts of revenge, like the Grand Prix results slip, until I think of something better.

Which is why, right now, I feel like one of the super-spies from one of my novels. I'm perched on the end of my sofa checking to make sure that Will's not coming up the drive. If we had net curtains they'd almost certainly be twitching as I survey the street.

I pick up the hallowed TV remote, which I so rarely get control of, and I sit on the floor, so as not to create a warm patch or dimples on the sofa that could incriminate me later on.

I bring up the planner and look guiltily over at the door. I don't know why, as I haven't done anything wrong . . . yet. I feel as if he's going to burst in at any second and catch me in the act. Yet what I'm doing *looks* innocent. It's not like we live in some sort of repressed household where I'm not allowed to use the TV unchaperoned. But I can't help but feel a teeny bit nervous about it.

I try and tell myself that I'm doing book research. After all, my unsuspecting heroine is always finding herself in tense situations, and this way I can learn how she feels first-hand. I'm not sure that Tom Clancy would describe one of his main characters as feeling like they were going to wet themselves with fear, or that they've put tissues under their armpits to start to mop up the sweat that seems to be pouring out of them, but that's what it feels like for me. Not the clammy forehead or the pounding heart that I've written about so often, which is a surprising revelation for me – see, it's like proper research.

The planner comes up and I scan down the list of things that are still to watch. Darts, boxing, football. It's a wonder he has time to go to work with this sort of a schedule. Not to mention why there's so much unwatched stuff on here that our capacity is teetering around the eighty-seven per cent mark.

I scroll down to last night's darts and select it. Taking a deep breath as I do.

Will's Friday night ritual is to come home from work, grab a cold beer from the fridge and veg out on the sofa for a while, watching the darts from the night before that he missed when playing five-a-side football. Occasionally, if I'm lucky, I get a 'Hi, honey, how was your day?' and a peck on the cheek, but quite often I'm ignored for a couple of hours. Then, at about seven thirty, like a bear awakening from hibernation he's his usual attentive self again.

We've been together long enough now for me to know that there's no point in trying to shake up the routine; it's like his way of shrugging off a tough week at the office and slipping into weekend mode.

Sometimes I bypass the whole thing and go to the gym. Although my bingo wings will tell you how often that happens.

I press the yellow button and something pops up asking if I'm sure that I want to delete it. Am I sure? I can't imagine what will happen to the beast if I mess with the routine. Am I shooting myself in the foot as I'll have to put up with a sulky man for the next two days? Or will he be unperturbed and find one of his saved games to watch, rendering my mini-revenge pointless?

I hesitate, but all it takes is a slight memory of that image on the text message and I press the button so firmly that I almost wedge it into the controller.

I let out a big breath and try to force myself to relax.

I seriously would not cut it as one of my kick-ass heroines. In my novels, they are always unexpectedly uncovering mysteries and taking down criminal masterminds, yet I can barely man up enough to delete a recording on Sky Plus. It's pathetic.

I don't sit around for too long as I don't want to be caught anywhere near the scene of the crime. I wipe the remote control over with my jumper, just in case I've left any lingering finger-prints, and position myself in the kitchen.

Since I was in alone last night, it's already tidy, so I wonder what I'm actually going to do with my nervous energy while I wait for Will to come home.

I even go as far as opening the oven door and peering in, wondering if I should clean that out. But then I remember I'm trying not to arouse suspicion, and I haven't cleaned the oven since . . . well, never.

I pick up my laptop and instead decide to pretend to be writing, although I'm way too jittery to actually concentrate on getting any words on the page.

The key goes in the door and I start to feel butterflies in my tummy. Not the romantic ones that used to flutter around when I first started dating Will, back in the Stone Age. They've long since disappeared, along with the flowers that Will used to buy me. No, these are nervous butterflies, wondering when he's going to discover what I've done. I tap noisily away at the keys, paying no attention as to what gobbledygook is appearing on the screen in front of me.

'Hello?' I hear him call, as he walks in the door.

Please don't turn on the telly just yet, I mentally plead. I don't think I'm prepared enough. I'm torn between faking my own pretend stomach problem, meaning I could go and hide in the toilet and not witness the fallout, and going into the lounge to distract Will from the inevitable disappointment that is coming his way.

'Hiya,' I say, as he walks into the kitchen before I can move. 'How was work?'

'It was all right, but thank God it's over. It's been such a long week. What with the illness making me miss out on the weekend, it seemed even worse.'

'Of course,' I say, through gritted teeth. Seriously, is he going to milk this forever?

'How was yours?' he asks.

'Yeah, same old. Nothing exciting to report.'

This is usually the point where Will does the obligatory peck, then retires to the sofa, before kicking off his shoes and slipping off his tie.

I brace myself for it, but he stays in the kitchen and doesn't even lunge for the fridge in search of a beer.

'So, I was thinking,' says Will.

A dangerous pursuit for any man.

'Damo has got some away tickets for the Southampton vs Swansea game and I wondered if we should go. I feel really crap that I had to let you down for the wedding, and I thought we could make a weekend of it.'

'Swansea?'

It's not quite Paris or Venice, is it? Even Blackpool has a certain charm for a dirty weekend – but Swansea?

'You wouldn't be expecting us to go on the supporter's bus, would you?'

I once had that misfortune on a five-mile trip to Portsmouth. There's only so many times you can hear 'Oh, When the Saints' without wanting to jump out of the bus window when you're hurtling down a motorway.

'No, we could take one of the cars, as we'd be staying over. It just seems a shame to give up the chance of the tickets; he's giving them away free.'

That is so typical of Will to think he's getting a free trip. He seems to forget the petrol, meal and hotel costs that go along with a weekend away. But sure, free tickets . . .

Maybe this is guilt again. It might not be Barbados this time, but he still wants to go away with me.

'Um,' I say, wondering if it's worth all the effort of travelling so far for a game of football, but then I start to think that at least it will be a weekend away.

'OK, why not?'

'Great, I'll have a look at hotels, then,' he says.

For a split second I forget about the football and get caught up in trying to remember when the last time we went on a mini-break was. But then I remember when we went to Edinburgh to watch the rugby. I'd been excited then too, thinking it would be a full of romance and sightseeing. In reality, we'd barely seen anything but the rugby ground and the Weatherspoon's next to our hotel.

'I'll do it, if you like?' I say, thinking that I don't want a repeat of Edinburgh. 'How about we go up on the Friday night and make a proper weekend of it?'

'Sure,' says Will, 'Why not.'

'Perfect.' I'll just make sure there isn't a Weatherspoon's in sight. And maybe we'll go for an out of town hotel, so that we're away from the other fans.

An idea pops into my head and I almost gasp at the mean-ness of it. What if I booked somewhere so far out of town, that it somehow means that we miss the game entirely? Not only would he miss a game, but he'd be so upset having travelled all the way there to watch it. That would definitely be fitting revenge for miss-ing Vanessa's wedding.

I sort of wish I hadn't deleted the darts now as that's a drop in the ocean compared to what I could do next week. I wonder if there's an option to get back what you've deleted on Sky Plus.

You know, like in your inbox where you delete an email and it goes into your trash folder and you've still got the opportunity to reverse your action before it disappears forever.

'Right then,' he says, walking over to the fridge.

It feels like he's going in slow motion as he retrieves a beer and walks past me and into the lounge. I feel like reaching out to him and trying to keep him in the kitchen. But what would I say? I almost take my shirt off, hoping that the boobs might work their magic, but a quickie on the kitchen table would only delay the inevitable.

He's got that Friday night look on his face, where he's wound up like a tight coil and desperate to relax.

Before I can think of a better plan he's walking through the dining room to the lounge. It's only a matter of seconds now until he discovers my guilty secret.

I hear the sounds of the television drift through to me and brace myself for the shout or scream that's going to come.

Three . . . two . . .

'Lexi!' he shouts almost exactly on cue.

I close my eyes and for a second I'm motionless. I wish I was anywhere but here. I chide myself for not leaving as soon as I'd deleted the darts. What a moron. I could have done the deed, then gone to the gym. Not only would I not have been here when he discovered the crime, but it would have given me the perfect alibi.

Rookie mistake. See, this is further proof that I suck as a thriller writer – a good heroine should be super switched on.

'Lexi,' he calls again.

Short of crawling into our wardrobe upstairs and hoping to discover Narnia, or scaling our ten-foot-high garden wall, I'm stuck.

I slowly drag my feet out of the kitchen and walk through the dining room into the lounge.

'What's up?' I ask, trying my hardest to keep my voice sounding normal, despite my pounding heart.

'I forgot to say earlier that Aaron and Becky wanted to know if we were up for going for a curry later.'

'Yes, that sounds fabulous,' I reply, happy to have any type of reprieve. Plus, I like Aaron's girlfriend Becky a lot. 'What time?'

'About eight? At the Jewel in the Crown?'

'Uh-huh, why don't we get ready and go for a drink beforehand? We could go to the White House. We haven't been there for ages and it's just round the corner.'

For a second I think I've got him. He looks tempted and I feel like he's going to prise himself off the sofa and head to the bathroom for a shower.

'Why not?'

I let out a sigh of relief and think that I've got away with him not finding out about the darts. I'm clearly not cut out for all this subterfuge.

'Great, I'll go and get ready,' I say, turning to leave.

'OK, but let's go out in about an hour,' he says, causing my body to go rigid. 'I'll just watch a bit of the darts first – you know, to relax.'

I'm desperately trying to get my feet to cooperate and hot step it out of the room before he finds out what I've done.

'What the fuck? Where's the darts?'

I try even harder to make my legs work but it's like they're stuck in treacle and I'm unable to lift them up.

'Lexi, have you been on the planner?'

'What?' I say, as casually as I can. I haven't turned to face him as I'm worried my face will give it away.

'The darts. They're on series link and it was supposed to tape last night, but it's not here.'

'Maybe it wasn't on last night?'

I really bloody wish I'd come up with some plausible-sounding excuses.

'Of course they were on. It was in Sheffield. Did you notice anything last night? Was there a power cut or anything?'

A power cut, now there's an idea . . .

'Did you press something on the TV?'

I turn to face him as I realise that in keeping my back to him, I'm acting suspiciously. Even though my boyfriend pretty much always misses what's right in front of his nose, I don't want him to put two and two together.

'I didn't watch telly in here yesterday. I watched an episode of *Mad Men* in bed.'

That much is true.

'I don't understand,' he says, scratching his face and wrinkling up his nose. 'It's never not recorded before. Perhaps we'll have to get the Sky man out. I mean, what if this had been something really important like a Southampton match?'

'Imagine,' I say, sarcastically. I don't want to point out that he goes to almost every match and watches them live. At some point someone needs to break it to him that he's not the coach and he doesn't need to rewatch the games on the telly to identify the team's weak spots.

'Why did it have to be the darts? Why couldn't it have been some shitty *Bake Off* or something that you watch?'

He's crossed into stroppy teenager mode now, and I try not to take it personally that he's called my beloved *Bake Off* shitty. I knew there was going to be some fallout from this. I've just got to suck it up and try to relish a little in the fact that it's pissed him off.

He pushes his bottom lip out and wrinkles his face in a way that reminds me of one of those Creature Comfort tortoises. I swear he's never looked hotter.

'Well, I guess we could go for that drink now, then,' he says with a sigh so big that it practically makes the framed pictures on the mantelpiece shake.

'I'll go and jump in the shower.' He sounds like Eeyore from *Winnie the Pooh*, his voice all sad and dejected.

'OK then, I'll go after you.'

I watch him walk out of the room and I have to take a seat on the sofa. I can't believe what's happened. Apart from a little grump, a couple of swears and him insulting *Bake Off*, that all went pretty smoothly.

My boyfriend has managed to get off the sofa on a Friday night a whole hour or two prior to what I thought possible, and we're going to spend a little quality time together before we meet our friends.

Perhaps I should do things like this more often. If this is the way to get my Friday nights kickstarted, then maybe a little sulk from the boy might be worth it.

I can't quite believe it, that's Lexi 2–Will's sports 0. And if it feels this good doing this, just think how good it's going to be when I enact the grand plan next week.

10

I'm looking for my laptop, about to settle down in an armchair for the evening, when I notice I've had a missed call from my parents on my mobile. I pick it up and call them back.

'Hello?' says my dad, as if he's not sure that's how you actually answer the telephone.

'Hi, Dad, it's just me.'

I'm ready for the usual – I'll pass you on to your mother – but it's not forthcoming.

'Oh, hi love. How are you?'

'I'm fine, thank you . . . Um, how are you?'

'Yes, fine. Good. Yes, fine,' he says.

'Great,' I say waiting to be passed across.

'Work OK, is it?'

'Same as always. That audit I was telling you about has started, but the guy doing it seems all right, so fingers crossed I won't be too affected.'

'Marvellous,' he says with enthusiasm. 'And Will, he's OK, is he?'

I glance across at my boyfriend, lounging on the sofa.

'Your mum said he missed Vanessa's wedding because he wasn't well.'

I grit my teeth.

'He's all better now,' I say, putting a fake smile on my face as Will's ears prick up at the mention of his name. I don't want him to know he was rumbled.

'Excellent.'

There's an awkward silence and I wonder how long my dad's going to talk to me for. It's not that my dad and I don't talk, it's just that we never do it on the phone and I have no idea what to say.

'So, is Mum there?' I ask.

'Actually, you've just missed her – she's nipped over to Jancie's. Shall I get her to ring you later on?'

'Yeah, that would be great.'

'OK then, love. Well, nice to talk to you.'

'Um, you too.'

'And give my best to Will.'

'OK, bye,' I say, hanging up and wondering what's happened to my dad.

'That was weird,' I say to Will.

'What was?'

'My dad actually spoke to me.'

'That doesn't sound that strange,' says Will as he picks up the TV remote and starts flicking through channels mindlessly in a way that really grates on me. I'm always telling him that if he wants to know what's on, he should just bring up the planner.

'Well, he sends you his best wishes. What's that about?'

'I don't know.' Will shrugs and continues his channel hopping. He can't be registering what's on each channel with the speed he's flicking through them.

'Perhaps it's because you invited him to the pub on his birthday.'

Will looks a bit uncomfortable at the mention of that night. I'm not surprised. I'm sure he didn't think that by inviting him he was going to make my dad think they were now BFFs.

That's probably why my dad was acting strangely. He's probably chuffed that someone took an interest in him. I smile at my boyfriend and think how much his little gesture must have meant to my dad.

Will's watching Sky Sports News and I decide to get my laptop out. Retrieving it from the bookshelf in the corner, I settle myself into the armchair to do a little research into the Swansea area. We had quite a busy weekend, and now I've only got four days until we're going, and so far I've booked nothing.

'I'm going to be sorting out the cricket games for Barbados tonight,' says Will. 'So how many matches do you think you'll want to come to?'

'How many matches?' I say, mumbling as my archaic laptop begins to boot up.

'Yeah, how many? They're only Twenty20 matches, so they'll be half-days.'

The home page finally loads and I stare at it for a second, wondering what I should search for, when what Will has said starts to sink in.

'Matches for Barbados?'

'Yes, matches,' he says, staring at me as if I'm mad.

'What are you talking about?'

I rub my furrowed brow.

'Barbados, you know: our holiday.'

'Yes, I know that bit.'

How could I forget our exotic holiday that's in less than four weeks. I'm ticking off the days earnestly on my work desk calendar.

'What does that have to do with cricket?'

'Um,' says Will slowly. 'You know, the Twenty20 Cricket World Cup – the reason we're going there.'

'What?' I almost scream. 'I thought the reason we were going there was to relax on a tropical beach?'

'It is, but the cricket's also on. I told you about that, when I suggested it.'

'No, no, you didn't.'

I'm sure I would have remembered that, wouldn't I? My thoughts drift back to that day when I was hauled up in bed with the mother of all hangovers. I can't remember him mentioning it, but I did get carried away in my little fantasy of us lolling about in the surf.

Will obviously senses the seriousness of the situation and he turns off the television.

'I definitely did. You were nodding along and everything.'

Oh, God. I remember nodding along, but I wasn't paying attention.

'Look, don't worry – it won't spoil the holiday. It's just a few games. Shall I get you tickets for say, two matches, and then I'll go to one or two on my own? Would you be all right by the pool by yourself for a few hours?'

Steam is practically blowing out of my ears. I've been duped. What I thought was some super-romantic trip to ease his guilt, was actually a trip to tick one of his many sporting dreams off his bucket list.

For a second I wonder if I should make him cancel the trip, but that's not really an option. It was paid for out of the joint account, and I'm sure we wouldn't get anything back on it if we cancelled now, so I'd talk myself out of a holiday and a big wad of savings. And if we stayed at home, there's always the possibility that Will would make me do the DIY.

A thought enters my mind, and I wonder if I'm missing a trick in only making him miss the Swansea game. Imagine how cross he'd be to miss a cricket match that he's flown half way round the world to see. But I know I'm not that mean.

I sigh loudly as I resign myself to the fact that our super-duper romantic holiday is going to be tainted by cricket.

'I'm sorry, honey,' he says, coming over and perching on the arm of the chair, 'I thought you didn't mind as you seemed so excited to go. Don't worry about the cricket. The matches only last three hours at a time, and I'll make sure that we don't go to two matches in a day, so that we always have at least half the day free. There will still be plenty of time for sightseeing, and whatever else you have on your agenda.'

He's nibbling my neck and trying to get round me that way, and I try not to get distracted.

'It's not some sort of barmy army thing, is it?' I shudder at the thought that my dream holiday is going to be spent with a whole load of fellow cricket fans in matching T-shirts. I can see myself now, sat on a coach looking out longingly at the scenery of Barbados as I'm bussed from cricket ground to cricket ground, while people are singing songs.

'No, it's just us. That's why I can choose the tickets. I reckon you might even enjoy it.'

'Ha,' I say, spluttering a laugh. I push him off my neck. 'I will not be wearing a cricket-themed T-shirt.'

I hold up my finger as if I'm dictating terms.

'But I saw a really nice purple one that would – OK, no T-shirt,' he adds hastily after I give him a stern look.

'You will not get drunk and leave me unattended at the games.'

'I wouldn't do that,' he says in almost mock horror.

'And when we're in our bungalow, there'll be no sports watching.'

'But how will I know what's going on with the tournament?'

I raise my eyebrow.

'Fine. No sports in the bungalow. Anything else?'

'I'm capping the limit of matches to three. I'll come to two with you and you can go to one on your own.'

He seems to be mulling it over. 'Is that it?'

I twist my mouth as I think. 'Yes, I think so.'

'Great, it's going to be an amazing holiday.'

'It better be.'

His kisses me on the top of my head as he retreats out of the lounge.

I shake my head. What a moron I am. When am I going to realise that my boyfriend is not the romantic man I want him to be? There is always some kind of sporting agenda running in the background.

I look back at the empty Google search box and think about our forthcoming Swansea trip. After finding out about the cricket, I'm more determined than ever to go ahead with my revenge. I type 'How to stop someone going to the football' but I'm inundated with pages about American football and something called 'running down the clock'. Not what I was looking for. Where are the forum posts by other devious sporting widows that have conspired to stop their other halves going to games?

Perhaps I need to think about where we'd stay. I bring up the map of the area and have a look. Swansea's close to the Gower Peninsula, where I went on a camping trip when I was at uni. It was so pretty, with its craggy coastline and rugged clifftops, not to mention remote. It's the perfect place to head to stop Will from going to the football, and I very much doubt there'll be another Southampton fan, let alone a Weatherspoon's.

I'm just bringing up hotels and cottages on TripAdvisor when Will walks back in. He hands me a hot chocolate and two Bourbon biscuits.

'Thanks,' I say, noticing he hasn't even got himself a beer. It's like a snapshot of what would happen if I told him I knew about his deceit at the wedding.

'What are you up to now? You fancy watching a *Game of Thrones*?' he asks as he settles back on the sofa and turns on the TV.

'OK then. I was only looking for somewhere for us to stay at the weekend, but I can do that later in the week. It's not as if it'll be busy this time of year.'

'I can help you look if you like?'

'No, no,' I say, shutting down the PC. 'I'll do it in my lunch hour at work.'

There's no way I want him to get involved. I wouldn't want him trying to get us to book somewhere close to the ground. If I'm going to be successful in whatever my plan is going to be, I've got to be in full control if I'm going to get even.

11

If I felt even the tiniest bit guilty about sharing my personal life via a blog, it all but evaporated when Will told me about Barbados. Now, as I turn up to the pub for writing group, I'm pleased that I posted it. Now, more than ever, it's true that I am a sporting widow.

It's been almost twenty-four hours since I found out about the cricket and I've calmed down a lot. I was just as angry at myself as I was with Will. I'm sure he did tell me about it, I was just too busy imagining the sand between my toes.

'At least you'll have a tan at Christmas,' says Cara, trotting out the reasons why I was so excited in the first place. I filled her in about the latest development on the way over.

'Yes, although these days I get more of a tan from a St-Tropez bottle than I do from the sun as I'm always in factor 50.'

She laughs, and I feel myself laugh too. I'm starting to relax again.

'So now that you've realised Barbados wasn't just his way of making it up to you, have you thought any more about telling him what you know?'

'Not exactly. After testing the water with the darts, I thought that I definitely need to get a bit even first.'

'Don't tell me, you're going to sabotage him watching the cricket in Barbados?' She says, her eyes widening in surprise.

'The thought did cross my mind earlier, but I don't think I'm that mean. No, I'm going to make him miss the game when we go to Swansea this weekend. I'm not too sure how I'm going to do it, though.'

'You could use your feminine charms and keep him locked in your hotel room?'

I roll my eyes at her. She is so predictable.

'I don't know if that would work. He'd probably just tell me that he'd see to me after we got back from the game.'

'Even if you bought something special for the occasion? When was the last time you took a trip to Ann Summers?'

'Probably in our first year of dating.'

Back in the days when we used to be at it like rabbits and sex was still a novelty, I used to dress up in all sorts of sexy teddies and nighties. Now, we're lucky if I take off my Winnie the Pooh pyjamas and he takes off his socks.

'Which means if you dressed up in something lacy and racy, I'm sure that Will would stand to attention and forget about going to some game.'

'Hmm,' I say, wondering if it would be that easy. I'm still feeling a little fragile in that department. It's one thing to be turned down when you're semi-naked and in bed anyway having made zero effort, but it's another to be all tarted up and still be rejected. I don't know if I could handle that.

'Oh, and I've got this great riding crop you can borrow, if you like.'

'No, thank you,' I say quickly, thinking that we're straying into the overshare territory. It might be an offer of a riding crop, but who knows what might be next. I know she has a drawer in her bedroom where she keeps all her stuff and it practically vibrates across the floor on its own.

'Suit yourself. But remember Alec the banker? Well, he used to go crazy for that crop. That and the –'

'I'm not listening,' I say, putting my fingers in my ears.

'Your loss,' she says. 'I'm just helping you to spice things up.'

'Thanks, but I'd rather put chilli on my bits.'

'Oh well, if you change your mind, you've still got a copy of my manuscript. Just go to chapter eight,' she says with a wink, 'that will sort you out.'

I dread to think what's in that chapter.

It's at times like these that I wished I didn't always drive to the writer's group meetings, as right now I could do with a stiff drink.

'Thanks, but I think I'll give it a miss.'

'Whatever,' she says, rolling her eyes. 'But if you're going to be prudish, just how are you going to stop him?'

Now that's the million-dollar question . . .

'I have no idea.'

It's only three more days until Swansea, and I keep hoping a plan will magically form in my mind, but time is almost running out.

'I'd been hoping to think about it at work, but we're all on such high alert because of the audit and I'm working harder than I have in years.'

'Oh, is that still going on? At least you get some eye candy to look at.'

I smile weakly. If only it was as simple as Robin and his model looks. It's funny as on a day-to-day basis we have quite a laugh and I actually like sitting opposite him, but then I remember why he's there and then the black cloud starts to hang over me.

'How's everything at your work?' I say, not wanting to dwell on mine.

'I won't bore you with what happened with Boring Belinda, but more or less the same as usual. No big leaps forward.'

We both sigh and drink our drinks. As well as being a ferocious man-eater, Cara is also a super-brainy scientist. She spends her days in a lab developing proteins that block cancer cells from developing. Or at least, that's her best attempt at explaining it in layman's terms for people like me to understand.

'Ah, looks like it's that time again,' says Cara, draining her wine.

Janet walks past, closely followed by Doom and Gloom, who are predictably as keen as mustard.

I stare at my watch. 'We've still got five minutes.'

Not that I'm trying to delay going in or anything.

'So how did you get on with your blog? What did you write about?' I say, carefully trying to finish my hot chocolate without burning my tongue.

'Oh, you know, it's like some sort of *Sex and the City* type thing. About being a single girl and my sexcapades. Although mine is a bit more bondage and a bit less shoes.'

I don't know why I even had to ask.

'And how about you?'

'It's really boring,' I say, fiddling with my empty glass. 'It's just about being a sporting widow.'

'That is so perfect. What is it, like some sort of survival guide for how to cope?'

'I guess so.'

I haven't really given it much thought since the first post I wrote.

'Have you told Will you're doing it?'

'No,' I say, shifting uncomfortably in my seat. I never used to keep any secrets from Will, and suddenly I'm starting to rack them up.

'You really are acting like a woman scorned,' she says, raising an almost disapproving eyebrow at me.

'It's not like it's revenge,' I say, justifying it to myself. 'I mean, I'm not going to write anything nasty about him. It's more about me taking the piss out of myself for putting up with it. Besides, it's not like he'd ever read it. You know Will; he thinks the Internet is only there to keep an eye on sports scores.'

'I guess so, and blogs can be anonymous anyway. Which is a good thing for me, as I wouldn't want to get myself a reputation.'

I splutter a laugh. 'Of course not.'

'Shall we go in?' she says, smiling wickedly as she slips on her cardigan.

'I guess so.'

We should really leave an hour earlier to go to the pub as we never get through gossiping in time.

'Welcome, welcome,' Janet says to us as we walk through the door.

The room's fuller than I expected; we must have been so caught up in our conversation that I failed to notice everyone else coming in. We're actually the last ones – ironic seeing as we were the first to arrive at the pub.

'Now, before we get started, any news?' asks Janet.

Her expectant gaze sweeps around the room but the rest of us stay silent.

'Maybe next week,' she says, ever the optimist. 'So, I hope we're all raring to go on the blogs.'

I close my eyes and wonder if I'm really brave enough to do this. It's one thing to hide behind my fictional characters, but quite another to read out something so close to home. Luckily for me, she starts at the other side of the room and I have more time to psyche myself up.

'Well, um,' coughs Janet. 'Thank you for that interesting insight into your life, Cara. I must say that I'm slightly glad of writing historical fiction as I think I'd be a bit lost in this Tinder-fuelled world that you live in.'

The room takes a collective breath, as if we've been too scared to breathe during Cara's blog post.

I know she said it was going to be a bit *Sex and the City*, but I think it was more *Secret Diary of a Call Girl*.

'Has anyone got any comments or feedback for Cara?'

I look around. Most people are still trying to get their cheeks to go back to their regular colour after they broke out beetroot red from the first line of Cara's blog. There's a fantasy writer at the back of the room who looks like he's itching to ask a question, or maybe for Cara's phone number, but he seems to think better of it.

'No? Well, thank you again for that, Cara. And keep up the hard work.' Janet coughs again nervously at the use of the word 'hard', getting a few sniggers from her audience. 'So, Lexi, let's hear yours. Now I'm guessing it might not be quite as X-rated as Cara's?'

'No,' I say, smiling at Cara, who is beaming with pride – she loves the attention she gets from being so provocative. 'Mine is not quite in the same league.'

'Good, good,' says Janet, fanning herself with a book.

I stand up and take a deep breath as I read out my blog post.

When I get to the end of it I stop and sit down, a little embarrassed to have spoken about me as a person rather than me as a writer.

Cara gives me a little nudge and whispers 'well done'.

'Well, Lexi, that was, um, interesting,' says Janet.

Interesting is never good. It's the lazy adjective you use when you're looking for a polite way to say something is boring.

'I would never have expected you to write something like that. It's so different from your usual thrillers; they're often quite male in approach.'

'But you said that it didn't have to be related to your writing,' I say, suddenly worried that I'd got the assignment all wrong.

'Of course it doesn't, but you've got to remember why you're doing the blog. It's all about gaining a following. You know I blog in my personal life about visiting stately homes and National Trust houses, trips to art galleries, that type of thing, but there's a lot of crossover for my target audience as readers of historical romances. My reservation with this type of blog for you, and your thriller writing, is that it doesn't seem to be a good marriage between you and your potential readers.'

I can feel tears welling up behind my eyes. I can't cry here. That would be ridiculous. Especially after all the group feedback I've managed to endure in the past.

I start to blink rapidly to try to keep the tears at bay.

'But that blog was really good,' continues Janet, and for a moment I think I've heard her wrong. 'It was engaging, witty and it got my attention. I think it shows real potential, and if I came across that blog I'd probably be inclined to try and remember to read the next instalment.'

I stop blinking and the tears seem to have stopped.

'Have you ever thought of writing women's fiction, instead of thrillers?'

I scrunch up my face.

'What, like chick lit?' I say, almost as though it's a dirty word.

I accidentally catch the eye of Angela, who writes those books, as she's giving me a death stare.

'Yes, Bridget Jones type humour. That's what that snippet reminded me of. And, you see, a blog like yours would sit beside and complement a romantic comedy novel very well.'

'But they always have some kind of rubbish happy-ever-after at the end,' I say, sighing.

Everyone knows real life doesn't have happy endings like that – my seven-year no commitment relationship is testament to that. And there's certainly no romance like you see in those books past the first year of a real relationship. No picnics in the park at night with trees decorated by fairy lights or romantic city breaks to New York with carriage rides in Central Park. Last week Will told me he had a present for me and conned me into pulling his finger.

'They're always so far-fetched,' I say.

Dr Doom laughs. 'Like your thrillers aren't? Come on, Lexi, didn't you pitch a novel that had a coven of modern-day witches trying to cover up an art heist in order to protect some medieval secret that would destroy religion and the world as we know it?'

I cringe as he describes it. It wasn't one of my finest assignments.

'I actually thought your blog was good,' he goes on to say, and I almost choke in surprise. 'I think Janet might be right.'

Janet looks equally surprised that he's agreed with her.

'Anyone else got any comments for Lexi?' she says as if she's trying to move on before his positive comments turn negative.

'Is it true? Did your boyfriend actually do this and you didn't confront him?' asks one of the sci-fi writers.

'Now that would be telling,' I say trying to retain an air of mystery.

The sci-fi writer shrugs her shoulders. 'Either way, I'd read it.'

I smile warmly at her.

'OK then, if we've got no more comments for Lexi, then we'll move on to Arthur, before we start looking at blog promotion.'

I can't help but grin. I've never had such positive comments for any of my writing before and I feel a swell of pride wash around my body.

I have to admit I don't hear much of Arthur's blog as I'm too busy trying to decide whether or not I could write women's fiction. It's been so long since I've read any and I don't know whether happy endings and me are a good mix, but it could be worth a go.

By the time the writer's group finishes I'm knee deep in thoughts of cupcakes and romance as I try to channel my inner girlie girl into ideas for a possible novel.

'So you must be pretty happy with your feedback for once?' says Cara as we walk out of the pub.

'I am. Can you believe it? Even Dr Doom said nice things.'

'I know, I thought Janet was going to fall backwards off her chair in shock. But they were right, it was good, and it did seem very natural. Did it take you long to write it?'

'No,' I say, shaking my head as I unlock the car and we climb in. 'When I started writing it just flowed. It was like my fingers were possessed and it wrote itself.'

'Maybe you're a natural fit for chick lit after all.'

'I don't know. I mean, I want to be an author, and if that's what I have to write to get started, then perhaps that's what I have to do.'

'It's a bit like with singers, isn't it? You start off doing mainstream pop, then after a few albums you get to put something weird out there. Like that Robbie Williams album? What was it, *Rudebox*?' I say.

'Probably not the best example, but yeah, I think there are lots of authors that write multiple genres so it's not like you'd be saying that you would never go back to writing thrillers, if that's where your heart is.'

'Exactly.'

I can feel the tingle of excitement about working on something new start to bubble up inside me. I've been trying to get the same thriller published for four years, and maybe it's time for a change.

'Any ideas for a story? You could always write about me if you want some single girl about town tales.'

'Um,' I say, trying to think of a diplomatic way of turning her down. 'I think the type of rom-coms I'd be writing would be a little less X-rated, but thanks anyway.'

'No problem,' she says, shrugging her shoulders.

We drive most of the way back to Cara's house in silence, as I force myself to concentrate on the road and not new book ideas.

'You could write about your big revenge plot,' says Cara as we turn down her road.

'I could, but I've got to come up with a plan for it first. I feel like I'm going to have to give up as I've only got forty-eight hours to think of something.'

I pull up alongside Cara's house and yank the handbrake up so severely that the creaking noise makes me wince.

'Well, I hope you think of something. You never know, your trip to Swansea might make it on to your blog next week,' she says, unbuckling her seatbelt.

'Ha, yes, if I ever think of how to keep him away from the footie.'

Cara smiles and opens the door.

'Drop me a text and let me know how your plan works out. That's if you're not in the middle of nowhere in Wales with no mobile signal.'

'I will do, see you –' I say, stopping short of finishing my sentence as I see her front door open. 'Cara, there's a man coming out of your house.'

I point at the man putting a bin bag in her wheelie bin.

'Oh, um. That's Dave. You know, the usher. Got to go. See you later.'

She practically runs down the path and I see him trying to give her a kiss on the lips as she tries to bundle him in the house as quickly as possible. But not before I get a glimpse of his slippers.

I chuckle as I pull away from Cara's house. Well, well, well, she kept that very quiet.

I'm midway through processing Cara's secret boyfriend when I'm struck by what she said about not having signal in Wales, and, like a bolt of lightning, an idea hits me. I know what I'm going to do this weekend, and I can't wait to get home to start sorting it out.

Let's just say, if I pull it off it'll make one hell of a blog post.

12

'Lexi, I'm ready for you now,' says Robin.

I look up from my screen and see him smiling his perfect smile – he always looks so good that it's as if he's got his own version of an Instagram filter applied.

'Lexi,' he says, reminding me that he's a real-life person.

'Right,' I say, blinking to remove the filters from my eyes.

'Are you OK?'

'I'm perfectly fine,' I say, standing up quickly.

I still get a little star-struck when he speaks directly to me. I know he's not a celebrity, but he's got this presence that makes you feel like he is.

I go to push back my chair, but it's caught in my bag, and I have to crawl under my desk to free it. Handbag untangled, I stand up and whack my head on my desk.

'Ow,' I say, rubbing the bump on my head.

I think Robin's taken pity on me, as by the time I get up to standing he's wheeled his chair round to my desk.

I try to compose myself and smooth down a patch of hair over the place where a massive egglike bump's probably going to appear.

'So,' he says, sitting down. 'I need to take a quick look into some of the projects that you've run over the last two years.'

He glances down his list and I get the sense that he's picking one at random.

'Here we go. The creative carnival.'

My heart sinks. Of course he'd pick that one. The one event that no one, bar my colleagues, came to.

'Now, I see that it didn't have a very good turnout.'

I'm going slightly pink. I even inflated the numbers to make it look a little better.

'It could have been better.'

He nods.

'I can print you a copy of the event evaluation, if you like?' I say, hoping that he's going to judge my performance on more than this one event.

'Great, that would be helpful, and then we can pick through the numbers.'

'Can't wait,' I mutter.

I locate the file on my PC and send it to the printer.

'Is that your boyfriend?' asks Robin, pointing at a photo of Will. I've had that photo on my desk for so long that sometimes I forget it's even there. It's covered in a layer of grimy dust, but you can still just about see Will's smiling face. It was on a holiday in Greece, and he's looking all sun-kissed and young.

'It is. That's an old photo, though,' I say, for clarification. I don't want him thinking that I'm cougaring some twenty-one-year-old.

'Oh right, how long have you been together?'

'About seven years,' I say, pretending to sound vague.

'Wow. That's a long time. And he's just a boyfriend?'

'We're going to get engaged,' I say, hastily covering up my naked ring finger as I see his eyes cast down to it.

'Right, of course, sorry.' He gives me what I hope isn't a look of pity as he stands up. 'I'll go get the printouts, shall I?'

I try not to watch his perfectly pert bum walk across the room, and instead search my desk for impressive-looking work that might make me look more competent.

He comes and sits back down and I offer him my stapler for the pages.

'Thanks,' he says, settling down to read it.

'You're like most people, surprised that we've been together this long without any rings,' I say, even though I should have probably let the topic go.

'I am a little, if I'm honest, but only because everyone I know seems to be in such a hurry to get down the aisle at the moment,' he says without looking up.

'I know that feeling. But Will *is* going to propose.'

'I'm sure he is.'

'And there's really no hurry. I mean, I don't understand why everyone's in such a massive rush.'

'Me neither,' he says, 'although –'

He shakes his head and doesn't finish his sentence.

'What,' I say. 'You can say it, you can pretty much guarantee my mum already has.'

'I wasn't going to say anything.'

'Yes you were. You can't start a sentence and then stop,' I say, slightly exasperated.

He takes a deep breath before muttering.

'I was going to say that I think he's mad for not being in a rush.'

'You do?'

'Uh-huh, I mean you're a pretty good catch,' he says with a slight cough.

'I am?' I feel my cheeks go a little pink.

I have to remind myself that Robin's a natural charmer and it doesn't mean anything.

'Yeah, I mean you've still got your own teeth and you've not got that much grey. And occasionally your jokes aren't totally rubbish,' he says playfully.

'Thanks,' I mutter, suddenly feeling a bit embarrassed that a man other than Will is talking to me like this. 'I'm sure Will knows all that. He'll get round to it.'

If he doesn't he's going to be in big trouble with my mother.

'I guess it doesn't matter,' says Robin, 'whether you're married or not. As long as you haven't slipped into one of those relationships where you are pretty much just friends. You know, as long as the passion's there, so to speak.'

I'm about to blurt out that of course we're not at that stage, but then I stop and consider when Will and I last had sex. Was it three weeks ago? Four? I'd planned in sexy time in my head for after Vanessa's wedding, but we all know what happened there.

'There's still lots of romance left in us yet. In fact, we're going away this weekend on a proper romantic trip. We're off to a country cottage on the Gower Peninsula.'

Where I'm now going to make sure that we have loads of sex in the midst of me getting my revenge – perfectly normal and romantic.

'You see, that restores my faith in relationships. It's nice to know that after all that time you're still really into each other.'

'Yes, yes, we are. The weekend was all his idea,' I say, leaving out the fact that Will still thinks we're off to watch a game of football.

I really hope, despite the revenge, that it turns about to be a more amorous adventure. After Will turned down sex a couple of weeks ago I've been feeling a bit fragile on that front, and Cara's always trying to get me to spice things up in the bedroom. What if Robin's got a point? I always thought that feeling so comfortable in our relationship is a good thing, but what if it's the very thing that's wrong with it?

'No, we're all about the passion,' I say out loud, a bit too forcefully.

I almost don't know what's worse, the fact that I'm blatantly lying or that I am openly talking about my sex life (or pretend sex life) at work. I'm sure I can hear Mike inhaling a breath at the desk next to me.

'Great,' says Robin. 'I'm sure that you'll have a great weekend. Now, I'll just have a read through this, shall I?'

'Uh-huh,' I say, relieved that he's going back to grilling my event figures, instead of my personal life.

While Robin reads my evaluation of the carnival, I try to pretend I'm busy, but I can't concentrate. I think of Robin's little compliment, and I almost wish that I could use it as a quote for a book jacket. Lexi Hunter – 'A good catch'.

'You're not going to go to the Southampton game while you're in Swansea, are you? Isn't that near the Gower? Or is my geography all out?'

I shift in my chair, and now it's not anchored to the floor by my bag, I jerk slightly into Robin's seat.

'Just a big coincidence,' I say, waving my hand dismissively. 'We're not going to the game.'

Not if I've got anything to do with it. Since Wednesday's writing group, I've prepped my revenge plan. As long as everything runs like clockwork, at game time Will and I will be stuck at our little cottage in the country with a broken-down car and no mobile phone signal.

'Oh, right. I just had him down for one of those super-fans after he went to the game rather than your friend's wedding.'

He's smiling in a friendly way, not knowing that he's hit a nerve.

'He is a big fan, but spending time together is just as special to him.'

If I have to manipulate it to get my own way, then it doesn't matter, does it? I mean, it's all the same outcome, whether it's voluntary or not. And this way it will make me feel a teeny tiny bit better about Vanessa's wedding. When I do tell him I know, and he apologises and I forgive him, at least I'll know that I'll have got my own back in some small way.

'Have you read the evaluation yet? Only, I've got quite a lot to do today,' I say.

I can't believe that I want him to read about the failed event, but it's preferable to having to talk about my love life.

'Of course. Sorry.'

It's seems to do the trick and he goes silent for a couple of minutes. Too scared to open up my inbox in case it's full of emails from Cara or Vanessa, instead I try to write a document to send out to local artists about a new private fund that might be of interest to them. It's a bit hard to concentrate, though, as I'm still thinking about my relationship with Will.

'Essentially, there wasn't a clear enough message in the marketing about what the event was or who it was aimed at,' says Robin eventually.

I nod.

'We're not running it again; we've decided to do a similar event, using the same resources produced for it, but as part of the larger arts week that we hold in May half-term. That way, we're almost guaranteed to attract an audience.'

'I see,' says Robin, making notes.

'You know, we don't run many other events, and those few that we do are generally well attended.'

'I'm sure they are. But unfortunately I can't only report on the good ones. As a value-for-money audit, I've got to look at all the aspects of the service we provide. Plus, if you look too good, then the councillors and my boss Beth tend to get a bit suspicious.'

I nod, wishing that my failed event didn't have to be the sacrificial lamb.

'Right then, let's pick through these details, shall we?'

I take a sharp breath and talk him through the awful day last April.

Twenty minutes later, when he's finished ripping the event to shreds and making me feel like I'm pretty crap at my job, he files away my evaluation and I breathe a sigh of relief. All I can hope is that he looks at more positive aspects of my work next.

'What about the arts week? Have you got some figures from last year for me? Or an evaluation of it?'

'I've got individual evaluations of each event we ran within it.'

'I'd like to see one with all the figures, so I can get an overview. How about you give that to me when you've put it together? If it's not too much work, I know you said you were busy.'

He flashes me one of his winning smiles, one of those ones you'd give anything away for.

'No problem,' I say, realising that in collating it together, it might look more impressive and make me appear more competent.

'Great. Would you be able to have it to me by tomorrow, or at some point on Monday?'

'Sure, why not,' I say, silently waving goodbye to the rest of the work I was going to do today.

'Great, thank you. Right then, that should keep me going for a bit.'

'OK, so there's nothing else you want to see from my work? Not the work I do with the artists themselves in supporting them? Not how much funding I've helped secure? The training sessions that I've run?'

I feel like I've wasted my one-to-one time with Robin talking about my personal life, when I should have been making a case for how bloody good I am at my job.

He glances over his notes before looking up and smiling.

'Not for now. At the moment I'm very much focused on the public events this department does, their spend per head, et cetera. I'm sure I'll get around to looking at the other little bits at some point.'

My heart sinks. I watch him as he makes a couple of notes in his diary and I'm waiting for him to leave to go back to his desk so I can wonder in peace what's going to become of my job.

'So how did you get into this? What did you read at university?' he says, looking back up at me.

'A lot of boring books,' I say laughing, before I see that he hasn't got my joke. 'I did English Lit.'

'Ah, I guess that figures. Was that one of the subjects with three or four hours a week?'

I know he's only making a joke, but I can't help but take it a little the wrong way. I always got defensive when people mocked my small timetable, as in my lightest final year I only had five hours a week. Yet, I spent hours upon hours reading.

'Yes, but that's because we had so many books to read.'

'Ah, those boring ones,' he says, laughing.

I try and hide a smile. I walked into that one.

'So what did you do, then?'

'I did Law for my undergraduate before doing Political Science for my masters.'

I should have known he'd done something super intense.

'So you did English Lit – have you always been a writer?'

I look around the office as I always feel a bit funny talking about it at work, like I'm cheating on my job by trying to write myself into a new career in the evening. Luckily for me, the office has thinned out as it's the start of lunchtime.

'I've always loved writing. But I only started writing in my *spare* time a few years ago.'

I enunciate the word 'spare', just in case my boss Jacqui happens to be walking past.

'You know, I wouldn't have picked you for a thriller writer.'

'Really? What would you expect me to write? Literary fiction?'

'No, I just thought you'd write rom-coms.'

'Because I'm a woman?' I say, mock-rolling my eyes.

'No, because you're funny.'

Ah, he's not being sexist after all.

'So what type of thrillers do you write, then? Psychological? Crime?'

'More adventure. Think Dan Brown, Sam Bourne.'

'Wow, OK. Have you been published?'

I almost splutter a laugh, as if I had, I'd probably have a framed photo of the book jacket sitting alongside the one of Will – I'd be that proud.

'No, but you never know, maybe one day. It's hard, getting a foot in the door.'

It's a patter I've said so often, to reassure myself and keep going. *It's a tricky industry to break into. They don't often take a risk on an unknown debut author.* I try to tell myself that everything's to blame except my writing. The thought that it might only be mediocre at best, or awful at worst, would be enough to make me give up.

'It's funny, though, that you should say that about writing women's fiction, as my writing tutor said that to me this week.'

'Well, there you go. It's a sign, then. Maybe you're the next Marian Keyes.'

'I don't know. I was excited about it at first, but now I'm not sure. I can't really think of an idea, and I don't know if I'm better off sticking to what I've been writing.'

Robin looks at me and narrows his eyes.

'Go on, say it.' I can tell he's itching to say something.

'I was just thinking that it seems a shame that you spend so much time helping others with their artistic dreams, but that yours aren't coming true.'

That's a really sweet thing to say.

'I'm sure I'll get there one day.'

'I'm sure you will. I always think that if you want something enough, you'll stop at nothing to get it.' He looks me firmly in the eye as if to emphasise how valuable a life lesson it is. 'I'm sure if you keep sending your book out for people to read . . .'

I don't have the heart to tell him that I haven't subbed it lately. In fact, I gave up a year or two ago. All that desperate checking of my inbox to see if someone's replied. My heart stopping as I notice I've got an email reply from an agent, just to see that it's a standard 'thanks but no thanks'. I shudder.

'I'd love to read it, if you'd let me? I love thrillers.'

'Oh, um, I don't really like people reading it.'

'Then, I've got news for you; I don't think you're going to make it as an author since that's sort of the point.'

I smile.

'I know that people will read my books *eventually*, but I want it to be deemed worthy first.'

'So nobody's read it yet?'

'Only Will and my best friend Cara.'

'And what did they think?'

'That is was good,' I say, shrugging.

'Well, if you want someone a bit more objective to take a look, then email it over to me. You never know, a fresh pair of eyes and all that.'

I'm not sure. I'm very over-protective of my book baby. But he's right though, as he always seems to be. If I want my book to be published I'm going to have to be prepared to let people read it.

'OK,' I say, taking a deep breath. 'I've got a copy on my memory stick. I'll send it over.'

'Excellent, I've got a pretty free weekend so that will give me something to read.'

'Just don't be brutal,' I say, wondering what I've agreed to.

'I won't, I promise,' he says, before he looks up and sees Jacqui's PA walking back over to his desk.

'Ah, Matthew,' says Robin. 'I need to catch him before he goes into a meeting with Jacqui.'

'OK,' I say, slightly relieved that he's leaving. I feel like I've been well and truly audited today.

'I'll have that other report over to you by tomorrow morning,' I call over my shoulder, as I almost run out of the office to get some fresh air.

I push round the revolving doors to find myself outside, taking a deep breath – what a meeting. It was almost as if he'd forgotten that he was auditing my work, and instead, he's auditing my life. First my relationship, then my writing career.

I know that he didn't mean to pick holes in either of them, but I can't help but feel he exposed problems that I've been ignoring. He's right, I should be doing more to get my book published, and my relationship with Will could be seen from the outside as being a bit stale.

Luckily for me, our upcoming trip to Swansea gives us the perfect opportunity to inject a bit of romance into our weekend. Especially if my revenge goes to plan, we'll have plenty of quality time together and I'll get even. It's shaping up to be quite the weekend.

13

'I'm glad that you suggested coming up tonight. I wouldn't have fancied going through those roadworks on the motorway tomorrow. We might have got held up and been late for the game,' says Will.

'That would have been awful,' I say, nodding my head in agreement.

I try and keep a straight face and not reveal that if my evil plan comes to fruition, he'll be missing the game anyway, traffic or no traffic.

'I can't wait to get there now. I'm gagging to crack open a beer.' Will's wriggling in his seat and like a contagious yawn, it's making me do the same. 'Satnav says we're almost there.'

I wish that was true, but we've still got to find our holiday cottage in the arse end of nowhere. It may be a fundamental part of my plan, but when you're three hours into a journey, knackered from a week of work and desperate for a pee, it doesn't seem like the smartest of choices.

I glance up at the screen and see that it says we're only two minutes away.

'Right, you'll need to get the directions from my handbag,' I say, pointing down at the bag at his feet.'

'What? Isn't the satnav taking us there?'

'Yes and no. It's taking us almost there, but apparently the road that the cottage is on isn't in the satnav, so we need the directions for the last five minutes.'

'Oh, great,' says Will, laughing and picking up my bag.

'They're on the two Post-it notes on the top.'

I try and point, but it's so bloody dark that I daren't take my eyes off the road for a second. I'm so used to driving around our light-polluted town with an abundance of street lights that I'm finding it really scary driving in the pitch black. I hate that I can't see where the road is really going in front of us, despite my headlights being on full beam. Usually on the wrong side of the speed limit, tonight I'm practically pootling along like my grandmother.

Will recovers the Post-its. 'These are the directions?'

It may be dark, but I can see him pulling a face.

'We're not going to get lost,' I say, 'we'll be there in no time.'

'Uh-huh, I've heard that before,' he says, chuckling.

To be fair, he has. Neither one of us is known for our sense of direction and we've been lost a lot over the past seven years. My map-reading skills are notoriously bad and Will's stubbornness and refusal to turn round when we've gone wrong is legendary.

'Right, here we are at the pub. This is where the directions start.'

My eyes fall on the well-lit pub – it looks so cosy and warm. It's bathed in a soft warm glow and there's a billow of smoke coming out of the chimney. I'd love nothing more than to pull in for a drink, but then we'd be even later getting to the cottage.

'OK, so it says here that from the pub we go back the way you came.' Will sighs loudly and looks at me. 'What sort of directions start like that?'

'Ones that will get us there,' I say hopefully, as I turn out of the pub car park.

'Take the second left.'

'OK,' I say, scanning the road. 'Uh, hang on, is that a left?'

'Um.'

I stop the car and we peer up in front to the left of us where there's a turning. There's no road as such, just a track that looks like it would hold a tractor.

'No, that's probably just field access,' says Will. 'Keep going. Ah, there's a left turn.'

'OK, so that's one. We're turning at the second one, then?'

I'm practically crawling along as we try and spot another left turn.

'How about that?' I say, wishing I'd eaten more carrots lately as not even the headlights are helping with this search.

'I think that's a footpath.'

I continue driving for another hundred metres and then I see a left turning that actually looks like a road. OK, so it might only be wide enough for one car, and there are no lines on it, but I can see some road amongst all the potholes.

We bump down the road (or track) and for a minute I start to regret bringing my little car. It's bouncing all over the place.

'Look out!' shouts Will.

I screech the brakes on, and realise we've come to a dead end. All that's in front of us is a gnarly old tree.

'That's odd,' I say, 'where's the cottage? What do the directions say?'

'They just say continue down the second left, then at the end of the road, turn to the right.'

We scan the hedgerows – there's nothing there.

'Maybe I should go back a bit.'

I put the car into reverse, hoping the turning is just before the end of the road. But there are only hedgerows.

'What about that gate?' says Will, pointing.

I look over the other side of the road at the big metal gate that's glimmering in my headlights.

'But that's on the left and there's no reference to a gate in the instructions. Not to mention that I can't see anything in those fields,' I say as I drive the car slightly forward and angle the headlights over.

'We're going to have to reverse,' says Will.

'Oh bloody hell, can't I spin it round?'

Will gets out of the car and he looks around him, before getting back in.

'There's nowhere wide enough to spin it round. You're going to have to go back the way we came.'

'But I can't see a bloody thing,' I say.

'Your reversing lights should help a little, and it is a straight road at least.'

I mutter all the swears under my breath as I crank the gear stick noisily into reverse. See, even my car is protesting at this plan.

'Just take it nice and steady,' he says, patting my knee.

I take a deep breath and try to relax as we bump along backwards. We finally make it back to the main road, or as main as it gets round here, and we go back in the direction we came.

The bumps are doing nothing for me needing a wee. I'd go by the side of the road if it wasn't so bloody dark and scary.

I'm about to suggest going back to the pub when I see the only other proper road we've seen and turn down it.

'Woah,' says Will, looking up from the directions. 'Where are you going?'

'I thought I'd try this. At least it's smoother than the other one.'

We get to the bottom of the road, and sure enough there's a right-hand turn.

'Great, so is the cottage down here?'

'Um,' says Will, shining his phone light over my scribbled notes.

'It says continue over the small hill and the road will curve round, then there'll be a track off to the left.'

I don't know if it's my imagination, but the further we drive down this road the thinner it's getting. I feel like the trees and the hedgerows are going to squash us at any minute.

'I'm getting the feeling that this is the wrong way,' I say, as we drive down the road. It's flat as a pancake – no hills in sight. What if we're going to be driving around these little roads all night?

I begin to feel my heart race. I don't know what scares me more, that I'm going to be lost here forever, or the thought that I might have to reverse down another road.

'It might have been easier if we'd stayed somewhere in Swansea,' says Will. 'We could have been all checked in by now.'

'It'll be worth it in the end,' I say through gritted teeth. Or at least it better bloody be. The cottage did look nice on the Internet and I think we've proved tonight that it's isolated, which is perfect for my purposes. 'Once you see how pretty it is round here, you'll understand why I booked it.'

'I'm sure I will. I can't remember the last time we went away somewhere rural.'

'Um, I think it was that trip to Devon.'

'Yeah, it must have been. What was that, three years ago or so?'

'I don't think we'd been together that long, so more like six or seven.'

'No way.'

He shakes his head and I can almost hear the cogs turning. 'You're right, it must have been. That was a great holiday. All that hiking.'

'Hmm, and all those post-walk massages.'

I'm suddenly quite glad I brought my walking boots.

'Oh yeah, I've never forgotten those. We should do that kind of thing more often.'

'Yes, we should.'

'Perhaps we could do this more often – you know, go to away matches but make a weekend out of it.'

I bite my lip. Not quite what I had in mind.

'Oh, would you call this a hill?'

We go over what appears to be a large bump in the road and immediately after the road bears round.

Will shrugs, and with me not really wanting to reverse, we keep on going until we see a track on the left.

'Is this it?' I say, glancing at the track and sucking in a breath as I do. 'Once I get down there I don't fancy my chances of getting back up.'

'If needs be I'll reverse it out, but I think this could be us.'

I turn into the track, and sure enough at the end of it I can see a little cottage tucked away.

I pull up the car in front of the cottage and yank the handbrake up, and as I turn the headlights off we're plunged into darkness.

'Keep the headlights on while we unpack the car,' says Will.

'OK,' I say, switching them back on.

We both get out and try to get our bearings.

The car is shining its lights on the side of the cottage. There's a picket fence running round the side and a small wooden gate with an ivy-covered arch over the top.

'Hideaway Cottage,' says Will, laughing and pointing to the sign on the gate as he swings it open. 'It's certainly that.'

I follow close behind him and try to spot the flowerpot that the key is supposed to be hidden under.

'The owner said she'd leave the key under the geranium pot.'

'What does a geranium look like?' replies Will.

'I have no fricking clue.'

The only thing our tiny patch of garden at home seems to grow is weeds.

It's pretty hard to see anything inside the garden, as the light from the car is obscured by the hedges. I'm hopping around from foot to foot trying not to wet myself and I bump into Will as he fumbles under a giant plant pot.

'Sorry,' I say.

'Not to worry. Got it.'

He comes up to stand and I can just about make out the key.

I hold on to his arm as he walks to the front of the house and finds the lock.

'You'd think they'd have left us a light on.'

'She did say something about having a torch handy and I forgot.'

Will pulls his phone out of his pocket and uses it to see the lock, and it isn't long before the heavy door swings open.

He quickly finds the light switch and I go in, desperately searching for a toilet.

The walls are thick white stone, with mismatched stone floor tiles. A narrow wooden staircase runs to one side, and straight in front there looks to be the kitchen. I spot a door under the stairs and my prayers are answered when I see it's a small toilet.

'I'll get the bags,' says Will as I shut myself in.

'OK,' I shout.

I'm sure I do a wee that could be entered into the *Guinness Book of Records*, it's so long, and afterwards I head into the kitchen, wrapping my coat further around me as there's a definite nip to the air. I gasp as I walk in – it's like my dream kitchen. Cream cupboards, dark wooden worktops and a large dining table. There's even a vintage-looking cream Aga.

I find the small utility room off the back and switch the heating on, as instructed by the owners, and as I walk back into the kitchen I spot the welcome basket on the windowsill, complete with a bottle of Prosecco.

'Excellent,' I say out loud. 'Just what we need.'

'What's that?' says Will walking back in.

I wave the bottle at him before popping it in the fridge.

'Perfect. I'll take the bags straight upstairs, shall I?'

'Yes, great. Did you get the food shopping out?'

'No, I forgot.'

'No, worries. I'll go and get it.'

'I can go once I've dumped these.'

'It's OK,' I say, a little too enthusiastically. 'I'll lock up the car while I'm there.'

'I don't think you need to worry about that around here.'

Will laughs and I head upstairs. Maybe not, but I need to put phase one of my plan into action.

It's a lot easier to navigate outside now that Will's switched on the external light. I head back to the car and see that he's already switched the headlights off. I sit down on the driver's seat and turn the sidelights on, before I switch on the light in the centre of the car and open the glove compartment.

With it being so dark outside it's practically like the Blackpool Illuminations now that I've turned all of these lights on, but luckily the cottage doesn't overlook the car, so hopefully Will won't notice tonight.

I retrieve the food shopping from the back seat and lock the car. I give the lights one last look before I go. I hesitate for a second, wondering if I've gone too far. What if there's an emergency and we aren't able drive out of here with a flat battery?

Then I laugh as in about ten minutes we'll have started to drink the Prosecco and will be unable to drive anyway.

'Find it OK?' asks Will as I walk back into the kitchen. He's digging around the cupboards and pulls out two champagne flutes.

'Yes, fine.'

I fill the fridge with the bacon and eggs for tomorrow's breakfast.

'It's a bit cold, but it's probably a bit late to light the fire in the lounge. How do you fancy taking this bottle up to bed? There's a great en suite up there, and I noticed it's got one of those corner baths that looks big enough for two.'

'Has it now?'

This cottage really does tick all the boxes.

'Uh-huh.'

He pulls the bottle out of the fridge. I'm about to argue that it's not had time to cool down enough, when he brushes past me and kisses me on the lips. And I sense that that warm Prosecco's about to be the last thing on my mind.

It looks like I wasn't totally lying after all, when I told Robin that I was going to have a passionate weekend.

14

I wake up on Saturday morning and for a minute I wonder where I am. Unlike my bed at home, there's no lumps in this one, and I feel like I'm being cocooned in softness. I open my eyes and take in the surroundings, before I remember.

'Morning,' says Will, rolling over and flopping his arm across by belly.

'Morning.'

It feels like I'm on that romantic mini-break in the country, rather than on a top secret mission to ruin my boyfriend's day.

'This bed is so comfortable,' I say.

'I know. I don't want to ever get out of it.'

That would make my revenge plan easier. That reminds me, I must go and turn the car lights off. But before I get up, I study Will for a second. He's got a cute sleepy look going on. His hair is all ruffled and his eyes barely open.

I can't help but edge closer towards him.

'Well, there's no hurry,' I say, trying to banish the memory of our last failed attempt at nooky a few weeks ago. But spirited on from our 'special bath' last night, I think it's worth a shot.

This time, his arm moves from my waist and grabs my bum and as he pulls me into him I soon discover that this time I'm not going to be turned down.

Maybe I've overthought my plan; maybe I can just get Will to stay under the covers all day . . .

An hour later and we're up and dressed and sitting at the kitchen table. So much for spending the whole day in bed. That's part of the problem with long-term partners, those long leisurely sex sessions of the honeymoon period have disappeared with the knowledge of each other's on switches. There's no need for exploration or discovery when you know where all the short-cuts are to get the job done.

But that's OK, a romantic mini-break is not only all about the sex, and this will give us some time to explore the area. It's half past ten now and the game doesn't kick off until one forty-five, so we've got a couple of hours before we have to leave. Or at least, try to leave, mwa-ha-ha.

'I bought the bits for us to have a fry-up as the game is at such an odd time,' I say going over to the fridge to retrieve the shopping I hastily shoved in there last night.

'Why don't we just go into Swansea now, and we could grab something there?'

Oh God. That is not part of the plan. Granted we might have trouble reaching Swansea if phase one has worked, but still, if we try and go there now there will be plenty of time to rectify the situation.

'But I'm starving,' I say, rubbing my belly. 'And I really fancied a little stroll around here before we go. You don't mind, do you? I mean, I am going to give up my whole afternoon to your football game . . .'

Or at least, give up my whole afternoon stopping you from going to the football game.

'OK, then. I guess that's only fair.'

Right now, Will's the only thing that can stop me from succeeding at revenge. I've just got to stop him from throwing any more spanners in the works before I officially start it.

I head over to the cooker while trying to keep calm. I still need to turn off the lights in the car, but I don't want to arouse suspicion.

'Hey, have you got any mobile signal?' Will says, lifting his phone high above his head and panning it round.

'Oh, I er, haven't checked.'

What's the point when I know that I won't get any reception within about three or four hundred metres of the cottage? Thank you Moodyman123 on TripAdvisor for that nugget of information.

'I might just go upstairs and see if I can get some.'

'OK, then,' I say, biting my lip. I can just picture him now hanging out of windows trying.

I've planned this trip with almost military precision. I've scoured TripAdvisor reviews, looked at public transport websites, done Google map analysis of the area. I might, according to the publishing industry, be a pretty crap thriller writer, but at least it's taught me how to research.

While Will's upstairs I sneak out to the car and hastily turn off all the lights and shut the glove compartment, making sure I leave the light in the centre of the car on.

I try not to feel too jumpy when Will comes back in. I've just got to relax and follow my plan. First step, long leisurely breakfast, followed by a walk to the sea, which might take us a little longer if I take a wrong path, meaning we arrive back here just in the nick of time to get to the game . . .

'Bloody hell, I thought that we were never going to get back,' says Will as we walk down the lane to the cottage. It's a bit easier to find in the day, and especially since we found a footpath that's a real shortcut to the coast.

For the first time ever, I've made it to Wales on a sunny and dry day. We were rewarded with the most breathtaking views along the cliffs of the craggy rocks down to the sea, and we had what can only be described as a delightful walk, even if it has made my legs ache. I hadn't realised, from the maps, that it would be such a steep or challenging walk. It made me realise that I'm not quite as fit as I thought I was. Perhaps I need to actually use my gym membership for more than a shower when I'm heading out straight after work.

After walking along the cliffs, we headed down some steep steps for a stroll along the beach, and we actually held hands as we did. It was really nice, if not a little clammy. I seem to have a real problem with revenge and excess sweating.

'We've still got plenty of time,' I say, trying not to rush.

'Yeah, just a quick pit stop and then let's get going. We want to make sure we're in and parked easily.'

'Uh-huh.'

I unlock the door to the cottage and after a quick bathroom break, pick up my bag.

'Right, I'm ready.'

I glance at the clock in the hall; we've got an hour until kick-off. My stomach starts to rumble like a washing machine and my cheeks start to burn again. I'm clearly never going to be head-hunted for MI5.

'Great, let's get this show on the road. C'mon the Saints,' he says, picking up the car keys.

I take a deep breath and hope that the car forums I've been on this week have been right. If the car starts we're in trouble, as unless there's some freak traffic jam, there will be nothing stopping us from reaching the game.

Will steps outside, gets into the car and places the key in the ignition.

I hold my breath and stare transfixed as the engine starts to make noises, only it doesn't turn over.

I almost do an air punch in celebration before realising that I don't want to give anything away.

'What the . . .' says Will, turning the ignition off and then back on again. The same thing happens – the engine makes a sort of whining noise but nothing kicks in.

He reaches under the steering wheel and pops the bonnet, before rushing out and opening it up.

I join him outside the car as he stares at the engine and pokes around.

'What are you looking for?' I ask, wondering where his sudden mechanical knowledge has come from.

'I was just checking nothing had come out.'

He slams the bonnet shut again and heads back round to the driver's seat. Another failed attempt and he hits his hand on the steering wheel.

'Bloody car, think the battery's flat.'

'How did that happen? Are the lights on?'

He looks round at them.

'No, they're off.'

'Oh, look,' I say, pointing at the light in the centre of the car. 'Do you think that would have done it?'

Now I know the answer to the question. The light possibly would have drained the battery, if it had been old, but luckily it was helped along by the side lights being on and the glove compartment being open.

'I guess it must have done,' he says, scrunching his eyes shut and sighing really loudly.

'Don't worry, we'll just phone the AA,' I say, pulling my phone out from my bag. 'Oh, no signal.'

I turn my phone round to show him, as if he needs proof.

'Fuck,' he shouts. 'What are we going to do now?'

He gets out of the car and pulls his phone out of his pocket and jogs around the garden holding it up like a wand, but – judging by the face he's pulling – to no avail.

I'm trying desperately not to laugh as I don't want to a) anger the beast, or (b) give him any idea of my role in this whole thing. Instead, I try my absolute hardest to remember my drama lessons from school and try to paint a look of concern on my face.

'Fucking hell. We're going to miss kick-off.'

And hopefully the rest of the game.

'I'm going to have to push the car.'

'What?' I say, genuinely confused.

'I'll push the car. You get in to drive it and when it picks up momentum, whack it into second gear and turn the key. There's a slight slope out of the drive. If we can turn the car round and get it facing in the right direction, then we might just be able to do it.'

Surely that can't work, can it? I thought that when a battery was dead as a dodo it was jump leads or nothing. What kind of sorcery is this, and why did no one mention it in the forums I read?

He gives me his phone as he goes and gets into position, placing his hands on the bonnet.

I pop his phone in my bag and reluctantly get into the car.

'Take the handbrake off,' he shouts.

This can't work. If he does miraculously get us going, how the hell am I going to stop him then?

'Is it off?' he shouts again.

I press the button on the handbrake and instead of taking it off all the way, I let it go almost half the way, to give it a little resistance.

I give Will a thumbs up and he bends over the bonnet and starts to push.

It's actually quite a turn-on seeing my boyfriend flexing his muscles and working up a sweat. After a few failed attempts at pushing, he gives up, and I make a point of pulling up the handbrake to cover my tracks.

'Why don't we try walking up to the main road, maybe there's a payphone somewhere? We could call a taxi,' I say, trying to help him along, even though I know from our little walk that there's no such phone box. I made sure that I scoured the landscape looking for one.

'Hmm, OK. Yeah, maybe we'll be able to flag down a car to jump-start us.'

Argh. God damn him and his ingenious ideas.

I throw my bag under the passenger seat of the car and get out, following Will, who's stomping down the drive.

At least when we're talking about a main road that's only in comparison to the unpaved drive that the cottage is on. It's hardly the M1 and, unsurprisingly, there's not a car in sight.

I breathe a sneaky sigh of relief and wonder what's going to happen now.

'Which way was that bigger road that we came in on last night?'

Will's spinning around as if he's trying to get his bearings. While I hadn't planned our dead-of-night arrival, it's served us well for getting totally disorientated as I have no idea which way we need to turn to hit the big roads.

'Shit, Lexi, which way? It's less than an hour until kick-off. What the hell are we going to do? We're never going to make it.'

No, Will Talbot, we're not. A cackle rattles around my brain.

'Let's not give up yet.'

I'm having far too much fun watching you squirm. If I'm going to get revenge, I might as well enjoy it.

'The bus stop,' he shouts, in a eureka moment.

'Ah, yes, the bus stop we passed at the beach,' I say, playing along.

I know that won't be of much help. I know for a fact that even if we catch one of the rare buses, it goes all round the houses before it gets to Swansea, then there's the trip from the town centre to the ground.

'Let's go,' I say, treating it as if it's some big adventure. I haven't had this much fun in ages.

15

It takes us fifteen minutes to reach the bus stop. Will's barely spoken in that time. He keeps mumbling something under his breath, but I can't quite catch it.

Whatever it is, he's not a happy bunny.

It's getting ever closer to game time and we're still miles away.

We reach the bus stop and I desperately try and hide my excitement as Will reads out the timetable.

'OK, so there's another bus in forty-five minutes. Bloody hell. The game will have started by then.'

His finger glides across the columns.

'And we wouldn't get into Swansea until twenty past three. The game would practically be finished by the time we get to the ground.'

He starts pacing the road, desperately trying to think of a plan.

I think he's done pretty well so far to come up with as many as he has. I know he was a boy scout when he was younger, but this is truly quite impressive. I'm glad that I didn't underestimate his determination to watch the game when I was doing my planning.

'Where's my phone? Maybe we can get a signal here,' he says, holding his hand out.

I look at my shoulder – pretending to look for my bag.

'My bag; I must have left it in the car.'

For a second I fear I've over-egged it as he looks at me suspiciously. My cheeks start to flush and my heart starts to race. Has he found me out?

'You mean you don't have it on you? What about your phone? Is that in the bag too?'

I nod my head slowly.

'I wasn't thinking; we left in such a hurry. I guess I was distracted by what was going on.'

'Fuck,' says Will, putting his hands on his head and shaking it wildly. 'We've got tickets and we're not going to be able to use them. I'm not even going to be able to follow the game as I can't get any bloody signal on my phone at the cottage.'

For a second I'm tempted to gloat and to tell him he deserves it, but I can't do that. Not yet. I've got to see this through to the end.

'What about that pub?' says Will, looking up at me hopefully.

'The pub?'

'Yeah, that one on the cliff that the directions started from. They'll be open now, and they probably have a phone. I'm sure we'll be able to call a taxi.'

Oh crap. The pub phone. Why did I not take that into consideration? I managed to find out that they don't show Sky Sports, but I didn't consider the whole phone thing. Balls, balls and more balls.

'Um, but how would we pay for a taxi? I haven't got my bag.'

'I've got my wallet in my pocket. Come on.'

He's already marched off and I've got no choice but to follow him.

I can't believe I'd almost succeeded, only for him to still find a way to get to his bloody football game. It took me so long to think of this plan and it's only going to work once. There's no way he'd let me take him away from civilisation on a game day again.

We hurry down the crumbly road towards the pub. All I can hope is that it's closed, but as it comes into view I can see the smoke escaping the chimney and there are quite a few cars in the car park.

Will starts to speed up and I can barely keep up with him. I'm definitely going to hit the gym harder after this weekend. I can feel my calf muscles burning.

I glance at my watch. It's about half an hour until kick-off. I guess even if we do get a taxi pretty much straight away we're still looking at at least forty-five minutes until we're at the game. So he misses the first fifteen – that's pretty crap revenge. I'm sure he misses that on a regular basis when he's finishing off his beer in the bar before he goes to his seat.

I watch in horror as Will pushes the big red door open and strides inside. That's that then. My dream of revenge is over.

By the time I walk in he's hunched over a payphone in the porch.

'How long?' he says incredulously. He sucks air through his teeth and my heart instantly soars again. 'No, don't worry about it, thanks.'

He hangs up the phone noisily and makes a weird roaring noise.

'No luck with the taxi?'

'No, it'll be an hour's wait for the local firm. So that's it,' he says, sighing heavily and shoving his hands into his pockets in defeat. 'We've come all this way to watch the Saints and we're going to miss the match.'

'Ah well, it couldn't be helped.'

Except it could.

'These are exceptional circumstances,' I say.

I'm beaming on the inside. My scheming has worked perfectly. I can't quite believe it. Who knew I had such a devious side to me? I feel like I'm wasted at the council, maybe MI5 might want me after all.

'It's just so fucking frustrating. I mean, we're so close. I know the cottage is lovely and it's great being out here in the country, but for a minute I just wished that we'd booked the Travelodge by the ground.'

Ooh imagine the romance that we would have had. Us staggering back from the game after a few beers along with all the other Southampton supporters who would probably be staying there. Heading for a romantic meal at the site Beefeater or Burger King, or a similar family-friendly chain restaurant attached to the hotel.

'Well, when I was planning it, I never dreamt that anything would go wrong with the car.'

I'm wondering if my nose is starting to grow like Pinocchio's.

'Un-fucking-believable,' he says again, shaking his head.

'Hmm.'

I'm wondering how long this will go on.

'Shall we get a drink while we're here?' I say, hoping we can get back to our mini-break again.

'I guess so.'

He's in a right sulk, with a big lip and slumped shoulders.

'Chin up, it's only a football game. I'm sure they'll win whether you're there or not.'

Will stops in his tracks and I wonder if I've gone too far. I may have pulled off the sabotage, but I might have fallen at the final hurdle by pushing him over the grumpy edge.

I'm half expecting him to launch into a proper rant. If he does I'll find it difficult not to gloat and tell him that I'd planned it all along. Now that would be a pretty silly thing to do. We're stuck on a peninsula surrounded by cliffs with a dead car battery. And even when we do call out the AA, we've still got to drive back. No, if I'm having this out properly with him then it's when I'm in the comfort of my own home, away from any danger of being pushed off a cliff.

But Will surprises me. He takes a deep breath, appearing to rise above what I said, and heads straight to the bar.

'What are you drinking?' he says, turning to me.

'A glass of dry white wine.'

Will nods and turns his attention to the barmaid, and orders us our drinks.

'I don't suppose you've got the Swansea game on anywhere, have you?' he says, the last hint of hope having departed his voice long ago.

'Sorry love, no screens in the pub.'

He nods as if he's resigned to the fact that his afternoon is ruined.

I sit down at a nearby table in the window, overlooking the sea, and Will comes over and joins me.

'So . . .' I say, wondering if this silence is going to hang over our whole afternoon. It's even more boring than being at a sodding football game. For a minute I wonder if I've got this revenge thing wrong. Maybe it's going to backfire and I'm going to end up punishing myself with having to babysit a sulky boyfriend. 'This is nice.'

'Yeah,' says Will, and I swear he giggles a tiny bit.

It starts slowly but then he starts to let out quite the belly ache.

I look around at the few other people in the pub, slightly embarrassed that I appear to have turned my boyfriend quite insane.

'Everything OK?' I say, risking a smile.

'I just can't believe today. I mean, it's been like something out of some Godawful comedy sketch. Every way we've tried to get to the game has failed.'

He continues to laugh and it becomes a little infectious and I start to laugh too. If only we'd been on some reality TV programme where the audience could have seen Will's face at every stage. The sight of him straining to push the car while the handbrake was on is enough to keep me giggling.

'If I didn't laugh, I'd be crying,' says Will. 'I guess there are worse places I could be. I've got beer, a good view and the pub's nice and cosy.'

I nod. It's a perfect Saturday afternoon pub.

'And I'm with you,' he adds.

I almost choke on my drink. It's a bit pathetic but that's one of the most romantic things he's ever said to me.

'Ah, thank you,' I say, leaning over and stroking his hand.

Don't feel guilty, he still deserves this, I tell myself.

'How about we finish these and go for a walk down to the beach again? It looked like there was another path over the other side.'

My calves desperately want to protest, but my heart is swooning that we're doing something as a couple.

'OK,' I say slowly.

There's something a bit unnerving about my boyfriend acting like this. First a compliment (he's barely drunk any of his pint and he's had sex this morning – usually his motivations for providing them), and now he wants to go for a walk, on a Saturday, when there are sports on. Granted, he'd have difficulty watching said sports, but he still could have suggested going back to our cottage and scouring the terrestrial channels for something.

'I really enjoyed going for that walk this morning,' he says, sipping his pint.

'Me too.'

There was something nice about being there with Will and having his full attention. Maybe I should confiscate his mobile phone more often. 'We'll have to go up to the South Downs for a walk sometime soon,' he says.

'I'd like that.'

I sip my drink and wonder if I've cracked the formula for how to have a romantic, interruption-free afternoon with my boyfriend. I'm not entirely sure that it's conducive from a time management perspective, having to spend all week planning and engineering things to go wrong in order to make the suitable environment, but at least I know now that it can be done.

'So cheers,' I say raising a glass. 'Here's to a lovely afternoon, maybe not one you planned.' *But I certainly did.* 'But let's hope it's a good one anyway.'

'Cheers.'

He chinks his glass and looks me straight in the eye, which we all know is the German key to not having seven years' bad sex. Hmm, I wonder if we didn't make eye contact at some point early in our relationship. But bad sex isn't the same as lack of sex, is it . . .? Oh well, perhaps we'll make up for it now. Well, a girl can dream, can't she?

16

'I can't eat another mouthful,' I say, pushing my plate across the table.

The chocolate mud pie in front of me was to die for and disappeared at a rate of knots. I think there are only two spoonfuls of it left, at best, but as much as it breaks my heart to leave it, if I put it in my mouth I think I will explode.

Will hovers his fork over my plate and looks carefully before I give him the nod of approval. I don't usually share my food, especially when it comes to sweet treats, but that pudding was far too good to go to waste. It's better in his belly than in the pub's bin.

We built up quite the appetite with our walk this afternoon and totally justified the humungous amounts of calories we've just consumed with our big fat pies and chunky chips, followed by orgasmic desserts.

'Mmm, that chocolate was lovely,' says Will.

'I know; it was delicious. How was your crumble?'

'Pretty good. It was nice not to have burnt, lumpy custard for a change.'

'Watch it,' I say, pulling at the edge of my plate. 'I can just as easily take this plate away again.'

Will laughs and holds his hands up. 'I take it back; your custard is just lovely. Lumps and all.'

I smile. I love desserts, but I fail miserably at custards. I even cock up the ready-made ones.

'I think you're going to have to roll me back to the cottage,' I say, wishing that it wasn't going to be a fifteen-minute walk back home. I could just do with someone picking me up and depositing me in a nice comfy armchair in front of the telly.

'It will be good for us to walk this off. Did you want to go back soon?'

'Yeah, we could do. I saw some DVDs in the lounge. We could curl up on the sofa and put one on.'

'Great, and I could even try and light the wood-burning stove.'

'Sounds like heaven.'

It's been such a lovely day and it's truly shaping up to be the romantic weekend away I told Robin it would be. I know it wouldn't have been Will's first choice of how to spend an afternoon, but I think even he enjoyed himself. I've been amazed at how little he's been moaning about missing the game.

'Can I get you any more drinks?' asks the barman, as he takes away our dessert plates. 'Coffees?'

'Actually, I think we'll be heading off pretty soon,' says Will, 'but that was fantastic.'

'Up for the match today, were you?' asks the barman, pointing at Will's Southampton scarf hanging over the back of the seat.

'Kind of. It's a long story but we missed it. Do you know who won?'

'Swans won 2–0. Cracking game.'

Well, we *were* having a lovely romantic weekend . . . at least I got a pretty good afternoon. I should be thankful.

The barman walks away and Will shakes his head.

'Maybe it's a good job we missed the game after all. It's bad enough that they lost, let alone having to watch them do it.'

Who is this man and what has he done with my boyfriend?

'Shall we finish these drinks and go? I need to walk off this food.'

'Yeah, sure,' I say, amazed.

We walk up to the bar to pay for the food.

'So are you staying nearby?' asks the barman, as he processes our card payment.

'At Hideaway Cottage.'

'Ah. Are you walking back? Got a good torch with you?' he says, chuckling.

Uh-oh. I hadn't thought about that. When we left this afternoon in our – or more correctly, Will's – frenzy, we hadn't planned to stay out the whole day.

'I've got a torch on my phone,' says Will, tucking his card back into his wallet.

'Your phone that's in my bag, in the car?'

'Oh.'

Oh indeed.

I'm trying to mentally walk the path. I know it's lined with brambles and blackberry bushes, and there were some stinging nettles. Then the memories of how dark it was last night in the car, even with headlights on, start to come back.

'How about I lend you guys a torch? You can drop it back tomorrow,' says the barman.

'Thank you,' I say in instant relief. 'We're going to have to come back to use the payphone to call the AA anyway. In fact, should we just book in for Sunday lunch?'

'Yeah, good idea,' agrees Will.

'Cool, I'll reserve you a table.'

The barman disappears out the back, reappearing with a wind-up torch.

'There you go. See you tomorrow.'

We walk out of the pub and I'm instantly glad of the barman's generosity. It's pitch black outside, thanks to a thick cover of cloud, and apart from the lights of the pub, there's no street lighting. Will takes my hand as we start to walk down the little lane. It's so ridiculously dark that the torch is barely illuminating a foot in front of us.

I cling on to Will for dear life and huddle in close to make the most of the small line of light we've got.

'Hang on a sec,' he says, winding up the torch, which whirrs noisily. 'OK, then.'

We set off once more, and I have to say I'm not liking this one bit. Anyone could be hiding on this path: murderers . . . rapists . . . snakes. I'm not sure snakes are nocturnal, but I decide to stamp my feet a little harder, just in case. Although with us tripping noisily over the tree roots and the whirring of the torch, I'm not sure we'd catch any unawares.

'How much further is it?' I ask, as I jump out of my skin at an owl hooting.

I clutch Will a little tighter.

'I think we've got another ten minutes or so to go. Here, why don't you walk in front with the torch, and I'll walk behind.'

We swap places, and I'm not entirely sure I want to be walking point with all the potential trip hazards, but Will places his arms firmly around my waist as we walk and it feels really safe and snug.

I'm feeling pretty tipsy from all the wine and what with my boyfriend pressing up against me, I'm sort of tempted to turn around and snog his face off, but I think better of it. There's no way that we're going to be doing anything al fresco. There are brambles everywhere, not to mention those snakes . . .

'It's lovely here,' he says. It's a very un-Will-like thing to say.

'Oh yes, the views are incredible through the torchlight.'

'Very funny. No, I mean generally. This is a really nice part of the world. Despite the disaster with the game, I'm glad you suggested coming here.'

I'm hit by a rush of love for my boyfriend. It's like this weekend, getting him away from his phone and all the sport, has made me remember what it used to be like when we first started dating. Back when we used to talk about things and actually listen to each other.

'Thanks. Isn't our cottage lovely? It's so cosy. I'd love to live somewhere like that one day. Not that we'd ever be able to afford it.'

I think of our little semi-detached, newish build on a faceless estate. It's nice enough, and we're lucky that we're on the property ladder, but it's not like a country cottage complete with beams and a secluded garden.

'Well, if you become the female Dan Brown then you never know.'

'Yeah, cos that's going to happen.'

'Don't be so hard on yourself. Your book's good and one day a publisher will realise that and publish it.'

'Thanks, honey.'

The mention of my book makes me think of Robin reading it this weekend and I suddenly feel a little nervous. What if he's reading it at this very second?

'I mean it. I don't know why you get so down about your writing. How many people actually finish a book that they write? You're the only person I know that has.'

'That's because none of your friends probably know how to write anything but an abusive rant on Facebook to an opposing football fan.'

'Very funny. But it's true. Even if you don't get that book published, I'm still proud that you wrote it.'

'What do you mean if I don't get it published?'

Will is my eternal cheerleader and super-fan – OK, my only fan – so him doubting that I'll succeed in my goal is unnerving.

'I don't mean you won't get published ever, I just mean with that book. You were saying the other day how you were thinking of writing something different. Maybe that one will be the one.'

'I guess.'

'Yeah, and then when it becomes a bestseller and you make millions, we'll buy a little cottage like that one.'

'Yeah, one day,' I say, laughing.

'And of course, you'll be able to buy us a box at St Mary's.'

'Oh yes, of course.'

'And the inevitable yacht to dock in the Hamble, as the Saints will be in Europe by then so we can cruise round to watch them at their UEFA matches. Imagine docking our own little yacht in Barcelona.'

He's almost making football sound appealing.

'Well, you better hope you've made an honest woman out of me by then, or else I'll be off with some Spanish stallion.'

He's so close behind me, that I can feel him tense up at the mention of marriage.

'Luckily for me, I think I've got some time, then, if you haven't written this bestseller yet.'

I try not to think about my conversation with Robin on Thursday. As I said then, we're not in a hurry to get married, so why should it matter if he takes his time? I try and push the thoughts out of my mind, as I don't want to ruin what's been a lovely day.

'Ah, here we are,' says Will, guiding me round to the little gate that comes out into the cottage garden. It's a good job he's with me as I'd never have spotted that and would probably still be walking round when the sun came up.

I retrieve my bag from the car as we walk past. Not that our phones are any use with no signal.

'So, let's get the fire going,' says Will. 'Do we have any wine?'

'Of course.'

I wouldn't have marooned ourselves in a cottage without any.

I retrieve the bottle and glasses from the kitchen and by the time I make it back into the living room, the fire's crackling into life.

'I didn't know you could do that,' I say, impressed that there's no end to his boy scout talents.

'Well, we don't have a lot of call for it with our radiators.'

I nod and sit on the sofa and he sits down next to me.

I hand him a freshly poured glass of wine and I naturally snuggle back into him.

'Thanks for a lovely day,' I say, breathing in the faint smell of his Hugo Boss aftershave. I tell myself that I should make more of an effort to snuggle in and smell it more often.

'Thanks yourself. All in all it turned out to be a pretty good day.'

I don't even feel the tiniest bit guilty about enacting my revenge as it truly was the best day we've had in a long, long time.

'And it's not over yet,' he says, stroking my stomach and grazing my boob, and gaining my attention.

Blimey, I reckon I'm going to get it twice in one day! It's a modern miracle. And totally justifies me having taken the time to shave my legs.

As Will leans over and kisses me, I can't help thinking that I should go on a campaign of revenge if this is what the outcome is. It's reminded me exactly how much I love him, something that's been easy to forget lately.

17

I waltz into the office and over to my desk, still gloriously revelling in the post-romantic haze that was my weekend.

'Someone looks cheerful,' says Mike, who looks anything but.

'Just an excellent weekend,' I say, as I sit down at my desk and switch on my PC.

Thanks to the bedroom activity, I haven't been this bow-legged since I bought the ThighMaster 3000 from an infomercial. I'm sure both causes of the John Wayne swagger were calorie-shifting, but I can tell you for sure which one I'd pick to do any day of the week.

'I'm going to make a coffee, anyone want one?' I say, jumping up.

Mike looks at me in shock.

Usually it's such an effort to even make it into work on a Monday morning, so when I arrive I stay glued to my seat and hold my mug out like a hitch-hiker hoping that one of my colleagues will take pity on me and bring me coffee. But not today. Today, despite my thighs aching, I seem to have boundless energy.

'I take it you want one?' I reply.

'Uh-huh.'

I pick Mike's cup off his desk and look over at Robin, who's staring intently at his screen, but I see that his cup is half full so I don't bother to interrupt. I try to tell myself that him ignoring me and being engrossed in his work does not mean that he's read my book and hated it.

As I walk into our kitchen and flick on the kettle, I think I might even go as far as to push the boat out and go down to the canteen to bring back Danishes.

I bend down to find the milk in the fridge, and when I come up to standing I bump straight into Robin.

'Oh, hello,' I say, beaming at him, and hoping that now he'll have to tell me whether he liked or hated the book.

'Morning,' he says, returning the smile. 'Had a nice weekend, then?'

'I did.'

'That's right, it was your mini-break. I take it all went to plan?'

I nod my head, thinking about my little act of revenge.

'To the letter.'

I get lost in a little daydream of being all curled up around Will on Sunday morning, and how we lay in bed just cuddling until we went for the pub lunch.

'You missed the football, then?'

'Yes, we went for a nice walk along the beach and then we went for a pub lunch. And the pub didn't even have the football on.'

'It's just as well since the match was dire. Sounds like you definitely had the better day. You've obviously got your relationship just right. I'm slightly envious; it's hard to find that balance with someone.'

I look up at Robin and I can't imagine that he has any problems finding women. The fact that he said he was between girlfriends when we first met indicated to me that he had an almost revolving door policy.

'Perhaps I need to get some tips from you. You could be like a relationship guru.'

I want to laugh at the thought. If you want to know how not to communicate with your partner or how to enact revenge, I'm your gal.

'Perhaps,' I say, making my coffee. 'So, um, I don't suppose you read my book, did you?'

I didn't mean to blurt it out quite as bluntly as I did, but I've been talking to him for two minutes and he hasn't mentioned it – it's all I can think about.

'Oh, God. Your book. No, I'm so sorry. I'd meant to send it to my Kindle, and then I completely forgot,' he says as if he's genuinely upset.

'Oh, don't worry. It's no big deal,' I say, lying. 'It was only because you'd said you were going to, but really there's no hurry at all. Just read it whenever,' I say casually. Even though I was sceptical at first of giving it to him, now that he has it I'm desperate to know what he thinks.

'I'll read it this week.'

'So what did you do at the weekend?'

I hope my voice didn't sound bitter, as if trying to find out why he was too busy to fit in my book.

'You know, the usual.'

I'm putting spoonfuls of sugar into Mike's coffee and I've lost track. I think I've put in two already, or was that three? I stare blankly into it, before adding half a one, just for luck.

'What's the usual?'

I feel like he knows enough about me, but I barely know anything about him.

'I went to visit my grandparents on Saturday morning to help them with their food shopping. Then I went to the pub to watch the football with my friends, before going round to another friend's for a dinner party. Then yesterday I did the obligatory cover-to-cover read of the papers before I went to the gym. Then I went and had a late Sunday lunch with some other friends.'

He shrugs.

'You know, the usual.'

I think he's just described a weekend fresh out of a Sunday glossy. And there was me thinking that they were the types of weekends men had in adverts and that didn't exist in real life.

I find myself wondering what my life would be like if I had a partner like that. Grown-up dinner parties and reading the papers.

'Not as good as yours, though. I'd much rather have been on a romantic weekend in the country.'

'So have you been single long, then?'

The words tumble out of my mouth before I can stop them, but while I probably wouldn't be so brazen in my line of questioning with my usual work colleagues, especially ones that I don't know so well, it feels like the usual rules don't apply with Robin.

'Not really. A couple of months? I'd actually been with my last girlfriend almost a year. It's not quite as impressive as seven, but it was a pretty long time for me.'

'What happened?'

'She asked me where we were headed. I told her I didn't know and she ended it all.'

'Wow, just like that?'

'Yeah, but she was right to. If we were honest, it wasn't going the way she wanted. I think I always knew I didn't want to marry her. I guess you get to that age where you can't keep plodding along. Not if you want kids and stuff.'

'I guess so,' I say, wondering what the cut-off age is. I try and tell myself that his is a totally different situation to mine. Robin's got to be at least a few years older than me. Plus, I know where Will and I are headed. We're living together. Marriage and kids are on the horizon – it's just that that's where they always stay – never getting closer.

'It's a big risk though, for her, isn't it? What if she never finds the one and ends up alone?'

'Isn't it worse to be with someone just for the sake of it? Besides, Victoria's not hanging around. She's already with some-one else.'

'And you only broke up two months ago? Wow. Fast worker. So you've not got anyone else lined up, then?'

I feel myself twiddling my hair round my finger and I instantly drop the curl I've formed. What the hell am I doing? Am I flirting with him? It's as if sometimes I can't stop my brain from thinking of him as the fit guy from the top rather than an actual person who I know and work with.

'I'm working on it,' he says, opening his mouth as if about to elaborate. Only he doesn't get the chance, as Mike walks in.

'I thought you'd gone to Kenya to pick the coffee beans yourself,' he says grumpily.

I hold out the coffee to him, and try not to snigger as he walks back out with it.

'Blimey, what's with him?' asks Robin.

'Ah, I'm guessing he had to spend Sunday with the mother-in-law. It's a once monthly grump that he gets. Don't worry, he'll be over it by lunchtime.'

'That's good to know as I've got a meeting with him this after-noon. So, I went through that report you gave me. It looks like your arts festival went well this year,' he says, as if drawing a line under the rest of our more personal conversation and snapping back into work mode.

'Thank you.'

I can't help smiling with a bit of pride.

'I'm sure that you'll be hoping that it goes equally well next year.'

'That's the plan,' I say, hoping that after his report I'll still have a job next year. Although the more I get to know Robin, the more I like him, and I can't see how he can be the axe wielder that I've feared he would be.

'Well, I'm sure that it will. You seem to work hard on it.'

'I do.'

He gives me a smile and with that he disappears out of the kitchen.

I stand there for a second hoping that I'm judging him correctly and that when it comes down to it, my job will be safe. I pick up my coffee and follow him back to my desk.

The rest of the day passes in a blur of work while my walking slowly gets back to normal. I no longer look like an extra in a cowboy movie.

I settle down into my armchair, balancing the laptop on my lap, determined I'm going to do another blog. Janet wants us to have put up another post by Wednesday, before we look at social networking and ways that we can drive traffic to it.

'Here you go, honey,' says Will, placing a mug on the coffee table in front of me. He goes and sits down on the sofa and assumes position with remote control in hand.

'Thanks,' I say, hoping he doesn't see my blog post loading. I glance at the mug that looks suspiciously like hot chocolate with marshmallows on top – a lovely surprise.

I feel a tiny bit guilty that I'm going to write another post, especially as we had such a nice time in Swansea. But I keep reminding myself that this isn't really about mine and Will's life, it's about getting published. The fact that I'm hamming it up and embellishing just reinforces the fact that it's essentially fiction.

My blog stats load and I stare in disbelief. I've had eight hundred views of my post. Eight hundred? How did that happen? I didn't tell anyone other than my writing group. So how did people find it?

I bring the post up and I see that I've got comments plural!

I hold my breath with excitement before I realise that the first one is an ad for Viagra. Great. I scan the next one, expecting to find another penis-enhancing drug post, only to see a genuine comment.

Oh my God – I would have killed my boyfriend if he did that. Can't wait to hear how you got him back.

Please, please, tell us what you did to get even????

What an arsehole. Why are you still with him?

I can't help but feel a little proud that people have read something that I've written and that they want me to write more. My cheeks start to flush and I feel the corners of my mouth widen into a big smile.

'Everything OK?' asks Will.

'Oh, yes. Just looking at the photos of Julie's baby on Facebook,' I say, knowing that he'll never ask to see photos of my uni friend's month-old baby.

'Ah,' he says, going back to his programme.

I go back to my blog and see that the little Twitter symbol at the bottom has the number 19 next to it. Nineteen people have shared links to it? I guess some people from my writer's group have shared it.

I almost want to squeal with delight, but I don't want Will to ask me what I'm up to.

I look up and see that he's firmly engrossed in the darts. Since we were away for the weekend, we're off schedule, so he's watching his usual Friday night recorded darts on a Monday. Which I'm not complaining about as it's stopped me from getting sucked into something like *Corrie* when I should be blogging.

Buoyant that I've now got people interested in my blog, I figure that I better get writing the next one. I've got to spread out my tales of revenge over the weeks, I can't just start with the Swansea weekend, so I decide to go back to the very beginning.

I've always been that dutiful girlfriend that doesn't interfere with the sports results. I never let it slip that I know the score of a game when he's watching it on replay or talk over the sports report of the news bulletins. But after my boyfriend's heinous behaviour two weeks ago (you can read all about that here), I deliberately turned up the radio when he told me to turn it off and the Grand Prix results were revealed in all their glory. I don't know what came over my hands, but it was like they were possessed. Well, you can imagine the mood he was in after that. He spent the whole of Sunday like a sulky teenager. As much as I had waves of anger for what he'd done to me, every time he grumped about the results I found myself with a twisted smirk on my face. It was definitely a case of Me 1– Boyfriend 0. And that's only the start of it.

I've started a campaign to well and truly get even. If he acts like that when a score is revealed, imagine how he'll react when a match he's recorded gets deleted or I stop him from going to watch a live game . . .

'What you writing over there?' asks Will. 'There should be steam coming out of that laptop with how fast you're typing.'

I look up in shock, for a second forgetting he was there. He's obviously on an ad break as he's busy fast-forwarding.

'I'm doing a writing assignment for my class,' I say, making sure I keep the laptop turned around so that all he can see from the sofa is the back. I don't want him accidentally catching sight of it.

The only reason I'm in the same room as him while he's watching sport is that I'm hoping that I can channel some of the sporting-widow angst, which is sorely lacking after our lovely weekend.

'I thought you might have been getting stuck into your new novel.'

I told Will about everyone's suggestions to try chick lit on the return journey from Swansea.

'No, I'm still not ready to start it.'

It's not like him to take such an interest in what I'm doing. I don't know if I'm imagining it, but he's been a bit more attentive since we got home yesterday. He kissed me when he got home from work tonight and he even bought home a packet of wine gums – my favourite sweets – as well as making me the hot chocolate.

'So what have you got to do for your assignment?'

'I've got to write a marketing piece,' I say, trying to make it sound dull. I can't tell him I'm blogging as he'll naturally ask what I'm writing about. And I guess I'm not technically lying – it is a form of marketing.

'Oh, well it's great that it seems to be going well.'

Eight hundred people well, I want to shout. But instead all I manage is an 'uh-huh'.

His attention switches away from me as he stops fast-forwarding and goes back to his programme.

I watch Will as he swigs his beer, captivated by the television. I can't help but feel guilty about what I've written. I know he'd never find or read it, but it feels like I'm betraying him by not only writing about our relationship, but by making him sound like a complete arsehole.

I hover my finger over the Post button wondering whether to delete it instead. But then I think about how much he's supported and encouraged me over the last few years with my writing. I'm sure he'd want me to do anything I can to get published. I'm sure if he knew he'd give me the green light. I mean, we all know it's fiction, don't we?

'Have you got much more to do?' asks Will.

'No,' I reply, as I hit Post and shut down the blog. 'How are the darts?'

'I've actually finished watching them.'

'Ooh, do you fancy watching an episode of *Game of Thrones*?'

I figure that my more attentive boyfriend might fancy curling up on the sofa like we did on Saturday night.

'Um, actually the Speedway is just about to start. Can we watch it after?'

'OK,' I say, almost laughing to myself. My boyfriend hasn't changed as a result of my revenge after all, his sporting affliction is still as bad as ever.

18

'I can't believe you went through with it,' says Cara. We drift into the pub and over to the bar. 'If I'm honest, I didn't think you had it in you.'

'I know, me neither. I was so scared he was going to find me out.'

We order our drinks, then settle into our usual table in the back corner.

'So I take it that as he took it so well, you got lucky, then,' she says, sipping her wine.

'Oh, yes. We had sex three times,' I say proudly.

I can't help grinning that we exceeded our monthly quota in one weekend.

'Wow, three times in a row. That's pretty impressive. I've only had one guy that had the stamina to keep on going that many times; I nicknamed him the Duracell bunny, and not because he went on and on, he also did this thing that was just like a rampant –'

'Ah, brain bleed! TMI! And I don't mean three times in a row, I mean over the weekend. Friday night, Saturday morning, then Saturday night. It was like it was one of our birthdays.'

'Surely that's what every weekend is supposed to be like? I thought the whole point of having a long-term partner was that you had sex on tap.'

'It is. That and you're not expected to shave your legs all the time.'

Cara rolls her eyes at me.

'But I did for this weekend, as we were going away.'

'Hmm, maybe there's actually a correlation between that and the multiple orgasms.'

Perhaps she has a point . . . Maybe it's not that we're in a relationship rut but rather it's the state of my hairy pins.

'So when are you going to have it out with him, then?'

I look at my fingernails and pretend I haven't heard her.

'You are going to have it out with him now, aren't you? I mean, you've done your little revenge, you've made him miss the football game. Surely that's enough?'

I shrug my shoulders and sigh.

When I got back I hadn't wanted to ruin the magic of the weekend away. We'd had one of those weekends we'll look back on and treasure. A big fight would only have spoilt it.

'It should be. But it was like we were in that giddy honeymoon stage where we couldn't get enough of each other and when we listened intently to what was being said. It showed me what our relationship could be like with a few little tweaks – it would be the perfect relationship.'

'But no relationship is ever perfect, is it? And I don't think carrying out acts of revenge behind his back are little tweaks.'

'Well, no. I guess not.'

'So, that's it, then. You're just going to draw a line under it and be done with it?'

I know I have to have it out with Will eventually. It's too big a secret for our relationship to bear. Not to mention if he thinks he got away with it, he might be tempted to do it again.

'No, I will talk to Will. I'm just not ready yet. I guess I can't help thinking that Swansea wasn't enough. I thought it would lessen my anger for what he did, but it still hurts.'

'You're going to get more revenge?' she says, sucking in breath as if it's the worst thing I've ever said.

'Yes, no, maybe. I haven't really given it much thought, but I don't feel like I've got even yet.'

'And this is nothing to do with the fact that people are reading your blog?'

I shake my head. Although it maybe should have. I've now had over a thousand reads of my latest post, and my readers are still baying for blood. I'm still yet to write about Swansea, and I can't help thinking people will think it's an anti-climax if that's the last one – as he seemed to take missing the football so well.

'Or your new chick lit book?'

'Ha, no. I still haven't worked out what that should be about.'

'Well, the offer is still there of inspiration from my single life,' she says.

'Ah, speaking of that. Seen anything of Dave the usher, have you?'

She picks up her wine and takes a large gulp. 'I might have done.'

She might be acting coy but I get the impression there's a bit more to this than she's letting on.

'Have you heard from Vanessa?' she asks.

It's not like her to be so silent about her love life. She's usually pretty vocal in telling me about her latest conquests and exploits (despite my protests). And now she's actively changing the subject. Either she's having normal-person sex (and therefore she thinks there's nothing to tell) or she might actually like Dave the usher.

'I have,' I say playing along and dropping the Dave subject. She'll tell me when she's ready. 'She sent me a WhatsApp message before they got on the plane. She said they had a lovely time and that she's looking forward to seeing us on Saturday night.'

'Oh yes, girls' night out,' says Cara, rubbing her hands together in excitement. 'We haven't been out for ages.'

'Ah, well, she wondered if we could have a night in and go out next week instead. Something about expecting to be jet-lagged.'

'Didn't she go to South Africa?' says Cara, wrinkling her brow in confusion. 'Isn't that pretty much in the same time zone?'

'Oh, yeah. Well, you know Vanessa, she probably just means she'll be tired out from the flight or the holiday.'

'Yeah, I imagine honeymoons are exhausting – all that shagging.'

Now it's my turn to roll my eyes at Cara.

'But a night in is fine. Do you want to do it at yours?' she asks. 'It's just, my place is a bit small.'

I want to point out that that's never stopped us going round there before, which just makes me ever more curious about her and Dave's new relationship. Maybe him and his slippers have moved in permanently.

'Of course. I'll check with Will, but I can't imagine it will be a problem.'

I wonder if Vanessa will know anything about Cara and Dave; after all, he was an usher so he's obviously a good friend of Ian's. Cara might be keeping quiet about it, but that doesn't mean to say Dave will be.

'That's a date, then – and quite frankly, with the week I'm having at work, it can't come quick enough,' she says, groaning.

'Why, what's happening?'

'Well, bitch Belinda –'

'Wait,' I interrupt. 'Bitch Belinda? Has Boring Belinda had an upgrade in nickname?'

'Uh-huh. We've been presenting our recent findings to the board and she's been taking credit for everything I've done. I know we're all working as a team and I don't mind *sharing* the credit, but I do mind her sounding like she's single-handedly responsible for everything. It's always the quiet ones you've got to watch,' she says, furrowing her brow.

'Sounds like you should have it out with her. You know, talk to her about it,' I say, parroting back the advice she gave me about Will.

'Or, I could just not say anything and bide my time until I can get my revenge.'

She pulls a face as if she knows what game I'm playing.

'Touché. But seriously, you need to do something, don't you?'

'Yes, probably. I'll just have to make sure next time we meet with the board I get in first and that I'm a lot more vocal about my contributions to the project.'

Our jobs may be like chalk and cheese, but we have funding challenges and fear of budget cuts in common.

'But the good thing is they've approved the use of the new protein in the trials, so they can go ahead.'

'Yay,' I say, in encouragement. I don't really have a clue what that means but she seems excited about it.

My phone beeps and I pick it up to glance at it, before seeing it's a message from my mother.

Lexi, Would you and Will like to come over for Sunday lunch before you go to Barbados? Mum x x

I love the way my mother writes her text messages like proper letters with our names top and tailing it, as if I wouldn't know who they were to or from.

My heart sinks at the thought of a roast. I always have to psyche myself up before I go. They're ridiculously formal affairs. We have to sit in the draughty dining room that's neglected the rest of the week, use the finest china and we're all required to wear our Sunday best. Just the thought of it is exhausting.

We should probably make the effort, since we haven't seen them since my dad's birthday. We've got two free Sundays before our holiday, so I'll let Will decide which one we should pick to see them.

'Everything OK?' asks Cara.

'Oh yes,' I say, texting my mother back. 'Just my mum. Sunday lunch plans.'

'Oh, fun,' says Cara, raising her eyebrows.

Over the years she's been dragged to a couple of our lunches and she knows what I'll be in for.

'Aren't they always?' I say, trying to laugh.

'It's a good thing that we're staying in on Saturday. At least you won't be as hung-over as if we went on a big night out.'

'That's true,' I say, shuddering. Hangovers and my mother really make for a bad day. Perhaps I'll strongly suggest Will picks this week. 'Speaking of Saturday night. Don't forget that you can't mention to Vanessa about Will going to the football instead of her wedding.'

'What? You're not going to tell her.'

'I can't. She'll be so cross and she'll have it out with him.'

'Isn't that more of a reason why you should tell him you know? Now you're keeping secrets from Will and your best friend.'

'I know, but it would really hurt her if she knew the truth. It's not my wedding he missed, is it – it's hers. That's such a personal insult.'

Cara sighs, she clearly doesn't agree.

'I'd much rather just not tell her about it, or the revenge.'

'Oh God, more secrets. So let me get this straight, can I mention Swansea?'

'Yes, as long as you don't mention the scheming bits.'

Cara shakes her head.

'This is all going to come back and bite you in the arse, and when it does, don't forget that I told you it would.'

I know she's right, but at the moment I'm just grateful she's agreed to keep her silence around Vanessa.

'Speaking of biting on the arse,' says Cara. 'Have I told you about the tip that someone left on my latest blog.'

I instantly try and tune out her voice; I'm pretty sure I'm not going to want to hear it. Instead I try and think about what I'm going to do about the Will situation. Just thinking about Vanessa's return brings the betrayal back to me, and I've got to remember that it's not just me he did this to, it was her, too.

While I'm sure Cara's right that I probably should confront him, I'm more convinced than ever that I need to do more to get my own back first. And you never know, whatever I do next might just have the same wonderful effect on our relationship as Swansea. Now that wouldn't be too bad, would it?

19

'I don't understand why you can't go over to Aaron's or Tom's to watch the fight,' I say, groaning, as Will gets ready to go and meet his friends in the pub.

Tonight is one of those nights where I really wish I had an under-the-thumb boyfriend that I could exert some control over. Instead I've got one who I only seem to be able to influence if I'm conducting revenge.

'Because Aaron's wife is pregnant and he says she's a hormonal nightmare that goes to bed as soon as it gets dark and Aaron doesn't want to wake her, and Tom's not got a sports package at the moment.'

What lucky women. One's not only got a ring but is also preggers, which gives her the ultimate upper hand, and the other is living the dream – no Sky Sports.

With neither a bun in the oven, nor time to cancel Sky Sports for tonight, I've got no legitimate reason that I can think of to stop him from having his mates over to watch a boxing match in the middle of the night. Apparently my sleep and sanity aren't good enough reasons. I've tried those before and was presented with earplugs.

All I'm thankful for is that it's not a weekly occurrence – and they're at least drinking in the pub first. Which might make it rowdier later on, but at least I won't be subjected to the testoster-one-fuelled pre-match banter in the run-up.

'I don't know why you're so bothered anyway. The girls will be long gone by midnight.'

'You don't know that; maybe we'll still be dancing and drink-ing margaritas.'

That's such a lie. I can't remember the last time the girls stayed round past eleven thirty. Ever since our clubbing days ended, we don't have the ability to stay out later than pub closing, no matter where we are.

'Please,' he says, slapping me playfully on the bum before giving me a kiss. 'When we get home I can guarantee you'll be tucked up in bed drinking Horlicks.'

Damn him, he knows me so well.

'Look, I promise we'll be quiet when we come in and you'll barely know we're here.'

I scoff, those boys sound like they're bulls in a china shop after a trip to the pub.

'We will,' he says.

I go and sit down on the sofa and pick up my drink and he bends down and kisses me on the cheek before he goes to leave. 'Have fun with the girls.'

He opens the door and bangs straight into Vanessa, who was about to ring the bell.

'Oh, hello,' she says.

'Hi,' he replies, looking like he's got the fright of his life.

Vanessa stares at him as if she doesn't know what to say and it takes me a second to figure out the root of the awkwardness: this is the first time they've seen each other since he missed her wedding. She seemed so relaxed about his absence on her big day, but now that the champagne's worn off, I wonder if she's angry. Imagine if she knew the real reason he hadn't come.

'Will, aren't you going to say how sorry you were for missing Vanessa's wedding?'

'Oh, um, yes of course. I'm so sorry. The food poisoning was just . . . dreadful.'

'Couldn't be helped,' she says, patting him a little awkwardly on the arm, giving me the impression she doesn't mean it. 'Hey, Lexi. Are you all right?' she says as she walks over to me. I realise that I've sucked my cheeks in like they're being pulled by a super-strong vacuum cleaner.

Seeing Will lie to Vanessa's face, without looking the tiniest bit shifty or guilty, has brought back my anger with a jolt.

He waves us goodbye and I manage to raise my hand, which is impressive as only my middle finger wanted to go up.

'So what have I missed while I've been away?' says Vanessa, settling herself into the sofa.

'Oh, not a lot. Will and I had a nice weekend in Swansea last week. We went hiking and drank lots of wine.'

I'm suddenly not in the mood to dwell on our nice trip away while this anger at him is flowing round my veins.

'And my work audit is in full swing with Robin, aka the fit guy from the top.'

'Oh, that sounds interesting. You can tell me more about that later,' she says.

I pick up the jug of margaritas I've made and go to pour Vanessa a glass.

'Not for me, thanks,' she says, holding her hand over it.

'Oh, did you drive over?'

'Yes, as I'm not drinking at the moment.'

'Oh, my God. You're not pregnant already, are you?'

I knew the plan was that she was going to start trying after the wedding – talk about honeymoon baby.

'No, not yet. But soon, hopefully. Do you know how much of a difference alcohol makes to your fertility?'

I top my glass up to the brim as luckily that's not something I need to worry about yet.

'No, I didn't realise.'

'Oh yes. So both Ian and I are dry for the foreseeable future.'

'Wow, that's dedication.'

I wonder if Will would give up his beer if it was us.

'Oh, yes. We're taking it very seriously. I've been taking my temperature and tracking my cycle, so that hopefully next month we'll be able to focus our efforts when we really know I'm ovulating.'

I almost choke on my margarita. Do people share that kind of information? I'm thinking that she's spent too much time over the years with Cara, whose oversharing has rubbed off on her.

'That's, um, great. Good luck,' I say, holding my crossed fingers up in support.

'Thanks. I know we've only been trying a couple of weeks, but really I had no idea there was so much to it.'

I'm hoping Cara will arrive pretty soon and rescue me from this conversation.

'So the wedding . . .' I say, as a way to change the subject.

'Oh, it was honestly the best day of my life.' She breaks out into a smile that is set off by her skin, which is glowing from her holiday. 'It was perfect. Wasn't it perfect?'

'It was.'

'If I had to do the whole day again, I wouldn't change a single thing.'

I don't know why I thought this was a better choice of topic. It's just serving to make me remember the moment I got that text from Mike and found out my boyfriend's awful little secret.

My doorbell rings and I scramble up to get the door, relieved for the distraction from wedding talk.

'Hi Cara,' I say, opening the door and dragging her in.

'Hiya. Hi Vanessa.'

She gives us each a quick hug before immediately picking up the empty glass and filling it up from the pitcher, kicking off her high heels and sinking into the sofa.

'Sorry I'm late,' she says, sipping her drink.

I stare at her – her cheeks are flushed and she's glowing a little. I could guess who and what had made her late.

'Have trouble leaving the house, did we?' I say, raising my glass at her in a silent toast.

'I was looking for my shoes,' she said.

'Ah, under the covers, were they?'

Now usually I wouldn't have to push Cara into telling us about her bedroom activities, but for once she's keeping shtum.

'What's going on?' asks Vanessa, raising an eyebrow.

'Nothing,' says Cara, 'Lexi's just referring to one of my stories for writing group. Aren't you?'

'Yes,' I say, curious. I would have thought that Vanessa would have been all over this information. It must mean that Ian is none the wiser, as I can't imagine he'd keep it a secret from her.

Vanessa bends down into her bag and Cara puts her fingers to her lips, giving me a look. A small smile unfolds over my lips as I nod in understanding. It looks like I'm not the only one keeping a secret from Vanessa.

'So Lexi and I were just talking about the wedding,' says Vanessa. 'Did you enjoy it?'

'I certainly did,' says Cara.

'Good, good. So you didn't manage to get your claws into my cousin Max, did you?'

'Unfortunately not. He said he has a girlfriend.'

'Yeah, he does – Louisa, and she is *so* boring. I would have loved it if you'd started dating him and been there for Ian's big family Christmas shindig.'

'Sorry to disappoint,' says Cara.

'Oh well. Let's just hope his stepbrother Dave's new girlfriend is more interesting.'

'Stepbrother,' I say, spluttering margarita everywhere. Trust me to be taking a drink when that nugget of information came out.

Vanessa laughs. 'Ian hates me calling Dave that, but it's true. His mum married his mate Dave's dad a few years ago so they're technically stepbrothers.'

I try to look at Cara, who has gone pale. I wonder if she knew the family tree before.

'I don't know why Ian hates it so much. Do you remember when we used to wish that our parents would get divorced so that my mum would run off with your dad?' she says, looking at me.

I giggle as the memory comes flooding back.

'I do,' I say laughing. 'God, didn't we get that from one of the *Sweet Valley High* books?'

'That or the *Baby-sitters Club*.'

'God you two were weird. I'm glad I wasn't your friend then.'

I met Vanessa on my first day of junior school and she became my best friend shortly after she showed me where the toilet was. Cara joined our merry gang when she transferred into our senior school in year nine.

'You were missing out,' I say, shaking my head.

'Hmm, but if your dad married Ness's mum, then that would have meant that my dad would have had to marry your mum,' she says, laughing.

'Why do you think I picked her dad,' says Vanessa, joining in.

'Oi! She's not that bad.'

I know she probably is that bad, but I've got to at least pretend to defend her.

Cara looks down at her empty glass and goes to refill it from the pitcher.

'Not for me, thank you,' says Vanessa, clamping her hand over the empty glass in front of her as Cara goes to fill it up.

'You not drinking?'

'No, I'm going dry while Ian and I try for a baby. Did you know how much of a difference alcohol can make to your fertility levels?'

'I'll go make you a cup of tea instead, shall I?' I say, standing up and hoping for some respite in the kitchen from the oncoming fertility lecture.

'No tea for me. I'm trying to cut out caffeine. A glass of water will be fine.'

'OK,' I call over my shoulder.

I walk into the kitchen and exhale deeply. Dave and Ian are stepbrothers – what a revelation. Now if Cara got married to Dave, would that make her and Vanessa stepsisters-in-law? Oh, how I wish I could get that thought out in the open.

I fill up a glass of water from the tap, and take a deep breath before I go back in to try and get the secrets straight in my head.

I go to fill up my drink with the new pitcher of margarita, and it slops messily on to the coffee table. My hand–eye coordination isn't great at the best of times, but this is the third pitcher we've made and with only me and Cara drinking, even with my buzzed brain, I can work out that means I've drunk far too much.

'So did Will see Vanessa when she arrived?' whispers Cara, as Vanessa heads upstairs to the loo.

'He did, and there wasn't even a smidgen of remorse in his voice about what he'd done when he talked about his bloody food poisoning.'

My nostrils are flaring and my eyes must look wild. I haven't been this drunk since the wedding, and it's as if the emotions I felt when I received that text message are flooding back.

'What I don't get,' says Cara, refilling her drink, 'is how he took missing the Swansea game so well, yet he wouldn't miss the match for Vanessa's wedding.'

'I know. I don't understand that either. To go through all that lying about his stomach just so he could sneak off to watch an ordinary game.'

I'm about to ponder it more before I wonder what the hell we're doing. Vanessa is out of the room, and we're talking about Will, when we really should be talking about Dave.

'So, I worked out that if you and Dave get married that you'll be Vanessa's stepsister-in-law.'

'How many of those drinks have you had? I don't think that's even a real term,' she says a little snappily.

'Isn't it? Wait, that's the point you're focusing on? Not the fact that I said if you *married* Dave. Hmm, interesting.'

I start humming the bridal march, and I guess in my drunk state I hadn't noticed Vanessa walking back in.

'What's going on here?' she asks, studying the scene of me humming and Cara looking like she's going to lump me one.

'Oh, you know. We were just talking about our favourite thing about weddings, and mine is that moment when the bride walks up the aisle and everyone looks adoringly at her,' I say, lying.

Vanessa looks like she's lost reliving the moment. Which is a good job too, as normally she'd have smelt a rat. Cara is about as allergic to wedding daydreaming as I am to using the gym, and with my situation with Will, it's a topic I barely discuss.

'My favourite bit about weddings,' says Vanessa, totally joining in our made-up game, 'is when you cut the cake and you have those little kisses when your mouth's full. Delicious. Or maybe it's when you say "I do", and the ring's slipped on your finger. Or the first dance. Or . . .'

I think we broke her. She's now standing in the middle of the lounge sobbing.

'Ness,' I say, putting my arm round her and pulling her down on to the sofa. 'What's wrong?'

'Nothing,' she says, dabbing at her eyes and trying to fan away her tears by waving her hand in front of them. It doesn't work and her mascara starts to run. 'It's just I've started taking these extra hormones, you know for the fertility, and they make me super-emotional. Right then I could feel myself back at the wedding and I got so overwhelmed.'

'And breathe,' says Cara, patting her knee. 'Let's talk about something else, shall we?'

She's saying it to Vanessa, but I know it's aimed at me.

'Fine,' I say, jumping up.

'Let's talk about your time in Swansea,' says Vanessa. 'I want to hear about that.'

'Oh, you don't really. We'd much rather hear about South Africa again instead,' I say.

Cara gives me a look of death. We've already had to watch a slideshow of over two hundred photos from the honeymoon. Will had me believe you could only cast sports matches from your mobile to our TV, but Vanessa managed to show us her whole honeymoon album in full widescreen glory. The only thing that made it mildly amusing was she'd accidentally left a few photos from the honeymoon suite in there. Let's just say we now have a very intimate knowledge of Ian, thanks to the millions of pixels on our telly that show everything in crystal-clear high definition. It brought the slideshow to an abrupt end.

'No, I think it would help to talk about something else,' she says between sobs.

'OK,' I say, sighing. 'So we went to this little cosy cottage and it had a log fire . . .'

'Stop! No, that's not doing it either,' she says. 'Too romantic.'

I'm relieved. I wrote the blog about my Swansea revenge today, and my mind is so fresh from retelling it that way, that in my drunken state I'd be bound to let something slip.

'So, Cara, I'm counting on you to tell me something from one of your latest conquests that will knock me off this romance cloud.'

'Um,' she says, struggling.

I can't believe she's been given the carte blanche to discuss her sex life and she's stumped. What is Dave doing to this girl?

'What about one of your blogs?' I say, prompting her.

'You're blogging now?' asks Vanessa.

'Yes,' says Cara. 'We both are. It's a project for our writing group.'

'And let me guess, you're writing about your sex life?'

'Uh-huh,' she says proudly. 'It's called Spanking in the City.'

Vanessa chokes on her water and mock rolls her eyes, before turning to me. 'So, what are you writing about?'

Oh crap.

'Um.'

'How she's a sporting widow,' says Cara quickly. 'You know, what she puts up with, how she copes.'

'It's a bit dull,' I say.

'But fun to write, I guess,' says Vanessa.

Despite how uncomfortable I am with the conversation, at least Vanessa's stopped blubbering. I stand back up and go and recover my glass of margarita from over on the sideboard and a couple of drops splosh out.

'Careful,' says Vanessa. 'You don't want to get your Sky box wet, you'd break it.'

'Couldn't have that when Will's coming back to watch the boxing,' I say, slurring slightly.

'Oh, could you imagine,' says Vanessa. 'Ian would hear the screams from our house.'

'Hmm, I better be careful,' I say, waving my glass around as if pretending I'm going to throw it over the box.

'Be careful, Lexi, that's a pretty serious thing to be joking about,' says Cara, arching her eyebrows to the sky as if trying to warn me.

She needs to relax, I think to myself as I place my glass down next to the box. It's not like I'm going to knock my glass over on purpose. I might want to get even with Will, but frying the Sky box isn't going to do that. After all, I can't imagine it would be cheap to replace.

No, Cara has nothing to worry about. I'm just going to pick my glass up calmly and . . . Oh shit!

I must have grabbed the stem of the glass too forcefully and the liquid seems to leap out in the direction of the satellite box. I lunge to try to stop it, and in doing so knock the whole glass of green margarita all over it.

It all happens in slow motion, but what feels like minutes is probably in reality only seconds as the liquid engulfs the box.

'Lexi!' shouts Cara in disgust.

'It was an accident.'

I try and protest but she gives me a scolding stare. She thinks I did it on purpose, and gives me a look that says you've gone too far. I'm in a sort of shock which is leading me to laugh out loud with a full-on manic cackle.

I might not have intended it to happen this way, but it looks like I'm one step closer to getting even.

20

I probably should have stopped drinking around the time I knocked my glass of margarita over the Sky box. Or looking back, I possibly should have stopped drinking long before that and then I might not have knocked said drink over. Either way, I didn't and I'm still doing my best to get through the pitcher.

'Are you sure you don't mind if I leave?' asks Vanessa as she slips her shoes on and picks up her coat.

'No, you go,' I say waving her off. Who knows what's going to happen when Will comes back from the pub, and should tempers flare, I'm not sure if I'll be able to keep my secret in any longer. 'I'll call you in the week.'

'OK, good luck, hun,' she says, giving me a hug as she leaves. 'Did you want a lift, Cara?'

'I think I'll stay for a bit, thanks.'

They hug goodbye and then Vanessa leaves.

As soon as the door closes, Cara gives me a look.

'It was an accident, I swear,' I say holding my hands up.

'Really? An accident? Convenient that when you're looking for ways to stop him watching sport, you suddenly ruin the box when he's got his friends coming over to watch the boxing.'

I close my eyes and wish I could turn back time.

'I really didn't plan it,' I say in as heartfelt a way as I can. I hold Cara's gaze and I think she realises that I'm telling the truth. 'Perhaps we should hide it,' I say, panicking.

'And that would be less suspicious? No, I think you should tell him the truth – if it really was an accident. He's got no reason to suspect otherwise, it's not like he knows about your plans for revenge.'

I go over to the Sky box and press a new tea towel on to it.

'Is it looking any better?' asks Cara.

'No, it's pretty wet.'

I'm wondering whether I really should have just legged it upstairs and pretended to have been asleep when the boys came back. I wonder if there's still time, but in answer to my question the front door opens noisily.

I freeze like a rabbit in headlights. I've got nowhere to run.

The boys are mid-conversation, arguing over who's the player of the season so far, when Will suddenly spots us standing guiltily over the Sky box.

'Oh, I didn't think you guys would still be up. Hey, Cara.'

'Hi, Will,' she says a little sheepishly. 'I'm going to leave shortly.'

She gives me a reassuring look as if to let me know that she's not going to abandon me in my hour of need. It's times like these when you know who's a true friend.

'No, hurry, you're welcome to stay and watch the boxing,' he says smilingly.

'Um,' I say, wondering just how I'm going to broach this topic. But it looks like I don't need to as Will is clearly more sober than

I am and he's looking down in horror at the tea towel I'm dabbing the Sky box with.

'What's going on? What are you doing?'

He comes over to examine the situation and I see his eyes nearly pop out of his skull.

'I had a little accident with my drink.'

He looks over at the box and gasps in horror.

'It's soaking. Oh God, how long's it been like this?'

'I don't know, half an hour or so; I've been trying to drain it out,' I say pointing to the sopping wet tea towel underneath it.'

He practically barges me out of the way and removes the leads quickly before cradling it and holding it tight like a newborn baby before he balances it on the radiator.

'Mate, have you got an airing cupboard?' says Tom. His face is showing the seriousness of the situation.

'No,' he says, shaking his head.

The three men stand over it like doctors examining a patient, and I know from their looks and the shakes of their heads that the prognosis is not good.

'Oh God, Lex, what have you done?'

He looks down at the box with such fondness and the same look he'd given me all last weekend on our trip away. I'm glad to know that in the ranked list of important things in his life, I seem to be roughly equal to a satellite box.

'I didn't mean to. It was an accident,' I say, shrugging and slurring, accidentally showing him quite how drunk I am.

'How are we going to fix this?' says Will, his voice a bit squeakier than usual as the panic starts to set in. 'The fight starts in half an hour. We're never going to get it dry in time.'

'We could put it in rice,' I say quickly. 'You know, like you do with a mobile.'

'Um, do you have a bag of rice big enough?' says Aaron, laughing.

I think about the tiny boil-in-the-bag sachets I have in the cupboard; they'd barely cover the base of it.

'We could go to the Asian supermarket down the road – they have those massive bags . . .'

Will rolls his eyes at me. 'Even if they were open at eleven, which they're not, a Sky box is not the same as a phone. It's got holes in it for starters, so the rice would get in.'

That told me, then.

'Of all the bloody nights,' says Will, holding his hand above the box to see if heat is radiating above it. 'Are you sure we can't go to yours, Aaron? Won't Becky be asleep now? Will she even notice we're there?'

'Oh, she'll know all right. Our flat practically has cardboard walls. Look, it's more than my life's worth taking you back there. Maybe you could come over tomorrow in the day when it's repeated?'

Will gives him the same look he gave me when I suggested he watch the Grand Prix when he knew the results.

'Well, the offer's there,' he says.

'Looks like we're not destined to watch the boxing,' says Tom, sensing the tension that's palpable in the air. 'I might just call a taxi.'

'I'll share it with you,' says Cara, who looks grateful for some sort of reprieve.

She mouths a sorry to me that she's going, but I don't blame her. I just wish I could too.

'Yeah, and I might just head home as well,' says Aaron.

Is it just me or do the other boys not seem that bothered about missing the boxing? Why are they acting like sane normal people when Will is acting like the Four Horsemen of the Apocalypse have just knocked on the door?

'There has to be something we can do,' says Will desperately as Tom pulls out his phone and rings a cab company. 'I've paid for the fight already. That's twenty quid down the drain.'

'I think that's the least of your worries. Sky boxes aren't cheap to replace,' says Aaron.

'I reckon it might just be covered on the house insurance. But I bet we won't be able to get an engineer out to fit a new one for ages. Which means I'm going to miss the Grand Prix *again* tomorrow,' he says, the rage audible in his voice. I'm pleased to see his nostrils are flaring in the same way mine were earlier when recounting his lack of remorse. 'That's the second bloody one this season that I'll have missed now.'

There are almost tears in my boyfriend's eyes. It's ironic that he's so upset over this, when I'd not actually planned it as revenge.

'And what about all my saved matches?'

Oh no, what have I done? Of course I don't give two hoots over his saved games, but what about all my saved programmes? I've still got half a series of *The Good Wife* to catch up on and tonight's *Strictly Come Dancing*. Now it's me that's nearly crying.

'The cab's going to be here any minute,' says Tom to Cara.

'Right, well I'm going to get going. Might earn some brownie points with the misses if I get home early.'

Will barely notices as his friend pats him on the back and slips out the door. He's too busy focusing his bulging eyes on his beloved box.

'Do you fancy waiting outside,' whispers Cara to Tom.

'Yeah, good idea.'

Cara gives me a warm hug and tells me to call her if I need her.

I nod my head, knowing that this is only going to get worse when they've left.

The door slams behind them and I'm wondering what I should do.

I don't really want to hold a vigil over the box all night, which is exactly what I think Will's got planned. Especially with all those margaritas sitting on my belly that are suddenly churning around. I desperately need to lie down and sleep it off.

'I'm really sorry, Will,' I say, going up and slipping my arms around his waist.

He sighs loudly.

Hmm. I get the feeling that this time a hug definitely isn't going to cut it. I can only think of one thing that would possibly distract him. As I contemplate dropping to my knees to give it a go, my stomach starts to churn quicker than a washing machine on a spin cycle. Controlling a gag reflex at the best of times is never easy, let alone after three pitchers of margaritas.

I'm just going to have to go to bed and leave my heartbroken boyfriend here with his apparent true love.

'We'll get an engineer out as soon as we can,' I say. 'I'm sure we could pay extra to get them out in a hurry.'

This is turning out to be an expensive accident. One to remember for any future revenge: prior research and planning are needed.

'Is there anything else you need me to do before I go to bed?'

Will shakes his head.

'No, you've done enough,' he says, scowling.

I might not have intended it to be revenge, but it seems to have turned out that way. Yet unlike my weekend away, I'm not left with any warm and fuzzy feelings.

21

This morning I've woken up with a huge sense of guilt and regret and it takes me a couple of seconds to backtrack through last night to remember why. Images of Cara and Vanessa pop into my mind, followed by the pitchers of margaritas. And, uh-oh – it hits me like a thunderbolt – the Sky box incident.

I can't even revel in the accidental revenge as I'm mourning the loss of the latest season of *Grey's Anatomy* that I hadn't caught up with.

I wait for the feeling of sickness, the bedroom spin or the pounding of drums to start. After the quantity of alcohol I drank last night it's inevitable that I'm going to feel like crap for the whole of today, if not the whole of tomorrow, too, given my hangovers of late.

I sit up slowly, cherishing what could be my last few minutes of being pain free, only to realise once I'm upright that I still feel all right.

Will had selected to go to my parents next weekend, thinking he'd be tired after watching last night's fight and would rather chill out on the sofa watching the Grand Prix and the footie. Now, with the satellite box ruined, his plans are also ruined and it means I can still salvage the day. If it was up to me how would we spend the perfect Sunday? I can't help but think of Robin. I can feel myself blushing a little as I imagine him padding downstairs in pyjama bottoms and no top (in my imagination he has a six-pack too). He walks into his kitchen and makes coffee from a fancy machine, before retiring back to bed with a tray of Sunday paper, coffee and croissants.

What I wouldn't give to have a morning like that.

But what's to stop me? Will's still sound asleep and snoring so it looks like I've got time to pull it off.

I get out of bed and realise that I don't feel too bad. I dress quickly, before my hangover has time to catch up, and decide there's no point showering if I'm off back to bed.

I quietly go downstairs and make a cafetière of coffee, letting it percolate while I go in search of the other ingredients. After finding my handbag, I slip out of the house to complete my mission.

I get back from the local shop ten minutes later, armed with fresh croissants and a selection of Sunday papers. I plunge the coffee, pour two cups and place everything on a tray before heading upstairs.

I'm beaming with pride when I walk into the bedroom.

'What's all this, then?' asks Will, rubbing his eyes. He sits up and readjusts his pillow behind his back, before propping mine up for me. 'Let me take that. Wouldn't want you spilling it all over me and the bed.'

He's holding his hands out and giving me a small smile.

I know I'm probably not forgiven yet after last night, but at least he's talking to me, which is progress.

'Peace offering,' I say, handing him the tray.

He looks down at the contents and nods his head in approval.

'Fresh croissants, and jam in a ramekin rather than the jar. You have made an effort.'

I shrug my shoulders, as if it was no big deal. Which in reality it wasn't. I should so do this more often. Who knows, this could be the start of our leisurely Sunday mornings in bed.

Will tucks straight into a croissant and I can't help but wince as the crumbs start to scatter over our white bedding.

I pick one up for myself, and hold a plate directly under my mouth to catch any flaky bits. It's not quite the relaxing care free experience I thought it would be.

'Great, the *Sunday Times*,' says Will, pulling out the paper. He starts to dissect it. 'What bit do you want? News, Travel, the Culture, the magazine?'

'Um, I'll go for the news first.'

Usually I'd pick the Culture, but today, as we're doing the grown-up coffee and papers in bed, I'll start with what I think a grown-up would.

He hands me the main section of the news before selecting the Sport for himself. No surprises there then.

He opens it up and starts reading.

We flick through in silence for a bit, before something leaps out at me.

'Oh, this is interesting,' I say, scan-reading a piece on fossils. 'It says here scientists have discovered a new dragon-like fossil in China.'

I look up at Will to share with him this amazing nugget of information, but he's not listening to me. He's engrossed in an article. How could he not be as excited as I am that they've found evidence of a real dragon.

I sigh, which again he doesn't notice, and then he practically hits me in the face as he opens his section up to full size.

I open mine up wider and we start to jostle for space to read. In the end he pulls his paper up like a defensive wall around him.

This is not what I had envisaged. In my head I'd imagined that we'd sit with a paper between us, picking out stories to read and discussing them while sipping our coffee. It would be a bit like the paper review on a news channel, only more cuddles and maybe a bit of nooky.

A hand appears from under the blanket and he retrieves another croissant from the plate on the bed. I can just see crumbs flying from underneath the bottom of his paper.

I try and turn my attention back to the news, but as I flick through it, it all seems so depressing and I've read most of the stories on my phone in the week anyway.

After ten minutes I've had enough. I wonder if I should try and initiate a bit of sexy time, but one look at the covers littered with crumbs and I'm freaked out by the mess.

'I'm going to have a bath,' I say loudly as I get off the bed. I turn and look at Will and he doesn't even acknowledge that I'm going.

Well, that didn't really pan out as I'd hoped. It wasn't quite the scene that Robin painted.

All I can hope is that when I get out of my bath, Will is finished with the sports pages and then I'll seize the day back into my control. It really was a rookie mistake on my part – I should have thrown the sports section out before I got home.

By the time the water has gone cold and I finally put my book down and drag myself out of the bath, Will's disappeared from the bedroom.

This is my window, I think to myself as I quickly get dressed and head downstairs.

I'm excitedly thinking about what we can do next when I hear shouting coming from the lounge. It's getting louder and more intense the closer I get.

'Take that,' shouts Will, before there's a large bang.

I'm wondering if he's smashing up the remnants of the satellite box as I hurry to see what's going on.

'What the –' I say as I walk in.

Will's sat on the poof in the middle of the room clutching a games controller.

This is not boding well for my romantic Sunday.

'What you doing?' I ask, despite the fact it's pretty obvious.

He pauses the game and looks up at me.

'I was reading the paper and they had a reference to an old FIFA game, and it made me want to get mine out and play it. Seeing as I can't watch actual sport.'

'Where was that thing?'

I didn't even know Will had it in the house. I remember him playing one when we first met and he lived in a shared house, but I didn't know he owned it.

Oh God, I can see my future. I'm sat on the sofa alone while my boyfriend is on the floor in one of those weird half-chairs, shouting orders to his friends through his headset. All I'll be good for is going to get him a beer or two out of the fridge.

I look round the room for the margarita glass. It worked once, right?

'Are you going to be playing this all day?' I say, wondering if I'll be able to prise him away from it.

'I was going to watch the Grand Prix, but you know, what with the box being fried . . .' he says, giving me a stare which lets me know that I am still firmly in the doghouse.

He un-pauses the game and starts moving his men around on the pitch. The sound of a crowd roars in the background and he's back to muttering and shouting at the screen. To be honest, it's the same soundtrack as if he was watching a game.

'I was thinking, perhaps we could go for a walk this afternoon and maybe go for a pub roast? Or out for brunch?'

Isn't that the thing that people do now?

He looks between me and the game, as if he's weighing up the options.

'OK,' he says quickly. 'But I'll just finish this season first.'

I look up at him in surprise. I can't quite believe that he agreed so easily.

'Great,' I say, turning and hurrying out towards the kitchen before he can change his mind.

Perhaps sacrificing *Grey's Anatomy* was a small price to pay to get some quality time together.

It turns out the season takes a little longer than expected. We missed brunch, and are now trying to find somewhere still serving a roast at two. I'm trying not to let my anger spoil the rest of the afternoon we're about to have. I'm determined that we're still going to have our roast, and go for our walk – the fat lady ain't singing yet.

'How about here?' asks Will.

I look up at the Swan before looking both ways down the high street, as if hoping to see another option. But I know that we've already exhausted the rest of the pubs.

My stomach growls at me, and Will's eyebrows are arched as he waits for my answer.

'OK, let's try.'

Will holds open the door and I walk over to the bar, hoping that they'll be full like all the rest.

'I just wondered if you were still doing your roast and if you've got room for us?'

'The restaurant is full, but you can eat in the bar,' says the barmaid as she unloads a full tray of steaming clean glasses on to the shelves.

'Perfect,' says Will, making a beeline for one that just happens to be under a giant TV showing the Grand Prix.

'Perhaps there's a quieter one,' I say, scanning the pub, but there's an abundance of screens and no matter where we sit we'll be able to see one.

'This one's fine,' says Will as he settles down, his attention already fixed on motor racing.

I bite the side of my mouth.

'If we're lucky and the food's slow, we might be able to watch the Spurs v Man City game,' says Will excitedly. 'Great suggestion to come here.'

I grit my teeth. I guess we're technically spending quality time together. 'I'll go and order us the food.'

I go over to the bar and console myself that at least my growling stomach will soon be cured.

'What can I get you?'

'We'll take two beef roasts and a G&T and a pint of Theakston's, please.'

'OK, there's going to be an hour's wait for food. Is that OK?'

My heart (and my stomach) sinks. What option do I have? We've already tried everywhere else.

'Yes, that's fine,' I say, lying.

I pay for the food and go over to tell Will.

'Yes,' he says, practically punching the air. 'It's almost better than having the Sky box working, isn't it? Food and drink on tap.'

'Hmm. But don't forget we're going for that walk later.'

'Yeah, that's fine. There's not much sport on later anyway.'

I'll say one thing for the pub: it did good food. I'm well and truly stuffed and Will practically had to roll me to the car. What I really want to do is go home and curl up in front of the telly. I couldn't think of anything worse than going for a walk, but having made such a fuss about it, I can't back out now.

We pull up at the car park of some nearby woods, and as we get out of the car I look up at the sky. It's been a gloomy grey colour all morning but now it's growing darker, and the wind's blowing colder. Even the elements are trying to tell me this is a bad idea.

'Let's go, then,' says Will, strolling over to the board of walking routes. This is almost on our doorstep, but it's been a while since we've been here. 'Shall we do this one? It says it should only take us an hour.'

I think an hour's pretty optimistic with my belly feeling like a lead weight, and looking at the clouds, I don't know if the rain will hold for that long.

We start walking towards the path when the heavens open. I run to a nearby tree and take cover, but not before I'm soaked.

'Holy crap,' says Will. 'Do you want to take a rain check – literally?'

'I guess so.'

Neither of us are prepared for the rain. I'm wearing a Florence & Fred parka, which is toasty warm but not particularly waterproof, and Will's not wearing a coat – only his large Southampton hoodie.

'Shall we make a run for it?' he asks.

The rain is bouncing off the car park, and I doubt that it's going to stop anytime soon. He hits the key fob and we see the lights flash.

'*Go go go!*' he shouts as he runs.

I pull up my hood and hope for the best as I follow him.

The car is less than a hundred metres away but I'm drenched by the time I get there. The faux fur trim on my hood is dripping, causing puddles on the few dry bits of my jeans.

'So much for that idea,' says Will, shaking his head like a wet dog.

He starts the car and drives us back towards home. It doesn't take us long and when we get in I go upstairs and change – it has definitely turned into a pyjama afternoon. I come back downstairs, about to suggest that we watch a DVD, but when I walk in the lounge I see that Will is playing his computer game again.

'Oh,' I say, frowning.

'Sorry, I didn't know how long you were going to be. You don't mind if I do another quick game, do you? I'd forgotten how good it was. Unless you wanted to do something else?'

I bite my lip.

'Well, we could, you know . . . if I closed the blind.'

I try to block out the voice in my head that sounds suspiciously like my mother, asking what our neighbours would say if we closed our blinds in the middle of the day.

'Um, couldn't we do that later? Score!' he shouts, cheering at his game.

He pauses it quickly and looks at me.

'I'm still a bit full from lunch, and I don't really think I'm up to it. But later, yeah? Tonight?'

'Fine,' I say sulkily. Although, to be honest, I don't really fancy it either, but I felt like it was my last hope to win back control of the afternoon.

Today's been a total write-off in the perfect Sunday stakes.

I go and settle on the sofa at the end of the room and pick up my laptop, thinking I could at least get some writing done. I have a quick check of my blog stats, and I find that my figures are at over three thousand. Surely that can't be right?

I read through the comments from people who are all desperately seeking the next instalment of revenge after Sunday's. I know me ruining the satellite box was an accident, but my blog readers don't have to know that, do they?

I start to limber up my fingers, wondering what I'm going to write, as from Will's point of view he appears to have rescued his Sunday quite nicely. I might need to use poetic licence for that, too.

Have you ever seen a grown man cry? Think the tears that are shed whenever England goes out of a World Cup after a penalty shootout and times it by ten. That's what happened to my poor boyfriend when I threw a glass of margarita over our Sky box. Not only did he miss the boxing that all his mates had come round specially to watch, but he also lost all his treasured saved games too.

Today he's been sulking like a teenager. Barely talking and wandering about in a daze, not knowing what to do with his time. It's fallen to me to re-educate him as to the joys of reading the paper, breakfast in bed and going out for lunch.

I swear he's starting to get the shakes, like an addict going cold turkey.

'Get in,' shouts Will, punching the air at whatever he's doing. He's worlds away from the man I'm describing. I seem to have turned Will into the ultimate pantomime villain, but it's surely the type of story that my blog readers (all three thousand of them!) are expecting. Without thinking too much about it, I hit Post.

I shut my laptop down and sit and watch my boyfriend direct his footballers on the screen. The revenge might not be working so well today in real life, but at least, for my blog, it worked well in fiction.

22

'So what's the state of play, then?' asks Cara as she puts her elliptical machine down a notch.

I follow suit, not wanting to make her feel bad when I burn more calories – I'm a good friend like that. Our writing group isn't on this week and Cara and I have decided to mix it up a little and meet on a Monday night, and in view of my poor level of fitness on the Swansea hikes, I convinced her to come to the gym with me. Although I don't really know why we're bothering, we're going that slowly – we're almost stationary – so that we can maintain our conversations without getting out of breath.

'Well, Will wasn't as grumpy on Sunday as I thought he was going to be. I did try and plan a whole romantic day – you know, breakfast in bed, pub lunch and a walk – but unlike Swansea, it all went wrong. He ended up digging out his long-lost Play-Station and playing FIFA, then the only pub still doing roasts was the Swan where there was sport on every screen, and then our walk got rained off.'

Cara's raising her eyebrow in a slightly smug I-told-you-so way. I still don't think she entirely believes me that I didn't mean to throw the drink over the box.

I've got to take time off work to wait in for the engineer, and then, perhaps worst of all, I've realised I'm going to have to watch *Bake Off* in the bedroom on our tiny TV.'

All those bakes, not to mention Paul Hollywood, deserve to be seen in all their HD big-screen glory.

'That doesn't sound ideal,' says Cara sympathetically.

'Er, no. I know I didn't plan it, but it's made me realise that I've got to be very careful with what revenge I seek. Especially if I want it to have the added bonus of Will and I spending quality time together. The only thing that's been getting any attention since the Saturday night is his PlayStation.'

'Well, at the risk of sounding like a broken record . . . you could tell him, you know. Turn the tables so that he's the one apologising.'

'I know, I know, I should.' God, I wish I'd chosen to go to the pub. Right now I could be sipping a nice glass of Pinot Grigio, but instead the only beverage I'm reaching for is my slightly off-tasting water from a reusable sports bottle. 'Do you fancy going and sitting in the juice bar for a bit?'

'Ah,' says Cara with relief, 'I thought you'd never ask.'

We walk over to the small juice bar in the entrance and I ponder what she's saying. I know she's right about the confrontation, but something's holding me back.

'It's just it was so good in Swansea,' I say, picking up a glass of something freshly squeezed and taking a seat in the corner. 'We had the best time. When I woke up on Sunday, I just assumed that with the satellite box out of action I'd be able to recreate the magic.

'Then after our abysmal day yesterday, I thought we could at least have gone to bed early, had a few snuggles as we watched TV, but it seems Will is taking his role of virtual football manager on his game far too seriously.'

'You see your problem's that you want two different things. Firstly, you want to get your revenge for what he did, which you know I think is wrong. And secondly, you want to recreate what you felt in Swansea. As I see it, what happened in Swansea is within your grasp all the time as, fundamentally, it was just you and Will spending time together.'

I nod my head slowly, trying to follow what she's saying. It's not like our relationship was dysfunctional before Will lied to me about the wedding, but having seen how it was on our weekend away, it's reminded me of what it used to be like.

'The methodology seems to be the same. In both the Swansea and the Sky box "accident",' she says, using her fingers to do air quotes, 'you removed sport from him in some form, yet the results were wildly different, which means you need to do better planning with your variables.'

Trust Cara to put it in a scientific framework, albeit a GCSE one.

'I just want us to be all in love and having all the good sex like we were in Wales,' I say, thinking that we're over-analysing it.

'Now you're starting to speak my language,' says Cara, raising an eyebrow. 'So, I think part of your problem with revenge is that you're putting obstacles in the way of the sporting events, but you're not really testing him. Wouldn't it be nice to know he'd choose you over sport?'

'Would it?' I gasp. 'What if he didn't?'

'Then I hate to tell you this, but if he doesn't, you've got a bigger problem in your relationship than you thought.'

I sigh. She's right.

'You said you wanted to have all the sex, so why don't you try to distract him with Sexy Lexi.'

After the weekend of three times in Swansea, I'm slightly less fearful of being rejected, but still, going head to head with sport is a risky venture.

'I don't know. He could still turn me down.'

'Really? Even if you walked into the lounge in some skimpy undies or starkers? I bet you'd be fighting him off.'

'Hmm,' I say, wondering if it would be that easy.

'There's always chapter eight,' she says, alluding to her work-in-progress that I'm reading.

'No, there's bloody not. I had to look *that* up on Urban Dictionary. There's no way I'm doing it as I'm pretty sure it's probably illegal in some countries. Have you –? Never mind,' I add quickly. I don't want to know.

Cara's giving me a smirk which leaves me in no doubt that she's done her research on the topic.

'You and Dave the Usher, huh?'

The smirk is wiped off her face. She hates being reminded of Dave, who from what I can gather has practically moved in with her.

'Well, if you're not going to read my tips, I can coach you, if you like.'

'Um,' I say, not knowing how I can be diplomatic about this. I'm practically a repressed Victorian compared to Cara. It would be like Eliza Doolittle being coached by Samantha from *Sex and the City*.

'I don't know if I need coaching. I do know how the birds and the bees work.'

'Oh, I don't doubt that. But I was thinking more along the lines of, I could take you to a couple of shops and help you pick out some bits that might get things going a little bit. You know, outfits, toys, accessories . . .'

I don't know what would be worse, going to one of those places or taking Cara the expert with me. Goodness knows what she'd convince me to buy. Not only that, but I'd be thinking anything she was recommending would have been tried and tested.

But in principle, seduction is not a terrible idea.

'I think I'd be all right on my own. I could pop in one night after work.'

I don't tell Cara that I've never actually been into an Ann Summers alone and I don't know if I'm brave enough to. It's the kind of place Will and I went early on in our relationship, full of giggles as we wandered round.

'OK, but you let me know if you need any advice. And if you go into the one in Southampton, go and see Sinita, and tell her I sent you.'

'Oh, I will,' I say, knowing full well that if I did manage to make it across the threshold, I'd be too embarrassed to enlist the help of any sales staff.

'And don't forget there's always my novel if you need more inspiration,' she says, winking again. 'Speaking of writing, I read your latest blog.'

'Ah,' I say, nodding. 'I, um, hammed it up a little. You know, to make it more interesting.'

'I wondered, as it didn't sound like the Will I know.'

I feel a bit guilty about portraying him like that again.

'Well, it is allowed to be a bit fictional, right?'

'Uh-huh. Half the stuff on my blog isn't true.'

'Thank heavens for that.'

'I've tweeted the link for you. Hopefully it might bump up your traffic a bit.'

'Oh, um, great. I checked my stats and I'm now up to six thousand views.'

'Holy crap. That's amazing. I thought I was doing well with a hundred.'

'That's probably because most of your keywords are banned from most search engines,' I retort.

'Ha, ha, very funny,' says Cara, sipping her drink. 'What about your new novel? Have you done anything on that?'

'Oh, yes, I've started it already,' I say, proud that I've been pro-active in my writing again.

'Brilliant. So, what's it about?'

'It's about a woman who's searching for her Mr Right. Isn't that what every chick lit novel is about?' I say, laughing.

I'm probably doing it a big disservice, but it's such a change from what I'm used to.

I've been pretty surprised that I actually quite enjoy writing it. It's really girlie and I'm worried that next week I'll be sporting shellac nails and buying Jimmy Choos.

'It's about a single girl who gets a job working for a specialist sports tour company and ends up falling for a sports-mad man, and it's about her coping with being a sporting widow.'

'So it's in no way autobiographical, then?'

'Of course not,' I say, pulling a mock-shocked face. 'I've written a few thousand words and so far it doesn't sound like mine and Will's relationship. For starters, they actually have sex.'

Cara giggles and I realise how desperately I need my plan to come to fruition. I can't believe that the only romance in my life since Swansea is the stuff I've written in that book.

Whatever might have happened since I discovered Will's lie, it's highlighted how comfortable we've become in our relationship. I feel like this revenge isn't only about getting him back for what he did any more, it's just as much about being a catalyst for rekindling our relationship.

23

Tonight is most definitely the night. My boyfriend is not going to know what's hit him.

Ever since Cara and I talked about it, I've had nothing else on my mind. Three days of thinking about sex – this must be what it's like inside a man's brain.

We grew out of that lusty stage where you had sex at the drop of a hat a long time ago and now we're lucky if we bump nasties more than once every couple of weeks – cough – once a month.

I'm sad to say that I gave up my regular trips to get my bikini line waxed and Will now finds me pretty much au naturel around there and usually with a fair amount of stubble on my legs.

But not tonight. Tonight I need to be like a goddess as I'm not being rejected a second time. I've gone well and truly above and beyond and got a Brazilian done at lunchtime. Now, I personally fail to see how having downstairs looking like a bald chicken is going to turn on my boyfriend, but according to my beauty therapist, it's the wax to have.

The irony that I'm trying to get revenge on my boyfriend and yet I somehow ended up spending the most uncomfortable half an hour of my life, is not lost on me.

'That was delicious,' says Will, pushing his plate away. He's practically licked the plate from the chocolate-and-chilli-laced dessert. I've been doing my research and both chocolate and chilli are aphrodisiacs. Add the honey chicken stir-fry I served for main, and I'm hoping that his libido is starting to warm up nicely.

'I know, it was. I'm going to have to cook that again.'

'You certainly are. Right, well, I'm going to go and watch a bit of TV in the front room, if you don't mind? I think I need to chill on the sofa and rest this belly.'

I watch as he sticks his protruding beer belly out in an exaggerated fashion. He's clearly doing the opposite of my seduction plan.

'No, that's fine,' I say thinking it's perfect since I need to sneak upstairs and slip into something more uncomfortable. All that I can hope is that the outfit I bought from Ann Summers gets ripped off in the heat of the moment, as it's a fishnet body stocking that I just know is going to ride up in all the wrong places. 'What time are you going out?'

'In about half an hour. The game kicks off at quarter to eight.'

'Right,' I say, rolling my wrist over to check my watch.

That gives me plenty of time to go upstairs and transform myself into someone out of one of Cara's naughty novels.

'Do you want anything while I'm in here?' he asks, as he grabs a beer out of the fridge.

'No, I'm fine thanks, honey.'

'See you in a bit, then,' he says, walking through to the lounge.

The sounds of Sky Sports News drift through to the kitchen and I hurry upstairs ready to put my plan into action.

Tonight is a midweek Southampton game, which of course their super-fan can't miss. It's a risky strategy – I'm trying to seduce the hell out of him to get him to stay in, proving that I am capable of persuading him to choose me over a game.

Again, the irony isn't lost that I'm taking my revenge by giving him an intense night of pleasure, but we'll gloss over that.

I slip off my work clothes and put my silky dressing-gown on, before applying the vampy make-up. I watched a YouTube vlog last night on how to create seductive smoky eyes, and I'm trying to replicate it.

By the time I'm finished I look a bit like I'm auditioning for an extra in Michael Jackson's *Thriller* video. It's not quite as subtle as the vlogger's. I take a cotton-wool ball and try to remove a bit, and *voilà*, I now look a little smouldering.

I stand up from the floor and head over to my dressing table where I coat my legs in baby oil, and take a deep breath as I pick up the body stocking.

It's a peculiar all-in-one thing. Once on it will look like I'm wearing a see-through teddy, with hold-ups and stockings. Yet, in reality, it's all connected, which means that getting into it is a tad tricky. I'll have to put my legs and bits through the right holes, which is going to be easier said than done since I have no idea which way up it goes.

I'm not usually a sheer tights kind of a girl. Whenever I put on anything that's less than 100 denier, it ladders immediately. And now I've got to get this whole thing on without laddering the stockings part.

What seemed like a bit of a bargain at the time, having everything all together, is in reality the worst nightmare for clumsy me.

I look down at my nails and wonder if I should cut them. On the one hand I'm guessing that my blood-red long nails look sexy; on the other hand, a run in my stocking will look pretty shite.

I shake my head at myself. Why the hell am I worrying about this? If Will is looking at a tiny hole in my leg, then the body stocking has really failed. There's going to be a hell of a lot better bits on show than that.

'Here goes nothing,' I mutter to myself as I realise that Will's due to leave in ten minutes.

While not really the intention of the baby oil, it actually helps to slide me into it, and it glides on surprisingly easily.

I look at myself in the mirror, trying to psych myself up to go downstairs without covering up. It certainly leaves nothing to the imagination. I'm almost embarrassed to show Will. How's he going to react?

I pick up a pair of heels that I can't believe I ever used to wear out and walk down the stairs with them in my hand. They've very much become bedroom heels as I doubt I'll be able to walk more than two steps in them without crippling my feet.

I position myself outside the lounge door and hear the TV still crackling away as I slip on the heels.

Why am I so nervous about being in front of him in something so revealing? After all, we've been together for seven years so he's seen me naked from pretty much every angle and in a lot more unflattering and compromising positions. I wonder if I'd feel less self-conscious if I were naked than in something that is so obviously trying to ooze sex appeal.

I put my hand on the handle and I hesitate. I put so much effort into planning this seduction, from the primping and preening, the outfit and the food we ate, yet I gave no consideration as to how I'm going to enter the room or what I'm going to say.

Then I panic. Did I shut the curtains when I came home from work? The lights in our living room are ridiculously bright and if the curtains are open, our nosy neighbour opposite is going to get a right eyeful.

My heart is beating ten to the dozen. I have no clue what I'm going to do and time's running out. The front door is through our lounge and if I don't make a move soon, then Will could shout a goodbye and be gone. Then all this effort would be wasted.

It's that thought that propels me through the door with perhaps a little too much gusto. The door crashes noisily into the wall, which at least gets Will's attention.

The only slight relief I have is that the curtains are firmly closed. Phew.

I take a deep breath and decide to go for a power strut, only my feet seem to have forgotten how to walk in stilettos and I'm worried the heels will mark the wooden floor. Not really the type of thing they teach you in seduction 101, but again, if I'd only given this part of the plan more thought.

My foot decides to buckle, and I realise floor marking is the least of my worries as I feel myself stumbling forward. I grab at the mantelpiece and cling on for dear life, sending one of our large candlesticks crashing to the ground.

'What the –' exclaims Will as I hang perilously off the mantelpiece, my legs slowly sliding into the splits. I try to style it out, as if I'm deliberately trying to look sexy. I stretch one leg out and tip my head back to push my boobs out.

What the hell am I supposed to do now?

I pout the best I can and narrow my eyes in what I hope is an alluring rather than needing glasses way.

'Lexi, what's going on?'

'I went shopping,' I say, trying to add a purr, but it just makes me sound posh. I'm not entirely sure why my inner mind thinks sexy is an RP English accent with a slight lisp.

'I can see that,' says Will.

I chance opening my eyes a little wider to look at him directly, and although he looks like he's been woken abruptly from a sleep, he's looking rather pleased about it.

'I thought maybe I could change your mind about going out tonight.'

I'm in serious danger of getting cramp and I try to pull myself up to a standing position. I'm still unsure whether to remain on this side of the room or to try and cover the two-metre distance to him on the sofa. I don't know whether my Bambi-on-ice type legs would make it.

Instead I channel my inner glamour model (little did I know she resided in me) and while making sure I hold one hand on the mantelpiece at all times for balance, I turn around, sticking my bum out and letting him get an eyeful of the back, which, aside from sheer stocking material and a whisper of a seamline that looks like a thong made of string, is bare.

'What do you reckon?' I say, turning my head to look over my shoulder at him.

He stands up and for a split second I think he's going to make a run for the door, but much to my delight he starts to walk over to me.

'You know,' he says as he pushes himself gently against me and traces his hands along the body stocking. 'It's a really big game tonight, and all the guys are going to be there.'

'That's a shame,' I say, wriggling my hips in a teasing motion against him. 'I guess I'll have to just hang out here in this and watch TV, then.'

I break away from him as if I'm going to walk off, but he holds me back against him and giggles.

'I'm sure I could text the guys and tell them I can't make it.'

'Maybe you can pretend you're ill,' I say, unable to resist the little dig.

He's silent for a second and I wonder if he's twigged. But before long he bends down and kisses my neck and mutters, 'I'll just tell them a better offer came along.'

He spins me round and sensibly keeps a hand on my back to steady me before looking at me again.

'Something better has definitely come up,' he says as he picks me up and I find myself with my legs wrapped around his waist. Blimey, I can't remember the last time he literally swept me off my feet.

'Now, then, where am I going to have my naughty girlfriend first?'

First? Now he's really talking. The last time we had sex twice in one night I'm pretty sure Labour were still in power.

Perhaps it's the honey, chilli and chocolate, or maybe it's the sheer fabric, but one thing's for sure: I think Sexy Lexi is going to make an appearance when he's supposed to be watching sport more often, revenge or no revenge. Who knew this would be all it took to turn my coach potato boyfriend into some sort of Lothario?

And as he starts to nibble me in all the right places, I can't help but think I'm on to something with this type of revenge, if only it could all be this pleasurable.

24

'Cheers,' I say, chinking glasses with Cara and Vanessa. It's not quite the same with Vanessa drinking soda water (not even a hint of lime – something to do with artificial colourings), but at least we're all out at the pub on a Saturday night for the first time in months.

'It's so busy in here,' says Vanessa as someone bashes past her and knocks into her elbow.

This is one of our favourite going-out pubs, and it appears that tonight it's everyone else's favourite too. There are no tables, and we've had to hover around a ledge that's en route to the bathroom, so consequently there's a steady stream of people going backwards and forwards.

'It's end of the month,' says Cara. 'Payday.'

Vanessa and I do a collective *ah* as it starts to make sense.

I start sipping my drink rapidly before I realise I've got to slow down.

'You're not allowed to let me drink as much as last week,' I say, thinking back to those margaritas and the trouble they got me into.

'Oh brilliant, you'll be on the soda water as well,' says Cara rolling her eyes. 'Don't tell me you're trying for a baby too.'

'God no, I couldn't think of anything worse,' I say, a little too quickly. I catch sight of Vanessa and she's not looking amused. 'I just mean, as I'd rather get married first.'

There I go with my spade digging myself out of a hole.

'No, I can't drink too much as Will and I are going to my parents' for lunch tomorrow.'

'Oh, can you tell your mum thanks for the card and gift? We're doing proper thank-you cards but it will be another couple of weeks as they haven't come back from the printer's yet,' says Vanessa.

'Of course.'

She'll be delighted with that – a natural in to a conversation about weddings.

'Thanks, hun,' she says sipping her drink.

'This is the start of a new era, then,' I say, pointing at her glass. 'First, you stop drinking, next there'll be a bump, and then you won't be coming out at all.'

'Hey, I'll have a baby, not be under house arrest. I'll still come out.'

'No you won't,' says Cara, laughing. 'You'll be going out with your new NCT buddies and you'll all be talking about stitches and baby poo, or whatever else it is that mums bond over.'

'That's not true,' she says, a little hurt. 'I'll still see you guys.'

I squeeze her hand. 'Let's hope so. Just think what it would be like having to listen to Cara the conquistador without you here to help change the subject.'

'That's true,' says Vanessa. 'Ian will have to get used to babysitting. Speaking of conquests, I feel like I haven't heard much about what's going on with you since I got back from honeymoon. Who's the latest victim?'

Her eyes widen as she stares at Cara, waiting for her to elaborate. It's funny as we both joke about not wanting to hear about her sex life, but it's a bit like rubber-necking at a car accident – you don't want to look, but you have to. Her stories might freak us out, but they can be bloody entertaining.

'Dave,' says Cara out loud.

For a second I'm shocked that she's admitted her relationship to Vanessa, when I realise that she's not talking about Dave, but to him.

'Cara,' he says, his face lighting up. He grabs her hand and goes to lean over before Vanessa interrupts.

'Dave?'

He freezes halfway towards Cara, and turns his head.

'Vanessa,' he says, putting on a smile. He's still got Cara's hand and Vanessa's looking at them closely. Dave styles it out by kissing Cara on the cheek. He then turns to me, grabs my hand and does the same, before finishing up with Vanessa.

Thank God he didn't do a Chandler in *Friends* and snog Cara, and then have to cover by snogging all three of us. The hand grab–cheek kiss combo was weird enough when I don't know him.

Vanessa scrunches her nose up as if she's trying to work out what's going on, and I think that the secret is blown. Cara obviously thinks that too as she looks like she's going to hyperventilate.

'What are you doing here?' says Vanessa. 'Aren't you out with –'

Her husband walks up behind, taps Dave on the shoulder and passes him a pint before he clocks who he's standing with.

'Ian,' she finishes.

'Ah, honey,' he says, looking shocked to see his wife. The colour drains from his face.

'Sweetie.' She leans over as if she's about to give him a kiss, then she freezes as her eyes fall on his hand. 'What the bloody hell is that?' she says, pointing to his drink. Her eyes almost glow red and I can see her nostrils flaring.

'I, um. It's just the one.'

'What's wrong with that?' whispers Dave to Cara and me.

'They're not supposed be drinking while they're trying to have a baby,' I say, filling in the blanks as Cara seems to be very focused on a spot on the floor.

'Since when?' he says, laughing.

'Since they got back from honeymoon.'

'Right,' says Dave nodding, and giving me the impression that Ian is not taking it quite as seriously as his wife.

I'm secretly glad he's rebelling a bit as it makes me feel better that Vanessa doesn't have much more control over her husband than I do over my boyfriend.

'It's not like I've had that many,' I hear Ian say grumpily.

I take a couple of steps away from them, as if to give them space, which in a pub this crowded is almost laughable.

'So, um. Dave, is it?' I say. I figure that if they're pretending they don't know each other, I'll join in the fun. But it's easy to play along as I've only ever met him in passing. Vanessa and Ian don't mix their friends very often, so I've only ever met him briefly at their engagement party and a couple of birthdays in the pub. I don't think I even spoke to him at the wedding.

'That's right, Lexi,' he says, giving me a little conspiratorial smile. It's then that I start to wonder how much about me he knows. From what I can deduce, Cara and him seem to see each other a lot. What if she's told him about what's going on with me and Will? And about the real reason that Will didn't go to the wedding? If he's friends – or stepbrothers – with Ian, what if he feels honour-bound to tell him?

I start to feel a little hot and flustered, before I calm down. If he was going to tell him, surely he would have done it already. And besides which, Cara's very much hoes before bros.

We stand there in silence, trying not to listen to Vanessa and Ian's argument, but her screeching voice is pretty hard to ignore.

'But you promised!' she shrills.

'So, Dave . . .' I say, looking at Cara, who is still looking at a spot on the floor. 'What do you do?'

'I'm a solicitor.'

'Oh, that's –' I struggle for an adjective other than 'grown-up'. 'Interesting. What do you specialise in?'

'Family law, so divorces, mainly.'

'Isn't that depressing?'

He shrugs his shoulders. 'It can be, but it makes you realise that you've got to be very careful who you end up with. And I guess it makes you realise that when you find a keeper, you cling on to them for all it's worth.'

'Right,' I say, nodding. It's not lost on me that he's looking at Cara as he says this. Bless him, he's really into her, and I'm guessing that the feeling is mutual as otherwise Cara would be on to someone else by now. I wonder why they're so intent on keeping it a secret?

I seem to have exhausted the conversation with Dave and we're left standing there awkwardly. This is not how I imagined girls' night would be. I'm sandwiched between warring newlyweds and a clandestine couple that don't appear to be able to acknowledge each other in public.

I look round the pub for an escape, when I make eye contact with Robin. I've never been so pleased to see anyone in all my life and I give him a friendly wave in the hope that he'll come over, but after waving back he goes back to his conversation.

I turn back to Vanessa and Ian, who have clearly made up as they're now smooching.

'That was quick,' I say, as they come up for air.

'Well, we've agreed that Ian needs to have a few drinks at the end of the week, and as long as I'm not ovulating, then it shouldn't be a problem.'

'See how easily things can be resolved when you talk about them?' says Cara, raising an eyebrow at me.

'Yes, you're right. So Dave, are you on the lookout for love tonight?' I say in order to get her back.

'Vanessa, did you want another soda water?' asks Cara loudly, before Dave can reply.

'Um, no,' she says, looking down at her large glass that's still almost full to the brim.

'Have you all met Dave before?' says Ian; it seems he's in the dark like Vanessa.

We all nod our heads that we've been suitably introduced (some better than others).

I'm about to announce I'm off to the toilet, to escape the boredom of girls' night gone wrong, when Robin walks up to me.

'Hey, Lexi,' he says. He leans forward as if to give me a kiss on the cheek, but then seems to think better of it and puts his hand out.

Flummoxed, I shake it awkwardly with my left one as I'm holding my drink in the other.

'Hiya, nice to see you.'

'Am I going to meet the famous Will?' he asks, looking around.

'No, it's a girls' night out.'

He looks at Ian and Dave in confusion.

'Well, it was,' I say hastily. 'My friend just bumped into her husband and his friend.'

'I'm Dave,' he says, holding his hand out for Robin to shake. Robin grins, and repeats his name as if cementing it.

'And you are?' he says, smiling at Cara.

'Um,' says Cara looking up from her spot on the floor and I see her eyes pop out of her head at the sight of him. 'I'm Cara. Lexi's very good friend.'

'Pleasure to meet you, Lexi's very good friend Cara.'

'And you are?' she says, tucking her hair behind her ear.

Uh-oh, flirt alert.

'This is Robin, my colleague,' I say, trying to take back control of the situation.

'Oh, *Robin*,' says Vanessa. 'Well, I hope that you'll be speaking highly of our Lexi in your report.'

She's like a lioness protecting one of her cubs.

'Don't you worry, I will be,' he says in full charm mode.

'I think we should be going,' says Dave.

I can see a look of disappointment on his face. Presumably because Cara hasn't taken her eyes off Robin since he started speaking.

'We wouldn't want to interrupt the precious girls' night,' he says almost bitterly.

'No,' says Ian. 'I'll see you later, sweetie.'

He leans over and kisses Vanessa, before giving us a quick wave goodbye, and they weave their way through the pub.

I see Cara visibly relax for a moment, before she pushes her shoulders back and her chest out and goes into what I've dubbed 'prowl pose'.

'So if that was your husband, then you must be Lexi's friend that just got married,' says Robin.

'Yes, that's me,' says Vanessa, flashing her finger proudly.

Robin takes her hand and dutifully admires the ring. I notice that it's not only Cara fluttering her eyelids.

I roll my eyes at the effect he has on everybody he meets.

'It sounded like an incredible wedding. I went to HMS *Warrior* last year on a tour and I thought that it would be brilliant to have an event there.'

'It was fantastic. And definitely all the more memorable because of the venue,' she says gushing. 'Wasn't it, girls?'

Cara nods, as if she's too far under his spell to speak.

'It was wonderful,' I say, nodding.

'The only shame was that Lexi had to come by herself.'

'Oh yes, she told me about that.'

It takes me a second before I realise in horror that Robin knows the real reason that Will wasn't there.

'So, Robin, are you out with –'

But I'm too late, as Vanessa gets in there first.

'Poor Will, I mean, getting food poisoning,' she says shaking her head as if it was too bad.

I groan. Any second now, Robin will tell her Will was at the football. I see a glimmer of confusion flash over Robin's face, before he replaces it with a smile.

'Yes, terrible thing to have been struck down with,' he says.

I breathe a sigh of relief and fight my impulse to hug him in thanks. Firstly because that would be inappropriate with a work colleague, and secondly with the look of lust that Cara is giving him she'd probably scratch my eyes out.

'Are you out with friends?' I ask, telepathically trying to thank him.

'I am. In fact I should probably get back to them, but I thought I'd come and say hi. It was lovely to meet you ladies,' he says and I hear them almost swoon as he flashes his winning smile. 'I'll see you on Monday, Lexi.'

'Will do,' I say, waving as he walks off.

'OK,' says Cara, the spell broken with his departure. 'When you said he was fit you never said he was like a walking flipping Adonis. You get to sit opposite him every day?'

'I must admit,' says Vanessa, 'that he is pretty attractive, and very charming.'

She looks a little flustered and I see her fiddling with her wedding ring as if she feels a little guilty that she's mentioned someone other than her husband is good-looking.

'Yeah, he is, but you sort of get used to it. At first it's quite easy to get sucked in, but you soon realise that he uses the same charm on everyone.'

'Hmm, well, I wouldn't mind seeing some more of that charm,' says Cara, practically licking her lips.

Poor Dave – I hope this isn't going to signal the end for their secret relationship.

'It doesn't seem like you have anything to worry about with your job, though, as he seems really nice,' says Vanessa.

'Fingers crossed.'

I know from experience that you can never be sure of anything when it comes to local government funding.

'But let's not talk about that,' I say, not wanting to dwell on work on a Saturday night. 'Let's get back to our girls' night out and for once, I've got actual news. Will and I did it twice in one night on Wednesday.'

'What?' says Vanessa, shocked. 'It wasn't his birthday, was it?'

'No, just a regular Wednesday night . . .'

I start to tell them edited highlights of the evening, obviously making sure that I don't overshare à la Cara or mention anything about it being part of my revenge. Either way the two of them are suitably impressed and I feel like our night is heading back in the right direction – giggles and gossip.

Now all I have to do is make sure I don't get too carried away and drink too much, or else it will make tomorrow's lunch with the parents even more painful than usual.

25

'Are you ready?' I ask, walking into the lounge.

Not that I really am, but unfortunately if we don't leave now we're going to be late for lunch with my parents. And being late is not an option. My mum refuses in punishment to pull things out of the oven until we're there, so if you're not careful with your timekeeping you end up with bone-dry beef and charcoaled roast potatoes.

I forwent giving myself plenty of time to get ready in favour of sleeping off my hangover, which means I'm leaving myself wide open to criticism from my mother about my appearance. With frizzy, non-blow-dried hair, dark circles peeking through my concealer and unironed clothes, she's got plenty to critique.

Will groans. It's the same noise I made when I got up this morning.

'I don't think I'm really up for it today,' he says.

'What do you mean you're not up for it?'

'I don't fancy going. Do you mind if I stay at home?'

Alarm bells are ringing in my ears. What sport does he want to watch? I know there's no Grand Prix this week, and I'm not aware of any football on until later. What could it be? Rugby?

American football? The start of the cricket tournament we're going to watch in Barbados?

'What sport's on?'

'What? Nothing. There's none on. I just don't want to go.'

I narrow my eyes at him. Ordinarily I'd think that he was telling the truth, but after his lie, I can't tell any more.

'Are you ill?' I practically shriek.

'No.'

'Then you can't stay at home.'

Will groans again, and still doesn't move. 'Couldn't you tell them that I'm ill? They wouldn't have to know.'

I bite my tongue as I was about to blurt something out, but I stop myself.

'No, but I would.'

Will shrugs his shoulders and sighs. I know he doesn't like going to Sunday lunch at my parents, but who does? All that fine china and formality – it's exhausting.

'Come on, Will. We've got to go. They're my parents and I'm their only child.'

I can't believe I'm using the same guilt card that my mum uses on me.

'Well, then you go on your own. I'll see them when we get back from holiday.'

'I can't go on my own.'

My mother will go into some sort of frenzied panic thinking that it signals the demise of our relationship if I turn up without Will.

'Look, do you think I actually want to go?'

Will looks at me and raises an eyebrow.

'Then let's both stay here.'

For the first time in the conversation his face lights up.

'We could curl up on the sofa and watch a movie. Or go back to bed and have croissants again like last weekend.'

There will be no croissants in our bed ever again. It was like sleeping on sawdust that night with all the crumbs.

But a movie on the sofa sounds tempting. I've got some popcorn in the cupboard and we could get the big fleecy blanket out to snuggle under. He obviously hasn't got a sporting agenda after all.

I almost slip my coat off, before I realise that my mother would probably disown me.

'Come on, we've got to go. We can do that when we get back. If we're lucky it will be a quick lunch and we'll be home by three.'

Will sighs. I think I've got him.

'I just can't face your mum today,' he says with an almost worried expression on his face.

This is probably because he knows she's going to be wedding hyper as this is the first time we've been round since Vanessa and Ian tied the knot and she's going to want to hear every little detail.

'Don't worry, she won't mention the wedding.'

'What wedding?' says Will, confused.

'Vanessa and Ian's. Isn't that why you don't want to come? Never mind. Let's go.'

I clap my hands in what I hope is an authoritative manner, hoping he'll get up. He's a thirty-four-year-old male who weighs about thirteen stone, so there's no way I'll be able to physically force him.

Luckily for me, he gets up and drags his feet to the car. I watch him slip a coat over his long-sleeved Southampton T-shirt. Ordinarily I'd point out that perhaps he'd want to change first, as my mum practically issues a dress code with the invitation, but I think that really would send him over the edge.

I check my watch as we pull up on to my parents' driveway. That was good going – only a couple of minutes late.

'Cheer up,' I say to Will. 'It might not be as bad as usual.'

He gives me a look.

'OK, it probably will be, but at least put a smile on your face.'

I climb out of the car and I'm halfway to the door before I realise that he isn't following me. He's still sitting there and for a second I think he's going to abandon me here and drive away. Why's he being so weird? He may groan about coming, but he never usually puts up this much of a fight.

I beckon him with my hand to get moving before my mum opens the door, which she does almost without fail.

'Mum,' I say theatrically, as I give her a more exaggerated hug than usual. By the time I pull out of it, I see that Will has joined us. Phew.

'Hello, William,' she says and then she hugs him like her long-lost child.

'Steady on, Mum. That's my boyfriend you've got your paws all over,' I mutter to myself. It seems it isn't only Will that's acting out of character today. Maybe there's a full moon.

She finally lets him go and we're led through to the formal sitting room. She only uses this room for guests. I've told her about a billion times that I'm not really a guest, and the cosy lounge at the back of the house would be much more comfortable, but she insists. I find it ironic that when I was younger I used to beg to be able to come in here and play, only to discover when I moved out and I finally earned the right to come in this room, that it smells a bit musty and the sofas are rock hard.

'There you are,' says Mum. 'I'll go and finish up.'

'OK, thanks.'

Something very strange is going on. She was too busy fawning over Will to look me up and down, meaning she hasn't commented on my appearance. I'm so glad that I didn't get up any earlier.

'All right, love,' says my dad, putting down his paper and standing up.

'Fine thanks, Dad,' I say, giving him a quick cuddle.

Will seems to be almost hiding behind me, forcing my dad to lean behind me to shake his hand.

My dad retreats back to his armchair and instead of picking up his paper like he usually would, he sits staring at us.

'Everything OK?' I ask, leaning my head to the side slightly, as if I'm missing something.

'Oh yes, fine, fine,' he says, nodding.

I turn to look at Will, to see if he's noticing any of this odd behaviour, pull a face at him, but he's sat with his head down fiddling with a loose thread on his T-shirt.

'So,' says my dad.

'So,' I say, wondering what on earth we should talk about.

In the end, when I can't stand the expectant look on my dad's face any more, I say 'How about the Saints, then?'

I have no idea what that really means, but I've heard him say that to Will often enough.

'Oh yes, they're doing nicely, aren't they, Will?'

Will jerks his head up at the mention of his name.

'Huh, what?' he says, a slight look of panic on his face.

'Um, we were just saying how well Southampton are doing this season.'

He seems to relax.

'Yeah, not a bad place to be.'

'Were you there on Wednesday? Did you see that goal; they think it'll be a contender for Goal of the Season.'

'Actually, I missed it. Something came up with, um, work,' he coughs.

I feel my cheeks flush at the thought of what we were actually up to on Wednesday. Definitely something I wouldn't want my dad to know about.

'I saw the goal on *Match of the Day*, though. It was amazing,' says Will.

Now usually if he'd missed such a goal it would have been the end of the world, but I think that night more than made up for it.

'Wasn't it?'

Now that Will's relaxed he seems quite happy talking to my dad.

I decide to leave them to it, and I go in search of my mum to see if she needs any help. I know that she'll say no, she always does, but if I don't ask her then she'll only moan when we sit down to eat that no one offered.

'Hiya, do you need me to do anything?' I say, strolling into the kitchen and sitting down at the table.

There's something nostalgically comforting about sitting here. Ever since they had the kitchen redone when I was eight, I've sat in the same chair, leaning up against the back wall. I only have to close my eyes and I'm transported right back there, sitting watching my mum in wonder as she effortlessly whipped up a huge meal for the (then) three of us.

'It's all under control, thank you.'

She opens the oven and I'm almost floored by the delicious aromas that escape. As much as I dread coming here, the food always makes up for the awkwardness of it all. She pokes around with a knife at her perfectly roasted potatoes and then eventually pulls the tray out.

'Is everything all right with Dad?' I ask.

She practically drops the roasting tray on to a trivet and it clatters down noisily. She's not doing anything to reassure me.

'He's fine. Why ever do you say that?'

'He seems a little odd today and he was weird on the phone the other day. I just thought he might be ill or something.'

It would be so typical of my parents not to tell me if he was.

'There's absolutely nothing wrong with your father, I promise,' she says, a smile appearing on her face. 'Now, can you pop these potatoes into a bowl for me?'

If I wasn't worried before, I'm really worried now. Mum actually wants me to help her. This can only mean one thing – she's trying to distract me.

I stand up slowly, recovering the bowl out of the cupboard, and I start to worry about what could be wrong with my dad. I carefully scoop the potatoes in one by one, so as not to damage them in any way. What if he's actually got some horrible, life-threatening illness?

'I think we're ready to go,' says my mum as she pulls off a tea towel that's covering the resting beef joint. 'Can you take those through to the dining room?'

'OK.' I've suddenly got the fear as I lift the bowl and take it into the dining room. My mother insists on using the dinner service that she got as a wedding present, which they stopped making in the mid-eighties, which means if there's an accident there's practically a steward's inquiry.

When Will first came over he chipped one of the gravy boats. He's never really been forgiven and, to this day, I have to pour his gravy on for him.

I set the potatoes down on one of the floral place mats in the centre of the table and I shiver. The dining room is always so cold as, like the formal lounge, it's only really used for Sunday lunches. The stupid thing is with just the four of us we could comfortably sit around the kitchen table. But I'm a guest now, which means dining room with the fine china and the solid silver cutlery. The only saving grace is that with all the food (and seconds) that I eat, I'm at least having an arm workout with the weight of the cutlery – bingo wings be gone.

I'm so slow at helping, that my mum's already bought the rest of the things in and I'm ushered to sit down while she retrieves the warmed plates from the oven.

'You OK?' I say to Will, as he comes in and sits down next to me.

'Yes, fine,' he says, looking a little more relaxed than when he first got here.

'Has my dad said anything strange to you?' I ask while it's just us the two of us in the room.

'No, why should he?'

I'm about to tell him what's going on, when my parents walk back in.

'This looks delicious,' says Will.

My mum beams with pride.

'Thank you. Now tuck in everyone.'

We jostle politely for dishes that someone else has as we make trades and try and find new spaces on the table for all the food. I do a quick sweep over the table to make sure I haven't missed anything. I once ate a whole roast dinner before realising I'd forgotten the roast parsnips – talk about disaster. Satisfied that I'm fully stocked, I pour mine and Will's gravy on and we're good to go.

'I saw Vanessa last night,' I say, as I start to tuck in. 'She said to say thanks for the wedding present and that you'd get a card in a few weeks.'

I figure that I might as well get this out of the way early. It's a bit like ripping a plaster off – get in quick and then it will be all over.

'Excellent,' says my mum.

I wait for her to make a dig about buying wedding presents for other people and not me, but it doesn't come. I know she asked me about the big day when I spoke to her on the phone a few days later, but still, it's not like her not to pounce on the opportunity to protest at the fact that I'm not engaged.

First she didn't comment on my outfit, and now this. There can only be one reason, Dad's ill and she's too distracted to be her usual delightful (i.e. critical) self.

'How's work, Dad?'

If they're not going to tell me then I'll have to go fishing.

'Oh, the usual, you know. Counting down the days to retirement.'

My dad's a civil engineer, which, despite him having done the same job since I was little, I'm still not entirely sure what that means. Whatever it is, he's just putting in his time now until he gets his pension in a couple of years.

'So you haven't been off work lately?' I say.

'No, we've got some holiday booked for next year. We're going to Greece again. In May,' he says slowly. 'But other than that . . .'

'Of course Zante won't be as exciting as going to Barbados, you lucky things. So romantic,' says my mum.

Will drops his knife and it crashes on to the plate. I hold my breath in case he's broken the plate, and I almost can't look. But my mother doesn't shriek so I figure it's safe.

'I can't wait,' I say dreaming of all the sand, sea and . . . you know. I can't think about that in front of my parents. 'It's going to be amazing.'

'Have you planned out what you're doing?' asks my mother.

'Not really,' I say. 'Of course we're going to the cricket on a few of the days, but other than that we're going to have a rest.'

'Sounds heavenly,' says my dad.

There is definitely something wrong with him. He never usually speaks at lunch, let alone uses words like *heavenly*. Not even I'd use a flowery word like that and I did a degree in English literature.

'We'll tell you all about it when we get back. Perhaps we can meet for lunch the weekend after?'

I really should spend more time with my parents – especially if there's something wrong with Dad.

'That's a great idea,' says Will.

'It is?' I say, wondering if he's being sarcastic, but he looks genuinely pleased about it. I'm pretty surprised considering how I practically had to drag him along today.

'Yes, it is,' he says, nodding and giving a finality to the subject.

Sunday lunch at my mum's is never normal, but today is one of the weirdest I've ever experienced. It's like everyone's had a personality transplant except me.

There's only one thing for it. I scoop some extra potatoes on to my plate. I'm going to have to put myself into a food coma to get through it.

26

'Someone's happy,' says Robin, looking up as I jump out of my seat.

Of course I am. I've just put my Out of Office assistant on, which means I'm officially on holiday. Whoop, whoop!

'You would be too if you were off to Barbados.'

'Ah, now that explains the spring in your step you've had all day,' he says, nodding.

Actually, it doesn't. That's due to the fact that it's the first time in a week I can walk without wincing. Let's just say my Ann Summer's purchase has been very good value for money.

It only cost me £35, which means so far I'm down to a £5 cost per wear. Not bad considering I've only had it a week. Although, can you call it a wear if you're only in something for a minute before it's pulled off? That thing now has more ladders in it than a London fire station. But hey, if it has that effect on my boyfriend, who cares.

Frequent sex *and* a holiday. It's as if Christmas has come early.

'I'll make sure to look out for you on TV,' says Robin, bringing me back from my daydream.

'I don't think there'll be that much cricket,' I say matter-of-factly. Now with Will's sexual reawakening, maybe we won't even leave the bungalow. Especially when he sees what I bought on my latest trip to Ann Summers. I've well and truly got over my fear of entering the shop.

Lingerie aside, I'm sure it's going to be a rerun of Swansea, just with more sun and rum. Thanks to my latest revenge, we're already on the right track; Barbados will just cement it.

I've already decided that despite my blog gaining new followers every hour, I'm going to stop it when I get home. I'm just going to do one final big act of revenge while we're away, as a finale to the blog and to make me feel like I've properly got even. Until I get out there and do a recce, I don't know how I'm going to stop Will from going to the cricket, but I'm sure it won't be that hard. If I pulled it off in Swansea, I can no doubt pull it off on a tropical island where everything's bound to be a bit more basic.

Then, as soon as we get home, I'm going to have it out with him once and for all. If I'm satisfied I've got my revenge, I hopefully won't be as mad with him, and we can talk like rational human beings about it, before moving on with our nicely rejuvenated relationship.

'No, not too much cricket,' I say for emphasis. 'We're thinking of going on a few excursions, seeing the island, trying the local delicacies.' I'm trying to sound cultured, but in truth I haven't so much as picked up a guidebook. The only research I've done for the holiday was finding out the best place for getting a bikini out of season. 'It's really only going to be one or two games max.'

'Wow, your boyfriend's a lot more restrained than I would be. If I'd gone all that way to watch it, I'd be making sure I saw as much as possible. You two really do have the perfect relationship.'

I smile a little weakly. We will have the perfect relationship, if I can help it along a little bit.

'I'm sure you'll have a lovely time. Barbados at this time of year is supposed to be nice.'

'Thank you. And I'll be thinking of you here slaving away over your desk.'

I look up at him as my computer finishes shutting down and I catch his eye. He's looking at me intensely and it causes me to blush.

'I mean, I'll be thinking of you *all* stuck here, while I'm lazing about in the sun.'

I turn round to find my coat, and hastily shove it on, before winding my scarf round my neck. I don't want him to think I'll be thinking about him while I'm away. I'll be far too busy relaxing and enjoying the sun, and having a romantic time with Will.

'Well, I should be finished with the leisure department audit by the time you get back.'

'Really, that soon?' I say, as I practically strangle myself with my scarf. I loosen it some more but keep hold of the long frayed ends.

I feel disappointed, and I don't know whether it's because the fate of our whole department and the twelve members of staff are dependent on his few weeks of evaluation, or whether I'm going to miss sitting opposite him.

'Yes, I think so. I've got a few facts and figures to get, but I think I've got all the information needed for the Value for Money study to report to the councillors.'

The hairs on my arms begin to prickle. I'm pretty confident that as the only arts officer my job must be pretty secure, but I've learnt that with the council there's no such thing as job security, and with the councillors' whims and the eternal budgets cuts, there's a perpetual axe hanging over our heads.

'So you'll be back to the big office upstairs, then?' I say a little sadly.

'Yes,' says Robin, nodding as he finishes highlighting something in the big pile of papers in front of him. 'Back to the executive, before I head over to the planning department.'

In the end it's gone really quickly him being here. I might have thought he was going to be a bit Big Brothery, but it hasn't been as bad as I imagined.

Robin's obviously shut his PC down too, as he stands up from his desk and puts his coat on.

I pick up my bag and slip it on my shoulder before I follow him out. I say goodbye to a few of my colleagues as I go.

'So are we all going to have jobs when your report comes out?' I ask as we make it out into the large stairwell and we start walking down side by side.

'You know I can't tell you that, it's for the councillors' eyes only. But wouldn't it do you a favour if you were made redundant?'

'Of course it would,' I say sarcastically. 'I'm sure my mortgage company would be thrilled.'

He's probably the sensible type that has a nice nest egg of savings, but it's not to say we all do.

'I didn't mean it like that. It's just, I finished your book last night and I really enjoyed it.'

'You did?' I start to feel a bit queasy and a little bit light-headed. Goodness, if I ever did become a bestselling author and people were reading my books, I'd be fainting all over the shop.

'Uh-huh.'

'Don't leave me in suspense.'

'Like you did for most of the book,' he says, laughing. 'I thought it was really good. It was perhaps a little rough around the edges here and there, and I noticed a couple of holes in the plot – ones I'm sure it would be easy to fix – but generally I thought it was really good.'

I let out the breath that I didn't even realise I was holding.

'I think you're pretty talented. That's why I think it's so ironic what you do. You're a creative person that wants to get your book published, yet you spend your whole day trying to get other people funding to help them realise their dreams, rather than making your own dreams come true.'

'It's not like I'm stopping them coming true. I can't exactly publish my book myself.'

'Um, I'm no expert but I thought self-publishing was really big nowadays?'

We push our way round the revolving doors and find our-selves outside the offices, a cool November breeze making me wish I had a hat as well as a scarf.

'That's not my dream. I want an agent and a publisher,' I say, trying to explain to him why I don't want to go it alone.

'Right, well, that's fine, but all I'm saying is, don't forget your dreams too. I mean, you are doing everything you can to make it a reality, aren't you?'

I hope I am. I've started to feel bad at how I'm portraying Will as the evil villain in my blog, and the only thing keeping me going at the moment is the thought that I'm helping my fledg-ling writing career.

'I'm trying new things, a blog and a women's fiction novel. It seems you weren't the only person to think I might be suited to it.'

'Good for you.'

'Yeah, well, I don't know if I'll get anywhere with it. It's still early days, but we'll see,' I say, shrugging.

'Don't be so pessimistic. Your novel was good; obviously it hasn't been read by the right agent yet. Do you know what I think your biggest problem is? It seems like you believe in and champion everyone else but yourself.'

I'm shocked and for a second I'm speechless. I've been so used to his charm over the last few weeks that I wasn't prepared for such brutal honesty.

'How soon are you going to be done with this audit?' I say jokingly, but desperate to end this conversation. I'm no longer comfortable with all this Lexi analysis. Perhaps it's not a bad thing that he's going to have left by the time I come back from Barbados.

He smiles his broad smile. 'Soon, but whether my findings are taken seriously is a whole other matter.'

I'm not sure whether we're talking about his official audit or the one on my personal life.

'Anyway, have a good holiday,' he says, turning to walk away. 'Don't forget to give the camera a wave if you find yourself being filmed for the TV.'

I smile, and shout, 'Will do.'

Then I turn and go in search of my car, excited that I'm not coming back to this place for another ten days.

Once home, I waste no time getting in the holiday spirit. I open a bottle of rum that's been lurking in our alcohol cupboard since our house-warming party four years ago. I give it a good sniff first to make sure it is OK. The smell of it nearly knocks me out, but I think that's what it's supposed to do. I'm sure that those types of spirits never go off really, do they? Ignoring any doubts, I pour in a little Coke, and *voilà*, Cuba Libra. As I take a few sips I can already feel myself drifting off towards the magical island of Barbados.

'Hi honey, I'm home,' shouts Will as he walks through the door.

He walks over to give me a kiss, and pulls me into a ballroom-dancing pose, before he proceeds to spin me around the kitchen.

'Careful, you'll spill my drink,' I say, laughing.

'Ooh, what you drinking?' he says, letting go of me and taking the glass out of my hand. 'Blimey, that's strong.'

He hands it back to me and goes to the fridge in search of a beer instead.

'Twelve hours and counting,' he says, doing a little wagging gesture that if I didn't know better I'd assume was him having a finger spasm, but unfortunately I know he's imitating the cricket umpire announcing a six (when the ball gets knocked over the boundary). If only this useless sporting information wasn't taking up all the memory space in my brain, I might be able to remember the names of all the Kardashians.

'Ah, yes,' I say, taking an extra big gulp of my drink. 'Speaking of the trip, Mike was asking me earlier what matches we're going to, and I realised I didn't know what tickets you'd got.'

More importantly, I need to work out which day my grand revenge is going to take place on, so I can start planning as soon we hit the ground.

'Well, we're going to go to one on Tuesday. England vs Australia, should be an absolute cracker, and then I've got tickets to go to Ireland vs India, by myself.'

'So just that one for me, then, and one for you?'

Will's poking around in the cupboard and I get the impression that he's not so much looking for something to eat as looking for a way out of the conversation.

'Um, well, I've got tickets for us two to go to England vs West Indies, which is going to be a huge game, and then I've booked New Zealand vs Pakistan for just me.'

Four games. I can hear Robin's voice in my head when he said that if he'd have gone all that way he wouldn't have been able to resist.

'Four games over four days. That doesn't leave us much time for sightseeing.'

'It's not every day, and besides, they're Twenty20 matches so they only last a few hours. If we go to a morning game then we'll be free to go for lunch and do whatever in the afternoon, and vice versa. It's going to be great, though, this holiday,' says Will, coming over and wrapping his arms around me. Clearly he's sensing I'm not happy. 'We'll have plenty of time to spend together and I've got a feeling it's going to be really special.'

'Why, are England going to win the bloody tournament?'

I pull away a little sulkily. I'd been so looking forward to this holiday and I guess I'd been so blindsided by the revenge and spending some romantic time with Will that I'd almost convinced myself that the cricket wouldn't feature much in our holiday. I'm never going to be able to keep him away for four games – I'm not that imaginative.

'Lex, I don't have to go and see all of the games, if you really don't want me to.'

My ears prick up. Did he actually just say that?

'Really?'

'Yeah, I can miss one of the matches.'

'Thanks, that would really mean a lot to me. I was looking on the Internet at lunchtime and there's a really great catamaran trip that we can do from the hotel on Friday. You go out to this bay and swim and apparently there are loads of turtles that swim round you, and –'

I stop mid-sentence as I can see him going a little pale. I can already guess what he's going to say before he says it.

'Actually, the Friday game is kind of the important one.'

I close my eyes for a minute and bite my tongue as I feel rage ripple over me.

'I'll change one of the others and we can go on the cruise another day.'

'But Friday is the only day that they go out to this little bay and . . . Never mind.'

He wouldn't get it. All he cares about is his bloody cricket.

I'm sure whatever I have to say would fall on deaf ears, so I turn and walk up the stairs.

I'd thought that the catamaran would have made a good end to the holiday. I could have got the revenge out of the way early on in the week, and then we could have ended on a high note.

I open up my suitcase and start chucking in the last of my freshly washed clothes. I don't bother to fold them nicely – what's the point when they're only going to get outings to a cricket oval.

I know I'm being petulant, that I'm sure we could do a tour on another day, but I wanted to do that one and with Will planning the rest of the trip round the cricket, I feel like I deserved one nice day.

I'm tempted to rummage through the packed clothes and take out my new lingerie purchases. But imposing some kind of sex ban would inflict just as much damage on me as it would on him.

I take a deep breath, thinking that I can channel all this fresh anger into revenge. If that Friday game means so much to him, then maybe that's the one he'll have to miss. If only there was some way I could trick him on to the catamaran and then we'd sail out to sea during his cricket game . . .

I shake my head. This is getting ridiculous. Perhaps I should simply tell him that enough's enough.

I could do what Cara's been telling me to all along – tell him I know. I could tell him that I don't want to be second fiddle to his sporting life any more, that I want to be put first, and demand that we go on the boat trip.

I stand up and exhale loudly. I'm going to do it, I tell myself as I go downstairs.

I grip hold of the banister as my legs suddenly become jelly-like and the nerves kick in.

'Will!' I shout.

He comes out of the living room sheepishly.

'We need to talk,' I say, giving him a look as if to tell him I know.

'I know, I'm so sorry,' he says. 'I really shouldn't have booked two games for myself. I just got carried away. I'll cancel one of the games, and go back to the original plan of two together and one by myself. Then you'll only have one morning by the pool on your own.

'I promise you, this holiday is going to be amazing. We'll both fall in love with the island and the games are so short, I'm sure you won't even notice them. It'll be the best holiday you've ever had. There'll be plenty of time for sightseeing, shopping and whatever else you have in mind,' he says, nuzzling my ear.

His forehead is resting on mine and I'm looking straight into his eyes. I feel myself blinking back a tear. I know then that I'm not going to bring up what he did at Vanessa's wedding. Not now.

'You promise, cricket won't get in the way?' I say a little feebly. It's as if I want to put him to the test one last time, see whether he can put us before his beloved sport.

'Promise,' he says, giving me a small kiss and rubbing my back. 'Now where is that rum? Let's start this holiday as we mean to go on.'

He takes hold of my hand and leads me to the kitchen. I try to relax as, after all, this time tomorrow I'll be in Barbados, baby!

27

The taxi pulls up to our hotel and for a minute I think there's been some mistake. A doorman opens our door, and I sit there frozen in shock and Will has to nudge me along.

I reluctantly step out, not believing that this is where we're supposed to be. The heat hits me immediately, like it did when I stepped off the plane, our bodies still in shock that we no longer need the winter coats and hoodies that we took to the airport.

The taxi driver unpacks our cases on to the gold-framed luggage trolley, before it's whisked inside by a porter.

'Right, then,' says Will, 'Shall we go and check in.'

I stand there motionless, trying to take it in. It's nothing like our usual holiday accommodation, which is usually a small shoebox-style apartment, picked for price rather than comfort. This resort's ridiculously fancy. When I'd checked it out on their website I'd just assumed that they'd used a very good photographer, but even those glossy images didn't do this place justice.

We move from white-walled covered walkway, which is lined with palm trees and plants with bright pink flowers, into the lobby.

I get my first glimpse of the pool beyond, which is glistening in the sunlight. My whole body is tingling in anticipation.

'Can I help?' asks the receptionist with a wide smile.

'Um, yes. I've got a reservation. The name is Talbot,' says Will.

The woman looks down at her computer screen and the longer she takes the more I keep thinking that she's going to tell us there's been some mistake, that we don't have a room here. It's all been some cruel trick and in fact our hotel bears the same name but is down the road.

'Ah,' she says nodding. 'Mr Talbot. Here we are. Let's get you all sorted.'

I practically shriek with joy when she confirms that we're going to be staying here.

As Will hands over his passport and fills out forms, I walk over to one of the comfy sofas in the corner and perch on a seat, helping myself to the complimentary mints in the centre of the table.

I try and stop myself from scooping up extra ones to put in my pocket for later. I'm sure that's not how one should behave in such an opulent resort. Instead, I peruse the book exchange in the corner, and try and pretend that I belong somewhere like this.

I see a man come to Will and shake his hand as if he's a long-lost friend.

'Mr Talbot, so great to welcome you to the hotel,' says the man in the suit.

'Thanks,' says Will, scanning the room to see me. 'This is my girlfriend, Lexi.'

He points over to me, and I get off the seat and walk over to join them.

'Ah,' nods the man. 'Lexi, nice to meet you too. You are very welcome to stay at the Tropical Beach Hotel.'

I smile. These five-star places are so welcoming. You don't get this type of introduction in your budget apartment – well, not unless it's from a rep who's trying to sell you an overpriced excursion.

'Now, I'm Joe, the concierge,' he says to me, ignoring Will. 'If there's anything you need during your stay, you let me know.'

'Thank you,' I say, beaming. The smiles here are infectious.

He pats Will on the back, and goes off to a desk in the corner.

'Shall we go and find our bungalow?' says Will, holding up the key.

'Absolutely.'

I'm trying so hard to keep a lid on my excitement as we walk past the sprawling pool in front of us. Jealous of those already soaking up the rays and sporting their spectacular tans. And wondering how long it will take me to find my bikini in my suitcase so that I can join them.

We head past the pool into the gardens, which are landscaped with a mixture of different types of palm tree and plants full of lush-smelling brightly coloured flowers.

'Look,' I say pointing in wonder at a little neon-green lizard that runs across our path.

'It's pretty cool, isn't it?' says Will, as if he can't believe it himself.

I know Will said he got a good deal, but I'm amazed he picked somewhere like this. It's the kind of hotel you'd expect the cricket team to be staying in, rather than the supporters.

I stop dead.

'Will, the English cricket team aren't staying here, are they?'

'Not that I know of. I'm sure they'd probably be staying at a Hilton or something.'

I relax and start walking again.

'Here we are,' says Will. '103.'

I look up at the bungalow. In my head I'd imagined more of a small chalet like you get in self-catering resorts in France, but this is a little whitewashed brick building that looks like a mini-villa. It's got a terrace at the front with a wooden table and chairs, and sliding French doors leading inside.

Will unlocks the doors and we walk into the lounge area, which has a large L-shaped white sofa with oversized fuchsia cushions. There's a small kitchen area to the far side, edged with a breakfast bar with high stools, and to our right a glass-topped dining room table and chairs.

'Wow, this place is great,' I say, dumping my handbag on the sofa and going through the door at the back of the lounge. I gasp as I see the four-poster bed, complete with white curtains tied up at the sides. I spot the little door to the bathroom in the corner and yelp as I see the wet room, decorated with camel-coloured marble tiles.

I'm suddenly torn between whether to test out the shower or the pool first.

I head back into the bedroom, and Will is tipping the porter who's deposited our cases in our room. Once we're alone, he gives me a big grin before diving on to the bed.

'Ah, man, this is comfy,' he says, groaning.

I can't help but jump on it too, and I land in a heap, bashing into him.

'You're like some fairy elephant.'

'Oi, watch it,' I say, grabbing a pillow and hitting him playfully.

'Oh, is that how it is? Don't make me tickle you.'

I go to squirm off the bed. I cannot stand being tickled by Will. He knows just the spot behind my ear that makes me go crazy.

He grabs my arm before I can make my mistake and pulls me towards him.

He runs his hand dangerously close to my ear before he strokes my face instead and kisses me.

'What do you want to do first? Go and check out the pool? Get something to eat?'

He goes to get off the bed and I pull him back down.

'How about we stay right here for a bit,' I say, snuggling into the crook of his arm and realising that I'm actually knackered from the flight. 'We've got all week to explore. Right now I don't want to move.'

'That's fine by me.'

He kisses me on the top of the head and gives me a squeeze and I wish we could stay in this magical moment for the whole holiday. No cricket. No revenge. Just me and Will.

It seems that I wasn't the only one that was tired after travelling. I woke up in Will's embrace three hours later, with a dead arm. The room was darker, and it took a while for me to work out where I was. I'd woken Will up as I wriggled out from under him.

After a not so quick shower – that wet room was every bit as fantastic as it looks – we've made it out for dinner and our first proper Barbados experience.

'Now, apparently there are some really nice restaurants across the road on the beach. Shall we go there?' asks Will, as he leads me through the resort gardens. The sun is starting to set, and the sky's gone a dusky red colour. The little lanterns along the path have lit up and are flickering like candles.

'Sounds perfect.'

I grab Will's hand and can't help swinging it as we walk along. We walk past the pool that's now empty and looking serenely still. There are a few people sitting at the wicker tables of the pool bar and the faint sounds of UB40 are drifting out.

'That looks nice and chilled.'

'Yeah, perhaps we can go for a drink there after.'

I nod and we walk though reception. Joe gives us an enthusiastic wave.

'Have a lovely evening,' he calls.

'Everyone's so nice and friendly,' I say.

'Uh-huh, it's their job though, isn't it?' he says, obviously not as impressed as I am. 'I can't wait to eat; I'm starving.'

'Me too. I didn't eat much of that chicken on the plane.'

'Me neither.'

We stroll hand in hand across the quiet road, and within a few steps down an alleyway we're on the beach.

'Wow, this is beautiful.'

There's a small sandy beach in front of us, with big waves crashing noisily in the surf. It's pretty much deserted, aside from another couple walking further down. There are a few small hotels lining the edge and a couple of restaurants with tables and chairs butting up against the promenade. It's as close to paradise as I think we'll ever get.

That is until I spot the first restaurant. My heart sinks as I see the giant TV screens hanging inside. The outside of it might look beautiful. It has a shabby-chic whitewashed wood exterior, no glass in the windows, and what looks to be fishing gear pinned on the walls and wine bottles on the tables with candles in. But if I'm not mistaken, and judging by the all-male clientele, this is very much a sports bar, and not what I had in mind.

I brace myself for Will to lead me in, but instead we walk straight past. He barely looks at it, and doesn't even remark on the fact that they're showing cricket. Instead, we go to the restaurant next door, which is beautiful in a completely different way. There's a large outdoor terrace that has white muslin drapes, like our bedposts, giving diners a sense of privacy, and the tables are surrounded by a mixture of blue and turquoise chairs that mirror the adjacent sea.

It's still fairly early, and with the restaurant being so empty the waiter seats us on a table overlooking the beach.

'I can't believe we're actually here,' I say, trying not to pinch myself as I sit down.

'I know.'

'Just think, we could have been at home stripping that awful wallpaper right now.'

'God, could you imagine.'

'It was your idea. Taking a week off to do the DIY,' I say, laughing.

'Well, we're going to have to do it at some point. I'm sure that alien wallpaper makes me have weird dreams.'

'Perhaps. I can do a bit over Christmas.'

'Yeah, right, as if you'd take time off from watching *The Wizard of Oz* and eating Quality Street.'

'Oh, that's a point,' I say, thinking how well he knows me. 'Can't mess with tradition.'

'I could always do it one weekend.'

'Ha, and miss the football?'

That's even more unlikely than me dragging my expanded post-Christmas belly off the sofa.

'I think there's a weekend in a couple of weeks' time where there's none on as they're playing midweek internationals.'

'Ah, well that's a date then.'

'Not the kind of stripping on a date I'd usually have in mind, but I guess needs must.'

I laugh. I like holiday us. The relaxed banter that flows easily and isn't interrupted by an argument over whose turn it is to unload the dishwasher or who used the last loo roll and didn't replace it. It's nice to sit and chat without being in a hurry to do something or go somewhere. Or, in Will's case, a game to watch.

We order our food and it isn't long before the waiter comes back over with our bottle of wine.

'Here's to a great holiday,' says Will, lifting his glass up.

I chink my glass with his and hold his gaze as I do, trying to work out what's happened to Will. He seems to have morphed into the perfect boyfriend, no revenge needed.

28

I curse Will as I shimmy myself into my slightly too tight but sod it I'm on holiday denim shorts, not because I can't fit into them (it's not like he's been force-feeding me the mahoosive ice creams I've been eating all week), but because he made me change in the first place. I give myself a quick once-over in the mirror. While I look pretty good – my white floaty top is setting off my tan nicely and doing wonders with hiding my stomach – I still think I looked better in the yellow dress I was wearing originally.

I stare at it, thrown over the chair in the corner, with wistful longing. It's the kind of dress that you can only really wear on those really rare super-hot days in the UK. You know, the ones where men seem to think it's acceptable to go round Waitrose without shirts on (FYI, it's never acceptable – unless you're David Beckham) and women are seen sporting bikinis in the park. As well as being linen and super summery, it's also classy. It was perfect for a trip to the cricket, but I've been forced to change as apparently in wearing it I'd look like I was pledging allegiance to Australia, England's opposition today.

I walk out of the bungalow and lock the door. As I walk round the pool to the lobby I see Will talking to Joe. He'd gone to get directions to get to the cricket ground, but from the animated nature of their conversation, I'd bet they've found some common sporting ground.

'Hiya,' I say, bounding up to them.

They practically jump back in surprise and immediately stop talking.

'Ah, Miss Hunter, nice to see you,' says Joe, beaming away.

'Call me Lexi, please,' I say, but then I feel guilty as he's already memorised my surname, and his mental Rolodex must already be chock-a-block full with all the guests staying here.

'Right, well, you two better get going to the match,' says Joe.

'Thanks, bye,' calls Will as he takes my hand and leads me out of the lobby. I do a little wave over my shoulder, but Will's leading me so quickly that I doubt Joe saw.

'You're looking pretty good in those shorts,' says Will, as he slows down and cups my bottom and nibbles my ear.

I playfully push him back. I'm well aware what often follows that move and it's not like that can happen here – we are in public.

'I still don't see why I couldn't wear my yellow dress. I've been working so hard over the last two days to have enough of a tan to wear it.'

'Then just think how much better it will look later on in the holiday when you're even more of a bronzed goddess. Besides, I think your shorts are way hotter.'

His hand reaches for my bum again and I can't help but giggle as I try and bat him away.

He's probably right that the dress will look better the darker my tan gets, but part of me is wondering if my outfit change will start me on a slippery slope. Was I going to be opening myself up to not being able to wear blue back home as I might be mistaken for a Portsmouth supporter (his beloved football team's arch nemesis)?

'So where do we go, then?' I say, looking at the main road in front of us.

'Right here,' says Will, grinning. 'Apparently we flag down a little bus when we see one. It'll be marked Bridgetown.'

My shoulders sink a little at the thought of how easy and convenient that all sounds. I've not given my revenge plan for Friday much thought, and I was hoping it would be easy to recreate a Swansea scenario again. I had been naively thinking that the island would be a bit of a backwater, but of course, Barbados has a pretty solid infrastructure and we're staying in a swanky five-star hotel where taxis can be summoned at the drop of a hat. I could have at least hoped to get lost on the way to the bus stop, but again I'm thwarted.

'Do you know how regularly they come?' My last hope is that they run on island time – like in the Malibu adverts – meaning they'll be late.

'Apparently they come past every five or ten minutes.'

'Great,' I say, before muttering all the swears under my breath.

'Ah, here's one now,' he says, giving it a wave as if hailing a cab.

A vehicle slightly bigger than a mini-bus stops in front of us.

'Here we go,' says Will.

'This is it?' I ask, as I follow him on.

'Yep.'

He pays the driver, who seems to zoom off immediately, leaving us to stagger back to two seats in the rear, crashing into passengers on the way. No one seems to mind, though.

The sound of hip-hop drifts through the bus and a few of the passengers nod along to it, while others have animated conversations. There are inevitably a few other cricket fans on the bus. They have bright yellow and green T-shirts and thanks to my wardrobe faux pas this morning, at least I know who they're supporting.

I gaze out of the window, looking at the hotels and shops that line the route. Occasionally, I'm rewarded with little glimpses of the sea, flanked between big hotels.

'That's where Tiger Woods got married,' says Will, pointing to a large resort on our left. 'It cost millions, apparently.'

I stare open-mouthed at the entrance to the resort. It makes our hotel look like we're staying at a Premier Inn.

'Trust you to know that,' I say, laughing.

'Yeah, well, it's got a famous golf course too.'

'Figures. Did they have anyone über famous like Beyoncé or Madonna play for them?'

'Dunno,' shrugs Will. Of course he doesn't. He's not big into celebrity gossip – just sporting gossip.

'You just remembered the important details,' I say, sighing. 'Aka the boring bits.'

I watch the scenery some more before turning back to Will.

'So have England got much chance of winning this game today, then?' I say, trying to psyche myself up for the game. Well, I at least should make some effort, as if my little revenge scheme all goes to plan later in the week (as long as I eventually come up with a plan), then this will be the only cricket match I go to.

'I think they've got every chance,' he says defiantly. I think he was a little hurt that I don't share his unwavering belief that England will always win at whatever sport they're playing. 'They've played some decent games already this tournament.'

I try not to smile. He's got the same enthusiasm he has through most of the football season until he reaches the point where no matter how many matches Southampton win and no matter how many goals, they're never going to chase down the leaders and win the title.

'Although the Australian side's pretty good too,' he concedes, a little more quietly.

'Fingers crossed, then,' I say.

Will nods, before looking up as the bus pulls over to the side of the road.

'I think this is where we get off,' he says.

His case seems to be based on the fact the guys in the yellow T-shirts have stood up and are getting off the bus.

'Come on,' says Will, pulling me out of the seat as he hurries off before the bus drives away.

We step off the bus and look around, trying to get our bearings. It isn't easy, as aside from the main road we've just come from, there are no hotels, only a sea of small houses with fenced gardens around us. I don't see any cricket ground.

I'm about to suggest we get back into the bus, but it pulls away leaving a plume of smoke in its wake.

'Um, why are here? Where's the ground?'

'Joe said to get off the bus as we come into town. He said we'd see the floodlights and to follow them, that it'd be a five-minute walk.'

Will spins round in circles and he can't see what he's looking for. I think perhaps we got off too early.

I'm beginning to think we might get lost in the suburbs and not make it to the game. Accidental revenge might strike again.

'Which way shall we go?' I say, looking round.

'Let's follow those guys,' says Will, pointing at our new Australian friends. They seem to be striding purposefully up a street running diagonally away from the road.

'Perhaps they're going somewhere else? We don't want to get lost. Maybe we should wait for another bus and go into the city, I'm sure we'd be able to get a bus straight to the cricket ground.'

'I think we're close, come on. We don't want to lose those guys,' says Will, marching off.

I have no choice but to follow him and we've only gone a hundred metres or so before he triumphantly points at the most enormous post of lights poking up from amongst the houses.

'Oh,' I say, a little defeated.

Within minutes, we're at the edge of the cricket ground. I'm going to have to think a lot harder about Friday's plan for revenge, as that was far too smooth a journey and I can't imagine any hiccup that would ruin it.

As we queue up to get in, Will gives me a manic grin.

'I can't believe we're here. I've always wanted to watch cricket in the Windies.'

I crinkle my nose up in confusion. 'In the where?'

'The Windies – you know – West Indies.'

'Oh right,' I say, nodding, pretending that I'm better up on my geographical knowledge than I am.

'You're going to love it,' he says. 'I reckon once you see this game you'll be begging to come back again on the next tour.'

A woman in front of us splutters with laughter.

'Sorry,' she says, smiling. 'I didn't mean to eavesdrop, but that's exactly the type of thing my husband said to me when we first went to watch the cricket.'

She affectionately rubs the arm of the man she's with.

'You know you love it,' he says, shaking his head. 'I don't know why you're always pretending that you don't.'

She winks at me and I smile back at her in solidarity. I can spot a sporting widow when I see one.

She pushes her Jackie-O type sunglasses on to her head, the gold-encrusted Chanel logo catching the light. She looks really familiar and I'm glad I still have my sunglasses on to hide my scrunched-up eyes as I try and place where I know her from. The glowing tan, her expensive-looking maxi-dress. Perhaps she's someone famous, you know, some Z-list celebrity from *Made in Chelsea* or something.

'You're staying at our hotel, aren't you?' says the woman. 'The Tropical Beach?'

'Oh yes,' I say, a little downhearted. Of course that's where I know her from. For a minute there I was hoping I could have had a celeb spot to send to *Heat Magazine* – *Spotted Z-lister at Kensington Oval in Barbados watching the cricket.* That would have made a change from the usual spots in Tesco's or at the airport. 'I've seen you round the pool.'

I watched her yesterday, jealously, as she read her book looking like she was posing for one of the hotel website's photos. She didn't have a hair out of place and looked to have a perfect face of make-up on. In total contrast to me, as I always look like I've got red war-paint on my face, as no factor seems to be high enough to stop my T-zone burning and beads of sweat rolling down my face. Although, now that I've spoken to her, and she seems quite nice, I feel a little bad that I was wishing bad tan lines on her.

'So you're a virgin, then?'

'I'm sorry?' I say, coughing and wondering if I've misheard her.

'You know, a cricket virgin out here? Sorry, it's just that it sounded like it was your first time.'

'You and your big ears,' her husband says, laughing.

She tips her head over to the side as she raises an eyebrow.

'Actually, yes, it's my first match abroad,' I say, trying to ease the tension before a full-scale war breaks out between them.

'Ah, well, probably much like when you lost your normal virginity. The best advice I can give you is to grin and bear it,' she says, giggling. 'Although, at least with this one you'll get to drink your way through it.'

'What is with you, woman?' says her husband, turning her round to face forward. 'I apologise for my wife. She's been drinking mimosas for breakfast.'

'Ah, yes, have you been to the little beach bar on the seafront? They do the most incredible bagels, and mimosas.'

'Oh, we haven't. Maybe we'll try that tomorrow.' Or Friday. We could get too drunk to go to the cricket . . .

'You should.'

There's a lull in the conversation and we shuffle forward.

'It's not too late for you to run,' she says as she hands her ticket over for inspection.

I smile. 'I think I can manage one game on holiday,' I say, laughing.

'Two games,' says Will adamantly, 'don't forget we're coming here on Friday, too.'

The couple go through the turnstiles and we hand over our tickets.

'Oh, yes, two games,' I say, as if I'd forgotten the other one, when in reality I'd almost revealed my little secret.

'Too late,' says the woman. 'Well, I hope you enjoy it. My top tip is to play the drinking game: take a sip for every four, and every six down your drink.'

'And that worked so well the last time in Sri Lanka,' says her husband.

'Ah, yes,' she says nodding and smiling as if lost in a memory.

'Come on, before you land this poor girl in hospital having her stomach pumped.'

'I only had a drip, not a stomach pump,' she says, as if that is better. 'Anyway, I hope you enjoy it, and we'll see you round the pool.'

'Thanks,' I say, waving as her husband marches her off.

Will walks us in the opposite direction, and I'm sad for a minute that I'm not going to be sitting next to her at the match. She seemed like a right laugh and even if my liver wouldn't have liked it, I would have done.

'Ah, here we go,' says Will, as we climb up the stairs into our stand.

I look over the cricket oval and take in the explosion of colour on the pitch. There's a steel drum band playing, with dancers dressed in carnival costumes shaking their tail feathers energetically around them.

'Did you want a rum cocktail?' asks Will waving a drinks seller over from the corner. The man has a tray strapped round him, and instead of holding ice cream like at a theatre interval, it is full of rum.

'That would be lovely,' I say. Talk about a tropical paradise. So unlike anything I've ever experienced at a cricket match before.

Will hands me a drink as he pays for them, just as the England players walk out on to the pitch and start to warm up. The crowd go wild, bashing inflatable paddles together and whooping loudly.

Will takes my hand in his and starts stroking it, and much to my surprise I find myself grinning in happiness – at a cricket match! I try and tone down the smile – as I don't want him to realise that I'm enjoying myself, or heaven forbid, I'll find myself on one of these holidays every year.

I'm enjoying the party atmosphere and I'm almost a little gutted that we're going to miss the game on Friday as this is actually fun – but ssh, don't tell Will I just said that.

29

I'm slightly out of breath as I race through the lobby, trying not to be seen by the ever-attentive Joe. I don't want anyone to know I've been off-site, or else it might give the game away.

I survey the pool for the right spot to plant myself, before spotting a hammock strung up between two palm trees.

I slip my summer dress off, to reveal my bikini underneath, and kick off my flip-flops. I try to work out the best way to get into a hammock, but fearing that Will's going to be back any minute, I straddle it and then plonk myself in. It takes me a few minutes to wriggle around getting comfortable.

'Can I get you anything?' asks a waitress, swinging by with a tray.

'I'd love a rum cocktail, actually two, and can I order bar food here?'

She nods.

'Some of your king prawns, then?'

The waitress walks off and I turn my attention to sorting out my bag. I pull out a book and bend the spine back to make it look like I've read more than the first page, and I litter the floor beside me with suntan lotion and magazines.

I let out a deep breath as I try to relax. I've made it back here before Will, that's the main thing. I want him to think I've been here for hours. He went off this morning to the cricket, leaving me the perfect window to research my final act of revenge. I've got to make it spectacular – I owe it to my new blog fans as well as myself (and Vanessa).

My first thought had been to 'lose' the cricket tickets for tomorrow's match. Only, when I rifled through the few possessions in our safe, they weren't there. Will obviously took them with him in his rucksack. I then decided that even lost tickets wouldn't stop a super-fan like Will, as he'd no doubt get his BFF, Joe the concierge, to source us some more.

Thinking I needed to think more creatively, I went for a long walk along the beach, where an idea hit me – literally. I tripped over a large blackboard advertising king prawns. How brilliant would it be to play him at his own game? I could fake my own food poisoning on the way to the game, and keep him waiting for me as I use every toilet from here to Bridgetown on our journey to the ground.

The waitress comes back over and hands me one of my drinks and I practically down it in one.

She raises an eyebrow but says nothing as she places the other glass by my feet.

I make a start on the second cocktail. I'm under no illusions that my boyfriend will come back from the cricket sober, and I want to at least be on a par with him.

I'm scanning the pool to see if the woman from the cricket is here, when I spot Will deep in conversation with Joe. It looks like an intense conversation, and I feel like I should go over and check everything's OK.

'There you are,' says the waitress, handing me a plate of grilled prawns still in their shells.

I smile my thanks, momentarily forgetting about my boyfriend's plight in the reception until I see Will and Joe walk out of the lobby and stop just before the pool. They shake hands before Joe walks off towards another part of the complex.

'Will!' I shout and wave, practically throwing myself out of the hammock, choosing to save the plate of prawns rather than my self-respect as I land on all fours.

'Hey, you,' he says, almost taken aback to see me there. 'I thought you'd have been having a little siesta in the bungalow.'

'I may have had one in the hammock . . .' Or I may not . . .

'Great, well I'm just going to go dump my bag, and then I'll come and join you while you eat.'

'Um, OK. Have you eaten? I say, almost protecting my plate with my hands, I can't let him have the same food as me or else my plan will be ruined.

'No, I ate, um, earlier. At the, um, cricket. Yes, I ate at the cricket,' he says nodding.

'OK,' I say slowly. There's something off with Will. He's all fidgety and twitchy. If anyone should be acting that way, it's me, I'm the one lying. 'Are you all right?'

I suddenly remember the concerned look on his face as he was talking to Joe.

'Yes, fine,' he says abruptly. 'I'll see you in a minute.'

I watch him head towards our bungalow. It's the way a commuter would walk for the train – head down and at speed. He practically pushes past a family coming towards him, making them veer off into the grass with their pram. Where's the laid-back holiday version of my boyfriend gone?

But I don't have time to dwell on it. I've got to eat these bad boys before Will comes back. I know he said he's eaten, but if he's sat here watching me eating, he might just be tempted to try one. And if he shares the prawns, then bang goes my food poisoning plan. I turn my attention back to shelling and eating my prawns. Suddenly ravenous after my busy morning, it seems to take ages for me to top and tail each prawn.

I'm making good progress when I see Will walking over. I've got three left and I start to panic. I quickly try to clear my plate, but the quicker I try to top and tail them the quicker they slide through my hands. Damn them. I just about finish cracking the last one before Will comes along and I hastily shove it in my mouth. So much for enjoying my delicious prawns – I practically inhaled them.

'Blimey, you ate them quickly.'

'Hungry,' I say, thinking I'm going to be sick. But that's far too early in the plan. 'So how was the cricket?'

'Um, yeah, it was good.'

'Who won?'

'I'm sorry . . .?' he says, distracted.

'The cricket, who won the cricket?'

'Um, I think New Zealand won.'

Is it just me, or is my boyfriend acting strangely?

'You think? Were you not at the match?'

I look at his face as if to find any clues.

'Of course I was. I mean, New Zealand won. Sorry, it's the heat getting to me.'

I'm wondering if he's just had too much to drink, but I can't smell alcohol on his breath.

'I'm boiling. I've got to go for a dip.'

He walks over to the pool and hastily strips off his T-shirt and shuffles out of his flip-flops before diving in.

Well, that was odd.

The waitress walks over and takes away my plate and after agreeing to another cocktail, I pull my tablet out of my bag. After realising that the only people that love me are ASOS and Debenhams, I bring up my blog dashboard. I have a quick look over at Will to make sure he's still in the pool. When his head bobs up in the deep end I bring up my blog page.

A slight ripple of naughtiness comes over me, as there's an excitement that I might get caught. I scan the comments on my latest blog and it's heart-warming to hear that I'm not alone in my sporting widow status. I click on the stats and I'm amazed to see I've had over seven thousand views. I feel my cheeks start to burn and it's nothing to do with the midday heat.

I log out of my blog, chuffed to pieces at my almost famous status, and pull up my Facebook page. I take a look at my notifications to see what people have written on mine and Will's cricket selfie. Mostly people telling us how great we look. I'm just congratulating myself on the wise decision to pack the hair straighteners, when I see there's a comment from Robin. I'd managed to block out thoughts of work while I was away, but seeing his name immediately makes me think about my job and what he's written about it in his report.

Robin Cassidy
Hope you're fitting in the sightseeing amongst the cricket!

From anyone else, I'd read that with a hint of sarcasm, but that's not really his style. I realise that it is a bit of a wake-up call, though, as in amongst all the sand, sea and, of course, sex, we haven't actually seen a whole lot of the island. Apart from on the taxi ride from the airport and the bus to the cricket. I'll be a bit embarrassed to go back to work and admit we didn't see anything.

I've still got time to put that right. It's only lunchtime – we still have the whole of the rest of today.

I go to get off the grass and I stagger slightly. These rum cocktails are a little stronger than I thought. I try to style it out, but as I look round everyone's too occupied with headphones in their ears or swiping away at their phones to notice.

'Hello,' I say, wading into the shallow end and swimming over to Will.

I give him an enormous smile and put my arms around his neck. He loops his hands around my waist, and taking full advantage of the buoyancy of the water, I wrap my legs around his waist.

'Well, hello yourself,' he says, giving me a kiss.

He playfully pushes me around in the water and for a minute I forget all the watchful, or perhaps not so watchful, eyes around the swimming pool. If only we were in our own private villa – I think this romantic interlude would have ended a bit differently.

'So what do you want to do for the rest of the day?'

'I don't mind,' says Will. 'But I feel like being busy.'

'Excellent. Why don't we go back to the bungalow, get dressed and head out,' I say, wondering if heading back to the bungalow is a good idea when we're clearly feeling frisky and I desperately want to go sightseeing.

I pull away from him and he takes my hand and leads me out of the pool.

'I'm so glad we came here,' I say to him.

'I know, me too.'

We wrap ourselves in our towels and I collect up my things before we pad back to our bungalow, dripping all the way. The maid is just leaving our place as we walk in.

'Ah, Mr Talbot,' she says before winking at him with a large smile on her face.

I look up at Will as she walks away.

'Why did she just wink at you?' I say, slightly outraged and suddenly protective of my boyfriend. Was she flirting with him? In front of me?

'I didn't notice,' he says, clearly lying. His cheeks are redder than my sunburnt nose.

He's gone all fidgety again, like he was earlier when he came back from the cricket.

My mind races, trying to connect the dots. The hotel concierge, the maid, him not remembering who won the cricket. But unfortunately no picture is forming in my mind.

'So the cricket today . . .' I say.

'I'm going to jump in the shower and get this chlorine off. I'll be out in a minute. And when I get back let's not talk about the cricket. After all, we said we weren't going to let it spoil our perfect holiday.'

I'd usually say amen to that, but far from thinking that my boyfriend has been converted, I'm wondering what's wrong. Perhaps he never went to the cricket, perhaps he's having an affair with the maid and they were off in some hotel room somewhere, doing the wild thing, and Joe caught them. That would explain him being fidgety, the need to jump in the pool and now the shower (washing off the smell of infidelity), and the desire to go out for the day (to get away from those who know his secret) and to not talk about cricket (his shame).

It makes sense for all of a second, before I realise that it's not really Will. We all know how difficult it is to get him away from sport.

I'm clearly reading too much into Will's behaviour. I try to switch my mind into holiday mode again. If I want this trip to be some all singing, all dancing romance, then I should be making it happen.

I hear the sound of the shower and I wonder what I'm doing when I could be in the nice warm wet room. I walk into the bathroom, pulling my bikini off as I go.

'Hello, again,' says Will. And the bathroom gets a whole lot steamier.

So we didn't actually see any more of Barbados today than we had already. Thanks to the shower incident, followed by the cuddle and unexpected siesta in the bed. We surfaced from our bungalow at five. Not many daylight hours left for exploring. Instead we headed to the shop, bought a bottle of Cava and plonked ourselves on the beach to watch the sunset before later going to one of the little restaurants dotted along the sea.

'Do you think we could stay here?' whispers Will into my ear.

'I wish.'

Our life in Hampshire seems worlds away from where we are now. It's so blissful here, without the daily grind, the pollution of television and our smartphones, which we're keeping mostly locked up in the safe in our bungalow.

'We could move here. I'm sure Barbados needs data analysts, and I bet there's an arts body you could work for. Or, you could work on becoming a bestselling author?'

'That would be a dream come true.'

'I couldn't think of a better place to inspire you. I mean, isn't this the perfect setting for a romance novel?'

I shift my bum in the sand. I'm feeling slightly uneasy about my writing at the moment, as my blog's such a central part of it. With Will being so sweet, I'm beginning to regret the villain that I've made him out to be.

I sink back into his chest and he squeezes his arms around me.

'Let's do it. Let's move away,' he says.

'But how would you cope without Southampton FC?' I say, giggling.

'Ah, I can't believe I forgot them.'

'You'd lose your number one fan status.'

'Yeah, we can't have that. Sorry, Lex, looks like we won't be moving here after all.'

'Ah, shucks. God damn the Saints,' I say, clicking my fingers and shaking my head.

Even without the move to Barbados, right now, my life feels perfect. OK, so Will still loves sports, but this trip has been proof that it doesn't have to take over our lives. We've only watched a tiny bit of cricket, leaving us ample of time to spend together. That's what matters, right?

I know I said I was going to confront Will when I got back, but what if I'm wrong about how he'll react to me knowing his lie? What if he doesn't just apologise and instead we have some massive row? This trip has proved more than ever that Will is my soulmate. I couldn't imagine losing him.

I shake my head.

'What's wrong,' asks Will, looking at me strangely.

'Just stretching?' I say, twisting my neck with exaggeration. But really I'm shaking my head to silence what's going on inside it.

My heart's telling me to let it go, that I've got even with Will already and now it's time to talk to him about it and move on. Our relationship seems stronger than ever and I shouldn't be putting the needs of strangers reading my blog first, but I don't think I can help myself. I feel like I need some big conclusion for the blog, and tomorrow's revenge I hope will make a good enough final farewell.

'Do you want to sit here a bit longer, or do you want to get some food?'

'Sit here,' I say. 'Just for another few minutes.'

I want to remember this moment forever, the moment I realised how wonderfully content I am with my boyfriend and my life.

30

'Good job that floor's tiled, as if it was a carpet you'd have worn it out by now,' I say to Will as I walk into the lounge from the bedroom. I've been watching him pacing up and down in there for the last ten minutes while I finished straightening my hair.

I've been trying to eke out getting ready for the cricket, so that my bout of food poisoning could come on just as we're about to leave, but it's as if Will can sense what I've got planned, as he's pacing about, eager to go.

'Huh? Oh, yeah,' he says distracted. 'I was thinking, if you're ready, we could go for a walk before we catch the bus?'

'Um,' I say, stalling as I try to work out if that helps or hinders my plan. I guess it could be a bit like Swansea if we went out further than expected. Then I can complain about my stomach problems near the end of the walk just before we get on the bus – yes, that works.

'OK, why not. Let's go, then,' I say as I pick up my bag. I'm about to walk out the door when he looks at my dress. My beautiful *yellow* sundress. Oh no. I don't like where this is headed.

'Do you have to wear that?'

'Why? It's not the same colour as the West Indies flag, is it? I thought theirs was purple?'

'Um, there's the sun on it and that's yellow he mumbles. Can't you wear those little shorts again?'

I stare at him. Aside from the plane ride home, this is the last chance for me to wear this dress. And it's not like it's going to matter what colour I wear to the cricket – we're never going to get there anyway.

'This isn't one of those stupid superstitions that just because I wore the shorts when England won on Tuesday that I have to wear them again, is it?'

He looks at me before slowly nodding.

'Yeah, I know it sounds crazy,' he says, wincing a little. 'But would you? I wouldn't ask but it's such a monumental match.'

I roll my eyes. I'm about to tell him that he's being ridiculous, but he's all jumpy and nervous about this game and I don't want to piss him off before I put my plan into action. So, instead of kicking up a fuss, I pad back into the bedroom and slip off the dress. I find the shorts in a heap of clothes at the bottom of my wardrobe. They're slightly less tight than they were earlier on in the week, which is a bonus. I hunt around for my floaty white top but it's stained with suntan lotion and – I sniff an odd brown patch before recoiling – rum cocktail. Yuck. I pull out a white sleeveless shirt, one of the few clean tops I've got left, and slip it on. It's not quite like the other one, but I'm sure Will won't notice.

As I walk back out into the room, I see Will visibly relax. My wardrobe selection has obviously passed the test.

'Right then,' I say, hoping it's a case of second time lucky.

I turn towards the door and see our maid standing on the terrace, her hand poised to knock on the glass.

'Hello, good time to clean?' she asks, smiling widely as I slide open the door.

'Yes, we're just going out,' I say, smiling politely back, but dragging Will away. I'm still wary of her after the winking.

We walk along the gardens towards the pool and Will's even more jittery than he was inside. I feel like I'm walking next to an overenthusiastic toddler.

'What's wrong with you?'

I grab his hand to try and steady him. We only make it as far as the lobby when I'm forced to unlock my fingers from his.

'God, your hand is so clammy,' I say, rubbing my now moist hand on my shorts.

If anyone's supposed to be all sweaty and acting guilty, then it's me.

'Sorry,' he stutters. 'It's probably a bit hot to be holding hands anyway.'

It is thirty-two degrees and stifling, but we've only been out in the sun for a few minutes – at this rate he'll be sweating buckets by the time we reach the cricket ground.

'So where did you want to go for a walk?'

'I thought we could go to the beach,' he says, grabbing my hand and pulling me across the road, as there's a gap in the traffic, before I can make a case for the shops.

Will drops my arm as soon as we're in the alleyway leading to the beach and he's practically running, I'm doing my best to keep up, my flip-flops echoing noisily along the path and the thong pinching between my feet.

I can't believe he's this nervous about a cricket match. I know England will have to win to get into the semi-final, but really, he's acting like he's going to be batting himself.

'Relax, Will. England will do it. I'm wearing my lucky shorts.'

He manages a half-hearted smile but marches on, still jiggling, still tense. Maybe a walk was a bad idea after all; perhaps we should go to the sports bar for a drink.

Yes, I know, a sports bar, but it's pretty and in a great location, so this once I'll let it go.

'Will,' I call as he rushes on past the bar. 'Why don't we stop in here for a drink?'

He spins round and looks at me.

'I want to walk,' he says, not evening glancing in its direction.

'OK,' I say, psyching myself up for a power walk.

He leans over to grab my hand, presumably to hurry me along, when I hear a shout.

'You-hoo!'

I look up and see it's the woman from the cricket; her husband's shaking his head in shame at her.

I wave back, and she's beckoning me over, so I obediently drop Will's clammy hand and walk up to them. They're sat on the bar's wooden veranda, and I lean over the balustrade.

'Hiya,' I say, smiling.

'Hey,' she says again. 'So how are you getting on? Having a good holiday?'

'Yes, thanks. Going home tomorrow.'

'Us too. Bummer, huh?'

'Yeah, wish we were staying forever,' I say, looking at Will who's come up beside me.

'Do you guys want to join us for a drink? I've still got loads left in my pitcher,' she says, holding up a jug of neon-red liquid with numerous umbrellas and glittery sticks in it. 'And Richard here is being absolutely no help.'

'I'm far too hung-over. I told you you should have stuck to a glass.'

I try not to giggle at their gentle bickering.

'I'd love one,' I say, eyeing it up. Not only could I do with a drink, but I could attempt to ply Will with so much alcohol that he forgets all about the cricket.

'Great,' says the woman, pinching a clean glass off another table. 'I'm Josie, by the way, and this is Richard.'

'I'm Lexi and this is Will.'

I go to walk round to the table, but before I reach the veranda steps Will puts his arm out and stops me.

'Actually, thanks, but we don't want a drink. We're heading off on a walk, remember?'

I stare at my boyfriend. That was just a little rude, seeing as we don't really know them and they're only being nice. Not to mention that I'm really parched.

'Speak for yourself,' I say, 'I'd love one.'

Josie goes to pour the drink.

'I don't think that's a good idea,' he says. 'You said you'd come for a walk.'

It's not often that a walk would win over alcohol, in either mine or Will's books, but the hurt puppy-dog look my boyfriend's giving me tells me exactly who I'm going to listen to. Besides, the further away we are from the bus stop, the more chance we have of being late to catch one.

'I guess you'll have to drink it up yourself,' I say, pulling an 'I'm sorry' face. 'We're on a bit of a tight schedule as we're off to the cricket this afternoon.'

I feel as if I need to justify Will's rude behaviour.

'You got tickets? Aren't you bloody lucky. We had no luck with those ones,' says Richard.

'Thank goodness.'

'I heard that, Josie,' he says in a mock-stern voice.

'Yeah, well, we better go, or we won't have time to use them,' says Will, grabbing my hand again.

'Perhaps we'll see you back at the hotel later for a drink?' I say as Will and his sweaty hand drag me along.

'Come on, let's get going,' he says, picking up the pace.

'I don't understand what all that was about. I thought you'd love a drink to relax.'

'I just don't feel like sitting. We'll be sat down all afternoon at the cricket. Best to keep moving.'

If only he knew that we're not going to make it there.

We walk in silence for a while, and I get lost staring out at the sea. It's so beautiful here, the way the light catches on the waves and the sand sparkles like diamonds. I'm going to miss this place when we go home tomorrow.

Will slows right down to a stop to stare into an open shop-front. He's looking at an easel with photos of beautiful beaches.

'Look how awesome that place looks,' he says, pointing at it.

'It looks gorgeous,' I reply, taking in the Robinson Crusoe beach with its uninterrupted golden sand and palm trees growing diagonally – their leaves hanging over the sea.

'Why don't we go?' says Will.

I look at the shop, noticing the ribs and jet skis lined up at the front.

'I don't think we'll have time tomorrow, what with us having to leave the hotel and get to the airport.'

I sigh slightly; if only we'd come for a walk here this morning and noticed this place. I'm sure I could have hatched a revenge plan where we rented jet skis and got marooned on a beach. I could have sent him off for a swim and siphoned off the petrol. Trust me to come up with a plan too late in the day.

'We'll have to come back on another holiday to do it,' I say laughing.

'Let's do it now,' says Will.

My jaw drops open.

'But we haven't got time – the cricket,' I say before I can stop myself. What an idiot for reminding him.

'Let's do this instead. There'll always be another cricket match, but how often do we get to go on a jet ski?'

I audibly gasp in shock. *There'll always be another cricket match*? Who is this man? My boyfriend would never say something so heretical.

Does he not know it's me, not him, that's trying to stop him from watching this game?

I have to admit I'm slightly pissed off since I never wanted to go to the cricket and would rather have gone on that catamaran trip to see the turtles.

I'm about to get a bit stroppy, but then I realise he's delivered me my final act of revenge on a plate. OK, so he stopped himself watching the game, but I'm sure with a little bit of creative writing I can spin it on my blog to make it sound like it was my idea. And maybe, just maybe, this is proof that my revenge has changed him – that my boyfriend is choosing us over sports.

'Let's do it, then,' I say, nodding, before Will has a chance to change his mind.

His face lights up and we walk straight into the shop.

Ten minutes later we emerge back on to the promenade donning life jackets and big smiles in anticipation of our big adventure.

'I can't believe we're doing this,' I say, my eyes widening as I look at the beast of a jet ski I'm about to be let loose on.

This is probably the most spontaneous thing we've ever done as a couple and I'm so pleased that it's come about with no meddling from me.

'We've got to stop meeting like this,' says Josie.

'Oh, hello again,' I say, smiling at her and Richard. They're obviously going for a post-lunch stroll.

'What are you guys up to? Taking jet skis to the cricket?' she asks, pointing at our bright yellow life jackets.

'Actually, there's been a change of plan. We're going to take some jet skis to some beaches instead.'

'What? You're not even going to use your tickets?' says Richard, a look of horror on his face.

'Oh, you know what, you should take them. Shouldn't they, Will? There's no point in wasting them, and you could still get there in time.'

Richard steps forward and kisses me overenthusiastically on the cheek, and as he steps forward to Will, I wonder if he's going to do the same to him, but he seems to change his mind at the last minute and settles on a back slap instead.

I grin as this truly is a win-win situation.

'Um, you can't,' says Will.

'But we're not going to use them,' I say, the smile sliding off my face.

'It's not that. I don't have them any more,' he says quickly.

'You what?'

'I lost them.'

'You lost them?'

I'm so stunned that all I can do is parrot back what he's saying to me.

Richard whistles through his teeth and shakes his head in disbelief. 'Mate, of all the matches to lose tickets for.'

'I know,' says Will, nodding.

'Oh my God. This is why you've been acting so weird,' I say, gasping as it all starts to make sense. Him pacing like a caged tiger. Him making me change into jet-ski-friendly shorts. Wanting to go for a walk. Not stopping for a drink. 'You lost the tickets and you thought you'd cover it up by taking me out on a jet ski?'

Will nods slowly as if embarrassed that I've worked out what's happened.

That's why I couldn't find the tickets in the safe the other day.

I stifle a laugh. Silly me for thinking that he was doing this because he'd changed; he was trying to cover up a mistake.

'Sorry, Lexi. I know I made a big fuss about not doing the catamaran so when I realised I'd lost the tickets I thought I'd try and make it up to you and I remembered about this place.'

'You poor thing, missing out on another game,' I say with a hint of sarcasm.

'I know, but I think the jet-skiing should make up for it.'

Richard splutters a noise as if to suggest that he doubts that.

'You're so right,' says Josie, seemingly happy that she's had a reprieve. 'I've always wanted to go on one of these bad boys.'

She mock revs the engine handle on one and makes a broom-broom noise.

'You should come with us,' I say, feeling a bit bad that I got Richard's hopes up and then dashed them.

'No!' shouts Will.

All three of us look at him, and I raise an eyebrow to signal how rude he's being.

'I mean, they've only got two jet skis left. Perhaps you could do a boat cruise instead?'

'But they can have one of ours and I'll share with you,' I say in slight relief. I was getting a little bit scared that I was going to zoom myself out to sea and not be able to get back again.

'Um, but you've been drinking,' says Will, pointing his finger accusingly at Josie.

'But I haven't,' says Richard. 'And I reckon that last night's booze will be out of my system by now. I think it's a great idea. I'll go and sort it out.'

He waves over the owner of the jet skis and starts to negotiate their trip. Will gets involved as the owner seems a bit worried that they're taking one of our jet skis, but a quick chat and it all seems sorted.

'This is going to be so much fun,' says Josie, squeezing my hand.

'I know,' I say, almost shrieking with excitement.

It's going to be great going out with them for the afternoon. I've always wanted to be one of those people that makes lifelong friends on holidays. And we already know that we've got lots in common. The boys and their sporting obsession. Us girls and our sporting widow status. We'll be BFFs by the end of the day, I just know it.

31

I watch Will and Richard zooming around on the sea in front of us. Is it my imagination or are they going a little fast?

They come speeding towards the shore and they stop a little way out, Richard spraying Will as he flies in behind him.

'Sorry, mate,' he says.

'No problem, mate,' says Will through what seems to be gritted teeth.

I think perhaps the boys haven't quite realised the BFF potential yet – but we've still got the rest of the afternoon to work on it.

The owner of the jet skis pats Will on the back and with a thumbs up wades back to shore. It looks like the boys have proved that they know what they're doing and we're being let loose on the ocean.

'Come on, ladies,' says Richard, slapping the back of his jet ski.

'Why don't I go with Will, shake things up a little,' says Josie as she splashes into the shallows and swings her leg over the back of his jet ski.

'OK,' I say, nodding.

'Yes, we like to get to know other people when we're on holiday,' Richard says, patting me on my thigh as I get on the jet ski behind him, making me think I'll grab on to the hand rails rather than his waist.

'Wouldn't you rather go with your husband?' says Will, only I don't hear Josie's reply, as Richard lets out the throttle and whoosh – we're off.

I immediately let go of the back handles and grab him, clinging on for dear life.

There was me thinking we'd be going on a nice gentle pootle up the coast, and now I'm clinging on to Richard, desperately trying not to be thrown off like I'm on a banana boat.

It's not long before Will and his jet ski appears in front of us, and I can't quite help wishing I was riding with him. Josie's sat very close to him and her hands seem awfully low down his waist.

But, as if he's in a bid to distract me, Richard's off again, over-taking, bounding over the waves, and I thud up and down on the seat as we do.

After what seems like hours, but is probably only minutes, we come to a stop.

'How about that beach?' says Richard, pointing.

It's not the beach from the photo, but it's still pretty. It's in a slightly sheltered bay with a wall of trees at the rear making it pretty secluded.

'Um, I think there's a better one just a little way up,' says Will, who's now alongside us.

'How do you know that?' I say, wondering when my boyfriend swatted up on his island geography, seeing as we've barely left the resort.

'I'm sure the one from the photos is around here somewhere.'

'But this one's so close, and I could really do with a pee. That tree over there would be a perfect cover,' purrs Josie.

'I told you, you should never have had a pitcher,' says Richard, as he starts up his jet ski and heads towards the beach. As soon as we come to a halt I jump off into the water, relieved to have stopped. I'm feeling ever so slightly seasick and I'm glad to be getting on to dry land.

Richard's already dragging the jet ski to the beach as Will pulls up. Josie hops off and runs to the tree.

Will seems to hesitate before dragging his jet ski out of the water.

Josie walks back over to us and leans down to wash her hand in the sea before standing upright and surveying the beach. 'Now, this really is paradise,' she says.

'Isn't it just?' I say, staring in disbelief that we're the only people here.

Will says, 'I think the other beach is supposed to be better, if we get back on the skis and –'

'Relax, we've got the whole afternoon,' I say. 'We can spend a little time here and then go on to the next beach. We're in no rush, are we?'

Will looks at his watch, and he starts to fidget.

'No, I guess not,' he says.

I look around before I sit down. There's not a lot to explore, so I might as well settle down and take in some of the view. Will plonks himself next to me and sprays me with sand that sticks to my wet legs.

I try and brush it off before taking off my life jacket, instantly regretting the white shirt choice. It's going see-through and it's not like I'm even wearing a bikini underneath. I guess that's the price to pay for spontaneity. I self-consciously fold my arms over my chest as Richard peers over.

'Now this is just what we've been looking for,' says Josie as she starts to strip off. She did remember her bikini, only she doesn't stop when she gets down to it. 'Be free my beauties,' she says, exhaling in relief as she throws her top on to the sand beside her.

Blimey, as if I wasn't jealous enough of her sunbathing when she has her bikini on – let's just say she makes my boobs look like I've got two fried eggs in my bra.

'That feels so much better. I can't believe they're so funny about topless sunbathing here. I mean, what sort of a country with such beautiful beaches makes it illegal?'

Josie sits herself down and lies back, propping herself up on her elbows. Richard starts to unbutton his shirt slowly as if he's doing some sort of a striptease, and then reaches for his shorts. Oh God. This is getting worse by the minute. The shorts hit the sand revealing a pair of tight swimming trunks, and I'm wincing thinking he's going to pull those off too, but luckily for me he settles down in the sand next to Josie – phew! It's not often that I'm pleased to see a man in budgie smugglers, but I'm willing to make an exception since the alternative would be unbearable.

'So, um,' I say, wondering what we're going to do now. I hadn't really thought this through when I'd invited them on our romantic beach trip. If it was just Will and I here then who knows what we'd have been doing now, but I'm imagining we might have ended up as scantily clad as the other two. But now it's the four of us, sitting pretty closely together with them practically naked, it's a tad awkward. I'm slightly scared after Richard's comments about getting to know people, and that thigh squeeze was a little close for comfort. I can't help thinking that I might be stuck on a deserted beach with a couple who are looking for some sort of *ménage à quatre*.

And the worst of it is, I'm feeling uncomfortable all by myself as Will doesn't appear to have noticed.

I'm usually not bothered by topless women sunbathing, but Josie's right next to me and I feel like I'm having one of those cringey communal changing-room moments. You know, the one when the whole changing room is pretty much empty yet you still end up sharing a tiny little changing bench with one of those women who likes to walk around letting everything hang out. When it happens to me, I do that terribly British thing of pretending I can't see. That's what I need to do now.

'So, you come on these sporting holidays a lot, then?' I say, as if I'm perfectly at ease hanging out with my semi-naked new friends.

'Oh yes, too many,' says Josie, rolling her eyes theatrically. 'We've come to a few in the West Indies, and we've done the Ashes in Australia.'

'Cover your ears, Will.'

And your eyes. Not that I needed to worry; he's staring intently at the sky.

'What was that?' he asks as he's clearly not been following our conversation.

I don't know what's he looking for as there's not even a cloud to see.

'Josie went to watch the Ashes in Australia with her husband.'

'For our honeymoon,' she adds.

'Oh, my goodness,' I say, laughing. That so could be us. 'Now that is dedication.'

'Uh-huh. I joke, but it was a trip of a lifetime.'

'Well, not really, as we're going to go back for our fourth anniversary when the next Ashes are out there,' says Richard.

Josie shakes her head.

'He's bloody sporting mad. You be careful, Lexi. You go on one of these holidays and then every holiday is based around another sporting event. I used to think that my holidays were the only escape from his sports schedule, but now they've just become part of it.'

Now this I can cope with. Us bonding over our sporting widow tales.

'Oh, come on,' he says. 'You love it just as much as I do. Remember the time we bumped into Jimmy Anderson at the bar? I don't remember you complaining then.'

Josie's cheeks colour and she begins to fan herself with her hand. 'Ah, Jimmy. Too bad he didn't take us up on our offer.'

I swear she has the same glint in her eye as I've seen in Cara's. It makes me think that I don't want to know what that proposition was, especially not when she's licking her lips, seemingly lost in a daydream. So much for safe ground.

'So, tell me about you two,' she says, as if snapping herself back to the present. 'Where are you from in the UK?'

'Just outside of Southampton, in Hampshire,' I reply.

'Near the Rose Bowl,' says the husband. 'Or what is it now, the Ageas Bowl?'

I nod. God, he sounds like Will. His UK geography is also based on sporting teams and venues. He so could be Will's BFF – if this whole slightly pervy side to Richard and the semi-nudity have so far meant that their couple BFF status is hanging precariously in the balance.

'What about you two? Where are you from?'

'Cheltenham,' says Josie.

'Oh, I like Cheltenham. Will and I went one December.'

'Let me guess, to the races?'

'Amazing, how did you know?'

'Just a hunch,' she says, and we laugh.

'So what do you do?'

'I'm an arts officer at our local council.'

'And she's an aspiring writer,' says Will.

I didn't realise he was even listening. He turns as he says it, for the first time breaking away from the sky and clearly noticing Josie's boobs. He immediately turns back to the horizon.

'Oh, that sounds intriguing. What sort of things do you write? Fiction or non-fiction?'

'Fiction. Mainly thrillers, but I've being playing around with writing something a bit more along the lines of a romantic comedy.'

I feel Will's hand grab at my leg as there's a rumble overhead, and I look up to see a passenger plane in the distance heading away from the island. That'll be us tomorrow, I think sadly. As quickly as he grabbed my leg, he pulls his arm away and loses himself once more in his sky watching. Don't tell me he's going to become a plane spotter as well as a sports fanatic.

'That's really interesting. I wish I could do that. I just would have no idea what to write about,' says Josie.

'It's not really the writing that's the hard bit,' I say, as if I'm the world's most knowledgeable writer. I dig my toes into the sand and watch as the crystal-clear water creeps ever closer towards us. 'It's the editing that's difficult. That's when you've got to transform the rubbish you've written into something intelligible. The ideas are easy to find when you start to look for them. Like the other day when we were at the cricket, I was wondering what it's like for the cricket WAGs. What they do when their partners are off on all their fancy cricket tours? Are they back at home looking after the kids, or are they flitting around the Caribbean with them?'

Richard picks up a bottle of suntan lotion and without asking starts rubbing it on Josie's back. She's starts moaning with pleasure and I join Will in staring at the horizon.

'Not much of a killer thriller in that idea,' says Josie, between groans.

'No, not so much. But, as I say, I've started to write a bit of women's fiction lately.'

I notice Will's started to dig a hole in the sand next to him. Maybe he's trying to dig his way out of here. With the erotic massage that appears to be going on next to us, I don't blame him.

'You all right?' I whisper, hoping he'll suggest we make a speedy getaway.

'Yes, yes,' he says. 'You know me, I'm not very good at sunbathing.'

'Right. Well we could always go and see another beach. Do some more jet-skiing.'

'But we've just got here,' says Richard. 'We've got the skis for another couple of hours so there's no rush.'

I'm hoping Will might suggest we go off and meet them somewhere else, but he doesn't.

'Yes, let's stay here for a bit,' he says.

I sigh. At least Richard seems to have finished with Josie.

'Lexi, do you want some?' he says, raising an eyebrow to the sky, a cheeky grin on his face.

'I'm fine, thank you,' I say, trying to remember when I last applied lotion. I think I'd rather burn.

'Suit yourself, but you're missing out on these magic hands,' he says, wiggling them.

I turn to look at Will and he's fidgeting, clearly as uncomfortable as I am. So why does he want us to stay?

'You know, you should write about this type of thing,' says the woman . . .

Being stuck on a deserted beach with a couple of semi-naked swingers.

'What? Chilling out on a deserted beach?'

'No, not this literally. I mean the sporting holiday. Write about being stuck on the sidelines.'

Little does she know how close to home that is at the moment.

'I can't imagine that would be very interesting for people,' I say, trying to steer the conversation away. I feel far too uncomfortable talking about this with Will sitting next to me.

'Of course it would. You probably don't realise it, but I bet you've got loads of anecdotes. I've recently started following this blog on the Internet about a sporting widow.'

I cough as I almost swallow my tongue. I can feel my face starting to burn and it's got nothing to do with the sun.

'Are you sure that you don't want to go back on the jet skis? I feel like I can hear the main road from this beach. Maybe we can find somewhere quieter,' I say, looking around and hoping the fear of people being nearby might be enough to get the others to move.

'Talk about bat hearing. I can barely hear it,' says Will.

Good to know he's still listening to the conversation.

'Oh, you should totally read it,' says Josie, ignoring me. 'I just can't remember what the full title of it is. But, you know, she's a proper sporting widow, just like us,' she says, elbowing me as she laughs.

I want to laugh her off as if to protest that I'm not one, but I can't. My throat seems to have gone very dry and I'm unable to talk. My stomach is churning now, really clunking around and I'm feeling like it didn't get the memo that I no longer need to have a stomach upset.

'I think it's got revenge in the title.'

Uh-oh. It has to be another one. Surely there are lots of other blogs about that. She couldn't possibly be one of the seven thousand people who has read mine, could she?

'Sporting Widow seeks Revenge,' says her husband, joining the conversation.

'That's it,' says the woman.

Oh, fuck.

I start to feel beads of sweat form on my forehead and my hands get as clammy as Will's were earlier. What are the chances of that? I look round for somewhere to go, but I don't think I'd be able to push the jet ski back into the water and I'm not that strong a swimmer. I look back at the trees at the edge of the beach. Perhaps I could make a break for the road?

Don't panic Mr Mainwaring, I say to myself as I try to remember to breathe. After all, it's a blog on the World Wide Web. She doesn't know I wrote it and therefore she doesn't *need* to know I wrote it. Will isn't going to magically guess from the title, as he is oblivious to what I've been doing.

'Have you read it?' says the woman. 'It's brilliant.'

I shake my head, lying. While I'm desperately uncomfortable with the subject matter, I can't help but be the tiddliest, tiniest bit pleased that she, a virtual stranger, has managed to find it on the Internet and read it. Not only that; she thinks it's brilliant. God, I'm so conflicted between wanting to jump up and down and scream that it's me that's written it, and wanting to run away for fear of discovery. And even though Will is heavily distracted, I don't think either of those responses would go unnoticed.

'I really fancy a drink?' I say to Will. 'Why don't you push me a jet ski out and I'll go and get some.'

'Ooh, rum cocktail for me,' says Josie, clapping her hands with delight.

'You can't take one of the skis out, you weren't given the lesson,' says Will, looking at me as if I've gone nuts.

'But I'm parched,' I say, trying to do a fake cough. 'Perhaps you could take me back?'

'Have some water.'

He digs around in his backpack with one hand while seemingly restraining me with the other.

'But it's warm,' I say, whining like a total diva.

'If you were really thirsty you'd drink it,' says Will, patting my hand firmly to end the conversation.

'But –' I say, going to stand.

'Just stay here,' he almost orders as he pulls me firmly down.

I look at him in shock. He's never physically restrained me before.

'We'll go up the coast in a bit, I promise. We'll see if we can find you a bar. But I feel like we should just wait here for a bit, OK? We don't want to miss anything.'

I look at the translucent sand, turquoise sea and baby-blue sky and out at the horizon. All have remained unchanged since we got here. I'm wondering what exactly he thinks we're going to miss if we go.

'But –' I start, unable to think of anything else to try.

Josie breaks out into spontaneous laughter.

'What's with you, woman?' asks Richard.

'I'm just remembering one of the blog posts. It was so funny.'

So we're still talking about this?

'I'm so thirsty, I really think we should get on the jet skis and –'

Will puts his arm around me and brings me into a big cuddle. I'm often moaning that he should hug me more, but really this isn't the time to start.

'Hang on, Lexi,' says Richard, jogging over to a jet ski.

I look up. While I don't really want to go on the the back with him again, but beggars can't be choosers. If it means escaping this conversation, I'll take a ride with him, thigh strokes and all.

I try and wriggle myself free of Will's surprisingly strong hug.

'Here,' says Richard, looking triumphant as he pulls a can of Coke out of a cooler box. 'The guy said he'd left refreshments in the back.'

He hands one round to each of us.

'There,' says Will. 'Problem solved, Lex. Thanks, Richard,' he says raising his can as he takes a sip. Oh great. Now they become BFFs.

Will releases his grip on me slightly and I take a quick sip of my drink. I feel well and truly hemmed in here now, with a half-naked woman who won't stop talking about my very secret blog and my boyfriend who's acting like a deranged prison warden.

Short of faking that food poisoning and disappearing into the bushes, the only way of getting out of this unscathed is to shut Josie up.

32

'So what do you do back home?' I say to Josie, trying to distract her in the hope she'll drop the topic of the blog and forget about it.

'I work in PR.'

'Ooh, that sounds glamorous.'

'Not really. I work for a frozen food company, so really it's all about managing spin about fish fingers and the like. The only exciting thing to happen at my work was the horse-meat scandal, and that was the first time I'd ever had a proper buzz from the media.'

'So did your company use horse meat?'

'No, thank goodness. But you know it's a sad state of affairs when that's the highlight of your working life. I sort of always dreamt of doing PR at a big firm up in London, and then I met Richard and it never happened.'

Josie looks wistful and I realise I shouldn't have such a big smile on my face as she goes on to explain her career woes, but I can't help it, I'm just so relieved at the change of topic.

'Do you think you need to redo your hair?' asks Will, as he glances at his watch for what seems like the millionth time since we got here.

'My hair?' I say, running my hand through my ponytail.

I'd spent all that time straightening it before we left the hotel, only to shove it up hastily before we went on the jet ski.

I look between Josie, who's now telling me about her under-graduate degree and the correlation between her drinking too much and her ending up in her job, and Will, whose eyes are fixed on the sky with such intensity that I can't understand how he's even noticed if I've got a hair out of place.

'Um,' I say, searching for words.

He's in such a strange mood right now that I obey him. I let my ponytail down before using my fingers as a rake to flatten it out a bit before carefully putting it back up.

'There,' I say, seeking approval.

'Better,' he says, barely nodding.

What has got into him?

'Richard has told me on a number of occasions that I should quit and start up my own PR firm. But you know, we'll be trying for a baby soon, and it's such a bad time to leave my job. Much better to stay at a company that has excellent maternity benefits. Don't you think?' Josie pauses for breath and gives me head-tilted stare which suggests she now wants my opinion.

'Um, yes, stay until after you've had your kids and they've grown up a bit,' I say half-heartedly, as I'm still trying to work out what's going on with Will.

'Yes. Exactly what I think.'

Josie rolls over so that she's leaning on her front. She's quiet for a moment and I don't want her to get lost in her thoughts again, as the last thing I need is for her mind to wander back to my blog.

'So, where's the best place that you two have been on one of your sporting holidays?'

It's not as far away a topic from my blog as I'd like, but it's all I could think of.

'Apart from the Ashes, our best trip was one to Dublin to watch the cricket. It got rained off and we spent the day in the Guinness Factory instead, followed by watching lots of live music in all the pubs. Fantastic place. Have you been?'

'No,' I say, shaking my head. 'But I'd love to.'

'That's your favourite trip? The one where we didn't watch any bloody cricket, with those tickets I'd paid a fortune for,' says Richard.

'Darling, it was the spending time together that counted. Isn't that what you always tell me when we're going on these trips?'

Richard mumbles as he stands up again. 'Anyone want another drink? Mate, do you want one?' he asks Will.

Will looks like someone's just called him back from the International Space Station.

'What's that?'

'Drink?'

'Er, yeah, yeah.'

'How about you, Josie?'

'Is there any rum hiding underneath the Coke?'

'I don't think so,' he says, poking his head in the cooler box. 'No. We so should have thought to bring rum, shouldn't we, Lexi?'

I nod. Right now a pitcher of rum might have been just what I needed to relax me.

'Lexi, your shoulders are looking awfully red. Why don't I put a little lotion on them?' says Richard, picking up the suncream again.

'Um, I'm sure I can do it myself,' I say, snatching it from him.

'Now where's the fun it that?' he says.

Uh-oh. Perhaps this is how the swinging starts.

'Will can do it,' I say, thrusting the cream into his hands.

'Huh?'

'Put cream on my shoulders. Apparently I'm going red.'

Richard settles himself back down on the sand next to Josie, realising he's not going to get anywhere. Will slops a bit of cream on to my back and starts gently massaging it in.

'Talking of sporting trips away. You know that blog I mentioned earlier? The woman went away for the weekend to watch the football and she plotted her revenge to stop him going to it,' says Josie.

I desperately hope Will's gone back into space.

'That's a bit mean, isn't it? he says.

He's looking directly at Josie. I guess now that she's lying on her front, boobs covered up, he feels safe to join the conversation.

Will finishes doing my shoulders and plants the cream back down into the sand.

'They went all the way there and she stopped him going. Guy must have balls made of sponge,' says Richard.

'What's that noise?' I say, cupping my ear to pretend I can hear something.

Will, who's been jumping at any rumble in the distance since we got here, hasn't registered what I've said and is looking directly at Richard.

'Actually, he didn't know it was her,' says Josie, 'It was all done as sabotage. She'd booked this cottage where she knew they'd have no signal, left lights on in the car and when the battery was flat they couldn't get anywhere. But don't feel sorry for him. You should hear what he did to deserve it.'

'I think my feet are burning. Richard, can you pop some cream on them?' I ask in desperation, hoping that he has some sort of foot fetish, or at the very least another man touching me might distract Will.

Richard practically leaps at the chance and picks up the lotion as he drops to his knees in front of my outstretched legs.

'And just how did he deserve it?' asks Will, seemingly unbothered that another man is caressing my feet.

'Well, that's the awful bit. He'd gone and faked a stomach bug to get out of going to a wedding with his girlfriend, and then he'd gone to watch his team play football instead. Talk about a rat.'

Oh God. Short of taking my top off and getting Richard to suncream my boobs, I can't think of any way of stopping the car crash that's about to happen.

'Yeah, but she's just as bad – she's flipping crazy,' says Richard. 'Can you believe she deliberately tipped a drink over their Sky box so he couldn't watch the boxing? As much as I love you, honey, if you did that it would end in divorce. Ow, fuck,' he shouts, as my leg kicks out in reflex – accidentally, of course.

'I'm so sorry, Richard, are you OK? Do you need to go back to our hotel, put some ice on it?'

'No,' says Richard, jumping up and hopping from foot to foot on the sand as he bites his lip and cups his manhood. 'I'm sure I'll be fine in a second.'

'I'm so sorry,' I say to Josie. 'Cramp in my foot. But really, I think we should perhaps pack up and go.'

I pick up my bag and start to stand up, but Will puts his arm out silently as if to stop me and it's enough to confirm that he knows.

Of course he knows. He's not an idiot.

'Oh, don't worry about it,' says Josie, laughing, 'he likes being treated rough.'

Her husband laughs slightly and winces as he sits down, and she rolls back round to face the sea, giving him a quick rub on the arm.

'So what else did this blogger do?' says Will in a quiet measured voice, looking between Richard and Josie.

I need to tell him it's not what he thinks, that the blog's been embellished and the line between fact and fiction well and truly blurred.

'There was that one about the sex,' says Richard. 'Now, I fully approved of that one. Getting all dressed up in sexy lingerie and trying to distract him from going to the footie. I'm still waiting for that to happen to me.'

'You'll be waiting a long bloody time,' says Josie.

I can't take this any longer. My cheeks are burning and I've started to shake. I turn to Will and he looks straight into my eyes.

'How could you?' he says in almost a whisper, before he stands up.

'How could you what?' says Josie, confused.

I'm momentarily stunned, before I come to my senses. Hang on a minute, buster.

'How could I?' I shout at him, the anger making my feet work again. 'How could I? What about you?'

'What about me?' he asks, turning to look at me again.

'What about you missing the wedding to go to a game? Don't you want to know how I found out?'

'I take it you saw it on Sky Sports?'

'Yes, I saw it on Sky Sports. Mike from the office texted me a screenshot when I was at the wedding. The wedding where I was at telling everyone you were practically on your deathbed.'

'You've known since then and you haven't said anything?'

His eyes are practically bulging out of their sockets. I don't think I've ever seen him so mad.

'Don't make this my fault. You were the one in the wrong. You're the one that lied to me. You had every opportunity to tell me on the Sunday.'

'Why didn't you just tell me you knew, instead of doing all those horrible things. Making me miss games. Messing up our Sky box. What else did you do?'

'Does it matter? I think you're missing the point here, that I would never have done any of these things if you hadn't been lying to me in the first place. What was so bloody important about that game that you had to miss the wedding and lie to me?'

'You should ask your dad.'

'Oh yes, because you Southampton fans all stick together. Well, I'm sure in this case he'd realise that you were out of order.'

'You wouldn't understand,' he says, sighing.

'Oh, of course not,' I say, rolling my eyes. 'How could I possibly understand anything as important as your sport. Do you have any idea what it was like for me to go to the wedding by myself? Or how awful I'd felt about leaving you at home ill?'

'I did feel bad, that's why I suggested going to Swansea. I was trying to make it up to you. But turns out I had no need to feel bad as what you've done is so much worse.'

'I was just getting even. I only stopped you watching a few games.'

'Do you think that's why I'm so mad? I'm not thrilled to know that we'd gone all that way to Swansea to watch the football and it was all thanks to you that we didn't even see the game, or that you fried a perfectly good satellite box – I might have seen the funny side if you'd told me. The reason I'm so bloody angry is that you told everyone in the world except me. That stuff is so personal. You blogged about our sex life, for crying out loud.'

'I wouldn't say I blogged for the whole world to see. I've been doing it mainly to help out my writing. It's not like anyone knows it's me. I changed our names, the sports teams, there aren't any photos. It's not even like that many people will have read it.'

'Um, well some people have read it, clearly, seeing as we're in Bar-fucking-bados and have met people who've read it. That sounds global to me.'

I'm about to point out to him that the Google analytics of the site wouldn't agree, but it doesn't feel like the time or the place.

I look at Josie and Richard. They're pretending not to be looking, but they're sitting so close to us they're probably getting sprayed with the spits of venom flying from our mouths. Now they're the ones trapped in an awkward situation with nowhere to go.

'I can't understand again why this is all *my* fault,' I say, thinking that I've finally got his betrayal out in the open. I've been waiting for so long for this to come out and now that it has, it's been turned on its head and he seems to be blaming me, like I'm the one who was responsible for him not going to that wedding.

'Because you ruined our trust.'

'No, you did. When you lied and told me you were sick and didn't go to the wedding. You started this. You . . .'

I look down at my finger, which is firmly pointing in the direction of his face.

'Well then, I'm ending it.'

He turns and walks over to his jet ski.

'What do you mean?' I shout.

'It's over, Lexi. Us, we're over,' he says, as he pushes the ski out into the sea.

There's a sharp intake of breath from Josie and Richard, but it's nothing compared to the gasp from me.

I can't believe he thinks it's all my fault. Or that he's broken up with me.

I'm too stunned to stop him from leaving. He starts his jet ski, and as it roars into life he pulls away.

'You all right, hun?' asks Josie, coming over and squeezing me into a hug. She's closely followed by Richard, who also comes over to lend his support, and I'm soon sandwiched between them.

If I wasn't angry enough with Will, I'm now fuming that he's marooned me here with these two and all their lumps and bumps pushing into me.

'I'm OK,' I say, lying as I try to wriggle out from between them.

I replay the fight with Will over in my head and the anger starts to boil up inside of me. Why can't he see he's in the wrong? And surely it should be me dumping him?

'Did you want me to take you back to the hotel, get you sorted?' says Richard, 'I reckon we could probably all squeeze on to the jet ski. We wouldn't mind squishing up, would we, Josie?'

'No,' I say practically running away. 'I reckon from what I can hear the main road is just through those trees. I'll go and have a look.'

'If it's the squeezing on,' says Josie, 'I can stay here and Richard can run you back.'

'It's fine. The road runs all the way down the coast, and there are all those taxis. I'll be fine.'

'We'll wait here for a bit, then,' says Josie, 'if you don't get a cab or can't get through, we'll work something out.'

'Thank you,' I say, as I slip on my flip-flops and storm off towards the trees.

'And thank you for the blogs,' she calls. I don't reply as I'm too focused on getting back to the hotel to talk to Will.

It doesn't take me long to walk through the trees, and I soon find myself on the main road. Our beach wasn't the secluded paradise we'd assumed it was.

Fuelled by anger, I flag down a taxi and as the driver pulls away I take a deep breath and try to work out exactly what I'm going to say to my now ex-boyfriend when I see him again.

33

I jump out of the taxi and practically throw dollar bills from my shaking hands. I'm yo-yoing between being furious at Will and desperate to patch things up. In all of our seven years together we've never had an argument like this, and I don't know what to do or how to fix it.

I dash through the hotel lobby and I'm past the swimming pool and heading to our bungalow in record time.

'Sorry,' I mutter, as I bash straight into someone.

'That's OK,' says Joe the concierge. His face lights up when he recognises me. 'Ah, Miss Hunter, or should I say the soon to be Mrs Talbot.'

I know people remembering your name is probably what you pay for in a five-star hotel, but if I'm honest I find it a bit overfamiliar, and I'd probably prefer softer loo roll.

I go to move around him but he puts his arm out to stop me, his face beaming like he's happy to see me.

'I didn't expect you back so soon. And where is Mr Talbot?'

He looks around behind me, as if I could be obscuring all six foot two of Will with my little frame. He's looking at me expectantly, waiting for an answer.

I wrinkle my face up, frustrated as I want to reach my bungalow and I'm in no mood to make small talk.

I force my lips into a half-smile to try and fob him off, and he beams back at me until he looks down and gasps.

'What?' I say, looking down at my front, wondering if my shirt's still see-through from all the water it took on board while jet-skiing. But a quick pat suggests it's all dry and as far as I can tell there's nothing out of the ordinary.

'Don't worry about it,' he says waving his hand. 'Um, why don't you come with me? I don't think the maid is finished with your bungalow yet.'

'Not finished? But she came in when we were leaving hours ago. It wasn't that unclean.'

I feel slightly affronted that the hotel thinks we would be that dirty to need a three-hour room cleaning.

I go to move round Joe, who is really beginning to hack me off, but he moves in front of me again.

'Free cocktail? It's happy hour and the first one is complimentary. Come join me.'

'I thought it started at six p.m.?' I say, confused. I'm sure it's only just after four now. That's one long hour . . .

'Free cocktail,' he says again.

For a second I'm tempted. I feel like a drink would calm me down a bit. I'm wavering, but then I remember Will. I've got to see him, now.

'Thanks, but I'll pass. I need to get back.'

'But,' he says, raising his arm in front of me.

'But nothing. I'm going to my bungalow.'

So what if the maid is still sodding cleaning. It's not like I've not seen a bottle of bleach before. I'm pretty sure I can handle it.

I practically push Joe out of my way, and I can hear him calling and stuttering in my wake, but I ignore him.

Unlocking the door, I immediately notice the rose petals. They're scattered haphazardly all over the floor. No wonder Joe thought the maid might be in here sorting it out.

'Will?' I shout. 'Will?'

Nothing. The bungalow is eerily quiet except for the noisy hum of the fridge.

I follow the trail of rose petals into the bedroom and freeze. Far from being haphazard in here, they are formed into a large heart on the bed. To the right is a bottle of Moët champagne on ice. There are unlit candles around the floor, and I immediately feel like I've walked on to the set of rom-com movie.

My hand flies up to my mouth, as it suddenly starts to explain Joe's odd behaviour. What was it he called me – the soon to be Mrs Talbot?

Oh God. He wasn't staring at my chest, he was staring at my naked ring finger. I run my hand over it and I suddenly yearn for what obviously should have been on it.

Will was going to propose.

I hear the door slide open, followed by noisy footsteps.

Will stops short when he sees me. He looks between me and the rose petals, and instead of anger there's just sadness in his eyes.

'I'd been hoping to make it back before you. I wanted to clear it up before you got a chance to see it.'

'You were going to propose?' I say, still not believing it could be true.

He doesn't answer me.

'Will,' I say, my voice softening. The anger that I'd been feeling starts to wain at the thought of him wanting to marry me.

He looks up at me and sighs.

'Yes, I was going to propose.'

'Here?'

I look around the room at the rose petals and the champagne, and I think how unlike Will this is. This is the kind of thing romantic men do, not my sports-obsessed boyfriend.

I look over, smiling at Will. But he's not smiling back; he's got a sad look etched on his face.

He picks his case up from the corner of the room and begins chucking his shorts and T-shirts into it.

'How were you going to propose?'

The words get caught in my throat. I can't believe I waited seven long years for the proposal and then right at the last minute it was snatched away from me.

But I still need to know how it was going to happen. It's as if I've seen the end of a movie without seeing the start. What was the story that I was going to proudly retell over and over again of how it happened?

He goes into the bathroom and I hear him clattering about. I'm too shocked to follow him. He returns a minute later, bottles spilling out of his wash bag. He shoves it in his case and presses everything down.

'Will, how were you going to propose?'

Was it here? At the cricket match if he hadn't lost the tickets? At the beach?

He sighs loudly. 'If you must know, the whole jet ski afternoon was planned. We were never going to the cricket. We were going to go to a beach further down from the one we ended up on, and a plane was going to fly past. You know, the ones with the messages flying from their tails.'

I blink back tears.

'It was going to say MARRY ME LEXI.'

'It sounds so perfect,' I say quietly. A small tear escapes from my eye, opening the flood gates. Before I know it, I'm sobbing. I ruined what would have been the best engagement story ever.

'But we can still get engaged,' I say through the sobs. Right now it's not just that I want that ring. I want my boyfriend back. I know he lied to me about the wedding and he was wrong to do that, but we've been together seven years and that's the worst thing he's ever done to me. It's hardly a basis for us to break up. And if I can forgive that betrayal then surely he can forgive me? So I disrupted a few of his sporting plans and I may have told a few people anonymously. No one knows it's about us. Well, maybe our new friends Josie and Richard do, but aside from them, to the other seven thousand we're strangers.

'Josie and Richard,' I say out loud. 'No wonder you were so weird about them coming.'

'Ha, I know,' he says, laughing almost manically. 'I thought they were going to ruin everything but it turned out they did me a huge favour. Without them, I'd never have known what you'd done.'

Me and my stupid big mouth. If I'd not invited them, then Will would never have found out. We could have got engaged, had a rational conversation about what happened with Ian and Vanessa's wedding and I could have deleted the blog before he was any the wiser.

'We can still get engaged. I still want to marry you.'

He looks up at me and laughs before shaking his head.

'Look what an amazing time we had this week. And over the last couple of months, it's like we've rekindled the magic of our relationship.'

'I wasn't aware that we needed rekindling. Are you trying to say that aside from those months the last few years have been pretty shit between us?'

'Well, no,' I say, thinking that I'm digging a deeper hole. 'But things did get a little stale, with your sports watching and me writing. I just mean that the trip to Swansea, and the little outfit from Ann Summers, you know, it all added to the spice of things.'

'You mean all the times that you manipulated me and then told the world about it so that they could have a good laugh.'

'No one was laughing.'

'Weren't they? Didn't Josie say she'd found it hilarious? I'm sure she wasn't the only one. For heaven's sake, Lexi. If you felt there was something lacking in our relationship why didn't you say so? "Hey, Will, why don't we go out somewhere instead of you watching the TV?" I would have agreed. It would have been nice to go out for midweek drinks, or for us to go away for more weekends. You didn't need to trick me.'

'Ha!' I laugh out loud, spluttering through the tears. 'I just needed to ask you? I'm constantly trying to get you to do things and there's always something. A match that you've got to watch or a game you've got to go and see.'

Does Will not notice that he's obsessed with sports? That his life is timetabled by them?

'It's always the sport, it always comes first.'

'If I had to choose between you and sports you know that I'd have chosen you.'

'Would you? Would you, really?'

I think back to the night I was going to seduce him in my sexy outfit. I really did think it was touch and go as to whether he'd choose me. And that's when I had my kit off. What about when it's only me on offer. No naked flesh, no sex on offer, just my dazzling personality? I've never been entirely sure.

'Of course I would.'

'Then what about Vanessa and Ian's wedding? You put the football first then.'

'Is that how little you think of me?'

He shakes his head.

'What an idiot I've been. All these months of planning this holiday, and this proposal.'

He throws the last of his clothes in the case and firmly shuts the lid.

'You mean, this was all planned before? The holiday wasn't because you felt guilty?'

'Of course it wasn't. I had nothing to feel guilty about. I'd booked it back in July when we'd agreed to take the week off work to do the DIY. I knew that if I didn't appear to do it as a last-minute thing, you'd suspect the proposal.'

All the pieces fall into place. I can't believe how long he's been organising this.

'But,' I say, my head spinning too much for me to think of a reply.

'It's too late now,' he says firmly.

I watch him as he zips up his case. I know I sabotaged my own relationship when writing the blog, but I can't take full responsibility for this mess.

'You still should have told me the truth about Vanessa and Ian's wedding. This whole thing would have been avoided if you'd been honest with me.'

He scoffs and as he pulls the suitcase off the bed it clatters noisily to the floor. I can't believe he doesn't want to talk about it.

'Will, look,' I say, as he goes to walk out the door. I'm getting pretty mad now. He can't just walk out. An hour ago he was planning to marry me – to be with me for better for worse. How can he just up and leave? 'Why don't we sit and talk about this like adults. Like we should have done after the wedding. We're both to blame. You should never have lied to me or gone to the football, and I shouldn't have tried to get back at you with the revenge, and I certainly shouldn't have written about it.'

Will freezes on the spot and he seems to be thinking about what I'm saying. His forehead unwrinkles and he looks at me calmly. For a second I hope he's about to unpack and produce the ring from his pocket.

'You're right. We should be rational. The whole situation is majorly fucked up and it just proves that we're not right together.'

I sniff loudly and wipe what is probably a combination of snot and tears on to the back of my arm – ever the attractive crier. But the rage is bubbling again and I don't care what I look like.

'Fine!' I shout. 'If that's how you feel, then it was a lucky escape. I'm glad that we missed your airplane flying past and that we aren't engaged. I don't want to spend the rest of my life feeling like I'm second fiddle to you and your bloody sports. So you're right: let's call it quits.'

'Fine by me!' he shouts as he picks up his suitcase.

The past seven years flash quickly before my eyes and just like that it's all over. Off he goes, out into the dusk.

I sit down on the bed, surrounded by rose petals, and I wonder what I'm going to do now. I'm all alone, thousands of miles away from my friends and family. My holiday BFF Josie is probably still on the romantic beach getting frisky with her pervy husband, and unless I go and take the concierge up on his offer of a cocktail, I'm all alone on the most romantic holiday I've ever been on. The only person that I'd want to be here with has stamped on my heart and abandoned me. So I do what any sane dumped woman would do, I pick the champagne bottle out of the cooler and pop the cork. I need to drown my sorrows, and fast.

34

I wake up the next morning with a wet pillow. For a second I wonder if I've cried that many tears that I've soaked it, but it smells strongly of chlorine. I shift slightly and realise that the pillow isn't the only thing that's wet. My whole bed is damp.

I roll over towards Will to get him to explain what's going on, but he's not there.

My head pounds as I furiously try and piece together what went on. The words of the argument float round the room as if on a loop. Him shouting, me crying.

I sit up and try and remember what happened after he left. There was the Moët that tasted pretty good, especially with the inclusion of a few salty tears as I drank.

But that still doesn't explain the bed being wet.

I hear a knock at the door. Ah, that must be Will, come back to grovel and to admit that he was totally out of order.

'Hello.' My voice is hoarse, as if it was used a lot last night. A vision of me singing pops into my mind. Me singing 'All By Myself', to be exact, à la Bridget Jones. The memory starts to become clearer, and I realise I was in a bar singing karaoke, belting out the song with a microphone in one hand and a drink in the other.

Uh-oh. Rum cocktails.

I hear the knocking again.

I cough to try to clear my throat.

'Hello,' I shout again. 'Will.'

I know I should get up, but the fact that I'm naked and lying on the bed with what is shaping up to be hangover of the century is doing a pretty good job of stopping me.

Besides, it's only Will.

'Hello,' calls a female voice as the patio door slides open.

It's not Will. I scramble to gather the sheets around me and make myself semi-presentable.

'Lexi?'

Josie's voice echoes around the bungalow.

'What if she's choked on her own sick,' I hear Richard say. 'We never should have left her alone.'

'And think how freaked out she would have been if she'd woken up with us and she'd been naked,' says Josie.

I pull the sheet firmly around me so that there's not an inch of flesh on display.

The door to my bedroom opens and they audibly gasp as they see me.

'Ah, Lexi, you're OK,' says Josie with relief as she sits down on the edge of the bed next to me.

How did they know that I was naked?

Oh God. Unless we did something last night. What if I went to their room to find comfort and I found something else.

I'm half expecting Richard to climb into bed. But he keeps a respectable distance behind Josie.

I must be looking at him in total panic as he narrows his eyes at me in confusion.

'Now that we know you're OK, Lexi, I think I'll go wait for you both in the restaurant,' he says.

'All right, honey, see you soon,' Josie says, turning round to Richard briefly, before snapping her head back to me. 'Are you OK, hun?'

I shake my head.

I am not OK. Not only do I have a raging hangover, I have not the foggiest clue what is going on and what we got up to last night.

'To be expected after all you've been through.'

'And what's that exactly?' I say, wrinkling up my face, wondering if my blackout isn't to do with a hangover but more that I've buried my memories in shame.

Josie stares back at me.

'You know, the break-up.'

'Yes, I remember that bit of the night. But I don't know what happened for the rest of it. I have a vague memory of karaoke.'

'Oh yeah, that was quite . . . special. I don't want to hurt your feelings, hun, but I don't think you'll be auditioning for *The X Factor* anytime soon. You remember being in the bar, right?'

I cast my mind back.

Apparently, one whole bottle of champagne, downed straight from the bottle, affects your judgement. I remember I went in search of more at the bar and that's when I saw the karaoke machine in the corner. It seemed like the perfect way to vent my emotions.

But that still doesn't explain the nakedness or the wet hair . . .

I try and pull the sheet further up over my head as if it's going to shield me from the shame. Josie tilts her head and pulls a sympathetic expression, and bam, it's like I'm back there in the bar. I remember.

As I finished my wonderful set on the karaoke machine, I spotted Josie and Richard walking past and I dragged them in. I made them sit there while I told them the whole sorry story – and not the exaggerated version from the blogs – as we all drank cocktails.

But that's as far as I can remember.

'Um, so last night, the swimming pool,' I say, as if testing the water.

'Uh-huh, that was fun, right?'

'Right,' I say. 'It was just us?'

'And the other people from the bar. You got us all in. Seemed like such a good idea at the time,' she says, laughing.

I try and laugh along, but a memory begins to knock at my mind. A boob here. A willy there. Uh-oh – we were all naked.

Joe's face pops into my mind.

I didn't make him get in too, did I? But then I remember him being pretty cross and saying something about getting in trouble with the police.

'You walked me home?' I say slowly.

'Yes.'

'And then you left?' I say, praying that the skinny-dipping was as bad as it got.

'Yes, of course. Why wouldn't we have?' she says, looking a little confused.

'Oh, I was just worried, as I can't remember ... And you know how yesterday you were telling us about propositioning Jimmy Anderson?'

I don't want to spell out exactly what I'm thinking.

'What, about me seeing if he wanted to join us for a nightcap?'

'A nightcap,' I say winking. 'Is that what the kids are calling it these days?'

'Lexi,' she shrieks. 'You did not think that we would do that, do you? What do you take us for, some sort of swingers?'

'No, of course not,' I say, trying to back-pedal.

'When you got back in here you stripped off yourself, and threw your clothes on the floor, before getting into bed. I then hung them out on the balcony to dry off as I left so that they'd be dry enough to pack in your case. That's why I came over, really. To check if you wanted any help packing?'

Packing? Oh no. We're flying out tonight.

'What's the time?' I say, in a sudden panic that I've slept most of the day away in a hung-over stupor.

'It's just gone eleven thirty. We're supposed to have been out of the bungalows at eleven, and when I checked out, I enquired at reception and they said you were still here. So I thought you might need help. I'm guessing you're pretty hung-over?'

'Yeah, pretty much.'

'Do you remember much of last night?'

'Far more than I want to,' I say, wishing I'd had a total blackout.

'Well, we worked out we're on the same flight back. You're going to get a taxi to the airport with us at two thirty. I've spoken to the manager and they're aware of your situation and they said they'd give you until twelve to get yourself ready. So how about you jump in the shower and I'll start to get your stuff together for you to pack? Then we'll get you some lunch and get you feeling a bit better. OK?'

I look at Josie and while on the one hand she's the reason that I'm here alone in the first place, on the other hand, if she wasn't here right now I'd still be wondering why my hair was damp, and would probably have been forcibly evicted by the cleaning staff. At least she has a plan.

'Come on, off to the shower with you. I'll start on the stuff in the lounge area,' she calls over her shoulder as she leaves the bedroom. I head into the shower, hoping that when I return I'm going to magically feel well and my mind will have been suitably cleansed of everything that happened the night before.

'Now, Miss Hunter, you make sure you come back some time,' says Joe as we leave the reception. 'And if you fancy a change of career, I'm sure that we could have an opening for you in hotel entertainment. Karaoke, pool games.'

He adds a wink to his beaming face and I want the ground to open up and swallow me.

I close my eyes for a minute and wish I was wearing ruby slippers that I could tap three times to find myself back at home.

But unfortunately for me, my espadrilles don't seem to hold any magical powers.

At least I'll never have to see him again.

I've had such a busy time of it this morning. Trying to scrub off the embarrassment of last night in the shower, packing up everything, while trying to rid myself of a hangover. Richard and Josie have been chivvying me along and keeping me company, so I haven't had much time to think about Will and our demise.

The hangover might have subsided, but I'm still angry with him and I can't imagine how I'm going to spend eight hours sitting next to him on a plane. Hopefully I'll get lucky, and there'll be a spare seat on the flight and the cabin crew might take pity on me. You never know, I could tell them my sob story at check-in and they might upgrade me to first class. With England having not made it into the semi-finals yesterday, maybe I'll sit next to Joe Root and we'll fall madly in love and therefore I'll get my ultimate sporting widow's revenge on Will. But not even that thought cheers me as I can't imagine being with someone else.

'Here's the taxi,' says Richard, bringing me back to reality.

He loads the cases into the car and Josie and I get into the back while he sits with the driver.

I spend most of the time on the ride to the airport looking out of the window. I try and drown out Richard chatting to the cab driver about the cricket. It's the exact same conversation Will would have had.

A pain burns in my chest when I think about him. As mad as I am for him blaming me, I still can't believe it's over. When we did this taxi journey the opposite way a week ago, I never in a million years imagined I would be coming back without Will.

A tear forms in my eye and I wipe it away quickly before it escapes.

'You OK, hun?' asks Josie.

'I think so.'

I'm lying, but I can't tell her how I really feel as if I start crying I won't stop for the rest of the flight.

I don't want Will to see me like that.

'You never know, you might sort things out on the plane.'

We could, or we could spend eight hours arguing. But after last night, I'm not sure if we have anything else to say to one another.

'Or we could always join the Mile High club? I wonder if the three of us would fit in the toilet?' says Richard, laughing.

Josie told him about my suspicions and he thinks it's hilarious, making jokes about us having threesomes wherever he can. The only upside is that he's not being tactile with me any more – maybe it made him realise how he came across.

Josie laughs at his joke, and I half smile, before I turn my head back to look out of the window.

I just want to be at home, but I've still got eight bloody hours on a plane before I get there.

I pity whoever is going to be in the seat next to ours. Even if we don't argue, there'll be so much tension in the air you'll be able to cut it with a knife.

'You know he came back for you yesterday, don't you?' says Josie.

'What? When? Last night?'

'No, when we were at the beach. Not long after you went off into the trees, he pulled up on the jet ski. He said he felt bad having left you.'

He was furious, and yet he still went to check I was OK. I couldn't work out how he didn't beat me to the room, but now I know. I feel my heart breaking that little bit more and I try to blink back the tears.

The taxi arrives at the airport and Josie and I split the fare, paying the driver while Richard wrestles with our luggage.

We walk into the large, bright terminal and I immediately start looking for Will. I scan the backs of the heads in the queue to spot him, but I can't. He probably won't turn up for a bit yet anyway – he always leaves it to the last minute.

We shuffle round the queue, my eyes remaining fixed on the airport entrance. Anytime anyone comes in, my heart races, just in case it's him. The queue behind us is getting larger, and I'm starting to get worried he'll miss check-in.

'Next, please,' bellows a voice from the desk in front of us.

I keep looking at the entrance, before Josie pushes me gently forward.

I wheel my case over and clumsily lift it on to the belt.

'I'm supposed to be checking in with my boyfriend, well, ex-boyfriend. There's two of us on the reservation, but he's not here,' I say quickly.

The woman behind the desk looks from my passport up to my face and raises an eyebrow as if to say she's heard it all before.

'I know that we've booked seats together, but I don't suppose there's any way that I can sit away from him, is there?'

I can't stand the thought of an argument, or worse, silence. Him ignoring me for eight hours would send me loopy. I'd rather have him out of sight, out of mind.

The woman looks back down at her computer and she starts tapping away at the keyboard.

'Let's see,' she says making a guttural noise. 'Ah, there's a note here. Apparently he changed his flight and went out this morning.'

'He what now?' I say, a little too loudly. I'm aware that probably everyone in the queue behind me can hear me.

'He changed his flight,' she says.

'But we've got the same reservation, how did he do that?'

'It seems he's an executive club member. He used some points and paid a balance.'

'So he's gone. Just like that?'

'Yes, he'll be landing at Heathrow in about half an hour's time. Not only will you not have to sit next to him but you'll have a spare seat next to you. Give you some room to spread out.'

She goes back to typing away and I'm left dumbstruck. I know five minutes ago I didn't want to sit anywhere near him, but I at least wanted him to be here. The fact that he's abandoned me in Barbados is too much for me to cope with and the floodgates fly open and the tears start to fall.

'There, there, Lex,' says Josie, passing me a tissue. 'You'll be home soon.'

She clearly heard everything when she was standing at the desk next to mine.

I take the boarding pass that the ground attendant gives to me and I clutch it to my chest, before Josie leads me to Departures.

I glance at the giant billboard of a perfect-looking beach, all white powdered sand and crystal-blue sea, and I instantly think back to my time with Will on the beach a few days ago. That magical moment where I'd realised how perfect my life with him had been. We couldn't be further from it now if we tried. I shake my head as I read the caption on the poster, 'Come back soon'. It's as if it's taunting me, as there's no way we'll go back to that moment, or that level of happiness, ever again.

35

I've often thought that they should ease you back in to work gently after you've been on holiday, you know, let you work two or three hours a day at first, adding a few more each day until you're back to normal hours. To go from lazing around, cocktail in hand and the only decision being how long you spend tanning one side, to having to use fully articulated sentences and, in my case, potentially helping to secure millions of pounds' worth of funding for a charity, is a major shock to the system.

And that's without factoring in a break-up. I don't know how I'm going to get through it. It's not only about putting up with my mind replaying what happened over and over, but it's also having to be normal and polite to my work colleagues, and doing actual work on top.

I get out of my car and walk towards the depressing sixties concrete monstrosity of a building that I work in. It looks dark and gloomy any day of the week, but it's looking even less inviting today under the dark and cloudy sky. It's as if the weather is matching my mood.

I'm momentarily dazzled by the ultra-bright strip lighting of the reception as I walk in. My eyes sting, still raw from all the crying I've done over the last two days.

I managed to keep it together on the flight home, but walking into my house – my cold, empty house – tipped me over the edge. Will had been and gone while I was on the flight home. He hasn't told me where he is, and I have no inclination right now to find out. I'm too hurt, angry and fragile, and a little thankful that I don't have to see him while I get my head straight.

'Hey Lexi, how was your holiday?' asks Nancy, one of my colleagues, as I walk into the leisure department. 'You look a fabulous colour. Take it the weather was nice?'

'Uh-huh, weather was great,' I say, in total honesty.

I continue walking over to my desk and as I go through the motions of switching on my PC, I look over at the piles of papers that have been left for me while I've been away, and then my eyes fall on the photo frame in front of me.

I look up at Will's face as he smiles away as if he doesn't have a care in the world. His skin is the same olive colour it was when he stormed out yesterday. It was taken on our first holiday together in Zante, all those years ago. It was when I first realised I loved him.

Next to that frame is a photo of him and me at one of his friend's weddings. We're looking blissfully happy, and I remember at the time thinking that we'd be next.

I blink rapidly, trying to stop the tears from forming. What the hell am I going to do with the photos? I can't keep them on my desk. I don't want them acting like a constant reminder that my personal life is in ruins.

I look around and wonder if I can hide them in a drawer where at least I won't have to look at them and I then I can take them home tonight.

'Hi Lexi,' says Mike, just as I've picked up the photo frames.

'Oh, hiya,' I say, trying to smile up at him as he sits down at the desk next to me.

I feel like I've been caught red-handed and in a panic I bring the photo frames up to my lips and breath on them to steam them up. I give them a quick wipe over with the sleeve of my jumper, transferring a grimy layer of dust on to my sleeve, before placing them back in their original positions.

That's perfect. Just what I wanted to do, see them more clearly. 'So, was the holiday good, then?' says Mike as he stands up from his chair.

'Yeah,' I say, putting on the best fake smile I can muster.

'The cricket was good, wasn't it? That England game against the Windies. Were you there?'

My heart sinks. That was the game Will pretended we were going to on the day he was going to propose.

'No,' I say, the words catching in my throat as the memories of the real story – the lost tickets and the jet ski excursion – flood my mind. The tears are going to start to fall any second. I can just feel it.

'Oh. Well, you'll have to tell me about the ones you did see later on. I'm going to make a cuppa. Do you want one?'

'Yes, please,' I say with relief.

Mike gets up to get our drinks and I immediately pick up the photo frames and shove them in a drawer.

It's one thing telling my best friends about the break-up, but at what point do you mention it to work colleagues?

Do I slip it into casual conversation? By the way, I'm single now. Will's moved out. Or, do I just go for the ghosting option? Pretend he doesn't exist. Don't mention the break-up or Will and hope that eventually everyone will cotton on without me having to spell it out?

'Hello, Lexi.'

I jump out of my skin and slam my draw shut as I look up and see Robin sitting down at the desk opposite me.

'Hello,' I say, in as composed a way as I can. 'I thought you were going to be gone when I got back.'

I could really have done without being sat opposite him today as he's another person I'm going to have to pretend to.

'Yes, just finishing up. I've got a couple of notes that I wanted to go through with you, actually, and then my report will be ready to go back to the exec's office. I should be out of your hair by lunchtime.'

Phew, I think. I'm sure I can put my best poker face on until then.

'Have you got time to go through the information with me now?'

'Yeah, I was about to tackle my in box, but it's probably best to help you before I get stuck into that.'

The sooner I help him, the sooner he leaves and I can relax my facial muscles. I'll be left here with Mike, and he's not the most astute of men when it comes to reading body language. Anything to do with emotions or feelings usually have him running to the kitchenette to make coffee.

'OK,' Robin says, standing up and taking hold of the back of his chair. 'I'll come to you.'

I'm a bit taken aback. Why does he need to come to my desk? Why can't I shout the information over to him?

I sigh as quietly as I can.

'I take it you're pleased to be back after your holiday?'

'Of course I am. Ready and raring to go,' I say, sounding like a cheerleader at a funeral.

'And I take it you had a good time? Enough sightseeing thrown in with your cricket?'

'There wasn't much sightseeing,' I snap, 'but not so much cricket either. Just a really lovely, romantic trip.'

I'm blinking rapidly, trying not to cry at the memory of how good it was before it all went wrong.

'Is that so?' says Robin, staring into my eyes as if he's burrowing down into my soul.

'Yes.'

I'm sure the weak wobbly voice is going to give me away.

'Then why have the photos of you and Will disappeared from your desk?'

I follow his gaze. All that's left where there was once a collection of photo frames are fluffy lumps of dust and dirt that had resided there unnoticed, probably for years.

'Goodness, you're like the council's answer to Sherlock.' I take a screen wipe out of my top drawer and try to remove the dust.

'Perhaps I wanted to update the frames with super-romantic photos of my holiday.'

'Or perhaps you've taken them away because things didn't go so well when you were away?'

'I – We –' I stutter, but it's no good. As a single tear rolls down my face, I tell him everything he needs to know.

'FYI, it wasn't the photos that gave it away. It's the look you've got.'

'The look?' I ask, as I try to wipe a tear away with my finger as subtly as possible.

'Yes. Your skin might be glowing with your tan, but your eyes look like you've done twelve rounds with Mike Tyson, and your jumper's on back to front.'

I look down, about to tell him he's wrong, but he's bloody right. The V-neck that's supposed to be on the front of this jumper appears to be missing.

I hastily pull my arms out of my jumper and spin it round.

What sort of a man notices a thing like that? He's clearly far more observant than Will is, or I am for that matter. I'm sure I would have looked in the mirror before I left the house this morning. I can't have been paying attention to what I saw.

'I'm sure you are better off without him,' he says, shuffling his papers like they do at the end of a news report. 'And you're not old, so you should be fine to meet someone and have kids.'

He's smiling as if he's trying to lighten the mood, but it's something I'd not even thought of. What if I am too old? I know I'm thirty-one, not fifty-one, but what still?

I start to do some fast-thinking maths, figuring out that if I met a new man next year when I'm thirty-two, we could only date for around two years, be engaged for another year, then we could totally have a honeymoon baby and I'd be a mum at thirty-six. That's about normal these days, isn't it?

My biological clock starts to tick loudly in my head. What if I don't meet anyone in a year? It's going to take me time to mend my broken heart and get over Will. Then I've got to find someone new who I want to spend the rest of my life with. What if we then date for a few years and he's not right either?

Oh God.

Or worse, what if I don't meet anyone at all?

I've been so focused on my break-up with Will that I haven't considered a future without him.

I start to practically hyperventilate and I see a flash of panic in Robin's eyes.

'Don't worry,' he says, placing a hand on my shoulder. 'Women like you don't stay on the shelf, trust me. Now, let's take a look at these figures, shall we?' he says slowly, as if he's treading lightly. 'I want to make sure I've got all the facts right for my report.'

He pulls a sheet of paper to the top of the pile and starts to read off things. I struggle at first to concentrate.

Mike walks over and offers me a temporary respite as he places a cup of tea down at my desk and engages Robin in a conversation about some rugby game. It gives me a moment to compose myself and to convince myself that Robin is right – that I will have no problem meeting someone.

'Let's look at those figures,' he says again as Mike walks back over to his own desk.

I turn my head and look at him.

'The figures,' I say, concentrating on what he's saying, if only because it's taking my mind off the sorry state the rest of my life is in.

Finally, the clock strikes five and it's a respectable time to call it a day. I managed to somehow survive without crying and without giving away any details about my holiday to the rest of my colleagues. Robin was the only one to mention the split, even if anyone else had guessed, and when he left the department later on that morning he took my secret with him, meaning I could go on pretending that everything was hunky-dory.

Now I can officially go home and wallow, at least until Cara and Vanessa come over and we start the break-up debrief.

I pick up my handbag and walk out of my floor. I've just started walking down the stairwell when I hear my name being called.

'Lexi,' Robin's voice booms from above, bouncing off the sealed walls.

I stop where I am, and hear him clattering down the stairs until he reaches me.

'How you doing?' he asks as we instinctively start walking down together.

I can feel the tears start to well up. I was so determined not to cry at work, but the slightest hint of compassion in his voice is enough to tip me over the edge.

'I'm all right, thanks. How's it feel, being back on the top floor again?'

'Feels great to get back there, you know, away from you slackers.'

'Of course,' I say. 'And we're enjoying getting back to all our tea drinking and sitting around playing with stress balls.'

I'm actually going to miss having him in our department.

'Well, I thought I'd give you a nod to say that I've finished the report, and you've got nothing to worry about. I obviously can't give you any details as it has to go to the councillors first, and what they do with the report is their business, but you'll be fine. Whether that's a good thing or a bad thing,' he says, raising an eyebrow. 'You know, lack of boyfriend, lack of job would have made for a good clean slate for you.'

'Yes, lack of job would be exactly what I need when I've got to pay the mortgage by myself now.'

I shudder at the thought of anything relating to the house. Although that's not strictly true. We'll both have to pay the mortgage until we sell the house. I definitely can't afford to buy him out and I don't think he'd have any desire to buy me out – and he'd never be able to afford the repayments on his own.

'Oh, yeah,' he says, nodding as if he hadn't thought that through. 'But you know, you might not need to worry if you become a bestselling author.'

'Cos that's so likely.'

'Actually, I wanted to talk to you about that. Please don't hate me.'

This doesn't sound good.

'But I sent the first couple of chapters to an old uni friend of mine who works in publishing.'

'You what?' I practically scream.

'I know, I should have asked you, but I'd forgotten all about her working in the industry until she posted something on Facebook about a book launch she'd been at, and I sent it to her on the spur of the moment.'

'I can't believe you did that,' I say, feeling a little violated.

'I know, and after you trusted me to read it, but don't you at least want to know what she said?'

'She's got back to you already?'

'Uh-huh, and she told me to pass on her details to you and for you to forward on the whole manuscript.'

'She what?'

My mouth drops open in shock.

'She really liked the opening.'

I'm so excited that I can't help but fling my arms around Robin and wrap him up in a big hug before I pull away all embarrassed.

'Sorry – I, um – Thank you.'

'You're welcome,' he says, beaming away. 'I'll forward you all the information.'

I nod and for the first time all day, my mind's racing with positive thoughts.

'Thank you. How am I ever going to repay you?' I say, realising that right now I'd give him a kidney if he wanted one.

'You could buy me a drink. It's my birthday on Friday and I'm going out after work if you're interested. It's mainly people from the exec's office, but Mike said he'd come and you'd be more than welcome.'

'OK,' I say, thinking that as well as thanking Robin, it will get me out of the house, the most depressing place on earth at the moment.

'Great. We'll be in the King's Head.'

'OK, see you then, then,' I say, with a wave. 'And thanks again,' I call.

I walk over to my car, now with something to smile about. What is that they say about one door closing and another opening? I might have broken up with Will, but I could be a step closer to getting my book published.

36

I walk through the front door and I'm hit immediately by the smell of Will. How did I not notice before that Hugo Boss permeates the whole house? I storm straight into the kitchen and search for something that will mask it. I'm not known for my cleaning prowess, but I do find a can of furniture polish and a bottle of citrus Dettol. Rolling up my sleeves, I decide to clean the man right out of our house. Or at least take the scent out of the air, as really I'm not ready to clear away his stuff just yet. It feels far too soon.

I flick on the radio, and get to work on the kitchen worktops. It's a full ten minutes later when I notice that I'm listening to 5 Live.

What the hell am I doing? Number 42 Springfield Crescent can now be a sports free zone. I go over to the radio and retune it to Radio 1, and I smile. Ever the optimist, I'm finding at least one silver lining to being single again.

I'm halfway through blitzing the kitchen when the doorbell goes.

My first instinct is to panic. What if it's Will? I look down at myself. Work clothes with bright pink marigolds on and my hair shoved up into the world's messiest top knot. I'm not sure if I even put make-up on this morning, but if I did I don't hold out much hope for what it will look like given that I went into work with my jumper on back to front this morning.

'Hello,' shouts Cara through the letterbox, forcing my legs to move.

Phew. I breathe a sigh of relief.

'Hey, you,' says Cara, wrapping me up into a big squeeze before I've finished opening the door.

Luckily for me and my circulation, she lets go and opens the door fully, pushing past me as she walks in.

'Oh my God, you really are in a bad shape; you're cleaning,' she says looking down at my worktops. It's the first time they've had anything more than a casual wipe since Will's mum last came to visit.

'I know, it's actually a bit therapeutic. Who knew?'

'Well, when you get into the whole baking is therapy thing, then let me know. I'm always up for cupcakes. In the meantime, I stopped by the shops and bought you some break-up essentials,' she says, holding up a shopping bag and placing it down on the table.

'Oh, booze and fags?' I say, hopefully, remembering that had been my staple diet during my last heartbreak, when I split up with my university boyfriend.

'Um, no. It's all clean eating these days, I've bought spiralised veggies and avocados.

'Just kidding,' she says, looking at my horrified face. 'I got a packet of chocolate fingers, some Ben & Jerry's ice cream, and a takeaway menu from the Chinese.'

'Thank God for that. And there's also booze in there, right? I can take or leave the fags, but booze?'

'Yes, a bottle of white.'

I take the bottle from her and instantly feel happy as I put it in the fridge. See, I can do this. I may be a bit rusty, but I'll get there.

'So, are you packing up Will's stuff as you clean?' asks Cara.

'No, I don't know what to do with it yet. I don't know which one of us is moving out or if we both are, or if he'll come back and get his stuff or if he'll want me to pack it up,' I say, taking off the gloves and diving into the chocolate fingers box.

'I can't believe you haven't talked to him. It's been how long since you broke up? Three days?'

I nod my head. Three days, although with the time difference in Barbados, it's only been two and a half, yet it seems much, much longer. It's the longest I've gone without speaking to him since we met.

'I can't face it. I mean, I've gone to ring him and then turned off my phone. I know we've got things to sort out but I need some time to get used to the idea first, I think.'

I scrunch my eyes at everything we'll have to do. There's the house, the joint CD collection, our joint bank account, his old T-shirts I wear as pyjamas. Where do we start? Our lives are so inextricably linked.

'But it's definitely over, then? No hope of any reconciliation?'

'None. I'm glad that it's ended. You know, it was inevitable really. What with him and the sports.'

'Was it?' Cara digs into the box of chocolate fingers more to avoid eye contact with me than to eat one. 'I mean, you were pretty set on getting your relationship back on track.'

'Exactly,' I say, slamming my hand on the table. 'That's the point. If we were so compatible, I wouldn't need to get it back on track. We'd have been click-clacking along in such track harmony that I'd never have needed to take revenge in the first place.'

I study Cara's face and notice her lack of eye contact as she stares intently at my clean table.

'What?' I say, hoping she isn't going to point out that I've missed a spot. Cara's one of the most outspoken people I know, but at times she can be particularly quiet. It's usually when you know she's going to say something that's hard for you to hear.

'I just think that Will was the one for you, that's all. When you told me you were off to Barbados I had an inkling that he'd propose and I was really happy for you, as I knew he'd make you happy.'

'But you're always the one that thinks we need to spice things up.'

She stands up and without asking goes and gets the wine from the fridge. She's a true friend as she clearly has mind-reading capabilities.

'I know I was, but that's just it, I didn't think that he was fundamentally wrong for you, I just thought you could get a little bit more action, as you made it sound like you were on some sex famine. I was only trying to help things along.'

I take the glass of wine that she hands to me.

'But you were always moaning about him and his sports. Telling me to put my foot down.'

'Again,' she says, sitting back down at the table, 'I didn't mean for you to break up with him. Every man has some sort of a vice. Be it sports, gambling, computer games. In the same way that

I'm addicted to Instagram and Tinder. There's something wrong with all of us. We're all guilty of neglect at times.'

I'm about to scream. All these years I've thought she was anti-Will, and now she sounds like his number one fan.

'I thought you'd be pleased.'

'What, that I've got competition for the ever-dwindling pool of available men with their own hair?'

I smile.

'I just think you should talk to him. Seven years is a long time to be with anyone, it seems such a shame to throw it all away over a blog.'

'But it wasn't just the blog. He couldn't understand that his missing the wedding had forced me to do the things I did.'

'They forced you to do the things you did? What, tip drink all over a perfectly good Sky box? Stop him from watching a game of football he'd travelled a couple of hundred miles to see? I would have thought it would have forced you to have it out with him.'

I snap the chocolate finger I'm holding in two.

'You mean you're going to say that this is my fault? That I did this?'

'Yes, I am.'

Cara looks me straight in the eye, and I try not to get too jealous of her perfect eyebrows as I stare back at her.

One of the things I value most in Cara's friendship is her honesty. And while most of the time it leaves me wanting to erase my memory from her talk of her sexcapades, it's usually refreshing to hear her tell it how it is.

Yet today it stings like hell.

The only thing that has been keeping me together post-Will is the fact that I've thought it was for the best. I've been clinging on to that idea that my life will be infinitely better without Will's super-fandom and sports obsession. Then for Cara to tell me that perhaps it isn't something to be thankful for, and that I caused this break-up, is a bitter pill to swallow.

'I mean, Lex, have you stopped to think about how he must be feeling about everything? How would you like it if you'd found out he'd been telling strangers all over the Internet about your life.'

'But you said me blogging about my life as a sports widow was a good thing.'

'I know I did, but I thought you'd set it up more as a tongue-and-cheek sporting widow's guide, all about tips and tricks to survive living with a fanatic. Not about you dressing up in your sexy undies and seducing him.'

I pick up the wine glass and practically down the contents. She's right. That's what it should have been, only I'd got carried away with sensationalising it to make it more readable.

'But he still started it,' I say, exasperated. 'Maybe I did take the blog too far, but he still started it with the lies when he missed Vanessa and Ian's wedding.'

Cara purses her lips. 'I admit he was wrong to do that. I guess he's not blameless in this break-up, but the point is you've been with him most of your adult life, and I just want you to be sure that you've done the right thing and that you're not throwing it away for nothing.'

I shake my head, clear in my mind.

'It's like Robin at work was saying, it's time to wipe the slate clean while I'm young enough to do something about it.'

'Excuse me? Young enough? We're only thirty-one.'

'I know, but in biological terms we're starting to be over the hill. This way I've still got time to find someone new and still get my happy-ever-after.'

'And you couldn't have got that with Will?'

'Enough about Will,' I say, slamming my wine glass down on to the table. I recoil slightly as I realise it should have been a little more careful, but luckily the glass doesn't break.

The doorbell goes again and I instantly freeze.

'That'll be Vanessa,' says Cara, as she takes it upon herself to go in search of her. She returns a minute later with Vanessa in tow.

'Hiya, sweetie,' says Vanessa, coming over and kissing me on the cheek. 'How are you holding up?'

'OK,' I lie.

'I still can't believe it,' she says, sitting down at the end of the table. 'It makes no sense to me why you two would break up like that out of the blue.'

Cara stares at me, raising an eyebrow, and I try and hold my own by staring back.

'Have I interrupted something?' says Vanessa, clearly confused as she looks between us.

'We were just talking about why it happened,' says Cara.

I shoot her a look. After all, Vanessa doesn't know what I've been up to, as I couldn't risk telling her about Will's fake food poisoning.

'Oh, come on Lexi, you're going to have to tell her the truth now. It's not like you need to protect Will any more.'

'Protect Will from what? Lexi, what's been going on?'

I sigh as I look at Vanessa.

'I didn't want to tell you this, but Will lied about having food poisoning at your wedding.'

I wince, waiting for her to start ranting, only she doesn't say a thing. She's fidgeting in her chair and she's barely acknowledged what I've said.

'You knew?' I whisper in disbelief.

She nods and I instantly look at Cara.

'Hey, don't look at me,' she says, holding up her hands. 'I haven't told anyone. Not even Dave.'

'Who's Dave?' asks Vanessa.

'Er –' stutters Cara.

If it had been any other time I would have quite enjoyed joining in asking who Dave is, but not now.

'Never mind who Cara's dating, how did you know about Will?'

'He told me.'

'He *what*?' shout both Cara and I.

'When?' I ask.

'You know the week of the wedding when I met you before your writing group at the pub? When Will came along to drop something off to you?'

'My assignment,' I say, nodding.

'Well, he was waiting in the car park for me when I came out, and he told me then about his predicament.'

'What predicament?'

'You know, about your dad?'

'No, I don't know. What's he got to do with it?'

I suddenly remember Will saying something about my dad when we were in Barbados.

'I'm so confused,' says Vanessa. 'I thought you said you knew all about him missing my wedding.'

'I did. He missed it to go and watch football.'

'Yes,' she says slowly, 'but only so that he could ask your dad for his permission to propose.'

'What?'

My jaw practically drops to the table.

'Apparently he'd been trying to get your dad on his own for ages, but it had been really difficult, so he thought he'd take him to a Southampton match. His friend Tom had to go on a last-minute work trip so he offered Will his season ticket, meaning he had to go the day of the wedding.

'He came to me to tell me he'd have to miss some of the day, but when we tried to think of a cover story for him to miss some of it and arrive late, we couldn't think of one. In the end, I thought it would be safer for him to miss the whole of it and I came up with the food poisoning. God, I'm so relieved it's out in the open. I've been feeling so guilty every time I've been in the same room with you two.'

And there was me thinking she'd been acting weird with Will as she was pissed off.

'So did you find out about it in Barbados?'

'No, I found out at your wedding. My work colleague took a photo of Will at the match on the telly.'

I instinctively reach over to grab my phone and hastily find the original message. There's Will in all his glory, there's a man I don't recognise to his left, and someone's arm dressed in a black coat to the right – presumably my dad.

'Oh my God. I did all those awful things in revenge thinking he'd gone to the football just to watch his beloved Saints, and that's what he was really doing?'

'What revenge? And who's Dave? Come on ladies. I think you need to fill me in.'

I hang my head in my hands and let Cara do the talking, as right now my mind's spinning out of control.

37

Nothing beats that Friday feeling. When the imaginary bell rings at clocking off time, there's always a buzz. And this week, after the week I've had, I'm more pleased than ever when five p.m. rolls around.

I'm not only relieved to be getting out of work, but also that I get to go to the pub for Robin's birthday drinks, meaning I can put off going home for another couple of hours. I only wish I knew more of the people going. I'm fine with a few unfamiliar faces, but when I only know one or two people, I tend to go all shy and clingy.

With Mike being the only person I know that's going, other than the birthday boy, he's set to become my new best friend for the night. I look over at him and I give him a big smile. He looks over before sneezing in my direction.

'Hat-choo,' he says noisily.

I shudder. My new best friend is a bit germier than I'd like him.

'Sorry,' he says, reaching over and grabbing a tissue from the box on his desk. 'I think this cold is getting worse.'

He sounds all nasally and looks really pale.

'Yeah, you're not looking too good,' I say, wincing. I can predict what he's going to say and I'm not going to like it.

'Um. I think I might just go home to bed. Get Laura to tuck me in with some Lemsip.'

I nod. I don't even try to persuade him to come; I don't want to be ill all weekend, especially now that I've got no one to look after me.

'That's a good idea. Get some proper rest.'

We stand up to walk out of the office together. As we emerge into the fresh air, I see my car and wonder if I could go to the gym instead. That would delay my return home, and it doesn't matter if I'm Billy No-Mates there. Or I could be brave and go back to the house and do some writing. I was going great guns yesterday, I'm sure I'd easily slip back into the zone.

'I'll just come in with you to the pub to tell Robin in person,' says Mike, as he keeps marching, past the parked cars.

'Oh, it's OK, I can tell him if you like.'

If he comes in with me I'll have to make up an excuse for Robin as he'd never believe me about the gym, as having worked with me for the last month he knows my gym membership is more about the free smoothies in the bar rather than the exercise.

'No, no, I'll do it in person. I don't want to piss him off. You know, with the report looming.'

'Ah, yes, the report,' I say, nodding. Even though I've been given unofficial confirmation that my job is safe, there's always that fear that Robin's interpretations of his findings may be very different to the councillors'.

We make it to the pub before I can think of an excuse.

We spot Robin immediately, and I look at the sea of unknown faces. I recognise some of them from working in the same building for years, but I've never met them before. I feel myself starting to get a little flustered and after giving the birthday boy a little wave, I make a beeline for the bar.

My phone rings in my bag and when I see that it's my mum I immediately feel bad that I haven't spoken to her since I got back from Barbados. I haven't known how to tell her and Dad that Will and I have split up, so I've put it off. I'm about to send it to voice-mail, as I can always pop round and see them tomorrow, when I realise that it could be an emergency. Perhaps something's wrong with my dad. He has been acting strangely. What if it isn't all down to him knowing about Will's plans? And if it was an emergency, it would give me a perfect reason for leaving tonight.

Gosh, I'm an awful person. I pick up the phone, praying that everyone is all right.

'Hi, Mum,' I say, trying to make my voice sound cheery.

'Lexi? It's your dad here.'

'Dad? Is everything OK?'

My heart starts to race as he hasn't phoned me since that time when my mum went away and he didn't know how to switch on the oven.

'That's what I was going to ask you. We haven't heard from you since your trip. Did you have a nice time?'

I look over at Robin surrounded by his laughing colleagues. This isn't really the time or the place to go into this.

'Um, yes and no,' I say.

'Ah,' he says and while I can't see him, I know he's nodding sagely. 'I thought as much.'

'You want to know why we're not engaged, don't you? Vanessa told me you went to the football with him.'

'What a treat that was. He didn't need to do it, though. He should have known he'd always have my blessing. But me and your mother did appreciate him asking.'

I scrunch my eyes shut to stop myself from crying.

'You don't have to tell us what's gone on, love,' he says, before he speaks again, presumably to my mother, 'No, she doesn't. If she doesn't want to say, she can keep quiet.'

'Sorry about that,' he continues. 'That's why I'm phoning and not her. We just want you to know we're here if you need us.'

'Thanks, Dad,' I say trying to keep the wobble out of my voice.

'It sounds like you're out, so I won't keep you. But come over on Sunday, for a cuppa? Yeah?'

'OK.'

'Great, love. Call us if you want us. Take care.'

'Thanks, Dad. Bye.'

I hang up the phone and stare at it. I can't believe my parents were complicit in the plot too.

I blink back tears. I don't think I can stay at the pub. I need to go home and be alone. I slip my phone back into my bag and turn to leave the pub, only to bump into Robin.

'Oh, um, happy birthday,' I say, trying to pretend I wasn't about to sneak out.

'Thank you! And thanks for coming, especially seeing as Mike's not able to.'

'That's OK. It's not like I've got any better offers.'

'Charming,' he says, smiling. 'So what can I get you to drink?'

'I'll get these,' I say, turning back to the bar. 'It is your birthday, after all. What do you want?'

'I'll have a Hoegaarden, thanks.'

I order his pint and a double vodka and Coke – well, I need some sort of Dutch courage to get me through the night.

'So, do you know anyone here?' he asks as I pass him his drink.

'No,' I say, shaking my head. I can't believe I've worked at the council for seven years and I only really know the people in my department and the odd person in finance and HR.

'Everyone's pretty friendly. Come on over and I'll introduce you.'

I follow him to the group of people standing around a tall table in the corner.

'Becky, Anita, this is Lexi; she works in the leisure department.'

The two of them look me up and down and purse their lips. 'Nice to meet you,' they chant in unison, in voices that sound frosty and cold.

'Nice to meet you, too,' I say, sipping my drink and looking at the clock behind their heads, wondering how long I have to stay.

I'm about to turn to Robin and ignore the frosty twins when he waves at someone coming into the pub and goes to meet them. I stand there awkwardly looking at the two girls as their eyes follow Robin's every move.

Ah, that explains it. I get the impression that these two want to be more than work colleagues with him.

'So, you've been working with Robin on his latest project?' says Anita.

Becky's raising an eyebrow and she looks like she's got the lasers in her eyes set to stun and ready to strike.

'That's right, total pain in the arse he's been. Demanding figures and files. I'm so glad he's gone back upstairs. Good riddance.'

I may have laid it on a little thick, but it seems to have done the trick. Anita has a small smile on her face and Becky's eyebrow is no longer lodged in her hairline.

'Well, we're pleased to have him back. It's never the same when he's not in the office.'

I observe as they dreamily watch him come back over. I'm almost imagining little love hearts floating along next to them like in a Disney cartoon.

I've been watching him over the last month and he makes everyone feel special. I wonder if Anita and Becky are too young and naive to notice that, and instead think he's only like that with them.

I consult the clock again. I've been here for all of five minutes. Still not a respectable enough amount of time to make an exit.

I turn back to talk to Anita and Becky, but they've gone – sandwiching themselves either side of Robin.

I'm left alone again. I do the only thing I can do. I spot another woman, sat on the periphery of the group, who is glancing around and casually swiping at her phone. She's probably one of Robin's colleagues' girlfriends, and doesn't know anyone either. When I sit down next to her she smiles, and I feel myself start to relax.

'You did not do that,' says the woman who I've decided will now be my new best friend. I feel I have an opening for one, what with Cara not approving of my new-found single status and Vanessa having kept the secret about Will's proposal for months. So far this woman's the prime candidate: she's laughing at my stories, she doesn't seem to judge me, and most importantly she's here in the pub.

'I did, well, apparently – I can't remember that much of it. I woke up the next morning with cold wet hair, in slightly damp sheets wondering what had gone on before it embarrassingly came back to me.'

The woman giggles and so do I. It's only the second time I've shared the story of my shameful Barbados night, only this time I'm finding it pretty funny. That's possibly something to do with the three double vodkas I've had.

'I think a little pee came out, and if I'm not careful I'm going to wet myself,' she says, standing up. 'You can tell me more when I get back.'

I grin. She's just got bonus points for her BFF application.

I watch her as she gives a quick peck on the cheek to a man, who I'm presuming is her boyfriend, and goes in search of the toilets.

'So, having a good time?' asks Robin, sliding into the woman's seat.

'Yes,' I say honestly, my cheeks hurting from having laughed for the last half an hour solid. I'm smiling and I feel pretty happy. Laughter really is good therapy.

'For the second time this week, I owe you a big thank you.'

'Did you email Sarah the rest of your book?'

'Yep, I sent it over last night, so fingers crossed.'

'That's great news.'

I nod. I know that nothing may come of it, but I feel pleased that at least something in my life is heading in the right direction.

'I'm really glad you made the effort to come tonight, it's been nice to see you out of work.'

'Yes, you too. I thought you might have melted, you know, like vampires do when they go into a church. Mr Corporate, going into a pub . . .'

'Ha, ha, very funny. I do like to unwind too. And away from work I'm a normal person, you know.'

'Nah, I'm not buying it.'

'OK, not normal, but you know, I'm different outside of work than I am in.'

I realise that I still know very little about Robin. He seems to have found out about my life in intimate detail, but I'm really none the wiser about his. I know he's single and he lives in one of the posh apartments overlooking the Hamble, but aside from that, I'm clueless.

'Let me guess, you wear tracksuits and race pigeons.'

'Got it in one. That's exactly how I spend my time,' he grins at me, flashing his perfect white teeth. 'OK, so there might not be pigeons, but I do own tracksuit bottoms. I laze around in them, like normal people, at the weekend.'

I let my imagination run away with itself as I picture him in loose tracksuit bottoms and a white T-shirt strolling over hardwood floors, his glasses balancing on the end of his nose as he carries the Sunday papers in one hand and a cup of freshly ground coffee in the other.

I snap myself back to reality and find that I'm sat a little closer to Robin.

I look around behind him, to see where my new BFF has got to. I spot her in the corner smooching her boyfriend. I try and see if there's anyone else I can turn to, but aside from the frosty twins, who are giving me evil looks, everyone seems to have gone. When did that happen?

'So what do you do in these tracksuit bottoms, then?'

'You know. I do a little piano practice. I work out.'

'I'm Sexy and I Know It' starts to play in my head, and weekend Robin from my imagination starts doing lunges, making my cheeks pinken.

As if sensing the mood has changed between us, he leans into me and the next thing I know his lips are on mine, and before my brain's caught up with it, his tongue, too.

I haven't kissed anyone other than Will for seven years, and I'd forgotten how weird it is. He's not doing it right and he tastes funny.

'Hey, hey. What are you doing?' I say, pushing him off me and trying to ignore the death rays emanating from the frosty twins.

'What? I thought that's what you wanted. I mean, you're single now and you came here – staying all night.'

He's wrinkling his face up as he scrutinises mine for signs of agreement.

'You think that because I'm single and I'm here that that means I want to kiss you? What about Mike? You invited him here too. And I bet you didn't stick your tongue down his throat before he left.'

'He had a cold,' Robin says drily. 'Look, I'm sorry, but I thought over the last couple of months you've been up for it. And then you hugged me the other day.'

'Because you'd done me a massive favour with your editor friend.'

'But I thought we got on really well. I thought I was helping you get your life on track with your writing and stuff.'

'You were, but I don't see how that has anything to do with you kissing me.'

'Well, you've always been flirty with me.'

'No, I haven't,' I say attempting to sound incredulous, but I'm not sure I believe myself. He's always had a bit of an effect on me, but I didn't mean to properly flirt, not when I was with Will.

'And then you split up with your boyfriend, and then you come here, what was I expected to think?'

'That I wanted to come and wish a work colleague happy birthday, like everyone else that was invited.'

I search around the chairs to find my coat and shimmy out of the seat.

'I'm sorry, I should have waited. It's probably a bit soon after your break-up. I should have given it a couple of weeks, then asked you out properly. I just thought that as your relationship has been pretty much over for ages, that you'd be ready for someone new.'

I stand up shakily.

'What makes you think our relationship's been over for ages?'

'The way you talk about him and his sporting obsession, like he'd put that first every time. It's so obvious to see from the outside that you're living your life on his terms. If you could only see what he's been doing to you for all these years, without committing to you. He's been stopping you from having the life you truly wanted, the one you deserve.'

'With someone like you?'

It's amazing how a sloppy kiss can be like being hit on the backside with an electric cattle prodder. It's just what I needed to sober me up.

'Yes, with someone like me. One day you'll look back on this and realise you've made the biggest mistake of your life. I could have been the one good thing that's happened to you.'

I look at Robin and I realise he's right. This is the moment where I'll look back and realise that I've made the biggest mistake of my life, but hopefully I've still got time to put it right.

I put on my coat and wrap my scarf around my neck before I turn to leave.

'Good luck, Lexi, with whatever comes your way. You never know, you might need it when the report comes out.'

'I thought you said that I'd be fine,' I say, turning back.

Robin shrugs and for the first time since I've met him his charming facade seems to drop. His smile has been replaced with serious look. 'It's amazing how you can spin any figures to get the outcome you want,' he says a little coldly.

I'm so shocked that he of all people could be capable of such malice and I'm about to reach over to grab his pint to tip it over his head when I realise that the woman I wanted to be my BFF has planted herself between us.

'Um, I hope you're not thinking of changing a report to settle a personal score,' she says, looking at him firmly.

He looks up at her in surprise and then back at me.

'Er, no, Beth,' he says, looking like he's been caught red-handed by his mother.

'Good, as if I read it and it's got any recommendations for the art development coordinator role to be amended, I might have to recommend my own staff changes.'

I look up at her in surprise. She's Beth? Beth his scary ogre-like boss? My mouth drops open. Oh good lord, I just told one of the high-ups in the council that I got everyone at our hotel bar to go skinny-dipping.

'Don't look so shocked,' she whispers. 'You were on holiday. Your secret's safe with me.'

I smile with gratitude before I remember what I've got to do. Robin might have acted like a total jerk, but I'll be forever grateful he's just reminded me of what's important in life.

38

'Hang on, hang on,' shouts Cara.

She opens the door and I immediately gasp.

'Um, I'm sorry, I'm looking for my best friend, Cara,' I say, laughing at her dressed in a flannel nightie and towelling robe.

'Very funny,' she says looking each way down the road before yanking me into the house.

'Nice slippers,' I say at the sight of her fluffy mules.

'Sssh,' she says, whispering as we walk past the bedroom.

'Who's there, Cara,' shouts a male voice, and I freeze.

'Don't worry about it. It's just Lexi. You go back to sleep.'

She pushes me down the hall into the kitchen and I'm still sniggering as she follows me in and closes the door.

'So I take it Dave's here, then?'

'I could have anyone in that bedroom. How do you know it's Dave?'

'Because the last time I showed up at your house unannounced at night you were wearing a leather catsuit and five-inch heels. Now you're in a grandma nightdress and slippers.'

'Hmm, but I'll tell you what – it's bloody comfortable. So are you going to tell me what you're doing here in the middle of the night?'

She goes over to the kettle and fills it up before switching it on.

'I'm sensing you've got something to say.'

She sits down at her breakfast bar, and I sit down on the stool opposite.

'I do. Robin kissed me.'

'Robin from work? The really super-hot guy?'

'Uh-huh, the super-hot guy that's actually a massive dick. When I said I didn't want to kiss him he told me he'd recommend to the councillors that my job be scrapped.'

'What?'

'I know!' I exclaim. Now that I'm sobering up the whole night seems pretty surreal.

Cara's face is a picture – a mixture of shock and outrage.

'Where is he? Is he still at the pub?' she says, standing up and looking like she's going to thump him one.

'Probably, but don't worry, his boss was there and she heard the whole thing. He muttered an apology and skulked away. Oh God. It was so embarrassing. I'd been talking to his boss – who's like our age, by the way – and telling her about the whole skinny-dipping in Barbados thing. I just assumed she was someone's bored girlfriend as she wasn't really talking to many people.'

'You see, that's where you went wrong, you've broken that fundamental rule of what goes on tour stays on tour. Did I ever tell you or anyone what happened on that holiday to Amsterdam last year?'

'No . . .'

'Exactly. What goes on tour, stays on tour.'

The mind boggles and I am actually quite pleased, in this instance, at her rules.

'But anyway, what happened with Rob the knob?'

'We were chatting and the next thing I knew he was sticking his tongue down my throat and it was all like this,' I say, sticking my tongue out in a rapid thrusting fashion. 'It was awful. And not just because he was a bad kisser, but because he wasn't Will.'

Cara smiles at me in a smug I-told-you-so way.

'You don't have to say it.'

It's one thing for her to think it, but it's another for her to say it out loud.

'I just don't understand what possessed Robin. I mean, did I really give him the signals? What kind of an impression must I have given him about my relationship with Will for him to think I was going to jump his bones a week after dumping him?'

'Um, firstly, men don't think, not when it comes to bones or boners.'

Trust her to make me laugh when things are so pitiful.

'I wondered if he liked you when we met him at the pub.'

'When you tried to shove your new boyfriend out of the way so you could flirt with him?'

Cara looks nervously over at the door.

'Yeah, I felt bad about that, but yes, that night he seemed to only have eyes for you.'

'But he was perfectly charming to Vanessa about her wedding.'

'Perhaps because you've been with Will forever you don't notice the signs like I do, and while there's no arguing that he could charm the pants off anyone – me included – or at least me before Dave became my boyfriend.'

'Your boyfriend, officially?' I shriek.

'Uh-huh, even Vanessa knows, and she's already bloody planning double dates and dinner parties, which is exactly why I wanted to keep it a secret in the first place. But, we can talk about that later.'

I'm about to protest, having momentarily forgotten about my problems, when she starts to talk about Robin again.

'But despite him having all the charm, he did look at you differently. And don't forget, he did send your book to that editor.'

'I know, but wouldn't he have done that for anyone he knew?'

Cara pulls a face. 'It's a pretty big favour to pull, unless the editor was a close friend. Was she?'

'I don't think so.' I got the impression from their email correspondence that she'd been a friend of one of his ex's.

'In my experience, men don't usually go out of their way to do nice things for women they don't have the hots for.'

'I can't believe how wrong I was about him,' I say, shaking my head in disbelief before sipping my tea. 'He was such an arsehole, threatening my job.'

'Yeah, I don't think he would have really done that, though. My guess is that he was a bit wounded. He's probably not used to getting knocked back, and the fact you rejected him probably made him lash out.'

'Do you think?'

'Yeah, but it's still a massive arsehole thing to do, though.'

I'm so glad I came over here. I'm starting to feel so much better already.

'Do you know Robin was trying to tell me that I deserved someone better, that Will didn't appreciate me, and it was like when he was telling me about the relationship he thought we had, it made me realise how wrong he was. I may have agreed with him a few weeks ago, that Will seemed unromantic and uncommitted, but now that I know the truth about what he's been up to and what he was planning I can see so clearly that he was anything but. And all the while I was getting my kicks out of planning the revenge and blogging about it.'

I collapse my head into my hands.

'What have I done? To Will? To our relationship? I can't believe I've been such an idiot.'

'Well, hang on. For starters, you're not an idiot. I mean, granted, if you had taken my advice in the first place and just told him when you found out about the food poisoning and the football thing, then you would have known his true reasons a whole lot sooner and you wouldn't have found yourself in this muddle. *But*, if you hadn't done the revenge you might not have realised that something was missing in the relationship. I'm not saying it was broken, but perhaps it needed a little bit of TLC.'

'Just like you were saying – spicing things up in the bedroom.'

'Exactly. I just think you lost your way a bit, forgetting why you were doing it all in the first place.'

I try and follow what Cara's saying, but my head is spinning and I don't know whether it's the fact that I'm still drunk or the fact that my emotions are whirling round my body.

'What the hell was I thinking?'

Cara gets up and reboils the kettle to finish making tea.

'Don't be too hard on yourself. You were really mad, and at the time we both thought you were deservedly so. How were you supposed to know that it was Vanessa's bloody idea all along?'

'Why didn't I just tell him that I knew what he'd done?'

Cara coughs politely and smiles.

'Yeah, you don't have to say it.'

I'm still not ready to hear I told you so, no matter how right she is.

'Look, there's no point beating yourself up about what you did and where you went wrong. At the end of the day, that's all in the past. What you need to do now is work out how you're going to put it right.'

'You don't think it's too late? I haven't spoken to Will since Barbados. I don't even know where he is. For all I know, he's glad it's over and that's the last I'll ever see of him.'

'Come on, for starters you own a house together, so I think you'll have to talk at some point. And don't forget, he hasn't been back to the house to get the rest of his stuff. If he really thought it was over he'd have been back to sort all that out. Maybe he just needed some time.'

'I don't know, he was so mad in Barbados. He wouldn't listen to anything I was saying.'

'Well, things are different now,' she says, pouring water into the cups. 'Don't forget, you didn't know why he really missed Vanessa and Ian's wedding.'

'I don't know. He didn't seem interested in working things out. I can't imagine him listening to me long enough to hear what I've got to say and for him to understand how much I know that I fucked up. I want to tell him that I got so carried away with the revenge that I ended up losing sight of why I was doing it.'

'I'm sure he'd understand if you explained it.'

I shake my head. 'No. I don't think that's enough. He was pretty clear about us being over. I've either got to accept it or . . .'

'Or what?' says Cara as she strains the tea bags and throws them into the bin, before passing me my cup. I take it from her, curling my fingers around it, scolding them slightly.

'Or I have to prove to him he's wrong.'

'And how do you plan to do that?'

'I've got to propose to him.'

Cara spits out a mouthful of tea all over her Formica breakfast bar.

'Are you having a laugh? After all the years of you waiting for your dream proposal, you're going to take matters into your own hands?'

'Uh-huh.'

'You're going to track him down to one of his mate's houses and drop down on one knee?'

She looks at me in disbelief.

'Oh no. It needs to be bigger than that.' I think back to his proposal that never was – he was going to write MARRY ME in the sky for goodness sake. 'No, I know exactly how I'm going to do it, but I'm going to need some help.'

I pick up my phone and scroll through my contacts. I hastily type a quick message and hit Send.

I fill Cara in on the details of what I want to do and how I'm going to put the plan into action, and her face lights up like all her Christmases have come at once.

'I'll put the kettle on again,' she says, practically leaping up, despite the fact that we're drinking freshly made tea. 'I'll make us some coffee. Somehow I don't think we'll be getting a lot of sleep tonight.'

I think she might be right. There's a lot to do in the next twelve hours. I close my eyes for a second and wish for my plan to work, as there's nothing I want more than to be back in the arms of Will this time tomorrow.

39

'Atchoo!' sneezes Mike into his tissue.

'You sound so ill, you should have stayed in bed,' I say, feeling awful that he left his house on my behalf.

'I wouldn't miss this for the world,' he says. 'Besides which, I thought it was easier to pull a few strings in person, than from my bed.'

I look up at him and smile. I can't believe that he'll never know that it was a text message from him that started us off down this crazy journey. If it hadn't been for him watching that Southampton game on TV and pausing it to take a snap of Will, I'd never have started the revenge or the blog. If he'd just gone to the kitchen at that moment to grab a beer, it could have all turned out so differently.

I think back over the last couple of months since that text pinged into my life, and actually wonder if I'd change any of it. I know it didn't have the greatest of endings, but some of the best moments of our relationship have happened since then. The trip to Swansea. The night of all the sex. The Barbados holiday – or at least the pre-life-shattering bit.

I know now we didn't need the revenge to turn our relationship into what it should have been. We just needed to work on it and give it some attention. But at least it's shown me that our relationship wasn't fundamentally broken and that makes it worth fighting for now.

'Right then,' says Amelia the events manager, click-clacking her way over to us in her high heels.

I look ominously down at the microphone she's holding in her hands.

'Nervous?' she says, smiling.

'Pretty much,' I say, thinking that the last time I spoke in front of an audience was a room of art curators at a conference. Speaking in front of my industry peers who are interested in the funding I'm talking about is what I'm used to. Speaking in front of a crowd of thirty thousand rowdy football fans, not so much.

'Right then, the whistle's about to blow for half-time, so we're going to whip you straight out before he's got time to go off to get a drink.'

'OK,' I say, trying to follow her as she leads me through a tunnel out to the ground. The noise hits me immediately. The chants, the clapping, the stamping. It's deafening and I have to strain to hear Amelia next to me.

'I'll do a quick introduction,' she shouts to me before bending down and slipping caps over her heels. 'Then you go straight into your speech. I told the boss you'd be quick, so you've got about two minutes before we break into the sponsors' messages.'

'OK,' I say, shaking slightly.

A whistle blows and the crowd cheers, and then Amelia grabs my arm and frogmarches me out of the tunnel, before I can bottle it and run. I try and make my legs cooperate but they're like jelly as we make our way over to the pitch.

'Your boyfriend's season ticket seat is over that way,' she says, pointing as we get to our designated spot.

The crowd are still clapping the team, who are slowly jogging off the pitch.

I'm just thanking my lucky stars that Southampton are winning, meaning that the supporters are at least in a good mood.

We get to where I'm making my plea from and everything seems to go into slow motion. I try and do that thing where you imagine the audience you're speaking to in their underwear, but faced with an array of men and their beer bellies, I quickly re-dress them in my mind. Instead I blur my vision to make myself believe that the sea of red-and-white football shirts I'm looking out on to are actually giant candy canes – albeit pretty sweary candy canes.

'Ladies and gentlemen,' begins Amelia, with a boom in her voice like a circus ring leader. 'Before you enjoy half-time, Lexi here has a quick something to say to one of our season ticket holders. Lexi.'

She hands me the microphone and I freeze like a deer in headlights. My hand is shaking so much that I can't keep hold of the microphone, forcing Amelia to wrap her hand around mine to steady it. She moves it right under my chin and she nods her head in encouragement.

I know the clock is ticking, and that Will and every other supporter has now seen me. It's too late to turn and run.

'Um, hello everyone,' I say unsteadily.

No one seems that interested in what I've got to say. People are starting to move and I see Amelia twisting her free arm over to check her watch.

'Have you ever lied to your other half so that you could come and watch a Southampton game?' I blurt it out so forcefully and confidently that I look over at Amelia in surprise, wondering who it was that said it. 'Well, that's what my ex-boyfriend, Will, did. He faked a stomach bug to get out of going to a wedding and he came here instead.'

A few ripples of cheers go up and I see that I've started to win my audience. Of course I have, their allegiance is going to lie with Will, but that's what I expected.

'Now, I'm sure if you can't imagine how mad I was, your partners might sympathise, but I wasn't too happy. I set out on a path of revenge that led me to make him miss matches and try to make him miss as much sport as possible. And not only that, I wrote about it on a blog for everyone to read.'

The crowd start to boo me, and I play up to it, as if I'm in a pantomime.

'I know it was an awful thing to do, especially as I recently found out he missed the wedding with the bride's permission so that he could bring my father to a game to ask him for my hand in marriage.'

The boos are replaced by gasps and groans.

'Believe me, I couldn't feel any worse about what I did. I know now that in trying to keep him away from his beloved sport, I ruined our relationship. I've learnt too late what I stood to lose, and I'm here now to put it right. To tell him that I love him and that I messed everything up.'

I give Amelia a grin, before I bend down on one knee.

I feel my knee sink into the squelchy mud and I wish that I'd thought this through a little better. But I'm too far gone down this route to change it now.

'Will Talbot, wherever you are,' I say into the mic that Amelia is bending awkwardly down next to me to hold on to. 'Will you marry me?'

There's a stunned silence in the crowd.

I can see a sea of heads turning round to see who this Will Talbot is and if he's going to come and put me out of my misery.

In my head I imagined the crowd would part and he'd come running down on to the pitch. He'd scoop me up and spin me round, screaming that of course he wanted to marry me. Then fireworks would start going off and Beyoncé would pop out and sing, and ticker tape would fall down and get stuck to our lips as we kissed. OK, so I may have got half-time at a English football league match confused with the Superbowl half-time show, but at the very least I expected to see Will. Instead there's no sign of him.

My knee is sinking further into the mud and I don't know what to do.

The crowd are starting to give me pitying looks.

It's then that I notice some manic waving in the middle of the stand in front of me. My heart starts to race as I imagine that it's Will.

I squint and look up and realise it's his best friend Tom. Tom, who Will sits next to. Only he's not there – the seat next to Tom is empty. I look round desperately trying to see where he's gone. Has he already started running?

Amelia puts her hand over the mic and bends down beside me.

'I don't think he's coming.'

'But he has to,' I say, my mouth going dry.

He has to come. I'll forgo the fireworks and ticker tape and settle for just Will. I can't have aired my dirty laundry to all and sundry for nothing.

Amelia goes to stand up and gently yanks at my arm to help me up too.

'He musn't be here,' I say, clutching at straws.

'We checked before and he scanned his season ticket.'

'Well then, maybe he's nipped to the loo or gone to the bar already.'

'Lexi, I think you're going to have to face it, he's not coming for you.'

The words sink in and reality hits. He's probably left in embarrassment at what I've done. I'm going to have to walk away and I don't know how my legs are even supporting me in my kneel, let alone how they'll walk across a muddy field.

I can't help looking at all the pitying faces, hoping that I've got it wrong and that I'm going to see Will's any second. But my head knows what my heart doesn't want to hear – he doesn't want me.

'Right, then, thank you to Lexi for being so brave. I'm sure you'll all give her a big clap as she leaves.'

Amelia, ever the pro, gives me a little shrug as if it wasn't that bad. That I didn't just lose my self-respect in front of thirty thousand fans. She pulls me back up to standing and helps support me off the pitch.

The crowd that's stood in front of me breaks out into an applause and it's the only thing that stops me from collapsing in tears. As we approach the tunnel I hear a couple of people tell me to keep my chin up, and a couple of other offers that I really hope I misheard. I try my best to keep my head held high and my eyes free from tears until we reach the safety of the tunnel.

'You did really well,' says Amelia, wiping her shoes on a mat. 'You were very brave.'

'I can't believe I did all that, and it was for nothing.'

'I know this is hardly a consolation, but I think you entertained everyone.'

The adrenaline that had pumped round my veins and allowed me to talk on the pitch starts to ebb and I'm left feeling sick and exhausted.

'Lexi, I'm sorry,' says Mike, walking over to us. He gives me a soft punch on the arm, which I think is the best he can do in terms of affection.

I nod in acknowledgement, but I've lost all power of speech. I stand there looking dazed and confused as he goes over to talk to Amelia.

'Thanks once again for the favour, Amelia, much appreciated. I'm just sorry that it didn't work out for the news story.'

Just when I didn't think I could feel any worse, I'm reminded of how Mike had pulled strings with his contacts at the club, with the promise that it would probably be a good PR piece for the local, if not national press. It was the only way we'd been able to get them to agree and at such short notice.

'Don't worry, it's got all the makings of going viral anyway, in fact it's probably better that he didn't appear and say yes,' she says in a whisper.

I know I look spaced out, but I can hear every word and my heart sinks even more with the thought that I'll be the butt of jokes on random people's Facebook pages and there'll be clever memes and gifs of me standing there with my soul bared and my mouth agape.

'Come on, Lexi,' says Mike, sneezing again. 'Let's get you home.'

Still mute, I follow him out of the ground. People offer me the odd 'cheer up' and 'hang on in there' as I go and worse, others deliberately turn their heads from me and avoid all eye contact, as if they're embarrassed for me.

Why on earth did I think this was a good idea?

This is why those half-time proposal things are a terrible idea. Or in fact, in my mind, why any large-scale public proposal thing is a bad idea, because if it goes wrong and the person says no, or, worse still, leaves you there alone like a total loser, it's not like you can shrug it off, when everyone knows your shame.

'Come on, Lexi. It's not that bad,' says Mike as we get in the car. 'I'm sure by next season everyone will have forgotten about it.'

I close my eyes. Next bloody season.

My phone beeps and I check, just in case it's Will, but it's a text from Robin:

Robin:
So I dragged my very hung-over (and very sorry) self out of bed to go to the football this afternoon. If it makes you feel any better, he's an idiot for leaving you there.

Of course he'd been there to see it. Just when I thought I couldn't feel any worse. It's reminded me that it isn't just strangers that are going to know what I did, but everyone I know.

I turn my phone off, not wanting to know who else saw it and the tears begin to fall. Mike lets me sob in silence as he drives me home, and I can't wait to crawl under the duvet and pretend this whole thing never happened.

40

'Thanks for the lift, Mike,' I manage to splutter through the tears as he pulls up outside my house.

It started drizzling during the drive, which suits my mood. At least it makes me appreciate that it could have been worse out there on the pitch – it could have been raining.

I walk up the path, trying to find my keys in the mess at the bottom of my handbag. When I finally find them I unlock the door and push it open. As I walk into the lounge I'm immediately hit by the smell. Something is burning. I'm immediately fearful that I left my hair straighteners plugged in, before realising that Cara did my hair at her house this morning, and I haven't used mine all week.

I hurry through to the dining room trying to work out what's on fire, and it's then that I see smoke billowing out from under the kitchen door. I hear noisy clattering before the smoke alarm starts ringing.

'Oh fuck!' shouts a voice in the kitchen and there's that banging again.

When you arrive home and discover your house is on fire and there's a man in the kitchen swearing and beating things,

I'm pretty sure you should vacate the premises immediately. But I don't, as the burglar in the kitchen sounds awfully like Will.

Either he was at the football and was so enraged by my embarrassing behaviour that he's come to burn the house down, or he's . . . I struggle to think of a more rational explanation as the noise of the alarm is so deafening.

I open the door and I'm greeted with not only the most extraordinary smell, but also with a sight that for a second I can't comprehend. The whole kitchen is on fire. It takes me a second to realise that there are tea lights burning – hundreds of them. Will must have lit them, but the one on the kitchen table is burning wildly out of control.

I look more closely. That's not a candle, it's my reed diffusing air freshener. Will is beating it fiercely to death with a tea towel, but it's clearly not working as the flames are spreading across the table top. The fire alarm is ringing and it's so high-pitched that it's impossible to think.

'Oh, shit,' says Will as the fire spreads from the table on to the tea towel, and he throws it on the tiled floor before slipping off his shoe and beating it.

'Lexi!' he shouts as he notices me hovering in the doorway. He's obviously so surprised to see me that he forgets he's beating the tea towel with his shoe and accidentally throws it. It narrowly misses my head and smashes a mug off our mug tree.

'I'm sorry,' he says, wincing. 'It's all under control.'

The smoke alarm in the dining room clearly doesn't think so as it goes off too, and the smoke slowly filters round the house.

'What the fuck were you trying to do?' I say, as he picks up a tea towel and beats the table again. I'm shouting as the fire alarms, which are annoyingly out of sync, are also ear-shatteringly loud.

I pick up the fire extinguisher that we usually use as a door-stop and stand over the pool of oil on the kitchen table. I pull the pin out and then stare blankly at it. We bought the fire extinguisher when we first moved into the house, when we were being proper grown-ups, but I have no frickin' clue how to use the thing. 'Were you trying to deliberately burn this place down?' I shout as loudly as I can.

'I was trying to propose in the most romantic way I could think.'

I forget that I'm holding the fire extinguisher and I let go of it. It falls to the floor hitting Will's foot (luckily the one still in a shoe).

'Ah, fuck!' he shouts, immediately hopping on to his good foot and clutching the injured one.

'I'm so sorry. I just can't believe you still want to marry me.'

He stops hopping long enough to retrieve the fire extinguisher. 'I do, it's just gone so wrong.'

He points the extinguisher in the right direction, clamps the handles together and a sea of foam splays all over the fire and the rest of the kitchen table. 'I'd forgotten we had that. See, everything's under control.'

I look down at our faux-wood IKEA table, and I beg to differ. Where there was once a curry stain, there is now a big black charred area in the centre, and the foam has splattered all over the wall covered in paint swatches. Now we're really going to have to decorate.

The fire alarms are still ringing and Will opens the back door and the window, while I stare at the table.

'I think it's going to take more than a tablecloth to hide that,' I say, prodding it, and instantly regretting it as it's still roasting hot.

'I think you might be right.'

I want to ask him what possessed him to set the kitchen on fire, while he's busy fanning the smoke alarm with another tea towel.

'Perhaps I should put out the other candles. We wouldn't want another attempt to burn the house down.'

The rest of the kitchen is still aglow with tea lights and I go round and blow them out one by one, wondering how long it took him to light all these sodding things. I try not to slip as also littering the floor are rose petals.

'There,' I say, extinguishing the last one in triumph.

I try and wave some of the residual smoke out of the way and as it dissipates I take in the scene in front of me. It's, um, so romantic – the rose petals, hundreds of now unlit tea lights, broken crockery and the sea of foam: not to mention the smell, which is like burnt toast times a million.

I look at Will's face and it's the same one he has when a football game gets postponed because of bad weather. It must have taken him ages to light all those candles and decorate the room, all for it to go up in smoke – literally.

'How did the air freshener catch light?' I say, still not understanding what happened.

'The what? That was an air freshener?'

I nod. 'It's a reed diffuser.'

'Oh. I thought it was a scented candle.'

I try and suppress a laugh, clamping my lips together to stop it escaping as he looks so hurt. But I can't help myself, and the giggle starts to erupt, and before long it's a huge belly laugh that has my whole body shaking.

'I'm sorry. It's not you – it's today. If you'd had any idea what I did earlier on, you'd be laughing too. I tried to propose to you too, and while I didn't do my best impression of an arsonist, it went pretty spectacularly wrong. I went to the football, and went on to the pitch at half-time.'

I close my eyes; it's too soon to relive it. The embarrassment's still raw. At least the only saving grace is that if he's here, he didn't see it.

When I open my eyes, Will's laughing too.

'I saw it. On YouTube about half an hour ago.'

FFS.

'It's on there already?' I say, sinking down on to one of the kitchen chairs and getting a wet bum thanks to the foam that is everywhere.

'Yeah, it's on there a few times. There's even one with you doing it to a Celine Dion "All By Myself" slash Beyoncé "Put a Ring On It" mash-up.'

I hang my head in shame. I can't believe it's gone viral already – I'm never going to live this thing down.

'How come you weren't there? You're always there,' I say, thinking that at least if he'd been at the game it wouldn't have been so embarrassing. 'They said your season ticket was scanned.'

'I lent it to Aaron,' he says, shrugging.

I gasp. In all the years I've known him, I've never known him to give up his seat to a game.

'I'd been doing some thinking and I realised I didn't want to let you go. You were right in Barbados about a lot of things. I do take you for granted sometimes and I do probably watch too much sport. But you were wrong, in that I wouldn't choose sports over you.'

'I know, Vanessa told me the real reason that you missed her wedding. If I'd known . . .' I trail off, thinking how different it all could have been.

He shakes his head as if to say it doesn't matter.

'I wanted to come here and propose again during match time, so that you'd see that you were more important. Only when I got here, you weren't here, and then Tom phoned me to tell me what happened.'

I'm about to open my mouth to speak when I'm hit again by the smoke and I start to cough.

Will slips his other shoe back on, before he puts some tea lights on a plate and pulls me up from the chair.

'Come on,' he says, grabbing my hand, taking me out of the smoky kitchen and leading me down the garden path.

It's still pouring and we're getting soaked, but luckily our garden is tiny and we soon reach our shed at the end of it, and he forcefully yanks the broken door open.

It's the first time I've been in the shed for a long time, since I tried and failed to cut the grass as I couldn't even get the mower out. In my defence, there was a spider's web so thick on the handle I got completely freaked out. From that moment on, I declared it a Will job and this became his space – and he's completely transformed it.

OK, so there are still far too many spiders' webs and unfathomable garden implements for my liking, but at least they're all tidied neatly away. There's about enough room to stand inside next to his deckchair and there's a little plant pot turned upside down with a radio on it.

It's not the man shed of George Clarke's dreams, but clearly Will's claimed it as his own.

'I like what you've done with the place,' I say, turning back to him.

He's lit the little plate of tea lights. And after moving the radio, he places them on the upturned flowerpot.

It creates a lovely warming glow, and, despite the wind battering at the plastic window and the roof, it feels pretty cosy.

Will bends down and I'm about to sit in the deckchair, thinking we're about to get settled, before I realise that he's down on one knee.

'What are you doing?' I say. My eyes can clearly see the ring box in his hand and logically I know what's going on, but I still can't quite believe it.

Could it be third time, or is this technically the fourth time, lucky?

'I didn't quite imagine it could go so badly,' he says. 'I mean, how hard is it to ask someone that you love to spend the rest of their life with you? But Lexi Hunter, will you marry me?'

For a second I'm too stunned to say anything. It's been a roller-coaster of a day. I feel ever so light-headed and start to feel a little sick, my heart racing furiously. I need to sit down before I collapse, and I propel myself a little too forcefully into the deckchair.

'Woah,' says Will, grabbing hold of it before it tips me backwards like Graham Norton's big red chair.

'We're not very good at this whole proposal thing, are we?' he says, laughing. 'You see, this is why it took me so bloody long to do it in the first place. All that pressure to make it spectacular and different.'

I look round at the shed, although trying not to look too hard in case I spot a big spider.

'I'd say this is pretty different. And one to tell the grandkids.'

'Oh, right, so we're having kids and grandkids, are we? That's good to know. Does that mean that it's a yes, as this concrete floor is bloody killing my knee, so it would be good if you could finally put me out of my misery.'

'Oh, yes, of course it's a yes.'

Will lunges forward and the deckchair collapses in a heap on the floor.

He finds my finger and slides on the most perfect-looking princess cut diamond ring and looks me deep in the eyes.

'I couldn't imagine spending the rest of my life with anyone else.'

He kisses me gently, and I shudder briefly at the memory of Robin's kiss. Cher was so right – it's totally in his kiss.

'You're more important than anything else in the world and I'd even give up my season ticket for you, if that's what you wanted,' he says as he pulls away from me.

'Really?' I say, raising an eyebrow. 'You'd give it up if I asked you to?'

He nods. 'Well, you know if you really, really wanted me to. You know, if it was *that* important.'

'Oh, right then,' I say, giggling and knowing full well that if he did I'd never hear the end of it. 'But, actually, I like you out of the house. When else would I get to catch up on all the TV that I record?'

The relief on his face is evident and he lets out the breath he's been holding. At least the thought was there, and I now know that if I really did want him to give it up, he would.

'You know, if you wanted me out of the house more, I could pimp out the shed. Put a big flat-screen in here and run a second Sky box. I could get that easy chair I've always wanted, and one of those little beer fridges. The boys would love it, what with Aaron's missus about to pop. Just think, we'd never disturb you again when we're watching a midnight boxing match.'

As tempting as that sounds, I can just imagine the muddy footprints all through the house as they traipse in and out of the garden. Not to mention, I see enough of Aaron and Tom as it is, let alone giving them some sort of designated clubhouse to indulge their brotherhood of sport.

'No, thank you. After a week of having full control of the telebox, I've decided that I don't mind sharing it with you. And besides, when we have kids there'll be no time for man sheds or sporting games anyway. The only thing you'll be watching is Mr Tumble on repeat.'

'Mr who? No no no. I'll be that guy at the football matches with a baby in one of those harness things dangling off him.

I'm sure babies get in free to matches if they sit on your lap. It'd be like two for the price of one with the season ticket. Might as well make the most of it, before we have to start paying for their ticket as well.'

'I'd never really considered that in having kids I might be spawning a mini-you,' I say, laughing. 'Is there time to change my mind?'

I go to pull the engagement ring off in jest, but as I catch a look at it, I get a lump in my throat. After all these years, Will and I are going to get married. I'm going to take him as he is, for better for worse, but at least I know what I'm getting myself into.

'Come on,' says Will, standing up again.

I'm quite liking his new taking charge attitude. We make a run for it back towards the house, and it smells no better than it did when we left it. I go to open the cupboard under the sink to make a start on clearing up, but Will slams it shut.

'We should celebrate our engagement, just us two. Let's go away somewhere for the night and we can come back to this and tell everyone later.' He goes over to the back door and locks it.

'That sounds amazing.'

I squeal with excitement as I walk out of the kitchen and go to climb the stairs to start packing.

'How do you fancy a couple of nights in Dubai – the golf's on – or a night up in London as there's a match at Twickers tomorrow . . .'

My nostrils flare, and I turn to see him laughing.

'Only kidding. How about a country hotel in the middle of nowhere, where the only sport is croquet?'

'Now you're talking. And no Sky Sports in the room.'

I see a twitch in his eyebrow.

'And no mobile phones,' I add quickly.

'Deal,' he says.

I go back over and give him a kiss.

I know I may be consigning myself to being a sports widow for life, but I have that glimmer of hope that sometimes – just sometimes – he may choose me over sports.

He scoops me up and picks up his keys from the worktop.

'What are you doing?' I scream, kicking my legs as he carries me through the house.

'I'm taking you away.'

'What about packing some stuff to take with us?'

'Ah, sod it. Let's buy stuff on the way. We're only going somewhere for the night and if I have my way we won't leave the hotel room. Besides, I'm being romantic. I'm carrying you over the threshold.'

'Um, technically you're supposed to wait until we're married and do it the other way round, in from outside.'

'Ah, sod you, then,' he says, dropping me before kissing me again. 'I won't pick you up again like that until we get married.'

'Get married,' I say, shaking my head, still not believing it. 'I can't believe we're actually going to do it.'

'I know,' he says opening the door, 'I had a look on the BBC Sport website and I reckon there's a two-week window next July if you fancy it.'

Ah, the romance of the BBC Sport website.

'Why not.'

If I can't beat him, why not join him? I'm getting married to my soulmate and who cares if it's based around the sporting calendar. The main thing is I'm spending the rest of my life with the man I love. And let's remember, this is the man that gives me the gift of time to myself and holidays to tropical destinations (as long as someone is playing cricket). Don't be jealous, I know I'm one lucky lady.

While I might always be a neglected girlfriend/fiancée/wife, I do at least now have a few tricks up my sleeve for how to cope with it. See-through underwear, clumsy fingers on the volume control . . . Just as long as I don't blog about it, we'll be fine, right?

Lexi's Sporting Widow Survival Guide

When you start dating someone obsessed with sport and find yourself in danger of becoming a sporting widow, then the best piece of advice I can give you is to run for the hills! Get out while you still can, before the commentary on football games becomes the soundtrack to your life, and your social calendar looks more like a 'What's On' guide for Sky Sports.

Only kidding. We all know you can't help who you fall in love with, but if you do end up with a sports enthusiast (and you don't share his passion), here's my guide to how to keep your sanity.

1. *Leopards don't change their spots*

We all know that you can't change men. Sure, we can tweak them and buff them round the edges, but it's pretty hard to get them to undergo a complete personality transplant. You'll be fighting an ever-losing battle banning them from watching sports. Instead, try to get them to watch less. Agree in advance which matches or sport he'll be watching over a weekend, making sure you create a balance between what you both want to do. It'll save so much frustration and arguing on a Sunday afternoon.

2. *Keep your arsenal well stocked*

When I first met Will, I didn't own a smartphone, and it was before e-readers. After ending up in the pub too many times when the football/rugby/cricket were on, I soon realised that I needed to carry a book around with me. Now, thanks to the wondrous improvements in technology, I no longer need a ginormous handbag. With my smartphone and e-reader always in my bag, there's no need to sigh if I'm being ignored in favour of sports, as I've always got something to entertain me at the click of a button.

3. *If you can't beat them, join them*

I actually don't mind going to watch live sport – sssh, don't tell Will. I'm not saying I'd like to go all the time, but it beats watching it on TV any day. Not only is the atmosphere better, but it makes you feel part of the game in a way you don't get in your front room. Will is always really appreciative if I keep him company at a game, too – earning me massive brownie points. It also means that I'm guaranteed to spend some time with him, even if I don't always have his full attention. My first sporting preference is cricket, as it's usually much warmer when you go to watch (or should be) than it is when the rugby's on. I always pick a Twenty20 game as it's over more quickly.

4. *Misery loves company*

You're not the first sporting widow, and you certainly won't be the last. If you're going to be dragged along to some match/game/event, then why not take someone along with you? I still think Josie and Richard would have been perfect for that – but unfortunately it didn't work out too well . . . It's also a good idea that if your home turns into man cave central when all the boys come over, that you invite their partners, too. That way you've got some company, and once the match is over you can all socialise together.

5. *Rules of engagement*

As much as I hate knowing all the sporting rules and regulations, I feel that it helps in my relationship. When Will's moaning about a game, or we're watching something live, I can have conversations with him – or at the very least I can understand what he's talking about. It's being supportive and taking an interest – earning those good old brownie points again.

6. *Gift of time*

Instead of sitting on the sofa getting the hump that the Speedway is on rather than Corrie, use the time wisely, and I don't mean by lusting over the lifestyles of non-sporting widows on Instagram. I never would have finished my first book without Will's dominance of the remote control. Is there a hobby you want to do? A fitness class you could go to, or a run you could go on? Coordinate things so that you have some 'me time' whilst your partner watches sports, and then carve out some quality time for the two of you after.

7. *Don't anger the beast*

When your partner's team loses and he's acting like it's the end of the world, try to remember that for him it is. Unless you want to provoke him, never trot out phrases like 'it's only a game' or 'there's always next week'. Let him wallow for a while, and eventually he'll snap out of it.

Good luck – and may the odds forever be in his team's favour, so that you have a happy partner!

The Bucket List of Sports

I'm sure that Will isn't the only sports-mad male to have a bucket-list of events and matches he wants to see. Countries aren't ticked off by visiting UNESCO World Heritage sites or iconic landmarks. Oh no, his is based on the sporting events that take place there. If you're threatened with such a sporting holiday, here are my top picks!

1. *The Ashes, Sydney, Australia*

Why not see the New Year in before anyone else does, whilst watching the fireworks over Sydney Harbour Bridge and the Opera House? Ok, so the slight compromise is that one of the tests for The Ashes is played in Sydney in the first week of the New Year. A day or two at the cricket seems like a small compromise for what could be an epic holiday down under. A boat trip around Darling Harbour, a hike up the Blue Mountains and a pilgrimage to Summer Bay (or Palm Beach, as it's actually called).

2. *Boxing in Maddison Square Garden, New York, US*

I hate boxing with a passion, but hello New York! I'm sure the atmosphere at 'the Garden' would be electric, and you've only got to watch twelve rounds . . .

Then for the rest of the weekend you can totally give Man vs Food a run for his money by tackling the massive portions of food on offer, before hitting up shopping meccas like Bloomingdales and Barneys. There are all those famous sights to see, plus with the Met, MOMA and the Guggenheim, there's something to please culture vultures, too.

3. *Monaco Grand Prix, Monaco*

If I had to go and watch a Grand Prix, this would be first on my list. Despite being forced to watch cars whizz round a track for a zillion laps, I imagine that you'd be able to soak up the glitz and glamour that seems to ooze from that place.

4. *Wimbledon Tennis Championships, London*

A sporting event where it's almost mandatory to eat strawberries and cream and drink Pimms couldn't possibly be bad. I've never been to Wimbledon, and whilst tennis isn't one of Will's must-watch sports, he'd love to go to this tournament, too. Unless you're lucky with the ballot, or super-lucky to get corporate tickets, you have to queue up and even camp overnight to get in – making it a quirky mini-break. Will and I plan to camp out one year for tickets – fingers crossed the rain stays away that year!

Acknowledgements

The first thing I should say is that this book is in no way biographical and any scenes that seem remarkably similar to my life are in fact a total coincidence. To my husband Steve – sports fan extraordinaire – thank you for helping with the accidental research for this book for the last eight years with all those trips to the rugby, darts, cricket, football and horse racing. Thank goodness I didn't actually know I was going to write this, as I'm sure you would have dragged me to many more events in the name of research. Also, thank you for all your help as usual tidying, looking after the kids and being my sports oracle. I hope you enjoy the book – and don't find too many sporting errors in it. Any errors (or minor tweaks to make it fit to the story) are all mine. To my children, Evan and Jessica, thank you for napping a lot so that I could write this, and thank you for doing such a wonderful job of being little at the moment, which is preventing us from gallivanting in the name of sports (long may it continue . . . !)

To the team at Bonnier – thank you so much for all you have done for me and my books. Thank you to Joel, my editor, for not only making me feel less alone as a sports widow with your anecdotes about your parents, but also for the brilliant notes and ideas for the story. Thank you also to Claire for the line edit and really pulling all those last threads together. Thank you to Emily Burns for your boundless enthusiasm for my last book. Also, thanks to Georgia Mannering, Nick Stearn, Nico Poilblanc and Vincent Kelleher. Thanks to the very talented Adrian Valencia for another wonderful cover.

One thing that's struck me when writing this book is just how many sporting widows there are and my agent Hannah Ferguson is (unfortunately?!) amongst them – and a good job too as it meant she totally got the idea for this book and championed it from the start. Thank you as always for everything you (and the rest of the team at Hardman & Swainson) do for me. Thank you to the Marsh Agency for my foreign rights deals. It's a dream come true to see my books translated into so many different languages.

Thank you to the Supporter Relationship Managers at Southampton Football Club, Khali Parsons and Daniel Whittington for answering my very random questions. While Lexi's proposal scene used a bit of poetic licence, it was really helpful to have your advice.

A huge thank you to all my lovely friends and family – your support, encouragement and enthusiasm always astounds me. Special mention to my mum (it's a bit of cliché but she really is my biggest fan), my parents-in-law Harold and Heather, my sister Jane (hang on in there, there will be a book dedicated to you one day – just waiting for the right one), Kaf, Hannah and Laura, whose cameos are yet to appear in one of my novels and Debs, Julie and Christie.

To the wonderfully lovely bloggers, authors and Team Novelicious that I tweet with – thank you for keeping me sane and entertaining me so much. To the bloggers and reviewers that take the time to review my books – a huge thank you and I hope you enjoy this one, too. Special thanks to Becky Gulc, Ananda, Chloe Spooner, Isabelle Broome, Rachel Gilby, Agi and Laura L.

Lastly, a huge thank you to you for reading my book! I do hope you liked it. There's nothing nicer than hearing from people that have read and enjoyed my books so do come and say hello if you use Twitter – @annabell_writes.

Want to read
NEW BOOKS
before anyone else?

Like getting
FREE BOOKS?

Enjoy sharing your
OPINIONS?

Discover

READERS FIRST

Read. Love. Share.

Get your first free book just by signing up at
readersfirst.co.uk